Your Secret's Safe With Me

Rosie Travers

CROOKED
CAT

Discover us online:
www.crookedcatbooks.com

Join us on facebook:
www.facebook.com/crookedcat

Tweet a photo of yourself holding
this book to **@crookedcatbooks**
and something nice will happen.

For my mum.

Acknowledgements

With many thanks once again to my fellow Hampshire writers, Ant, Grethe, Gill, Sally, Anne, Avril, Tania, Linda and Julie, and to dear friends Tracey and Yvonne for their encouragement and support. Thanks also to my quizzing buddies, Pauline, Cliff and Andy for their company every Monday evening and for inspiring a small, but very significant, part of this story. Special thanks to my sister, Carrie, my first reader, and, of course, to Neil, Ellen and Zoe. I couldn't do it without them.

And a big thank you to Crooked Cat for putting their faith in me once again.

About the Author

Rosie grew up in Southampton and loved escaping to a good book at a very early age. As a teenager she landed her dream Saturday job in WH Smith and scribbled many stories and novels, none of which she was ever brave enough to show anyone.

After several years juggling motherhood and a variety of jobs in local government Rosie moved to Southern California when her husband took an overseas work assignment. With time on her hands she started a blog about the trials and tribulations of ex-pat life which rekindled her teenage desire to become a writer. On her return to the UK she took a creative writing course and the rest, as they say, is history.

Rosie takes inspiration from the towns and landscapes of her native south coast and enjoys writing heart-warming stories sprinkled with mystery, comedy, tragedy and a dash of romance.

Follow Rosie at **www.rosietravers.com**

Your Secret's Safe With Me

Prologue

Pearl

Was there an easy way to drop a bombshell? Not that Pearl considered the announcement she was about to make a bombshell, more a stroke of amazing good fortune, but she knew how it would be received in certain quarters. Was it best to prepare the ground with a little foreshadowing, a few clues of what was to come, or should she just dive straight in? The reaction would be the same whatever. Pearl had never been good at subtlety. Life was too short to worry about other people's sensibilities. It was probably best just to get it over with. Adopt the brace position, hope for the best and expect the worst.

It took two attempts for Becca to answer her call. She sounded tired and disgruntled. 'Don't you know what time it is? I thought we had this rule...'

Pearl glanced at the jewelled watch on her wrist. Surely Becca wasn't tucked up in bed already? It was just coming up to one in the afternoon in San Diego. Did that make it after ten already in London?

'Sorry, darling, you know me. Anyway, just wanted to let you know that I'm back on *terra firma*. The cruise was marvellous but there's been a slight change of plan.'

'Oh? Change of plan?' Pearl detected the escalating irritation in Becca's voice. 'What do you mean?'

'I won't need you to meet at Heathrow tomorrow. I'm not coming back to London; at least, not straight away.'

'Oh?'

'Look, darling, I had an absolute ball on the holiday. The *Majestic Oceans* is a fabulous ship, and as for South America, what an amazing continent – the landscape, the festivals, the people. You'd have loved every minute of it, but the thing is something rather exciting has happened.' Pearl took a deep breath. 'You'll never guess what, but I'm going to be getting married.'

The silence said it all. Pearl could picture Becca's face. Her dark eyebrows would be knitted together and her mouth pursed tight, an expression she'd perfected as a fractious toddler. That tiny child, body rigid with rage, was now a thirty-nine-year-old woman whose fuller figure – it was the politest term that sprang to mind – would be taut with disapproval, or as taut as such curves could go.

'I know what you're thinking, but it's not like that at all,' Pearl continued undeterred. 'I've met the most marvellous man. His name is Jack, Jack Robshaw. He's from Hampshire and is something big in the yachting world. He owns a marina, or a boatyard; something nautical. Anyway, he proposed last night, our last night on the boat, and I said yes. We've been inseparable since we met at the single travellers' gathering.'

It seemed an age before Becca spoke. 'But you've only known this man eight weeks. How can you possibly—'

'Eight weeks is long enough at my age,' Pearl cut in. 'Look, we're not planning to get married immediately. Jack's got this wonderful place on the coast. Apparently, there are beautiful gardens overlooking a river. He suggests we wait until summer and have a big celebration there, on the lawn, surrounded by family and friends. That'll give you plenty of time to get used to the idea, and to lose a couple of pounds. I want you as my Maid of Honour, of course.'

'Of course.' Becca's voice was brittle. 'Well, that's wonderful, that's wonderful news. I'm very happy for you.'

She sounded anything but. Poor Becca harboured a grudge, not just against marriage but men in general. She was never going to greet the news of anyone's impending nuptials with rapturous delight. In the circumstances, it was the best Pearl could hope for and it could have been a lot worse. At least Becca was still talking to her. Just.

'Well, thank you, darling. The thing is, Jack's invited me to accompany him down to his house when we get back to the

UK. Rivermede, it's called. Isn't that a wonderful name? And I mean, why not? If it's going to be my new home, I want to see it. He's been on his own for a few years now, and it's bound to need a woman's touch. I want to get cracking.'

'You mean you aren't you going to come back here first and see me? What about Freddy?'

'What about Freddy? You're both grown-ups. You don't need me around, do you? I want to see Jack's place, he's told me so much about it.'

'Right. So, you're going to go straight down to Hampshire? And that's where you plan on living in the future?'

'Well, obviously if I'm going to be getting married, I want to be with Jack and it makes sense to stay in his place. It's bigger. Look, I haven't worked it all out yet.'

'No. Obviously not. You're just rushing straight in again.'

'I'm not rushing into anything.' Pearl tried to retain her patience. 'Come down to Hampshire and see us in a couple of days' time when we've had a chance to get over the jet-lag. We can talk properly then. I'm going to need you to bring me some suitable clothing anyway. I've only got my cruise outfits with me for now. I'll need some sensible sturdy footwear for the countryside, and maybe some slacks and jumpers. Have a rummage through my wardrobes and bring a selection. You know the sort of thing I'll need.'

'Of course. Whatever you say, *Mother*.'

Mother! Pearl winced. Perhaps she should have checked the time before she rang. Becca was never at her best last thing at night; she valued her beauty sleep. All work and no play, that was her trouble, and as much as Pearl appreciated the commitment Becca had shown to her career – their joint career – over the years, it had been at the detriment of her social life and her sense of humour.

Rivermede couldn't have reared its idyllic, picturesque head at a better time. A change of scenery was probably just what Becca needed. Jack had already said he was happy to have them all on board. He was generous to a fault, and who didn't aspire to a house in the country?

'Good, well I'm glad we've got that settled,' Pearl

concluded. 'I'll see you soon, darling.'

Becca ended the call without another word. Pearl shook her head and slipped her phone back to her handbag. She glanced across the crowded airport bar to where Jack sat by a window table. He caught her eye and threw her one of his dazzling smiles. Her heart gave a somersault of excitement. She walked back to his side and took his hand. She didn't need Becca's approval. This time she knew she'd got it right.

Chapter One

Becca

'I don't know why you're making such a fuss about it.' Freddy yawned as he spoke, and his words, like his arms, stretched towards the ceiling. 'Maybe this'll be third time lucky. Don't you want her to be happy?'

'You think this toy-boy will make her happy? I've Googled this Jack Robshaw character. Look, Freddy, look at him.' I held out my phone, thrusting the screen into his face. 'A former world championship powerboat racer? Twenty years her junior. Is that what you want for a step-father?'

Pearl's phone call had left me shell-shocked. *How could she do it again?* I'd fended off palpitations with deep breathing exercises, whale songs, and a mug of camomile tea, but it had been impossible to get back to sleep. I'd called Freddy first thing to impart the news and he'd very reluctantly agreed to meet me for lunch to plan a campaign strategy. His lack of concern was demoralising. He could hardly keep his eyes open despite a second coffee.

'I am not going to let her make another disastrous marriage,' I continued. 'I can't bear the thought of another gold-digger like Dieter coming into our lives. This guy is hardly her type, is he?'

'Who knows what Pearl's type is?' Freddy replied, brushing my phone away. 'She's had her fair share of oddballs over the years.'

This was true, although luckily none of them had hung around for very long, least of all Dieter, the last husband. The aftermath of Pearl's catastrophic second marriage had heralded a horrendous period in our lives. Freddy, now twenty-one and struggling through his final year of an art degree, was the one positive to come out of that whole sorry episode. At least Pearl had now reached the age when childbearing was no longer an option.

She referred to Dieter as her cloud, and Freddy our silver lining. I'd been a teenager at the time, unaware of the financial implications of my mother's messy divorce. Now, I was an adult and very conscious of the consequences. Jack Robshaw wasn't so much a cloud as a potential thunderstorm.

'This is all Aunt Phoebe's fault.' I was determined not to be side-tracked from my mission. 'If she hadn't had that angina attack, she would have been able to go on the cruise, too, and then Pearl wouldn't have gone to the singles' meeting and she wouldn't have met this Jack.'

Pearl had encouraged Freddy and me to call her by her first name from a very early age. Since I'd taken on the role of her PA, it made perfect professional sense, but our personal relationship had suffered as a result. Right now, I felt more like my mother's keeper than her daughter.

'You could have gone with her instead; you have before.' Freddy looked amused. 'I know Aunt Phoebe can be a bit of a pain, but I don't think you can hold her entirely responsible, Becs.'

'I couldn't go away for eight weeks, not with deadlines looming. It wasn't like she had a lecture schedule to deliver. I thought she was safe on her own.' I heaved a huge sigh. 'I've promised to go down to Hampshire in a couple of days, because not only does she now need an entire wardrobe of country casuals, but I've got to get her to approve these manuscripts I've been working on. It would be nice if she could show a bit of enthusiasm for her own books. She didn't even mention them. Not a word. At this rate, I might as well write them myself.'

'I thought you already did?' Freddy smiled. 'You're part of a team. Isn't that what she says? Pearl gives you the outlines and you fill in the gaps?'

'Yes, and in recent years there have been far more gaps than outlines. There's only so many times an author can regurgitate a familiar plot. I've tried to spice things up a bit for her. But it's not just the books, Fred. What's going to happen to Beech Mews?'

'Well, surely she's not going to do anything with that, is she?' Freddy at last showed a smidgeon of unease. 'I mean, sure she might want to go down and live in Hampshire with this guy, but Beech Mews is our home, isn't it? She wouldn't dream of getting rid of it.'

'Wouldn't she?'

It was hard conveying the depth of my anxiety. I'd Googled the name Jack Robshaw the second I'd ended Pearl's late-night call. Dieter – a Germanic blond playboy in a ski-suit who had emptied the contents of her bank account with the same speedy dexterity he applied to negotiating black runs in St Moritz – had come along in the days before internet stalking. Now it was much easier to check people out surreptitiously. *Something big in the yachting world*, Pearl had said. What was it about my mother and her predilection for athletic types? It had to be the attraction of opposites. I immediately pictured Henri Lloyd and deck shoes, but the reality was much worse.

'We're going to be united on this, right?' I insisted. 'Pearl is a wealthy woman. I don't care if this guy has got world championship powerboating medals, he's not getting a penny of her hard-earned cash.'

'You mean your hard-earned cash?' Freddy raised an eyebrow. It never failed to surprise me that sometimes he could be far more astute than he looked.

'Yes, exactly. I've invested a lot of time and effort into maintaining Pearl's career. Anyway, what have you been up to, Fred? You've been very cagey about your movements of late, and you look like shit.'

'Thanks for the compliment.' He brushed his long artistic fingers through his floppy blond fringe. 'I ain't been up to anything.' He had dark circles under his eyes, and his pallor, as always, was deathly pale.

'How's work for your degree show coming on?' I enquired. Freddy had just scraped through his second year at Goldsmiths, and was now nearing the end of his final. I wished I could share his nonchalant approach to life. There was no sign of the last-minute graduation nerves that had plagued me during my last term at uni.

He gave a shrug. 'S'okay.'

'You haven't gone back on the weed, have you? You did promise.'

He held his hands up. 'Don't you start. It's like having two mums.'

I smiled at him. 'That's what big sisters are for.'

I'd been eighteen when Freddy was born, Pearl in her early forties. We were a tight-knit family trio. Pearl had always declared my father had been the love of her life – young, vibrant, and horrifically injured in a motorcycle accident when I'd been less than a year old. Paralysed from the chest down, he'd subsequently died of pneumonia some eighteen months later, consigned to a nursing home. Struggling on her own, Pearl had taken a job as a typist for a publishing house and, armed with a vivid imagination and a gritty resolve, she had risen rapidly through the ranks to fully fledged novelist.

By the time I started primary school, Pearl was churning out two or three books a year, bestsellers that ensured I spent a childhood closeted in an eclectic circle of publishing friends and colleagues, literary celebrities who hit the headlines in the heyday of the hefty sexy saga. It was the era of big things – shoulder pads, hair, egos. Pearl had been easy prey to the charms of Dieter, fifteen years her junior; a scriptwriter, or so he'd told her, in the film industry. He promised that her books would grace the silver screen and Hollywood would fall at her feet. Of course, it didn't. Twenty-one years later and I'd yet to see Dieter's name appear on any cinematic credits. After Pearl, he had moved on to a model from Hamburg.

It was hard not to feel over-protective. The cavalier attitude my mother adopted for the world was all for show. Beneath that brash exterior, she was just as vulnerable as the rest of us. Her relationship with Dieter had cost her dearly. He had encouraged her to live extravagantly. She'd rented a house in the Hollywood Hills in anticipation of the film contracts that never happened. She undertook ill-advised investments, lavished Dieter with material gifts and undeserved affection, before returning to London alone, pregnant, and broke.

'You just need to stay calm,' Freddy said, as if he could see my mind racing ahead to the worst-case scenarios. 'You're getting too het up about this, Becs. If she'd met some benign old bloke on this cruise, as opposed to this flashy forty-year-old playboy sailor, you'd probably be welcoming him into the family with open arms. Are you sure you're not just jealous?'

'Of course I'm not jealous.' The reply came out far too quickly. 'The very idea, Fred. What are you thinking of?'

He gave another infuriating shrug. 'I'm jus' saying. You know Pearl, Becs, once her mind is made up, it's made up. You go in all guns blazing like this and you'll be waving a red rag to a bull.'

I never liked acknowledging that Freddy was right, but he had a very valid point. Pearl was notorious for behaving like a petulant teenager. Any sign of dissent and she'd be bringing the wedding forward, not putting it off altogether. I had to tread very carefully.

Chapter Two

My invitation to Rivermede arrived a few days later. Pearl suggested I stay for an entire weekend, and after reeling off a list of everything she required transporting down from Battersea, insisted on giving me lengthy directions, despite my protestations that all I needed was the postcode.

'What if your sat nav stops working?' she said, 'You know my feelings on modern technology. It's not foolproof.'

I listened with half an ear on how to negotiate the junction off the nearest motorway and how not to take a road to the right that involved crossing a ford.

'If you miss the sign for the village of Kerridge, you could end up in this godforsaken place called Helme Point and you'll disappear off into the marsh never to be seen again,' Pearl chuckled. 'I'm told it has happened. This place is so interesting, Becca. You're going to love it. I'd forgotten what it was like to be in the country, the peace and quiet, the gentle ebb and flow of the tide. We're right on the river here, on a creek a couple of miles inland from the estuary. The gardens overlook the water and the views are stunning.'

'Has he taken you out on his powerboat yet?' I asked, unable to contain my sarcasm. I tried to block out the mental image of my mother donning a bikini and standing at the wheel beside the sun-kissed, dark-haired Jack Robshaw. Google images had provided nothing up-to-date; Jack had disappeared off the racing circuit some ten years or so ago. Pictures of a virile bare-chested twenty-something posing in his record-breaking speedboat were all I had to go on.

'Oh, Jack doesn't own a boat himself,' Pearl replied, somewhat to my surprise. 'But he is a member of the local yacht club. I suppose we could always borrow something off

12

the marina if we wanted to.'

Had Jack Robshaw, former champion, fallen onto such hard times that he could no longer afford his own boat? No wonder he had jumped at the chance of ingratiating himself with my mother. On the other hand, if he was that broke, what was he doing on an eight-week South American cruise, apart from using it as an opportunity to hook a wealthy widow or divorcee?

I trawled through the internet in an attempt to discover what I could about my mother's new home. According to Wikipedia, Kerridge was situated on the eastern bank of the River Deane, historically famous for its boat-building industries, although – as my mother had hinted – now more renowned as a south coast sailing centre. I located Jack's marina on Google Earth and learned that Robshaw Marine Holdings handled new and used boat sales as well as offering berthing and storage facilities. It was a world away from our life in London.

Pearl explained she was not going to make a public announcement of her engagement just yet. Jack, she confided, was a private man who had no wish to become caught up in the inevitable 'celebrity whirlwind' once the press got hold of her story.

Although I was relieved at my mother's uncharacteristic discretion, I felt Jack's reluctance to make a public announcement probably stemmed not from wish to remain out of the limelight, but from a desire to avoid pressure from Pearl's friends who would inevitably try and talk her out of another disastrous marriage. From his point of view, the less people who knew about the engagement, the better.

I highly doubted Pearl's nuptials would carry an awful lot of credence in the newspapers. However, her inimitable observations on popular fiction and literary classics had made her a popular guest speaker at various public events, and led to a regular slot on local radio and the occasional guest spot on daytime TV chat shows. It was possible the story could fill a few inside page spaces. She had friends in the media and colleagues in high places who she wanted to invite to the wedding.

'But only after I've talked over my plans with you,' she promised.

Despite my efforts to cajole, Freddy refused to join me on the trip down to Hampshire. An all-night rave in Lambeth took priority over sibling solidarity. I half-hoped if *Jumpin' Jack Flash* met his stepson-to-be, he might think twice about taking Pearl on.

The sat nav did indeed take me on a wild goose chase along the road with the ford, but as the weather had been dry for several days, the route was passable. I decided not to mention the technological error. Pearl would be beside herself with glee.

Rivermede was situated on a twisting country lane, bordered by hedgerows just coming into bloom. I drew up outside the imposing wooden gates that heralded the entrance and pressed the visitors' button on the keypad as directed. The gates swung open to reveal a sweeping gravel drive across an expanse of green lawn, dotted with ornamental fir trees and early spring blossoms.

Pearl had referred to the house style as 'Palladian'. I didn't know an awful lot about architecture, but it was grand as opposed to imposing, and not particularly vast. I pulled up outside a stone-front portico bearing classical ancient Roman and Greek influences. There were outbuildings to the side – a more modern addition of a garage, possibly converted from a former stable block. The lawn sloped down to the river, the vista only broken by a long straight hedge. It looked remarkably well-maintained for the home of a man who had fallen on hard times.

Had I Googled the wrong Jack Robshaw? Before I had time to re-assimilate, my mother emerged to greet me at the top of a magnificent set of stone steps. It was a relief to see she was alone.

'*Darling*, you're here.' She was dressed casually in a pair of jeans and a positively subdued grey jumper. Her hair, which she'd had re-touched into her favourite shade of honey blonde for her cruise and usually framed her head like a well-coiffured helmet, was just starting to reveal its grey roots. The less manicured look softened her features.

My mother was a diminutive woman; I'd been taller than her since the age of eleven and had always struggled to emulate her sense of style. Instead, I opted for the clean business-like approach and dressed predominately in standard issue black trousers and a selection of muted coloured tops, much to her – and, in truth, my own – despair. I'd given up even trying to do something with my hair and kept it to a manageable shoulder-length bob. Unadventurous and unstylish. Pearl was always quick to voice her disapproval. Today, she looked positively relieved and very pleased to see me, casting barely a glance at my sensible attire.

'Let me get Neville to help with the cases,' she gushed. 'Can you believe it, Jack has staff? I have a housekeeper and a butler-cum-handyman.'

It was as if she had fallen straight into the pages of one of her novels.

'Staff?'

'Yes, isn't it fantastic? Leave the bags in the car. Neville can take them straight up to my room. You have brought everything I asked?'

I assured her I'd fully fitted her out for spring in the countryside. My eyes swept through the magnificent hallway as Pearl's kitten heels clicked on the black and white checked tiled floor. A stone staircase swept up to a galleried landing. Photographs of racing yachts and motor cruisers adorned the walls – mementoes, no doubt, of Jack's glory days.

'Jack's in the drawing room,' Pearl said. 'He's dying to meet you. What do you think of the house?'

'It's very impressive,' I remarked, not knowing what I thought at all. So far, the décor and the furnishings I'd seen suggested an occupant far older than a flashy forty-year-old powerboat racer. I wondered if he still lived at home with parents, in which case I had even more reason to be worried. Did he see Pearl as his 'sugar mummy'? I felt my hackles rise.

The drawing room was at the front of the house; a beautiful

15

airy room with French windows overlooking the lawn. A handsome silver-haired man sat in a wheelchair admiring the view. He wore grey trousers and a canary yellow sweater.

'Jack darling, she's here.' Pearl rushed to his side.

'Becca, how lovely to meet you,' Jack Robshaw said, manoeuvring his chair to greet me. 'Pearl's told me so much about you.'

I wished I could return the sentiment. I was completely thrown off-guard. This was definitely not the Jack Robshaw I was expecting. He had to be at least seventy. We shook hands.

'Have you asked Heather to bring us tea?' Pearl asked.

'Of course.' Jack returned her indulgent smile before turning to me. 'Pearl's not used to having people to boss around.'

'Really?' I remarked. 'I'm surprised. Pearl is usually very good at bossing people around.'

'I told you she had a way with words,' Pearl retorted.

Right on cue, a smart slender woman in her early fifties arrived bearing a tea tray. I was glad of the interruption. Pearl and I sat on one of the three floral sofas and watched while Heather the housekeeper poured out our tea and handed around a plate of biscuits. I realised I'd got this all so wrong, but I still wasn't convinced Pearl should be rushing into marrying anyone, despite the obvious displays of affection. It was all far too soon.

She hadn't mentioned Jack had been confined to a wheelchair. I wondered about the extent of his disabilities. I didn't want to do Pearl an injustice, but as a young woman she'd been unable to cope with my father's injuries, and as a consequence he'd remained hospitalized for the rest of his life. Was this some sort of attempt to make amends, to take on another invalid?

Jack's grey eyes twinkled, and his conversation was sprinkled with intellect and humour. Yes, he had thoroughly enjoyed his cruise – all the more for having met Pearl, of course. South America had been fascinating, so much to see and do. He agreed eight weeks was a long time to be at sea, but he and Pearl had filled their time with Spanish conversation lessons, Scrabble, and afternoon tea.

'We managed to keep ourselves occupied, didn't we, dear?' he chuckled. Pearl blushed like a schoolgirl. It was a relief when he suggested she give me a guided tour of the house and grounds.

The master bedroom was situated on the ground floor – an enormous room with heavy festooned curtains and an entire wall of mirror wardrobes.

'It's just for Jack, for now, obviously,' Pearl remarked. I wasn't sure why she was bothering with the pretence. It was quite apparent from the paraphernalia lying around in the room that they were already sharing.

The en-suite was furnished like something out of a bad seventies' porn movie, or one of Pearl's *Hollywood Heroes* novels. A large walk-in-shower and a sunken bath, surrounded by yet more mirrors.

'The last thing we want at our age is to be reminded of our wrinkles from every angle,' Pearl grimaced. 'Jack's first wife must have been a complete narcissist. It's all going to have to go. Jack says we can get an interior designer in.'

Warning bells sounded again. It was right not become too complacent. Although it was hard to picture the congenial senior I'd just met as a serious threat, did Jack have his eye on Pearl's money after all? If he thought she had enough to invest in rejuvenating his property, he was very much mistaken.

We poked our heads around the door of Jack's study – an untidy, masculine room filled with bookcases and filing cabinets. There was a snug, a cosy room with a large screen TV, a conservatory, and a dining room with a hugely ornate walnut dining table and seating for at least twelve, then a few steps down to the large kitchen, utility and boot-room.

'Heather and Nev's domain,' Pearl said. 'We won't disturb them.'

'Do they live here, too?' I enquired.

'Yes, but not in the house. They have a cottage in the grounds.'

Upstairs, there were several more bedrooms. Apart from the one Pearl had requisitioned for her belongings, and my guest suite, all were either empty or very modestly furnished, complete with jaded out-dated décor. There was a further floor and attics, but Pearl ran out of steam at the thought of yet another staircase.

'Nothing much up there,' she informed me. 'Just the old servants' quarters and the former nursery. I don't think any of the rooms have been used for years.'

'You said Jack had been married before?' I ventured. 'He has children?'

She nodded and lowered her voice, even though we were well out of hearing of the drawing room. 'He lost his wife Mary to cancer five years or so ago.'

'And the children?' I prompted.

'Just the one son, Jack Junior, although everyone refers to him as JJ for short.'

Jack Junior. Realisation dawned. 'Does he live nearby?'

'Unfortunately, yes. He and his wife have their own apartment, the West Wing, here in the house. Hopefully, they'll be moving out soon. JJ's having this monstrosity built on some land his mother bequeathed him. You can just see it from one of the side bedrooms. Come and take a look.'

Presumably Jack Junior was the former powerboat racing champion; an easy mistake to make. Pearl took me to one of the sparsely-furnished rooms on the far side of the house. A shell of a building was just visible through the tree tops, a steel and glass rectangular block, incongruous in its fairy-tale woodland setting.

'He's having hell with his builders,' Pearl said. 'It took him years to get the plans approved. Not that Jack objected, obviously, but apparently there were plenty of others in the village who did. You can see why, can't you? Talk about out of character with its surroundings.'

'What does JJ think of your engagement?' I asked.

'Let's just say he's not overjoyed,' Pearl replied.

'Oh dear.' Secretly I was delighted. If Jack's son opposed this marriage as much as I did, we could put on a united front and hopefully talk some sense into our parents. 'It is only natural to have reservations,' I pointed out. 'You and Jack have only known each other for a few weeks. I am sure he is just concerned for his father's welfare.'

'Welfare?' Pearl pouted. 'What does he think I am going to do to his father? I don't know what's up with you young people. Don't you want us to be happy?'

'Of course we do,' I assured her, patting her arm. 'I do want you to be happy, I just don't want you getting hurt. You shouldn't be rushing into something you might regret. Remember what happened with Dieter.'

'Jack is nothing like Dieter,' Pearl retorted with a snort. She pulled her arm away. 'Honestly, Becca. Do you think I'm totally stupid?'

The tour of the house was complete. Pearl had never been a great walker. A twenty-a-day habit which I'd been nagging her to give up for years and which she now appeared to have miraculously kicked overnight, had left her not only with a trademark husky voice, but breathless at any kind of exertion. Our expedition around the grounds was confined to the immediate garden surrounding the house. There were a couple of statues and a broken fountain, a rose arbour, and traditional flower beds. It was obviously well-tended but did not contain any great extravagance. The term functional came to mind. Jack had obviously never been a keen gardener and I again wondered about his lack of mobility. I decided I had to broach the subject.

'*Mum*...' The word rolled off my tongue a little awkwardly, but given the delicacy of the situation it seemed the most appropriate term to use. 'About Jack's disabilities.'

'I see the man, Becca, not the chair.'

My mother had a writer's talent for conveying a great deal with very few words. The message was quite clear. I knew not to press her any further.

Heather delivered a plate of sandwiches to the conservatory for lunch and Pearl informed her that it would just be the three of us for dinner. JJ and his wife Marguerite would join us on Sunday.

'Jack wants us all to become better acquainted,' she grimaced. 'I must admit the only saving grace is that their wing is fully self-contained – separate entrance and everything – so we don't actually have to see a lot of each other.'

I looked forward to having the opportunity to test the water with Jack's son and gauge his views on his father's marriage. I was pleased to hear that no arrangements had yet been cast in stone for the wedding, so at least I still had time on my side. Towards the end of the afternoon, Pearl acquiesced to cast her eyes over the manuscripts I'd brought with me. She refused to correct her drafts digitally.

'You are getting so much better at this than me,' she conceded. 'I seriously think it might be time to quit.'

'You want to quit writing?'

'Well, now I'm here, with Jack, it hardly seems worth the bother, to be honest.'

'It's hardly any bother. I've done all the hard work for you.'

'Yes, I know, but then we'll have the launches to organise, and the publicity. I'll have to go up to London and do signings and interviews.'

'I thought you liked giving signings and interviews?' I argued.

'Well yes, dear, but it has all got rather tedious over the years, and now I've got Jack.' She smiled across the room to where Jack sat at a small table puzzling over a crossword. 'I'd rather be here with him, to be honest, than having to trail up to London.'

'Jack, what do you think?' I turned to the man who had seemingly charmed my mother into an unnatural state of domestic docility. 'Surely you don't expect Pearl to give up her career just because she's found you?'

'Pearl has to do what she thinks best,' Jack replied. He returned Pearl's soppy smile.

'I think I'll make these two my last,' Pearl said, shuffling up the reams of paper having barely lifted her pencil. 'Can you draft a note to Anita, telling her?'

I opened my mouth to protest but shut it again. Anita was our agent. I would speak to her personally before I drafted any notes. It was little consolation to know that my concerns for the future were well and truly justified. If Pearl Gates gave up writing novels, what was I going to do for a living?

Chapter Three

Saturday evening at Rivermede was uneventful. Heather rustled up a very tasty lasagne and salad, and I retired early to my guest room for a somewhat surprisingly restful night's sleep. The following morning, I hoped all thoughts of a resignation letter had slipped Pearl's mind, but they hadn't. Straight after breakfast – a full English, served by Heather in the conservatory – she mentioned it again, and then dropped her second bombshell.

'I've decided to put Beech Mews on the market,' she announced.

'What?'

'Now, don't look like that, Becca, it's not as bad as it seems.'

Pearl was wearing tweed trousers and a caramel coloured blouse, as effortlessly elegant as always. Heather arrived to clear the table. I'd already discovered Heather and Nev shared an ability to turn up without warning. I found their presence intrusive, but Pearl had slipped into her role as lady of the manor with ease. Jack was nowhere to be seen.

'In what way is it not as bad as it seems?' I demanded, once we were alone again.

'We don't need it any more,' Pearl replied.

'Yes, we do. It's our home, my home, Freddy's home. He finishes college this summer. Where is he going to live?'

'Here, of course. He can come here to live with Jack and me. You both can.'

A far more pressing danger had arisen than literary oblivion. Why did Pearl think either Freddy or I would want to move to the countryside?

'Freddy won't want to come and live out in the sticks like

22

this,' I replied. 'He's going to be job hunting. He's going to need to be in London if he wants to get private commissions.'

'Oh, come on, darling. We both know Freddy has about as much chance of winning a private commission as I do of being nominated for the Man Booker prize.'

I applauded my mother's sense of realism, but this wasn't the time I wanted to hear it. I did my utmost to keep my voice rational. I might have felt like a whinging teenager, but I didn't want to sound like one.

'You've only known Jack a few weeks,' I pointed out. 'It's far too soon for you to be making big decisions like this. I like him, seriously I do, but can't you just date for a bit, live together if you have to, but keep the flat as security? What if it all goes pear-shaped?'

'It's not going to go pear-shaped,' Pearl replied. 'We had a long chat last night and we've decided to set the wedding date.'

'What?'

'It's going to be midsummer, 21st June. We're going to have a quiet civil ceremony at the registry office in Southampton, and then back here to say our vows and have a garden party. Jack's out in the grounds now with Nev, looking at the logistics of putting up a marquee.'

'Oh, I see.'

'You could at least look pleased.'

'What have I got to be pleased about? You're doing me out of a job and out of a home.'

'I told you, you've got a home here.'

'And my career?' My frustration bubbled over. 'Of course, I'd forgotten. Kerridge is overflowing with publishing houses looking for editors, and writers looking for PAs. Can't you see I need to be in London if I want to find work?'

'London's only just over an hour away. You do most of your work on your lap-top. You're always telling me I'm a positive dinosaur because I like an ink pen and piece of paper. When you work online, it doesn't matter where you're located, does it?'

'And my social life?'

'There's the sailing club. They put on a good do every now and then; we went to one just the other night. And there's a couple of nice pubs, and that reminds me, I need to tell you about the pub…'

'Are you being serious?'

I could have throttled her. Almost as if he could sense his fiancée's life was in peril, I heard the sound of Jack's wheelchair approaching along the corridor. Nev wheeled him into the conservatory.

'Good morning, Becca dear,' Jack said. His greeting contained genuine warmth, and Pearl's face lit up at his arrival, once again rushing to his side. I turned away, ashamed of my outburst.

Jack reported that he and Nev had earmarked the perfect spot for the marquee while Heather had been charged with investigating local catering companies. After lunch, Pearl insisted we sit down with a stash of bridal magazines, and in an attempt to redeem myself I tried to look interested as she offered up suggestions for bouquets and dresses.

'I hope you've started that diet I recommended,' she said. 'You don't look like you've lost any weight yet.'

I felt positively inspired to put more on but quashed all thought of rebellion. I did need to lose a few pounds. Pearl was the one who'd been on an all-you-can-eat cruise, yet she'd returned looking trimmer than ever. In her absence, I'd been tucking into calorie-laden comfort foods.

'I originally thought of yellow for the colour theme,' she mused, flicking through pages of glossy photographs of beaming brides and their handsome grooms. 'An homage to spring. I quite fancied a maypole and floral bunting, but I suppose now we've decided on June, the maypole idea is out. So, I'm veering towards purple, with sprays of cornflowers and hints of lavender. Or is that too similar to what we had for you? What do you think?'

I replied I thought purple would be just perfect, but felt tears smarting in the corner of my eyes. I felt totally deflated. Confused and deflated. It was all too much. 'Do we have to do this now?' I muttered.

'Of course we do. You of all people should know these things take meticulous planning. Do you think I should ask Freddy to give me away, or Laurie?'

My honorary 'uncle' Laurie was an old family friend. He'd been Pearl's first boss in publishing, and had later taken me under his wing. He had stayed in touch over the years, checking up on Pearl every now and then out of a sense of misplaced loyalty. As a child, I'd often dreamed that sensible Uncle Laurie would one day see the light and marry my mother, but of course he was far too sensible for that. Thankfully, when Pearl's world imploded, as it did every so often, he was still there to pick up the pieces. I'd always suspected Uncle Laurie was a little in love with Pearl himself, so it seemed somewhat insensitive to ask him to give her away, but right now my mother's lack of sensitivity had reached boiling point. Finally, she took the hint.

'Freddy,' she said decisively. 'I expect he'd relish the task.'

'Not when you're about to diddle him out of his home.' I was unable to stop myself.

Pearl pursed her lips. 'I'm not diddling anybody out of anything. I don't know how you can say such a thing, Rebecca. After all I've done for you.'

I blinked away the tears. My mother was being incorrigible. It was as if she had absolutely no idea the impact her behaviour was having on me. I was floundering in an alien world, staring into a black hole. I'd dedicated the last fifteen years of my life to creating stability from chaos, and my mother had quite literally just pulled the rug from under my feet. The need for a quiet word with Jack's son to discuss a joint plan of action was now paramount. I would grab him at the first opportunity.

Dinner was arranged for six – Pearl never enjoyed eating late, and it appeared Jack shared her views. As much as I hated to admit it, they were extremely well suited.

JJ Robshaw oozed the type of confidence and demeanour that came from a public school education, easy wealth, and a handsome visage. He had the physique of a rugby player and, although slightly stockier than those images I'd seen on the internet, he was still a good-looking man – and knew it.

His wife, Marguerite – Rita, for short, according to Pearl – was a slender blonde, perhaps some ten years or so his junior. She wore a black and white polka-dot jump-suit, an outfit which wouldn't have looked out of place on a children's TV presenter. Even Jack looked taken aback as the couple made their entrance, while Pearl couldn't hide her amusement.

JJ barely glanced in my direction as his father introduced us, although Rita broke briefly free from his arm and air-kissed my cheek.

'How lovely to meet you,' she said.

They both made no move to greet Pearl, but she seemed unfazed by their behaviour.

'That's quite an outfit, Rita,' she said, helping herself to another glass of Prosecco from the bottle Nev had opened earlier and left cooling in an ice bucket on the cocktail cabinet. 'Did you buy it locally? And how's the house coming on, JJ? Has the problem with the glass for the windows been resolved?'

JJ and Marguerite continued to ignore her, and I immediately felt insulted on her behalf. Even if they resented my mother's arrival at Rivermede, there was no need for such blatant rudeness. JJ turned to speak to Jack while Marguerite asked Neville, who was hovering, if she could have a G&T.

Pearl gave a shrug and came and sat on a sofa beside me. 'The house is a bit of a sore point,' she explained, as if that justified their behaviour.

'So, what do you do for a living, Becca?' Marguerite asked after a dainty sip of her G&T.

'I'm Mum's PA,' I replied. 'I handle the business side of her writing.'

'I didn't know you wrote, Pearl.' Marguerite's ignorance seemed quite genuine.

'She writes trashy romance novels,' JJ broke in. 'I did mention it. You won't have heard of her.'

'I might,' Marguerite contradicted. 'What's your pen name?'

26

'I write under my own name,' Pearl replied.

'Oh, don't tell me Pearl Gates is your real name?' JJ snorted. 'It's made up, surely? Nobody is born Pearl Gates.'

'When you are gifted with a name like mine, you don't change it,' Pearl said with a fixed smile.

'Oh, don't be daft,' JJ spluttered. He turned to his wife. '*Pearly gates*, get it, Reet?'

Marguerite looked quite blank.

'Not familiar with the Bible?' Pearl raised an eyebrow. 'Now there's a surprise.'

'Oh, those pearly gates. I hadn't thought of that.'

With a discreet cough from the doorway, Neville announced dinner was about to be served in the dining room. Pearl whisked Jack off in advance while I helped myself to another large Prosecco. As I headed out into the hallway, I caught Marguerite's peel of girlish laughter.

'Do you think the daughter has a husband?'

'Well, if he does, I already feel sorry for the chap,' JJ replied.

Conversation over dinner remained strained and somewhat stilted. Jack and JJ spent some time talking business, while Rita periodically looked up from pushing her food around her plate to comment on how many calories she had consumed already that week versus steps on her Fitbit and how many more exercise classes she would need to attend to counter-balance the effects of the tomato consommé and gorgeously succulent roast chicken, which had barely touched my sides.

'So, do you have a partner, Becca?' Rita asked, eventually pushing her chicken to one side.

'A partner?' I'd been waiting for the question to arise since we'd sat down. 'You mean like a business partner? I could certainly do with one to help manage Pearl's commercial affairs. A successful novelist can keep one PA incredibly busy.'

'No, I mean like a husband, boyfriend?'

'Oh. I see. No, I'm happily single.' I gave her what I hoped was a pleasant smile and asked Jack to pass me more gravy.

'I'd have thought an attractive, intelligent woman like you

would have had no trouble finding yourself a young man,' Jack remarked, sadly ignoring my attempt to draw him into a conversation about Heather's culinary skills.

'I'm more than content on my own,' I assured him.

'She always says that,' Pearl interjected. 'I don't believe her. Ever since she was jilted at the altar, she's been off men.'

'You were jilted at the altar?' Rita's face was agog with interest. 'Oh, go on, do tell. When was this, Becca? Recently or—'

'A long time ago now,' I replied. 'This roast chicken really is excellent, Jack. How long has Heather been working for you?'

'Oh, don't change the subject,' Rita whined. 'I'm enthralled. Was it really at the altar, Pearl?'

Pearl put down her knife and fork. She could never pass up the opportunity to revel in her lost mother-of-the-bride moment, especially after a drink or two. 'Yes. We were all there in the church and her Uncle Laurie had walked her up the aisle, and the next thing we know she and her fiancé are having a slanging match in front of the vicar. Two minutes later, she comes storming back down the aisle and announces the wedding is off.'

'Sounds like some young man had a very lucky escape,' JJ smirked.

Rita nudged him with her elbow. 'So, was it you who decided not to get married, Becca, or was it him?'

'Yes, actually it was me. I wasn't jilted at all.' I glared at Pearl. 'I discovered my fiancé had been sleeping with my best friend, so I decided all men were bastards and I haven't touched another one since.'

To my surprise, Jack gave an approving nod. 'Nothing worse than being betrayed by a loved one,' he grunted.

Rita seemed determined not to let the subject drop. 'Why did you wait until you got to the altar? Why not call the whole thing off beforehand if you knew he'd been cheating?'

'Because I'd spent a lot of money on that wedding,' Pearl interjected, 'and I wasn't going to let it go to waste. The very least she could do was walk up the aisle for me. We had friends coming from miles around, people booked into hotels. I didn't want to let them down.'

'What, you made her do it? You knew she didn't want to marry him, yet you made her go through with the ceremony?' Rita looked astonished.

'Look really, I don't want to talk about this,' I said, pushing my plate away. 'It was nearly fifteen years ago. I was very young.'

'I think that says it all, Dad.' JJ leaned back in his chair. 'What sort of woman is this that you want to marry? Forcing her daughter to suffer that indignity and humiliation just because she wanted to wear a posh frock and show off in front of all her friends? How shallow is that. You heard her. Let's drop this charade now.'

'Don't you start on that again,' Jack growled. 'Can't we have a civilised meal?'

'I don't think we can. I don't think there is anything civilised about Mrs Pearly Gates,' JJ sneered.

'That's enough!' Jack slammed his fist down on the table. 'Do you hear me, boy? Enough.'

I had intended suggesting to JJ that we devise a joint strategy on how best to dissuade our parents from marrying, but the battle lines had clearly already been drawn. JJ seemed intent on attacking Pearl's integrity at every opportunity. I doubted he would approve my idea for a subtle approach.

We carried on in silence until Jack needed the bathroom. Pearl ushered him out of the room towards the ensuite. JJ turned to me the minute we heard the click of the bedroom door. 'How much money do you want?' he demanded.

'I beg your pardon?'

'You heard me. How much money are you two after?'

'I'm not after any money,' I said.

'Oh, come on, look at my father, your mother. Do you honestly think this is a match made in heaven? They meet on a cruise ship and the next thing we know is he's proposing marriage. A week later, she's moved in lock, stock and barrel. The last thing my father needs at his time of life is a gold-digging divorcee. I'll pay you whatever it takes to get your

29

mother out of our lives.'

'I'll have you know my mother is a wealthy woman in her own right. You honestly think she's after his money? Does she look cash-strapped?'

Rita tapped her husband's arm. 'That scarf is Hermes, JJ, I did point it out.'

'Are you worried Pearl's going to show you up at the yacht club? Is that it?' I attempted to fix a polite smile on my face.

'Don't be ridiculous,' JJ snapped. 'I said I'll give you money to take your mother away from Rivermede and not bring her back. She might well have made a fortune from writing that romantic shit, but you look like you could do with an extra few bob or two. Come on, just name your price.'

I'd thought Jack's son and I would be allies, not adversaries, but I'd never taken such an instant dislike to anybody in my entire life. The last thing I wanted to do was align myself to such an obnoxious man. My mother had been on her own for a long time and she deserved to be happy. My own fears for the future paled into insignificance.

'I think Jack and Pearl are absolutely perfect for each other,' I announced, as I heard the bedroom door re-open and the soft whoosh of the wheelchair on the tiled hallway floor as my mother and her fiancé returned. 'In fact, I don't think this wedding can happen soon enough.'

Chapter Four

It was almost a relief to speak the words out loud. There, decision made, no going back. I had to accept that Pearl would come to live at Rivermede, marry Jack, and our lives would begin a new phase. I hadn't yet worked out exactly what that new phase would entail, but at least it felt as if I was back in control in the driver's seat, even if we weren't travelling in the direction I'd originally planned.

I hadn't intended to head back to London until Tuesday. The next morning, I accompanied Pearl on another walk in the grounds, this time to check out the location for the marquee as suggested by Neville, and then to discuss the merits of releasing balloons versus doves to celebrate the vows.

'I meant to tell you about the pub, didn't I?' she said as we strolled past the defunct fountain. 'Do you remember Stella Markham?'

Somewhere in the dark recesses of my mind, the name rang a bell, but not in the context of any authors or anyone in my mother's immediate social circle.

Pearl digressed to poke at the flaking stonework on the fountain. 'I must ask Nev to look at this fountain,' she said, 'it needs a good clean out. We want that working on the day, don't we?'

'Yes, we do,' I agreed, mainly because it was always easier to agree with Pearl than to argue on matters that were unimportant. 'Who is Stella Markham?'

'Owen Markham's wife, or ex-wife, rather.'

Owen Markham. That name certainly rang a big bell. He was a celebrity chef from the era of my childhood, a trademark moustache and the dress-sense of a swashbuckling buccaneer. He'd earned the nickname '*Captain Cook*' after a TV series followed him around the globe, catching and cooking exotic seafood from the back of his yacht, tossing red snappers and sea urchins into a frying pan and declaring we should all be able to emulate his skill with little more than a packet of frozen scallops from the local supermarket. Re-runs of his programmes still occasionally cropped up on lifestyle and cooking channels.

'You might not remember, but he and his wife had that very public bust-up,' Pearl said. 'They were both sailing mad, and she made the headlines for winning a big yacht race and it all blew up her face. There was a huge scandal. Owen accused her abandoning him and her children. It was all over the press.'

I shook my head, although the story sounded vaguely familiar. 'Before my time,' I pointed out. 'What's she got to do with the pub?'

'She owns it.' Pearl lowered her voice. 'Her and *her girlfriend*.'

So, that was the scandal; hardly a scandal these days, but thirty years ago it might have been pretty shocking.

'Anyway, the thing is, Stella might be able to help you.'

'Oh?'

'She and Jack are quite pally. He likes to pop in for a drink every now and then, and the food in the pub is pretty good. He took me there when we got back last week.'

'Oh, I see. So how could she help me? Has she offered me a job in the pub?'

'No, listen. We were having a chat and we got round to the bit about me being a writer, and you being a brilliant editor, and how you would need to find some work once I've retired. And guess what, she'd like you to ghost-write her memoirs.'

'Are you being serious?'

Pearl looked a little bashful. 'Well, she didn't actually say she wanted you to ghost-write her memoirs, but she did say she'd like to tell her side of the story, put things straight after all these years. I suggested you could meet to see if there is a potential book there. Why not, Becca? Why are you looking at me like that? What else have you got to do?'

I hadn't actually given a thought to what I was going to do

if Pearl followed through her retirement plan. I was still living in hope she'd pull out of it. Just because I'd relented to the marriage, it didn't mean I endorsed everything else that apparently came with it.

'I don't need you interfering in my life any more, thank you,' I said. 'You've done enough damage already.'

Pearl looked quite hurt. 'What does that mean?'

'You know what I mean. Selling my home, giving up your career, putting me out of a job. Okay, I understand why you want to stay here. Rivermede is a lovely property, but does this have to be the end of your writing? Surely you can find inspiration here for some new stories? Just because you are marrying Jack, it doesn't mean it all has to stop, does it?'

'Yes it does, Becca. I'm afraid it does. Jack needs looking after. I want to look after him, and I don't want to be constantly thinking about writing, and about all the publicity stuff we have to do to go with it. I've already told you. I want to immerse myself in village life, join the gardening club, the WI, take art classes.'

'Oh, come on,' I said, 'this isn't you. You shouldn't give up your career to join the village gardening club.'

'But I want to give up my career,' Pearl said. She patted my arm. 'I'm sorry, darling, it's over. I know you're upset, but you're a great writer yourself. Talk to Stella, see if you can make something out of her story. Who knows? This could be your big break. She's a fascinating woman.'

I sighed. With no other work on the horizon, what real choice did I have? I agreed to talk to Stella Markham and Pearl settled on doves rather than balloons, as I always knew she would.

The community of Kerridge covered a wide area. There was no high street as such, but the church and its adjacent hall appeared to constitute its centre, with a village green surrounded by sprawling chestnut trees. Clusters of chocolate-box cottages juxtaposed by modern detached designer properties dotted winding lanes along the river valley. According to Pearl, most of the action in Kerridge took place on the waterfront but I had yet to see the delights of Kerridge Hard, as she referred to it – home of the marina.

It all looked and sounded very charming, but it was impossible to imagine my gregarious, cosmopolitan mother being happy in such a sleepy backwater, despite her protestations to the contrary. When had Pearl ever been interested in gardening? We didn't even have a window box in Battersea, and the house-plants were plastic imitations for ease of maintenance. As for the WI, a few months ago the mere mention of the organisation would have sent her into spasms of mocking derision.

The Ship of Fools was situated on the outer regions of the village, in a picturesque spot on a bend of the River Deane. Pearl's directions were not easy to follow, and my sat nav directed me over the ford once again. The pub's sign depicted three colourful court jesters in a sailing boat, one of whom bore more than a passing resemblance to Owen Markham. History had never been my thing, but I was pretty sure waxed moustaches weren't popular back in medieval times.

I had to stoop to enter. Inside, sloping black wooden beams dominated an interior decorated with fishing nets, lobster pots, and ships' lanterns. A fire roared in the grate, giving the pub a cosy, smoky, atmosphere. For six-thirty on a Monday evening, it seemed remarkably busy; there was a small crowd at the bar and several of the tables were already taken.

At Pearl's insistence, I'd conducted some online research so that I was already prepared with the background to Stella's story. Owen Markham didn't have a good word to say about his ex. What should have been seen as major triumph for amateur sailor Stella, captaining an all-woman crew for the Tri-Island long distance yacht race – Isle of Wight, Madeira, The Azores – had been overshadowed by a vicious dissecting of her personal life and accusations, later proved to be totally unfounded, of cheating.

She was serving behind the bar; a short, rather dumpy woman of about sixty, with a greying, pudding basin haircut. She wore a black and white striped T-shirt with jeans. It was easy to picture her stood at the helm of a yacht, battling the elements, but totally impossible to imagine her ever being married to a flamboyant character like Owen. Her skin was weather-beaten and her face devoid of any make-up. She was aided behind the bar by a young man in his twenties, bearded and pierced, and eager to serve.

'What can I get you?' he asked with a smile.

'I'm actually here to see Stella,' I said, nodding in her direction, 'but I'll have a small white wine, please.'

Pearl had phoned ahead to let Stella know I was my on my way. 'Are you Pearl's daughter?' she enquired with a beaming smile. 'I'll get this, Ben. Can you take the wheel for a while?'

'Yes, of course,' he grinned.

'You look very busy,' I remarked as Stella handed me a large glass of white wine.

'It's quiz night,' she replied. 'We do a pie, chips and quiz special on a Monday. They're all regulars, so we're in control. Pearl said you were heading off back to London tomorrow so tonight was our only chance for a chat.'

I nodded. 'Yes, but I suspect I'll be coming back to Kerridge fairly regularly.' More than regularly, if Pearl had her way and the Battersea flat was sold, although I fully intended to make Beech Mews as unsellable as possible – a major task, considering our flat was in one of the most desirable blocks in the area. I would put off contacting estate agents for as long as I could, and I certainly had no intention of 'staging' anything, as Pearl had suggested, to make the flat look more attractive. Potential buyers would have to view it warts and all. I was definitely not going to waste my time whitewashing Freddy's black bedroom walls.

Stella suggested we head to a small table well away from the bar in the quieter end of the pub, hidden away behind a couple of cross-beams.

'Pearl thinks my story could make a good book,' she began as we sat down.

'They do say everyone has a book in them,' I smiled, 'and you've certainly led an interesting life, that's for sure.'

'You think?' Stella grunted. 'It's been pretty hellish a lot of the time, to be honest. Besides everything else that went on, it's not nice being accused of cheating, you know. That smear never wears off.'

'Well, maybe it is time for people to hear your side of the story,' I suggested.

'That's what your mother said.' Stella gave a shrug. 'Do you think you can make it a bestseller?'

'Oh, I'm not sure about that,' I confessed. I didn't want to give Stella the wrong impression. I wasn't sure the name Owen Markham carried enough kudos any more to create a great deal of interest from the paying public. Many other celebrity chefs had come and gone since his glory days. 'It's very hard to predict what will make a bestseller and what won't,' I told her. 'Sadly, it's a lot more to do with marketing hype. I suppose that's another thing you have to consider. Are you prepared for the inevitable publicity?'

'Well, that's just it, isn't it?' Stella replied. 'I'm not sure I am. Chloe and I live very quietly here in Kerridge, and part of me would like it to stay that way. On the other hand, I suppose it would be an opportunity to tell the truth about everything that happened, put the record straight.'

'So why not do it then?' I suggested. 'Have you given any thought to what sort of format this book could take?'

'To be honest, I'd not thought about any of it for years, until Pearl mentioned it,' Stella admitted. 'At the time it all blew up, I did try and cobble some notes together, but I couldn't get a publisher to touch it. I've kept a lot of the old newspaper cuttings about the race itself and all the build-up, because I was pretty proud of that despite Owen's accusations, but I certainly didn't keep any mementoes of the fall-out. You'd have your work cut out making my original scribbles into something readable, that's for sure.'

'Have you still got the notes?' I asked hopefully. 'It would give me something to go on.'

'I'll have to have a dig around,' Stella said, 'and see what I've got up in the attic.'

'Great.' I couldn't help but feel Pearl's suggestion of writing Stella's memoirs was nothing but a ruse to keep me in Kerridge. However, it could be something worth pursuing.

'Look, I'll probably be back down here in a few weeks,' I told her. 'Why not have a good think about whether you want to proceed? The newspaper cuttings and photographs would help me to get an understanding of the facts, give me some idea of whether the project could work. Maybe you can send me what you've got? I'll give you my email and postal address. In the meantime, it wouldn't do any harm to jot down some retrospective thoughts about the emotions you felt at the time, the high obviously of winning that race, then how it felt afterwards to be vilified by your husband in the press. I'll do a bit of online research, too. If we do go ahead, what about your ex? How would he feature in this?'

'As little as bloody possible, I hope,' Stella grumbled. 'I haven't spoken to Owen for years.'

'We might just have to warn him about the book, if it gets as far as publication. We have to be aware of the libel and defamation laws.'

'He didn't seem to worry about that when he slagged me off to all and sundry,' Stella pointed out. She looked up at the bar. 'Look, I'd best go and help Ben out. I'll have to discuss it with Chloe anyway, see how she feels about everything coming back out into the open.'

'That would be a good idea,' I agreed. I knew from my research that Owen Markham's sous chef, Chloe Poole, had been his rival for Stella's affections. Together, the Markhams had owned a top-end restaurant in Cowes on the Isle of Wight, a popular haunt of the sailing fraternity. Chloe had accompanied Stella on her infamous yacht race. The fact that she and Stella were still together thirty years later was testament to the strength of their relationship, although it had been a double whammy for Owen. He hadn't just lost his wife, he'd lost his top chef, too. No wonder he'd been so bitter.

'Chloe is with you here tonight, I take it?' I asked.

'Yes, she's in the kitchen, as always,' Stella smiled. 'This joint is hers as much as it is mine. I don't suppose I could interest you in our pie, chips and quiz deal, could I?'

Pearl had already extolled the virtues of The Ship of Fools' extensive menu, and I'd made no arrangements to be back at

Rivermede for dinner.

'Sure, I'd love to,' I said.

Chapter Five

Stella insisted on fixing me up with a quiz team, even though I assured her it wasn't necessary.

'I'm quite happy to sit here eating on my own,' I protested.

She wouldn't hear of it. 'The Twitchers are a bit thin on the ground tonight. Let me introduce you.' Somewhat reluctantly, I followed her through the pub to a table in the nook by the fire place. I noticed she walked with a slight limp, as if she had seized up from sitting down.

There were three people sat at the table, all tucking into their pies – a couple in their early sixties, wearing matching navy sweatshirts; and a younger man, bearded, with scruffy collar-length dark hair, his shoulders hunched.

'Sorry to interrupt, Twitchers, but you don't mind Becca joining you, do you?' Stella announced.

'Not at all,' the woman in the blue sweatshirt smiled.

'Take a seat,' her partner added, waving his fork at the vacant chair. 'I'm Craig and this is my wife, Chrissie.'

'Pleased to meet you,' I said, as Stella headed back to the bar.

The third occupant of the table looked up from his meal. Our eyes met. Locked.

It was inevitable that along life's journey you encountered people you never wanted to see again, people you went out of your way to avoid, crossed over to the other side of a road or hid in a shop doorway to avoid; those kinds of people. And then there were people who if you didn't know they had already left the country, you would seriously consider moving to the other side of the world to avoid, people who you had vowed never to speak to again because they had betrayed you, hurt you, and humiliated you so much. The kind of people who didn't just break hearts, they destroyed them. The kind of people like the third member of the Twitchers' quiz team.

'Where's your manners, Alex,' Craig laughed, giving his teammate a nudge. 'You don't mind Becca joining us, do you?'

I could almost see the cogs turning in his brain, whirring at top speed, his mind running through the same dilemma, questioning the unlikeliest of scenarios, how we two people had ended up here in the same room, in the same pub, in the same village, miles away from where we both lived, fifteen years after our last encounter.

The last time I'd seen 'Alex' was when I'd flounced down the aisle of St Mary's Church in Battersea, and he certainly hadn't been called Alex then, although it might possibly have been one of his middle names. Nick Quinlan could well have a double, but from the look on Alex's face, Nick's doppelganger was not currently sat having a pie and pint in The Ship of Fools in sleepy Kerridge. This was the genuine thing, my ex, in the pub, pretending to be someone he was not, and by all accounts he was as horrified to see me as I was to see him.

He regained his composure first. 'No, not at all. I'm Alex McLean,' he said, holding out his hand. 'Pleased to meet you, Becca.'

No appropriate, polite, words of introduction came into my head as I shook that firm, familiar hand.

'How are you on TV soaps?' Chrissie asked, resuming her dinner and filling the awkward silence. 'We always fall down on the soaps without Mark and Marie. Mark and Marie are on holiday, which is why it's just the three of us this week. Alex is our music buff, and Craig knows his sport. I'm okay with geography and history.'

'I'm sorry, I'm probably not going to be much help at all,' I told her, wondering how I was going to get through the rest of the evening. Not only did I have to display some sort of intelligence during the quiz, I also had to maintain a polite conversation with Nick Quinlan sat next to me. It was going to be impossible. 'I'm not a great TV fan either.'

'What brings you to The Ship on a chilly night like this, Becca?' Nick asked. The message in his introduction had been perfectly clear. *You don't know me.*

40

'Umm, Stella invited me,' I replied. It didn't take much to guess the reason for the assumed name and that unspoken request for my silence. I knew what line of work Nick had been in fifteen years ago; there was no reason to assume he had changed careers, despite a sojourn overseas. I quashed the temptation to blow his cover. Revenge was always a dish best served cold, or at least well-calculated.

'Are you a friend of Stella's?' he enquired. His expression had returned to inscrutable benign politeness.

'Not really,' I smiled. 'We only met earlier this evening.' I turned to Chrissie and Craig. The matching navy sweatshirts bore the emblem of the RSPB. 'So, what's with the team name? Twitchers? Isn't that something to do with bird-watching?'

'Oh yes,' Craig enthused. 'We get a wide variety of wild fowl down here on the salt marshes. We're all very keen amateur ornithologists.'

The Nick I knew had absolutely no interest in birds, of the feathered kind at least. 'You too, Alex? How interesting. Tell me, what's the rarest bird you've come across in Kerridge so far this year? I'd love to know.'

Before Nick could come up with an answer, Craig interrupted with an entire catalogue of seabirds which over-wintered at Helme Point.

'Yes, all of those,' Nick murmured in agreement when Craig had finished reeling off his list.

'Alex is always out there on the marsh with his binoculars,' Chrissie added. 'Do you have an interest in ornithology, Becca?'

I shook my head. 'Oh no, sorry.'

'So, how come you're in Kerridge?' Nick enquired. 'Are you just visiting?' It was a perfectly reasonable but totally loaded question.

Stella had appeared at the table bearing a huge plate of food. 'Becca's mother has recently moved into the village,' she answered on my behalf. 'She is one of our new neighbours. You've got our last chicken and leek, Becca, hope that's okay.'

'Thanks, Stella.' The pie was enormous. Pearl would never

have fixed me an appointment with Stella if she'd known how much pastry was going to be involved in the negotiations. Even Nick appeared defeated by the walls of crust on his steak and kidney, and a good third remained un-eaten on his abandoned plate, although perhaps that was just because he'd lost his appetite.

'Oh, are you Pearl Gates' daughter?' Chrissie exclaimed. 'Why didn't you say? Did you know we now have a famous author amongst us here in Kerridge, Alex? I'm surprised you've not come across her yet when you've been out on your walks.'

'No, I don't think I've had that pleasure,' Nick replied. 'Your mother is here in Kerridge, Becca?' His discomfort was just starting to show, although he was playing his part very well. Years of undercover work had probably prepared him for every eventuality, although probably not an unwanted encounter with a vengeful ex-mother-in-law-to-be. I may have forgiven Nick for his defection, but Pearl hadn't. Her mention of him at yesterday's dinner table had been evidence of that. Nick hadn't just deprived her of her big day; in Pearl's opinion, he'd turned me off men for the life.

Nick stood up abruptly. 'Another drink, Becca? Can I tempt you with more wine?'

'Oh, I'm sure you can.' I smiled.

'How about you come and help me up at the bar?'

'The poor girl's just got her meal,' Chrissie said, waving him away. 'Craig will give you a hand. Let Becca enjoy her dinner.'

Chrissie had a point. I caught Nick's expression. The request to join him was not so much a suggestion but a command. *Tough.* I was enjoying watching him squirm.

'It's very tasty,' I replied, cutting through the layers of carbohydrate. 'I'm on the Sauvignon, Alex; the French, not the Chilean.'

I concentrated on my pie, scooping out as much innards as I could and leaving the outer wall. Nick had aged well over the last fifteen years. The beard, just showing the first few flecks of grey, coupled with the longer hair gave him a ruggedness he'd lacked before when he'd been a sharp-suited police detective. He was still a good-looking man, several inches taller than Craig, having to bend his head to avoid the beams at the bar. I wondered how I appeared to him. Even today, for my meeting with Stella I'd opted for my uniform of black trousers and a simple lightweight cream sweater; my efficient, professional look. I didn't want Nick to think I'd let myself go – but there was no stopping the tide of time. I'd lost the exuberance of youth and any sense of fun and frivolity.

'So, are you all regulars?' I asked Chrissie. 'I take it you all live in the village?'

'Craig and I are old-timers. We've lived here for nearly thirty years. As I said, our friends, Mark and Marie – the M&Ms we like to call them – are currently on holiday. Alex is a relatively new addition to the team. We saw him up on the marsh for the first time a couple of months back and realised he must share our love of bird-watching. Then we just bumped into him here one night and got chatting.'

'So, Alex lives in Kerridge, too?'

'He's on the marsh. Stella rents out a houseboat down at Helme. He needs the solitude. He's writing a book.'

'Oh, really?' I wondered where he'd pinched that idea from.

'Yes. Perhaps your mum could give him some tips,' Chrissie suggested.

'I expect she'd relish the opportunity,' I replied.

Nick and Craig returned to the table with the drinks.

'I hear you're writing a book, Alex,' I said as he sat down. 'How interesting. What's it about?'

To my disappointment, Nick's answer was drowned by an ear-piercing whistle from the PA system.

'Phones away and pencils at the ready, everyone,' Stella called out.

Chrissie had meticulously marked out the team's answer sheets. I'd never experienced the world of the pub quiz before and was amazed when a tense hush fell over the bar. Craig and Chrissie had their heads bent, pens poised. I glanced sideways at Nick, who glanced sideways back at me. The chance for conversation was over.

Chapter Six

As predicted, I was no help at all with the inevitable TV soap question, but the art and literature round fell into my hands. At halfway point, the Twitchers were in joint first place.

I ignored Nick's suggestion of heading out for some fresh air during the break and remained firmly in my seat. He changed his mind and decided to stay at the table with me. Chrissie was keen to show off photographs of her latest grandchild, and I feigned an interest. The inevitable question arose about my marital status. which I played down with a quick, 'I'm currently single,' which at least implied I hadn't always been.

'What about you, Alex?' I asked. 'Are you a family man?'

Nick shuffled awkwardly on his seat as the sound system switched on again. A quick shake of his head left me confused as to whether he meant no, he wasn't a family man, or no, I shouldn't have asked. Another static scream signalled the start of the second half.

At least Chrissie and Craig appreciated my contribution to the evening. A final round of pot-luck questions saw the Twitchers win by a point.

'I hope you'll join us next week,' Chrissie beamed, counting out the cash prize into four equal piles. 'I can't believe we beat the Bloodhounds. They're too bloody clever for their own good.'

'I won't be in Kerridge next week, but I'd certainly love to join you whenever I can,' I told her, deliberately avoiding Nick's eye. We had matters to discuss. I knew he wouldn't let me out of his sight.

He caught me up in the car park. I allowed him to take my arm and lead me to a secluded spot behind a bin store.

'I suppose I should thank you,' he said.

'For what? Knowing that *croquembouche* is a desert made out of choux pastry balls as opposed to *croque monsieur* which is cheese on toast?' I replied.

His face was deadly serious. 'You know exactly what I mean.'

'Oh, for not blowing your cover? You are here working, I take it?'

'You know I can't say.'

'Well, you're going to have a harder job keeping your identity secret if my mother bumps into you,' I pointed out. 'I might have forgiven you for saving me from a fate worse than death and becoming Mrs Nick Quinlan, but she hasn't. You spoilt her big day, and not only that, deprived her of the potential for any grandchildren, and an entire crime series she'd been planning, entitled *My Son-in-law, The Ace Detective.* I take it you are still in the police force?'

Again, he didn't answer my question. 'Where is Pearl living?'

'A house called Rivermede, in the village. She met this old boy on a cruise and moved in with him a few weeks' back. Now they're planning a wedding. I'm not totally happy about it to be honest but—'

'She's at Rivermede?' Nick interrupted, 'with Jack Robshaw?'

I nodded. 'Yes. Do you know him?'

Nick shook his head, not in answer but with a look of disbelief. 'Tell me you are not serious?'

'Yes,' I replied. 'I wish I wasn't.'

'This can't happen, okay. You have to get her away from that place.'

'Excuse me?'

'You can't let her marry Jack Robshaw. You have to get her away from Rivermede.'

'Why?'

'I really can't tell you, just trust me.'

'Trust you?' I couldn't stifle the giggle. I'd been knocking back the wine all evening and any hope of a serious, sensible conversation was long lost. How on earth was I going to drive home? I steadied myself, clutching hold of the nearest wheely bin. The irony of trusting Nick Quinlan. 'You can't tell me what you're doing here, you can't tell me why my mother shouldn't marry Jack Robshaw. I just have to trust you?'

'Yes. Please, believe me, Rebecca, you cannot let your mother marry that man.'

Rebecca. Only two people ever called me by my full name. My mother was one and Nick had been the other. *Rebecca.* He'd had a way of saying it, of making it sound sexy and sophisticated, evoking images of the desirable, haunting, *femme fatale* in the Daphne Du Maurier novel I was named after.

'S'what's wrong with him?' I slurred. It was almost as if I had forgotten just twenty-four hours ago that I'd had a list of reasons as long as my arm as to why my mother shouldn't be getting married to Jack Robshaw.

'Just please take your mother away from Rivermede,' Nick said. 'It's for her own safety.'

'You're just saying that because you want her out of the way, so she doesn't see you and blow your cover for whatever it is you're really doing here in Kerridge,' I accused.

'Becca, please.'

'Why would I trust you, Nick? You slept with my best friend the night before our wedding. You're the last person I'd trust on earth.'

I hadn't meant to sound hysterical. There were still a few patrons milling about in the car park. I could hear car doors shutting, friends calling goodbyes.

'Keep your voice down,' Nick hissed. 'You don't want to draw attention to yourself.'

'You mean draw attention to you?'

'Yes, exactly, to me.' His face was a dark scowl. 'I'm doing something important here, of national importance, that's all I can say, and I can't afford to let you, or your mother, mess it up.'

'Oh, don't worry, your secret's safe with me. I'm not planning on spending a great deal of time in Kerridge so hopefully our paths won't cross again. But I've no intention of putting off my mother's wedding. You already denied my family one big day, Nick Quinlan, you are not going to deny us another.' I wasn't Pearl's daughter for nothing. I gave him a haughty glare and began to stumble across the car park towards my car.

'Becca, what are you doing? You're in no fit state to drive.' He caught up me with me again.

'Arrest me then, *Officer*.' I held out my wrists. 'Still got your handcuffs?'

It was an old private joke, reeled out many times during our relationship. Every policeman probably got fed up of hearing it, but Nick never seemed to. He'd kept a pair of handcuffs by his bed – not exactly police regulation, but a very good mock-up – and we'd had great fun using them.

'Sorry,' I said, dropping my hands as an instant picture came into my head of all the other women – one in particular – who had probably been teased and charmed by the same method. 'I shouldn't have mentioned the handcuffs.' I shouldn't have reminded myself. I shouldn't have reminded him.

His body language changed at the same time as mine. 'Let me walk you back to Rivermede,' he sighed.

'I don't know the way,' I admitted with a hiccup.

'Well, fortunately for you,' Nick said, holding out his hand, 'I do.'

Despite all my reservations and pledges never to speak to him again, there was no denying I had quite enjoyed baiting Nick during the quiz. For once I'd had the advantage, and it was extremely satisfying to hold the upper hand after all the previous pain he'd put me through. Power was a wonderful aphrodisiac. One word from me and whatever he was doing in Kerridge could all come crumbling down. I just couldn't believe it was anything to do with national security. That was typical Nick, playing up his own personal self-importance. He'd always been very good at putting himself on a pedestal, although a rapid rise through the ranks of the Metropolitan

Police had certainly helped to boost his already over-inflated ego. He had been one of their rising stars.

Nick was heading down towards the river.

'So, if what you're doing here is all hush-hush, how come you teamed up with the Twitchers to play in a pub quiz every week?' I asked as we slipped through a kissing gate and onto a gravel path. There were no lights, but Nick used his phone for a torch. The tide was up, and the River Deane glistened in the darkness.

'Oh, don't ask.' There was just a hint of humour in his voice. 'I bumped into them on the marsh. I had to come up with some excuse as to why I was lurking in a gorse bush with a long lens camera and a pair of binoculars, so I said the first thing that came into my head, I wasn't to know they were amateur bloody ornithologists. Anyway, after bluffing my way through a conversation about Brent geese and widgeons, I then ran into them again at the pub and they insisted I join them. Stella owns the houseboat I'm renting. I'd made the mistake of popping into see her on a Monday evening because the toilet wasn't working properly. It's all to do with pumps and it was pretty unpleasant, I can assure you. She suggested I stop for a pie and pint, and the next minute Craig and Chrissie and their regular partners – the dreaded M&Ms – turn up. To have declined their invitation would not only have seemed rude, but it could have aroused suspicion. To them, I'm just an ordinary bloke taking a bit of time out to get back to nature and write a book. Plus, it was a foul night and I was looking forward to some decent food.'

'Is that your disguise, an ordinary bloke?'

'Don't I look like an ordinary bloke?'

'Nick, you've always been just ordinary bloke. You're not anything special.'

'I really pissed you off at some point, haven't I?'

'Really? You don't say.' The path had become very squelchy underfoot. 'Are you sure this is the right way?' Up ahead, I could see very few lights.

'Yes, don't worry. You'll recognise where you are in a minute. This is just a shortcut. You'll be back at Rivermede before you know it.'

Almost before he finished speaking, we left the course of the river and headed through woodlands. Within minutes, we reached the lane that led to the house.

'So what about your family?' I realised with an unwelcome sense of dismay we were at the point where Nick would soon turn back. 'You managed to avoid answering earlier. How is Saskia?'

'I've no idea how Saskia is,' he replied. 'I haven't seen her for years.'

I tried to hide my surprise. 'Really?'

We came to a standstill. 'Yes, really. Saskia and I were never a couple. We were not compatible in any way, shape or form. It was all a huge mistake.'

The words I'd always longed to hear, just fifteen years too late.

'But you went to Texas with her,' I pointed out, trying to keep my voice under control. Nick sounded very matter-of-fact, as opposed to full of regret and remorse. I didn't want to let him know he'd just catapulted me into an emotional frenzy.

'When everything blew up, at first I blamed you,' he said, 'then I blamed her, then I realised the only person who was really to blame was myself. I went to Texas with her because I didn't know what else to do, and me being me, I had to save face. I tried to contact you when I came back to the UK, but you wouldn't take my calls or answer my letters.'

'Why would you think for one minute that I would? Saskia attempted to befriend me on Facebook years back. She never said you'd split up. She had pictures of herself with kids—'

'Not my kids,' Nick cut in. 'As I said, it was all a big mistake.'

Nick was a good liar; a trained liar. I shouldn't believe a word he said. I'd seen several pictures of Saskia's children over the years, because she sent friend requests on a regular basis and her social media privacy settings were minimal. One child had a definite look of Nick. *Untrustworthy*.

The gates of Rivermede loomed up ahead. 'I can manage on my own from here,' I told him.

'Are you sure?'

'Yes.' I realised I sounded ungracious. 'Thank you.'

'The pleasure was all mine,' he remarked. 'Seriously, Becca, about Pearl and Jack Robshaw.'

'I have very little influence over my mother,' I said, stopping him before he could say any more. 'As you must surely be aware, Pearl has always been a law unto herself.'

He didn't turn away. As the electric gates closed softly behind me, I was aware of his presence, lingering in the shadows of the trees outside in the lane. A surge of comforting warmth swept through my body. It could have been the wine, but I had a horrible suspicion it was something else entirely.

Chapter Seven

The following morning, despite a thumping headache, I crept out of Rivermede at first light and retrieved my car from the pub car park. Just as I was driving back up the lane towards the house, I caught a glimpse of Nev scurrying through the trees, as if he too had been out on some clandestine assignation. He was dressed in what appeared to be a wet suit, and had an oar tucked under his arm. Naturally, when we met at breakfast neither of us mentioned the sightings. Nev was far too well-trained. He lurked with not so much an air of menace but ingratiating politeness, and I had no intention of letting on to my mother I'd been too drunk to drive home. It would have led to far too many awkward questions.

When I finally made it back to Battersea at lunch time, Freddy was ensconced in his black bedroom.

I knew he was back in the flat because he'd left his moped in my parking space. The moped had always been a major bone of contention. Pearl had been distraught when he'd bought his first one. My father's accident always haunted her. The current model, a vintage Lambretta, was his third.

I expected to find him raiding the fridge; instead he was in bed. I woke him up with a shove, before heaving open his sash windows in an attempt to dilute the odour of stale sweat and alcohol.

'What are you doing here?' I demanded.

He looked dreadful, even darker black circles under his eyes than usual, his hair a badly bleached bird's nest of a mess.

'I've got a bit of a confession to make,' he mumbled, looking surprising pleased to see me. 'Where have you been?'

'I've been down in Hampshire seeing Pearl. I did tell you. You didn't want to come, said you had a rave or something to go to.'

'Oh yeah, the rave.' He shivered. 'Can't you shut the windows a bit?

'No. You stink. Have you been arrested? Chucked out of college? Come on, what is it?' After the shenanigans of the previous day, I really didn't want to listen to any torrid tales of woe, but Freddy looked quite traumatised.

He struggled to sit up. 'Can we go into the other room? I need a coffee.'

Freddy had a hangover that equalled mine. I made us both a coffee while he took a quick shower. He re-emerged five minutes later, smelling of exotic *Mon Guerlain* shower gel and wrapped in one of Pearl's dressing gowns.

'So, spit it out,' I said, as we sat opposite each other on the large floral sofas.

As I waited for him to reply, my eyes skirted around the room, wondering how it would appear to a potential buyer's eye, and how I could make it less appealing. It was a beautiful room with huge bay windows looking straight over the park. Even if I painted every wall the colour of Freddy's bedroom, I highly doubted it would discourage a sale.

'I got this girl pregnant.'

'You what?'

For some time now, Pearl and I had been hedging our bets as to whether Freddy would make an announcement about his sexuality. Gay sons were very fashionable in Pearl's immediate social circle, and Freddy hadn't mentioned girlfriends since primary school.

'Oh, don't make me say it again,' he muttered, 'you heard. This girl says I got her pregnant.'

'This girl? A girl? Not a girl you love, or have been dating, or have had any kind of meaningful relationship with?'

'Well, we were sort of seeing each other, a few times.'

'And did it ever occur to you to use any kind of contraceptive?' I hated myself for sounding like a disapproving headmistress. Having plucked up the courage to make his confession, it was hardly the response Freddy would have been hoping for.

He couldn't hide his embarrassment. 'She said she was on

the pill. I didn't think I needed to do anything else.'

'So, all those talks you had at school about Chlamydia and STDs didn't ever resonate with you, then? You didn't think you needed to protect yourself as well as the girl?'

Freddy looked down at his size thirteen feet. 'What do you think Pearl is going to say?'

'Oh, she's going to have a field day with this one,' I replied. 'She's been harping on at me for years to produce a grandchild for her.'

Freddy's flush deepened. 'I mean, Ruby and me, we're not together.'

'No, of course not. Why would you be?' I was beyond the realms of rational speech. I had to keep calm. 'Freddy, exactly what are you and this girl, this Ruby, doing about this baby? Does she plan on keeping it?'

'I think so, yes.'

'So, you will have to accept some sort of responsibility for it, won't you? You'll have to provide financial support.'

'How am I going to do that when I don't have a job?'

'You might have to think about getting one. You've more or less finished at Goldsmiths now, apart from your final project. Why don't you start looking?'

'I wanted to go off travelling for a bit over the summer.'

'Freddy!'

He scowled at me. 'What now?'

'You can't, can you? You've got no money, no visible means of support. How an earth can you expect to afford to go off travelling?'

'I could sell the Lambretta, and Pearl gives me money.'

'Pearl gave you money to live on while you are at uni. It's not to fritter away on a bloody gap year, especially not now, not with this. Who is this Ruby, anyway? Is she at college with you?'

He nodded. 'She's a second year.'

'And when is this baby due?'

'Next month.'

'Next month? Jesus Christ! And she's only just told you?'

'Well, no, I've known for a little while actually.'

53

'Oh Freddy.' No wonder he'd been so cagey the last few times I'd seen him. He'd had this hanging over him for months. 'Why didn't you say anything before?'

He shrugged. 'I dunno. Didn't know how to tell you, I s'pose. But with this thing happening with Pearl, I thought you ought to know.'

'Oh, thanks very much. So the baby will be here before the wedding?'

'Is it definitely going ahead? You couldn't stop it then?'

I smiled. 'Jack Robshaw is a benign old bloke she met on a cruise. It's his son who is the powerboat champion.'

Even that couldn't coax a smile onto his face. 'Oh. So how do you think she is going to react to my news?'

'You know Pearl. She does tend to take things in her stride.' There was no point making a bad situation worse. The fact that Freddy had told me first confirmed my suspicion he was, and always had been, slightly in awe of Pearl. It seemed quite sad that we both had such a strained relationship with the woman who had only ever done what she thought was best for us. 'What do Ruby's parents think of the situation?' I asked. 'Have you met them?'

Freddy shook his head. 'No point really, if me and Rubes aren't together.'

'What a mess, Freddy.'

'Sorry.' He looked totally pathetic, wrapping Pearl's pink quilted kimono around himself. I swapped sofas and came and sat beside him, putting my arm around his shoulders. To my surprise, he suddenly buried his head in my chest. Was he actually crying?

'Oh Fred,' I said. 'Don't worry. We'll get through this. We'll manage. Nothing's insurmountable.' I tried to sound confident, but it was hard not to feel overwhelmed by the course of events of the last few weeks. It was as if I'd been caught up in a whirlwind, a tornado, and deposited in a parallel universe. Where was my *good witch of the south* when I needed her? Or more importantly, why couldn't I wake up and discover it had all been a bad dream?

I took Freddy out to lunch, by which time we had both consoled each other, sobered up, and attempted to plan a strategy. Topping the list was the need for Freddy to get a job. Over our roast vegetable paninis, we scoured the internet. Freddy's fine art degree – 2.2 hoped for, but a 3 more realistic – had equipped him for very little in terms of south London employment opportunities, but he was surprisingly open to my suggestions that he should at least follow up a couple of leads for bar work.

After lunch, Freddy hopped on his scooter and zipped across London to his digs in Newcross, while I returned to Battersea and flopped onto my bed in a state of nervous exhaustion, only to be woken within half an hour by the doorbell.

In anticipation of my reluctance to put the flat on the market, without any warning Pearl had gone ahead and contacted a local estate agent. Magda Pepowski announced she had been instructed to carry out a preliminary valuation and showed me a copy of my mother's email to prove it. I scrutinised the message. Pearl had never emailed in her life without my say-so. Jack had obviously set her up with a new account.

With a weary sigh, I let Magda in – my only saving grace being that both my bedroom and Freddy's were in a state of complete disarray, although the open window policy had eliminated the foul smells in Freddy's. I wished now I'd left the window closed. Unfazed, Magda Pepowski shoved dirty cups into the dishwasher, wiped work surfaces, dusted, vacuumed, and made up the beds before taking numerous photographs.

'I'll be in touch with your mother,' she said. 'I've got clients queuing up to buy places like this. I could sell it ten times over in a week.'

The very words I had feared.

If Pearl was now capable of engaging an estate agent, she was equally as capable of sending her own letter of resignation to Anita. Still in a state of shock, I sat down on my bed and dialled Anita's private number.

I came straight to the point. 'If you receive a message from Pearl telling you she's quitting, ignore it. She says she wants *Single in St Johns Wood* and *Welcome to Weymouth Hill* to be her last two books. You've got to convince her to keep going.'

There was a very pregnant pause before Anita replied. 'What's brought this on?'

I couldn't betray Pearl's confidences before she made her official announcement about the wedding. That would be unforgiveable. 'It's just a blip,' I assured Anita. 'She's just back from that long cruise, remember, and it seems the time away has dampened her enthusiasm.' I resisted the temptation to add *and resulted in a complete personality transplant*.

'Well *Divorced in Dulwich* didn't last as long in the bestseller charts as we'd hoped,' Anita said. 'Churning out three or four books a year is a big commitment.'

'Yes, but her fans expect it,' I pointed out.

'The market has become very competitive,' Anita replied. 'There are plenty of other authors ready to take up Pearl Gates' crown. Sales of the last Christmas book were below par.'

'That's because the market is flooded with seasonal specials, spin-off novellas, and celebrity biographies,' I argued. Anita knew I put a great deal of effort into sustaining Pearl's career, but perhaps she didn't realise just how much my own life was invested in it. I handled all Pearl's correspondence, maintained her website, interacted with readers, travelled to conferences and seminars, arranged book tours, wrote speeches. It was almost impossible for me to envisage a life where those tasks no longer existed.

I pressed on with my case. 'I just feel this all a bit premature. I think Pearl's career could go on for many more years yet. She still has a lot to offer. She's only just started on the radio and TV circuit. Look how popular she is proving with a whole new audience.'

'I appreciate what you are saying,' Anita agreed. 'But maybe there has just been a little bit of originality lacking in her writing of late.'

I decided it was time to be brutally honest. 'Look, Anita, the fact is, if Pearl quits, I'm out of a job.'

There was another very pregnant pause. 'You won't be out of a job, Becca. You're a brilliant editor. You could get any amount of freelance work. Please don't take this the wrong way, but you've allowed that one unfortunate incident in your past to cloud your whole judgement on life. You are a clever, talented writer, yet you hide behind your mother and use her like a crutch. This could be just the opportunity you need to get out there from behind her shadow and start making a name for yourself in your own right.'

It wasn't quite what I wanted to hear. I thanked Anita for her time and stretched out on my bed, not knowing what to do next. It was almost if Pearl and Anita were on the same page, while I was still a chapter behind.

Chapter Eight

My life was spiralling out of control. Resilience could well have been Pearl's middle name, but it wasn't mine. I wasn't good at accepting change. I liked a fixed schedule, a six-month plan. Now I couldn't even predict my movements for a week ahead. I had no idea what the future held.

Pearl expressed her satisfaction with Magda's valuation, and an open house was arranged for the following weekend. She wanted to take Freddy shopping for his wedding suit, and Freddy needed to break the news she was about to be a grandmother. It made sense to head back to Rivermede.

The weather forecast was looking good; perfect conditions for a walk and further exploration of Kerridge. I threw my wellington boots into the back of the car. Since the encounter in the pub, I'd been doing my best not to think about Nick. I didn't want to examine my feelings. Seeing him again had opened up an emotional maelstrom I'd spent the best part of the last fifteen years trying to suppress. I told myself I didn't want to run into him again, and yet I knew in my heart of hearts I did.

We had unfinished business to discuss. I wanted to get to the bottom of what he was really doing in Kerridge, and I needed to know why, and when, it had all gone so very wrong between him and Saskia. Not that I had any idea where Stella Markham's houseboat, and Nick's stake-out, was moored, but as Freddy and I set out in the car for the drive down to Hampshire, I realised the possibility of bumping into Nick was the one aspect of the whole weekend I was actually looking forward to.

I was glad to see Freddy had made a small effort to spruce himself up for our trip to Rivermede. He'd had a haircut and removed his lip piercing. Although when I remarked on the improvement, he explained it was only a temporary arrangement while his mouth ulcers cleared up. Freddy's attempts to find work had so far proved fruitless but he told me somewhat proudly that he'd had two interviews.

'And?' I asked hopefully.

'They said they'd get back to me,' he replied with a nonchalant shrug. His enthusiasm of the previous week appeared to have worn off.

We arrived at Rivermede just as Heather was preparing lunch. I was immediately despatched to the kitchen to request more sandwiches, while Pearl fussed over her darling, and not seen for ages, little boy.

When I returned to the drawing room, Pearl announced she had already commissioned a local dressmaker to design her frock, and waved some sketches and material swatches at me.

'These are her ideas for you,' she said. 'You need to choose one and then we can arrange a consultation. Once Nev gets back this afternoon, I'll get him to run us into Southampton for Freddy's suit fitting.'

'I thought your fiancé was called Jack, not Nev?' Freddy looked confused.

'Nev's our butler-cum-handyman,' Pearl explained. 'He's had to take Jack to an appointment this morning, but they should be back soon. We can head out after lunch.'

Heather brought the sandwiches and was introduced to Freddy. Freddy seemed awestruck that Pearl now had staff.

'Wow, Pearl, what does this bloke Jack do to earn the money to run this place? He must be worth a packet.'

'Jack's retired now,' Pearl explained patiently, as Freddy wandered around the drawing room devouring his hastily prepared tomato and lettuce sandwich as if he hadn't eaten for a week – which he quite possibly hadn't.

'What did he do before he retired?' Freddy asked

'He owns a boatyard,' Pearl said. 'His late wife inherited it from her father, together with Rivermede. There's no boatbuilding now, though. Jack apparently put a stop to that because the company was making such a loss. The old boatbuilding sheds were knocked down and Jack turned the site into a marina. His company buy and sell boats, and carry out a few repairs and lease moorings. After we've been to Southampton to look at clothes, we can always ask Nev to give you a guided tour and then you can see it for yourself.'

So, Jack had waved his magic wand and turned a loss-making boatyard into a profitable marina. I was keen to learn more, especially in light of Nick's warnings. I had arranged to meet Stella later that afternoon and made a mental note to ask her what she knew about the Robshaw family history. She had sent me the draft notes she had commenced previously, together with some photographs and photocopies of newspaper cuttings from the time of her sailing triumph. There was no need for me to accompany Freddy and Pearl on their shopping trip – especially not now Pearl was becoming an independent woman. She seemed a little put out when I mentioned this, as did Freddy.

'Oh, you have to come, Becs,' he whined, 'otherwise she will choose something hideous for me.'

'Your opinion might be quite helpful,' Pearl agreed.

'Take photographs of Freddy modelling potential outfits on your brand-new iPhone and send them to me,' I suggested.

Over coffee, I kept trying to catch Freddy's eye, hoping he would take the hint and break his news to Pearl. He kept his eyes averted. When we heard Jack and Nev arrive in the hallway, he looked like a prisoner receiving a last-minute reprieve from the gallows.

'When are you intending to tell her?' I hissed as Pearl hurried out to greet Jack.

'It don't feel right, not yet,' Freddy replied. 'After we've been shopping, or this evening, maybe.'

'You should tell her when you are on your own, not when she's with Jack,' I pointed out.

'I'll do it in my own time,' he muttered.

'Here he is, here's my boy,' Pearl gushed, wheeling Jack into the room. She draped herself over Jack's shoulders like a human shawl. 'Isn't he the most adorable young man, Jack?'

Jack eased himself out of Pearl's embrace. It was obvious

from his expression that he thought Freddy anything but adorable, but he soon replaced his look of horror with a smile.

'Welcome to Rivermede, young man,' he said.

'Thanks, Jack,' Freddy replied. 'It's a great place you've got here. Have you lived here for a long time?'

'Only fifty years or so,' Jack chuckled. 'Have you had lunch already, Pearl?'

'Yes, sorry,' she said. 'You didn't say what time you'd be back.' She turned to me. 'Jack can be very secretive about his whereabouts sometimes. He and Nev are as thick as thieves.'

Jack tapped the side of his nose and gave Pearl another one of his indulgent smiles. 'Never you mind what I've been up to, my love.'

Freddy looked as if he was about to throw up.

'I want Nev to take us into Southampton to look at morning suits,' Pearl announced.

'Yes, of course,' Jack replied. 'Are you all going?'

'No, I've got some business to sort out in the village,' I said.

'Good on you,' Jack winked. 'Can't stand clothes shopping either. Well, we'll catch up at dinner, young Fred.'

I waved Pearl and Freddy off, and then set out for The Ship of Fools. I could have driven, but I decided instead to walk.

I followed the path along the river. The track seemed much shorter in daylight, and the tide was out. The River Deane was a dirty brown channel, dribbling tributary rivulets through the seaweed and the mudflats. At various points along the bank I could see the kelp-encrusted reminders of former landing stages and piers, remnants I presumed of the Deane's boatbuilding past. The eerie skeletal remains of long abandoned vessels protruded from their muddy graves.

The pub was quiet. Stella took me into the kitchen and introduced me to her partner, Chloe – a truculent, ferocious-looking woman who kept her hand firmly on the meat cleaver while we spoke. Stella suggested we continue discussions upstairs in her private office.

'I'm having second thoughts,' she confessed straight away.

'As you might have just gathered, Chloe doesn't think this book is such a good idea.'

After reading through the paperwork Stella had mailed, I was half-tempted to agree. But the story had potential, and right now it appeared to be my only future employment prospect. Stella's account of the race itself was far too technical to be of any interest to anyone who wasn't a sailing fanatic, and she had made no attempt to refute Owen's allegations of cheating. It was as if all the fighting spirit had been sucked out of her. The book could be her opportunity to recapture it.

'Is Chloe worried about the consequences?' I asked.

Stella nodded. 'Chloe is concerned that there might be an impact on our business if this all gets raked up again. What if we start losing customers? It's not just that. There's the other side of the coin. We don't want to be a freak show, have people coming to the pub just to ogle at us.'

'I totally understand that,' I agreed, 'but the whole point of the book would be to put the record straight. I've had a look online. Owen's rants in the press were very personal. I realise his pride was hurt, but I don't understand why you didn't do more to defend yourself?'

'Against Owen? He was the wronged man whose wife had a lesbian affair whilst sailing halfway around the world, leaving him sick with worry on the mainland with two kiddies. Back then, Owen was a bit of a national treasure, wasn't he? He had everyone on his side.'

'And where are your children now?' I asked, wondering if the children could be coerced into telling their side of the story. It could add a whole new level of interest.

'He wouldn't let me have anything to do with them,' Stella said. 'He got a lawyer involved, it all turned very nasty. He poisoned them against me. I thought... I hoped,' she gulped, and her eyes filled with moisture, 'when they got to eighteen, they might try and find me.'

'Do you mean to say you haven't had any contact with your children since your divorce?'

She shook her head. 'No. I haven't seen them for years.'

'They haven't tried to find you?'

'No. I'm not that well-hidden, am I? I run a pub not a million miles away from where we used to live. If they Googled hard enough, they'd know where I was.'

I was appalled. 'Oh Stella, I'm so sorry.'

She gave a shrug. 'Don't worry. I've developed a very thick skin. I've learned to live with their loss.'

It was as if she had suffered a bereavement. No wonder she had lost her spirit.

'I'm not surprised they turned against me,' she continued. 'Owen knew how to manipulate the press. The nationals lapped it up. I was a callous woman who had put her ambition before her family, just because I wanted to win a bloody yacht race. Do you know what he said to me? *I let you go off chasing a whim, and this is how you re-pay me.* Can you believe in the twenty-first century a man would actually say that about his wife? *I let you* go. After all the support I'd given him over the years, helping set up the restaurant business and then making it easy for him to have this marvellous TV career, and he accuses me of abandoning my children.

'Do you ever read anything like that about all those men who on go on these fantastic adventures, setting endurance records or trekking across the Antarctic? No, you don't, do you? Because it's okay for men to go off chasing whims, isn't it, but not us women?'

'He sounds like a bit of a tyrant,' I remarked.

'Oh, he was,' Stella agreed. 'Forget that cosy image he created for the cameras, glugging back his Merlot as he tossed a mackerel onto the hot coals. He was a resentful and jealous man. This wasn't about Chloe. This was because I won that race and for once he wasn't the star of the show. Do you know, he'd actually taken part in the Tri-islander a few years earlier, when he was nobody, and his boat didn't even finish.

'He couldn't face the fact that for once I had done something better than him. I would never abandon my children. I'd made full arrangements for their childcare while I was away. They had loving grandparents on both sides of the family, aunts, uncles, and friends. I recruited a whole team to look after them in my absence. I'd drawn up a bloody wall-planner, for Christ's sake; I had to. Owen was flying out to Madeira to meet me halfway, and again for the final in the Azores. Although by then, of course, he'd started his smear campaign. He told us not to come back to the restaurant, banned me from my own home.'

It was no wonder Stella was bitter.

'And your parents, the extended family, they didn't help to put you back in touch with your children?' I asked. 'Even after it all blew over?'

She shook her head. 'They all took Owen's side. My parents were old-school conservative; in fact, I'd describe my father as homophobic, if the word existed back then. In any case, he died ten, fifteen years ago and my mother shortly after. Of my siblings, only one sister keeps in touch − a birthday card and an Amazon voucher at Christmas. One of my brothers did suggest that if I dumped Chloe, he might condescend to visit, but I decided I would rather have Chloe.'

I tended to agree with her. She had chosen her love for Chloe over her family. That took some guts, but then it also took some guts to sail halfway across the Atlantic, and break records to boot. She'd accomplished a lot but been reviled rather than applauded. That was definitely something worth telling.

Owen Markham still ran the restaurant he'd started with Stella. How was he going to react if his story was dragged up again after all these years?

'You know Owen remarried?' I asked.

'Oh yes,' Stella replied. 'And no doubt the second Mrs Markham is a far better mother to my kids than I would ever have been.'

'What did you have, children I mean?'

'Boy and a girl. Tristram will be thirty-five now, Emily thirty-two.'

'Have you tried Googling them?' I asked.

She looked at me as if I was stupid. 'Of course I have, but I can't just barge back into their lives, can I? I know they won't want anything to do with me. Owen saw to that, just as he ensured my sailing achievements were belittled.'

It was quite possible Stella's children were still on the Isle of Wight. Surely it wouldn't be that difficult to track them down. Was a reunion possible? Could I persuade them to forgive and forget? Could Owen Markham be exposed as an ogre who had kept a good, honest woman away from her family for thirty years out of spite? Was I up to the task? I was used to assisting my mother with her light fluffy romances. I'd always been the sort of person who avoided challenges like the plague; I liked my security blanket. But that was the old me, and this was the new one. The one without a job.

'Look, I'd really like to have a go at this,' I told her. 'How about I draft some chapters out? If you're not happy with what I come up with, we'll forget the whole project. But I think we should at least try.'

'I'd have to discuss it with Chloe,' Stella frowned.

'Stella, this is your story,' I reminded her. 'You were the one who lost your family, not her.'

'That's true,' Stella mused. 'Okay,' she said decisively. 'Why not? Like you say, if I don't like it, we don't proceed?'

'Exactly,' I told her.

I persuaded Stella to hand over the one precious album of family photographs she had retained, along with an entire folder of newspaper cuttings she had surreptitiously collected of articles relating to Owen's career and his restaurant.

'Occasionally he mentioned what the kids were up to in his interviews,' she confessed, 'especially early on. It was just my way of keeping tabs.'

It seemed a very sad way to have to stay in touch.

'No letters?' I asked. 'No birthday cards?'

She shook her head. 'Obviously I wrote and sent cards to them, but I never received anything back.'

I thought of Nick's attempts to contact me after we first split up. I'd felt too hurt, too broken to reply, but Stella's children were too little to have felt so betrayed. Her husband had been a vindictive man indeed.

As she walked me out to the front of the pub to avoid the kitchens, I asked her what she knew of the Robshaw family.

'Not an awful lot, I'm afraid,' she replied. 'JJ was into powerboat racing as a youngster, made a bit of money on the circuit but I imagine he frittered it all away. As for Jack, I understand his first wife, Mary, belonged to the Dimmock family. Presumably, that's why he got the house and inherited the boatyard business. The marina was well established by the time Chloe and I arrived in Kerridge. If you're interested in local history, pay a visit to Portdeane library. There's an exhibition there; they've got loads of lovely old photographs of all the old boat-building families. Dimmocks were based in Kerridge for years but I don't think they could compete with the bigger firms down in Portdeane. I suppose Jack saw the commercial potential in developing the waterfront into a marina.'

'Where's Portdeane?' I asked.

Stella pointed towards the estuary. 'Opposite Helme Point. There's a couple of boat-building firms still based down there.'

'Helme, isn't that where you keep your houseboat? I understand you rent one out?'

'Are you looking for somewhere to stay?' Stella laughed. 'Sorry, but *The Solstice*'s already taken. Another writer, in fact. Alex, you met him here on our quiz night. I rent a mooring at Chapman's Wharf, hidden away in the marsh. It's a lovely spot.'

'How long would it take to walk there from here?' I asked.

'If you cut up through the village and take the road by the church, you'll be there in thirty minutes,' Stella replied. 'It'll be quicker than heading along the course of the river. There's far too many inlets and creeks between here and Helme Point.'

I thanked her and set off with a renewed vigour.

Chapter Nine

I only made it as far as the church before Nev's familiar white Range Rover drew up alongside me.

Pearl leaned out of the window. 'That's a bit of luck. Hop in.'

It would be positively dangerous to reveal where I was heading or, more to the point, why. Fortunately, Pearl was too impatient to off-load the traumas of suit shopping to have any interest in what I was doing wandering around Kerridge in the middle of the afternoon. It was apparent Freddy had not yet broken his news. He sulked beside me in the back seat while Pearl unleashed a tirade on the horrors of finding suitable wedding attire.

'The boy is too lanky,' she complained. 'We're going to have to have something made-to-measure. Nothing fitted – arms, legs, all too short. He looked like a scare-crow.'

'I looked like a bloody trussed-up penguin,' Freddy corrected. 'I'll never live it down if any of those photos get onto Facebook.'

'I would imagine that would be highly unlikely,' I assured him. Despite her new iPhone, Pearl had not yet mastered social media and I had no intention of posting anything to do with the upcoming nuptials, even though I had given Pearl my blessing. Weddings were firmly off my radar. Most of my friends knew better than to invite me to share their big day. It wasn't that I didn't wish them well, but for obvious reasons the thought of being present at any kind of formal marriage ceremony tended to bring on flashbacks and palpitations. I was doing my best to keep a calm head at the thought of Pearl's impending celebrations. Freddy's schoolboy attitude wasn't helping.

'Trussed-up penguin or not, you will wear the outfit I

choose,' Pearl insisted. 'This is my big day and I won't let you spoil it.' I couldn't help but feel the second half of the sentence was directed me. One wedding day had already ended in tatters – mine. Hers was not going to befall the same fate.

Freddy continued to sulk, but cheered up over dinner when Heather dished up a vegetarian curry.

'Isn't there something missing?' Jack asked after a couple of mouthfuls.

'Freddy's a vegan,' Pearl informed him. 'I almost forgot to mention it to Heather, but she's come up trumps again, hasn't she?'

'Vegan?' Jack grunted. 'What's that mean?'

I could see Freddy itching to begin his spiel. He could talk for hours when it came to promoting his cause.

'Did you tell Pearl you were applying for jobs?' I broke in before he could start.

'Jobs?' Pearl paused. 'You're not telling me there's a chance you'll get a private commission?' I could hear the hint of hope in her voice.

'What is it you do exactly, boy?' Jack asked, perhaps also seizing the opportunity to forestall a lecture on the wonders of veganism.

'I told you he's a painter,' Pearl replied.

'Well, our bedroom could certainly do with decorating,' Jack said. 'I had thought about getting someone in.'

'No. Art, you silly old thing. I'm sure I've told you, Freddy is studying fine art.' Pearl gave Jack a playful shove.

When Freddy had announced his intention to study fine art, my mother had imagined a modern-day Constable or Turner, or at the very least a Jackson Pollock. Instead, Freddy's forte was 'conceptual installations', an idea I was convinced originally stemmed from a trip to A&E at the age of twelve when he had broken his femur playing rugby. It had been a serious injury and ruined whatever hope Freddy, or at least Pearl, might have had that he could pursue an international sporting career. It had, however, resulted in a fascination with Plaster of Paris – an obsession which one of his art teachers had unfortunately encouraged when it became clear that

Freddy had very little talent for anything else. Freddy's POP and chicken-wire creations had adorned our living room shelves for several years.

Freddy liked to 'create', but it wasn't necessarily art as Pearl and I knew it. He wanted to 'open' our minds to the 'unimaginable', and over the last four years had produced a collection of obscure videos, audio recordings, collages, and mash-ups of still-photographs which made no sense to me at all. 'That's the whole point,' he argued.

'The stable block will need a bit of a spruce up if Becca wants to move in,' Jack continued. 'I'm serious, by the way, about the decorating.'

'Who said anything about moving into the stable block?' I asked.

'You're going to need somewhere to live when Beech Mews is sold,' Pearl pointed out. 'Jack has very generously offered to put you up in the flat above the garage.'

'These things can take months to go through,' I said, not wishing to sound ungrateful. 'I've got plenty of time to look for something to rent in London. You know I'd prefer to stay up there.'

Pearl looked unimpressed. 'The change of scenery might do you good,' she said. 'I feel positively invigorated since I've been on the coast.'

'What about me?' Freddy asked. 'Where am I going to go? I was planning on moving back to Battersea. I can't afford to stay in my digs without my student loan.' He looked hopefully up at Pearl. 'Unless you want to carry on paying my rent?'

'No, she doesn't, boy,' Jack retorted. 'Sounds to me like you've had years of bumming around on your backside, living off your mother's charity. You should be looking for a proper job. JJ can find you something on the marina. I'll give him a ring later this evening. There's always boats that needed hosing down or barnacles scrubbing off. A monkey could do it.'

'It sounds right up Freddy's street,' I said with a smile. 'Seriously, Jack, do you think you could get Fred a job in the boatyard?'

'If I ask JJ to take the boy on, he'll take the boy on.' Jack gave an assertive nod of his head. 'Bit of hard work never did anyone any harm. Be physical, mind. No disrespect to you, Pearl, but he doesn't look very robust.'

'That's what veganism does to you,' Pearl said with a shake of her head. 'I have told him in the past. But still, Freddy, you could do it, couldn't you, at least until something else turns up? It would be good for you to learn a bit about Jack's business. And you could also come and live here with us. You can have the old nursery on the top floor.' She beamed around the table. 'Isn't that wonderful? We'd be a proper family again. One big happy family.'

I almost willed Freddy to tell her then, on the spot, about the impending new addition to our one big happy family, but he looked so shell-shocked by his sudden promotion from art student to barnacle scrubber that I didn't have the heart.

We were due to return to London on Sunday evening. Although there was no pressing need for Freddy to return with me, he'd arrived at Rivermede with no evidence of any change of clothes, so I assumed he was only planning on staying the one night.

Jack announced over breakfast in the conservatory that he'd already spoken to JJ, and Freddy should report to the office on the marina at eleven.

Freddy was still in bed.

'You're not expecting him to start straight away, are you?' I queried, slicing the top off my boiled egg with great gusto.

'Does he want a job or not?' Jack grunted. 'Marina operates seven days a week.'

'I'll go and wake him,' Pearl offered, folding her napkin. The napkins were pure Egyptian cotton. I dabbed at a spot of egg yolk I could feel on my chin. I briefly wondered if Jack's offer of accommodation above the garage included participation in Rivermede's full-board dining arrangements. Pearl had certainly got used to being waited on hand and foot, but I didn't relish the thought of Heather and Neville watching over my every move. Pearl seemed to think the stable block flat was self-contained. It wouldn't do any harm to take a look.

Don't be tempted, Becca, I told myself. *Don't be swayed. It's not what you want.*

The truth was I wanted my old life back, the familiar routine. I wanted Pearl back in Battersea, and Freddy out of sight out of mind causing havoc in the creative art studios at Goldsmiths. The reality was, though, that what I wanted wasn't going to happen. Freddy needed to have a job on the marina because he would soon have a child to support, and Pearl was getting married. It was time for a new start – for all of us.

Freddy emerged from his room in a state of confusion. Pearl plied him with coffee, reassuring him that this was just an interview, and no, of course no-one expected him to work on a Sunday.

I Googled Chapman's Wharf and calculated it was no more than a fifteen-minute walk from the marina. I offered to drive Freddy to his job interview.

'I'm not really going to be washing boats, am I?' Freddy asked.

'It's either washing boats and living rent-free here, or it's washing beer glasses and paying your own rent in London,' I pointed out. 'If you think you can earn enough by being a kitchen porter in Soho, then go for it.'

'Okay, okay, you've made your point.'

'I'm sure there's more to the job than washing boats.'

Robshaw Marine Sales occupied very prestigious offices at the entrance to the marina. A vast selection of boats of all shapes and sizes were offered for sale – everything from the smallest rib to a large cabin cruiser, propped on steel cradles and girders. I'd never seen so many boats on dry land.

I knew from discussing the situation with Jack the previous evening, after Freddy had retired exhausted to his guest quarters, that JJ was in charge overall and took personal responsibility for the brokerage side of the business, buying and selling new and used yachts and motor boats. A foreman was responsible for the dry storage area and on-the-water berthing facilities. Various other marine-related businesses leased workshop and office space from Jack.

Adjacent to the marina was the public slipway known as Kerridge Hard. This area was also home to a yacht chandlery business which doubled up as a general store and newsagent, and a café/bar, The Jolly Jack Tar. There was an area of public seating and car parking. Pearl had said the Hard was the 'hub' of Kerridge, although in my book, one café, one shop, and an ice-cream van hardly constituted a hub in terms of what I'd been used to in Battersea.

As soon as we arrived on the marina, JJ strode out to greet us, almost as if we'd contaminate his domain if we stepped foot inside the door of his plush sales office.

'Rebecca,' he said, giving me a cursory nod.

'It's Becca,' I corrected him.

'Yes, of course.'

Apart from our first meeting, our paths hadn't crossed at Rivermede.

He gave Freddy a look of pure disdain. 'You've done this sort of work before, right?'

'No, of course he hasn't,' I said on Freddy's behalf.

Freddy was like a rabbit caught in a headlight. The marina was a very alien environment. Both Freddy and I had been brought up in the city, the lake on Battersea Park the nearest we got to any waterborne activities. I was slightly concerned at the close proximity of heavy lifting equipment, forklifts, and yacht hoists. Men were working underneath large vessels, sanding hulls and dismantling keels. Enormous cabin cruisers were propped up on little more than railway sleepers and metal joists. Two youths in blue overalls were hosing down a catamaran. They were muscular and tanned. Freddy looked like a teenage vampire in comparison.

Out on the water, dinghies. Kayakers, and canoeists snaked their way between the larger yachts. Freddy's eyes nearly popped out of his head when a shapely blonde teenager strode past us in the skimpiest of shorts, despite the chill of the spring day, effortlessly carrying a paddle-board under her arm.

'All right, JJ,' she called cheerfully.

'Morning, Kimmi,' JJ replied, forcing a smile onto his face.

'Let me get one of the lads to help you with that.'

'No need,' the girl replied with a swing of her hips. 'I can manage.'

Freddy and I both watched in awe as Kimmi continued onto one of the pontoons, lowered her board and stepped onto the water. As JJ gave a brief run-down on health and safety in the yard, calling over one of his underlings to kit Freddy out in some appropriate workwear, Kimmi paddled away without so much as a life-jacket in sight. I promised to collect him at one.

Chapter Ten

I set off to explore. I asked the two lads washing the catamaran for confirmation that I was heading in the right direction to Chapman's Wharf.

'Go round past Sailor Gerry's barge and follow the gravel track for a couple of hundred metres,' the more sensible of the boys replied.

'Sailor Gerry's barge?' I queried, wondering if he was referring to some sort of rum shack.

'The old rust bucket over there,' the less sensible one said.

What could possibly have been an old frigate or coastguard vessel was tacked onto the very last pontoon of the marina. It was indeed a rust bucket, slate grey, and totally out of kilter with its swish shiny neighbours. I was surprised JJ allowed such a ramshackle vessel anywhere near his premises. The pontoon was in a state of disrepair, while on board, a grubby tarpaulin covered much of the deck, half exposing a pile of black bin bags. I could just make out the boat's name – *The Regatta Queen*. She had clearly seen better days.

The gravel track soon petered out into little more than a metre-wide path, bordered on one side by the river, and on the other by reed-beds. Up ahead in the distance, I could see a handful of boats moored in an inlet. *The Solstice* was a traditional barge painted in a delicate shade of New England blue. It looked quite deserted, but its location was the perfect writer's retreat. I was actually quite jealous.

If this was Nick's hideout, what was he really up to in Kerridge? The idea that anyone in Kerridge warranted police surveillance seemed very far-fetched. Was Nick even still in the police force? He could be working for anybody. Perhaps he had befallen some fate that meant he'd had to adopt a whole new identity. Perhaps he was in witness protection. I'd inherited my mother's vivid imagination. It came with the territory of being a writer; in fact, it was an essential skill. I was about to turn away, when the cabin door opened and Nick emerged onto the deck.

'I thought I saw someone spying on me,' he called. His greeting seemed friendly enough. 'You're still here then, you didn't listen to me?'

I shook my head. 'I'm just visiting again. Freddy has a job interview on the marina.'

'Freddy? Freddy is at Rivermede, too?' Nick's expression changed. He hopped off the deck and joined me on the path. He was dressed in a pair of baggy old jeans and an Arran sweater. The clean-cut Nick I used to know would never have dressed so casually, not even on his day off. 'You are winding me up now, aren't you?'

I shook my head. 'No, he needs a job. He got his girlfriend pregnant and he needs to earn some money.' The words tumbled out before I could stop myself.

'What? How old is he?'

'Twenty-one going on sixteen. I shouldn't have told you that. Sorry, forget I said anything.'

'So, you're going to be a…' Nick faltered, as if struggling to find the right word.

'An auntie, yes.' I smiled. 'He hasn't told Pearl yet. That's why I bought him here this weekend to break the news she's about to become a grandma, but he chickened out. But he does need a job. Jack suggested JJ could find him something on the marina.'

'So, will he be staying at the house, too?'

I nodded. 'I expect so. There's more than enough room for him and he can't afford to stay in London. Pearl's decided to sell the Battersea flat. There's every chance I'll end up at Rivermede as well, unless I can find enough work to afford to rent somewhere in the city.'

'Rivermede isn't safe,' Nick said again. 'None of you should be there.'

'Oh, don't worry, I won't break your cover and Freddy

75

certainly won't remember who you are even if he does bump into you,' I assured him. 'As for Pearl, seriously, she never walks anywhere, she's hardly likely to come this far down the river.'

'That's not the point.' Nick's face was set in a frown. 'Christ, Freddy, here. How old was he at our wedding?'

'We didn't have a wedding,' I reminded him. 'Six.'

'I can remember turning round and seeing him walking up the aisle behind you in that ridiculous sailor suit, picking his nose.'

'Yep, sounds like Freddy, although he's gone all Goth now. Pearl is kitting him out in another ridiculous outfit for when he gives her away. Let's hope he won't be picking his nose as he walks up the aisle this time.'

Nick smiled. 'You haven't changed, Becca.'

'Oh, yes I have,' I assured him. 'According to Pearl's agent, Anita, I'm a bitter and twisted spinster who refuses to allow the scars of the past to heal. I enjoy picking at my scabs and using my oozing wounds as an excuse not to move on.'

'That's a very graphic analogy,' Nick remarked.

'And that's a very big word for you. Okay, Anita didn't actually say all that; she didn't have to. I know exactly what I am and what I do, which is more than I can say about you. Nick, why are you in Kerridge?'

For one moment he looked as if he was about to confess all, but then he shook his head. 'I really can't tell you,' he said.

'But you are here working?'

He nodded. 'Yes, and as I said at the pub, it's vital that my cover isn't blown. But that's not the reason I want you and Pearl, and now Freddy, out of Rivermede, Becca. I am genuinely concerned for your safety.'

'You can't expect me to believe that Jack Robshaw is about to bump us all off? The man's an invalid.'

'It's not Jack Robshaw I'm worried about.'

'JJ?' It was a lot easier to believe JJ could be mixed up in criminal activities. Nick remained silent. 'Rita, then? Do the fashion police want a few words with her?'

'Listen, Becca, I'm trying to be serious here.'

I was fed up with his riddles. 'Why should I believe a word you say, Nick? Why should I trust you? You lied to me. You told me you weren't sleeping with Saskia, and then you turned up reeking of her. I could still smell her on you when you stood at the altar. How do you think that felt? Why should I trust you? Why should I believe a word of this stupid, stupid game, or whatever it is you're playing?'

I turned to walk away, but he grabbed my arm to stall me. 'I'm not playing any games, Becca. What happened between us happened fifteen years ago, when I was a different person – a very young, stupid person, I'll admit it. But we're in a totally unique situation here. I'm saying what I'm saying because I don't want to see you or, believe it or not, your mother or Freddy hurt. I want you all out of harm's way, and I'm sorry if you think I'm not telling you the truth, but the fact is I can't tell you the truth. I can't risk you knowing what is really going on.'

I shook him off. 'Stop playing secret squirrels, Nick.'

'Secret squirrels? You think that's what this is. Some sort of game of tit for tat?'

'Tit for tat? Why would you say that?'

'Well, you're the one with all the secrets, aren't you?'

'What do you mean?' I was totally lost.

'When were you planning to tell me about Freddy? On our wedding night, or when you moved him in to live with us.'

'Freddy? What's Freddy got to do with any of this?'

'You go on about not trusting me, but you couldn't even tell me you had a child. What sort of basis was that for a marriage?'

I stared at him, speechless, churning over the implications of his words. *He thought Freddy was mine*? What on earth had given him that idea? *Who* had given him that idea? I certainly never had.

I shook my head in exasperation. Nick could live with his fantasies; I wasn't going to belittle myself with a reply. I turned away and began to head back along the uneven, rutted path, slipping and sliding in my haste to make a dignified retreat. I wished I was the one dressed casually in walking boots, old jeans, and comfortable sweater, my resentment brimming over as I stumbled along in my smart business trousers and two-inch heeled boots. Nick had so obviously managed to change his life and move on into a different world, while I hadn't. It was so unfair.

'Becca!' he yelled after me. 'Becca, we need to talk.'

No, we didn't. Freddy and I didn't even look like each other. We both looked like our fathers, although sadly Pearl had very few photographs of mine to prove it. Neither of us bore a great deal of resemblance to our mother.

If Nick was trying to drive another barrier between us to ensure I didn't expose his cover, he was doing a very good job, but I was having serious doubts about his sanity. His intimation that he was on a top-secret surveillance mission was all starting to sound very dubious. Was he delusional? Had Nick suffered a major trauma whilst serving in the police force, and lost touch with reality? Was he suffering PTSD? For all I knew, he could be living in a fantasy world funded by social security.

By the time I reached the comparative safety of *The Regatta Queen*, I decided that despite my better judgement, I might well take up Jack's offer of the stable block flat. I didn't want either Freddy or my mother running into Nick, who was quite clearly deranged. And if they did, I wanted to be close by to smooth over any repercussions.

It was a relatively easy decision to make, and hardly my decision at all when Pearl called me on her brand-new iPhone at ten the following morning to announce she had accepted a cash offer on the flat. The open house had been an overriding success. The buyer was eager to take possession as soon as possible, and Magda Pepowski had promised to expedite the necessary legal formalities. With no mortgage on either side, she hoped to have the paperwork ready to complete within four weeks.

'Four weeks?' I had hoped for a longer reprieve.

'Can you get some quotes for removal companies?' Pearl enquired. 'Jack says there's space in one of the outbuildings for anything we can't squeeze into the nursery for Freddy or the stable block for you.'

I'd given the stable block flat a quick look over before driving back up to London. Poky was the word that sprang to mind, but then I was used to living in the light, airy space of Beech Mews. JJ had generously allowed Freddy seven days' grace to finish his final art 'installation' before starting his new job as general dogsbody/marina assistant. Nev would drive to Newcross to transport the few personal belongings Freddy kept there down to Kerridge. Freddy would follow on his Lambretta.

'Just got some re-recordings to do,' Freddy had mumbled as I dropped him off at his flat-share on Sunday evening. We'd spent the majority of the journey up from the coast in silence when it transpired he'd decided there was no need to tell Pearl about her impending grandchild after all. 'I mean, if me and Rubes aren't together, what's the point? It's not as if she and the baby are ever going to meet.'

'And do you have any intention of meeting this baby?' I asked him. 'Or are you just going to let this poor girl struggle with motherhood on her own?'

He hadn't answered, although he had looked pretty dejected throughout the journey. It was only after I had reached the rapidly evaporating sanctuary of Beech Mews that I wondered if Freddy actually wanted to be involved, and maybe it was Ruby who wasn't letting him.

Reluctantly, I hired a removal company and gave notice to all the utilities. Neighbours were informed. Many wished us well; others, I was sure, were glad to see the back of us. Pearl had been rather fond of throwing raucous parties. Several expressed regret that they would not have the chance to say goodbye to her personally. I suggested she might wish to come back up to Battersea to sort through the flat before everything was packed, but she was adamant it wasn't necessary.

'I can go through it here just as well as I can there,' she argued. 'Even better here, because Nev can take anything we don't want to the local household recycling centre. We'd have to pay the council to take it away in London, wouldn't we, or a hire a skip?'

Pearl had immersed herself in country life, in Rivermede, and it seemed nothing could lure her back to London.

With the flat cleared, I spent my last couple of nights in Battersea in a local hotel. I needed to supervise the contractor hired for the last-minute clean and be on hand to pass the keys over to Magda. It was impossible not to shed a tear. My mother might not have regrets and had cast off her old life with ease, but I had serious misgivings. I hadn't chosen this move to the south coast; it was almost as if it had chosen me.

I put on a brave face, aka a thick layer of make-up, and had a last lunch with Anita. I wanted to briefly touch on the subject of Stella's memoirs and also sound her out about any potential future jobs. Pearl, now master of her own administration, had indeed sent Anita an email informing her that she fully intended to quit writing, and didn't even wish to fulfil her contract for the two novellas I'd spent winter nights re-hashing while she'd been sitting up on the deck of the *Majestic Oceans*.

'She said she couldn't face the media circus surrounding the launches,' Anita remarked with a sympathetic smile. 'She does sound like a changed woman.'

Changed beyond all recognition. I'd never felt so lost and alone.

Chapter Eleven

'How's your diet coming along?' Pearl asked when I arrived at Rivermede, ready to begin my new life. She regarded me sceptically. 'There's a Slimming World class in the church hall on a Monday evening. I think you should sign up. I don't want you bursting out of your bridesmaid dress.'

'I don't need a Slimming World class,' I told her, looking around for Nev to help with the bags. 'I'm not overweight. You're starting to sound like one of those obsessive bridezillas. Where is Nev, by the way?'

'Oh, he and Jack are out somewhere,' Pearl replied. 'I suspect they'll be gone all day. Leave the bags in your car, Nev can bring them up when he's back.'

I didn't want to wait. I wanted to unpack straight away, to make my new flat seem like home. Pearl stood by and watched as I completed several journeys up and down the external staircase to the flat. I was pleased to see the items from Beech Mews I had marked 'stable block' for the removal company had been deposited in the right place, including one of Pearl's big soft sofas, which took up most of the living area. I listened with half an ear as she chatted on about her new social life in the village.

'Of course, I'm winging it with the bridge,' she said. 'But I thought if I got in with the jazz choir, they could do a couple of songs at the wedding on the cheap. I want *Love Lifts Us Up Where We Belong* and as Jack's a big Andy Williams' fan, a rendition of *Moon River.*'

'On the cheap?' I was surprised Pearl was concerned with saving the pennies.

'Well, you know, as a favour. The bill is starting to add up, and we're not made of money.'

'You could scrap the whole thing and just have the registry

office ceremony without all this palaver,' I pointed out.

Pearl raised an eyebrow. 'Your father and I did that forty years ago,' she said, 'and I've regretted it all my life. Two years later, he was dead, and what mementoes have I got of our special day? A couple of snaps taken by relatives, that's all. We didn't have a proper photographer. I've hardly got any pictures of the guests, and only a couple of me and Tony. It was raining cats and dogs, so we had to run from the car to the registry office, and then back to the car and straight to the pub. It was a shambles. *This time*,' she emphasised the words to make her point, 'I'm having the whole works.' She didn't need to say any more. She'd planned the whole works for me and it hadn't happened.

It was on the tip of my tongue to mention her email to Anita and her reluctance to take part in the 'circus' surrounding the launch of her books, when she was seemingly planning a major performance of her own. But I sensed the irony might be lost. Pearl was determined to have the wedding of her dreams, limited budget or not.

I spent most of the afternoon cramming crockery into the severely restricted space in the kitchen cupboards. The flat was open-plan apart from the bedroom and bijou ensuite shower room. The kitchenette barely took up a corner. Pearl jumped up off the sofa at five o'clock on the dot.

'That'll be Jack and Nev back,' she said, peering out of the kitchen window. I hadn't heard a thing; the Range Rover shared Nev's ability to arrive by stealth. 'I almost forgot, I've arranged a little dinner party tonight to celebrate your arrival.'

At five, it was too late to protest. Pearl knew how to play her game.

'A dinner party?'

Her words were almost lost on the stairs. 'Just a few of our new friends and neighbours, nothing too formal,' she called. 'See you for drinks at half six.'

Half six. An hour-and-a-half away. I had been looking forward to a quiet night in my new home, a bottle of wine, feet up, watching mindless TV or even reading a book, maybe even starting to plan my new career. Anita had mentioned a couple of editing jobs she might be able to put my way, and was prepared to cast her eye over Stella's memoirs. My desk from Beech Mews was far too big for the stable block, but I had requisitioned Freddy's old computer workstation, and that now had pride of place under the living room window. The flat had been decorated with a quick coat of magnolia paint since my first viewing. According to Pearl, Nev and Heather had lived in the stable block when they'd first arrived at Rivermede, but had quickly opted to move to the old gardener's cottage on another part of Jack's estate. I could quite see why they might wish to have more substantial distance of separation from Pearl.

As I crossed the drive to the front door, bracing myself for the evening's entertainment, Freddy pulled up on his Lambretta, having just finished work for the day.

'How's it going?' I asked. He'd been on the marina for less than three weeks but already he had developed some colour to his cheeks. Even his spindly white legs, incongruous and unfamiliar in the marina uniform of baggy regulation shorts and workmen's boots, seemed to have gained a bit of muscle.

'I hate it,' he replied. 'I hate being outside all the time, the weather's been bloody awful all week. JJ's a right bastard, everyone hates him. Look at my fingers.' He held up his hands which were red with blisters. 'I'm not cut out for manual work.'

'Think of the money,' I reminded him. 'You'd best hurry up and get yourself tidy. You are coming to my welcome party, I take it?'

'No, I'm bloody not,' he grunted. 'I'm shattered. I'm having a bath and going straight to bed. I'm working tomorrow morning at six.'

Nev, in full butler attire, waylaid me in the hallway. Freddy stomped upstairs while I was escorted into the drawing room. The French windows were slightly ajar, soaking up the warm early evening air. There was no denying this room was the *piece de resistance* to the house, the views of the river were spectacular, and at their best this time of day.

I was not the first guest. I was surprised but pleased to see the Twitchers, Craig and Chrissie, perched awkwardly on the edge of a sofa, while a plump but jolly-looking woman in her early seventies had requisitioned Pearl's favourite armchair next to Jack's crossword puzzle table. A man I assumed to be her husband was dissecting the weekend sailing forecast with Jack.

'Come on in, Becca darling, let me introduce you,' Pearl fussed. She was in a yellow cocktail dress, something she'd picked up for her cruise. I had swapped regulation office wear black trousers for an evening version of the same thing, coupled with a sheer burgundy silk vest. Chrissie was in white slacks and a sequin-embellished white T-shirt, while Craig wore jeans and a grey polo shirt. The older couple were smarter, but they all fell way below Pearl's standards. Chrissie looked particularly uncomfortable, but Craig seemed non-plussed.

'Hello again,' he said, jumping to his feet and stretching out his hand. He turned to Pearl. 'We've already met.'

'You have?' Pearl looked surprised. 'How come?'

'Quiz night,' Craig replied. 'We could have done with her again this week. We had another food and drink round. If it isn't made with hops or doesn't come with chips, we're flippin' useless. I don't know a lot about the culinary arts, I'm afraid. Becca was brilliant last time.'

'I'm so pleased the expensive education in Switzerland is finally paying off,' Pearl mused. 'I always knew that Cordon Bleu cookery course would come in useful.'

Chrissie gave me a welcome hug, and Heather appeared by my side bearing a tray of something sparkling. Chrissie and I both grabbed one. I wondered briefly whether the remaining member of the Twitchers' quiz team had been included in Pearl's invitation to dinner, but of course if he had, 'Alex' could hardly accept. In any case, Pearl didn't know him, which made me wonder how she had become acquainted with Chrissie and Craig. They weren't her usual type, but then, I didn't know my mother any more.

Before I could enquire further, Pearl ushered me over to the other side of the room. I gave Jack a brief kiss on the cheek and was introduced to the other two guests – Commodore Stevenson, who was apparently something high up at the local yacht club and didn't appear to have a first name, and his wife, Judy. Judy explained that she and the Commodore were Rivermede's closest neighbours.

'We're in Honeypot Cottage; you'll have driven past it, at the top of the lane.'

I had indeed. Although it had a partly thatched roof, Honeypot was hardly a cottage. I had admired the sprawling mansion many times.

Another couple was escorted into the room and provided the connection between the rather oddly-matched guests. It transpired the new arrivals – Pete, also something big at the yacht club; and his wife, Natalie, at least fifteen years his junior – were members of the '*Kerridge Pops*' choir, as were Chrissie and Judy. Pearl really was going all out for that freebie musical interlude at her nuptials.

'Just JJ and Rita to come now,' Pearl said. She turned to me with a grimace. 'Jack insisted.'

Despite living on the premises, JJ and Marguerite were late. Rita, wearing another designer jumpsuit, was profusely apologetic. Some drama on the marina had delayed JJ.

'Nothing to do with young Freddy, I hope,' Jack guffawed.

'Sadly not, otherwise I'd have a good excuse to give the boy the sack,' JJ muttered. 'Buyer pulled out of the Beneteau 40 last minute, which means I'll have the damn thing sat on the forecourt for the next month and I've got two new cruisers being delivered at the end of next week. Don't know where I'm going to put the ruddy things now.'

'How's business going?' the Commodore asked. 'I'd heard sales have slowed right down at Graysons in Portdeane. Economy's up the spout, isn't it? Government hasn't got a clue.'

Pearl took me to one side. 'Don't get anyone started on politics,' she chuckled. 'Can you just go and check on timings with Heather? I think we're ready to sit down.'

I wanted to point out that she was the hostess and I was

supposed to be the guest of honour, so it wasn't my job to do the running around, but Pearl had always been very good at delegation and it was very hard to break the habits of a lifetime.

Everything appeared calm in the kitchen. A large pan of fragrant soup was bubbling away on the stove, whilst I could smell something equally as aromatic in the oven.

Nev was helping himself to a can of beer at the kitchen table while Heather was surrounded by battalions of regimentally-chopped vegetables.

'You look very much in control,' I told her. 'Pearl says we're ready.'

'Right, I'll bring the soup through,' Heather said. 'Nev, you best go and sort the wine out.'

The dining table was sumptuously laid with silver cutlery and cut glass. The dinner service was Royal Doulton, edged in gold leaf.

'Only the best for you, dear,' Pearl whispered when I murmured my appreciation. 'You'll be amazed what treasures I've uncovered ferreting around in Jack's cupboards.'

To my relief, JJ and Rita were placed at the opposite end of the table, alongside Natalie and Pete. To begin with, the conversation focussed on the food – Thai fish soup followed by Oriental spiced chicken with jasmine rice. Heather was clearly an accomplished cook.

'Compliments to the chef,' Judy said, echoing my very thoughts.

'She's a marvel, isn't she?' Pearl agreed. 'We're so lucky to have her. She cooks everything from scratch. Not that I've been down to check it out, but apparently Nev's transformed a patch of the old kitchen gardens into a flourishing allotment. In future, everything will be home-grown.'

I made a mental note to take a wander through the grounds to take a look for myself.

'Where did you find this marvellous couple?' Judy enquired. 'It's so hard to get good staff. We're on our third cleaner in almost as many months.'

'It was through JJ,' Jack replied. 'Some people he knew up in London were letting the pair of them go. Their loss, our gain. Nev's been a godsend since my hip went. I don't know how I'd have managed without him. We only had Norah Morland before that. If it wasn't for Marguerite being on hand, I don't know how I'd have managed.'

Marguerite looked up at the mention of her name and beamed. JJ gave a mock shudder. 'Norah Morland was the housekeeper from hell,' he muttered.

'Norah was Mary's old nanny,' Jack explained to Pearl. 'I kept her on out of the kindness of my heart. We should have let her go long ago.'

It was the first time I'd heard Jack mention his late wife. I'd not seen a single picture of her in the house – presumably that was Pearl's doing. Another mental note: find out more about Mary.

'How long have Nev and Heather been with you?' I enquired.

'Eighteen months maybe,' Jack glanced at JJ. 'Would that be about right?'

JJ nodded. 'They came with excellent references.'

'And you can certainly see why,' the Commodore said, patting his stomach. 'That was excellent, Jack, Pearl, thank you.'

'Well, it's not finished yet.' Pearl smiled. 'We've still got dessert to come. Always my favourite part of the meal.'

'So, tell us about the Cordon Bleu lessons, Becca,' Craig said, making a valiant attempt to contribute to the conversation. 'You're a bit of an amateur cook yourself?'

I shook my head. 'I'm not any great shakes, but I did tend to be in charge of all the cooking at home.' I'd always thought Pearl had been rather fond of my attempts in the kitchen, but I sensed my achievements had been surpassed.

'Well, somebody had to be, darling,' Pearl said with a chuckle. 'Jack's certainly not marrying me for my culinary skills.'

'Makes one wonder exactly what he is marrying you for,' JJ murmured under his breath, but quite loud enough for everyone to hear.

Diplomacy could have been Judy's middle name. 'I think Jack and Pearl are made for each other,' she said, smoothing over JJ's rudeness. 'It's such a breath of fresh air for us to have you here in Kerridge, Pearl, and you, too, Becca. I hope you are going to fully embrace village life, just like your mother. Do you sing?'

I shook my head. 'Not in public, Judy.'

'So, are you single, Becca?' Natalie asked. I'd almost forgotten she and her husband were present at the far end of the table. Natalie had spent most of the evening engaged in a whispered conversation with Rita. Both women had succeeded in consuming very little, while Pete had been far too busy doing the opposite to stop and talk. Rita was looking very smug

I smiled through gritted teeth. *Here we go again.* 'Footloose and fancy-free, that's me,' I said cheerfully.

'Are there any eligible bachelors in Kerridge?' Pearl asked. 'Becca's not had much luck with men in London, have you, darling?' She could learn a lot about diplomacy from Judy.

'I believe Sailor Gerry is still unattached,' Rita replied, wiping her mouth on her napkin to disguise her snigger.

'Sailor Gerry?' Pearl turned to the Commodore, her voice full of hope. 'Is he a friend of yours at the yacht club?'

A ripple of laughter fluttered around the table. Pete almost choked. Even Judy couldn't contain her mirth. 'Gerald Kimble is a stalwart of Kerridge waterfront,' she replied, 'but he's not exactly yacht club material. It's a nickname, Pearl, dear. He's an old chap who used to work at the boatyard. The Kimbles have been in Kerridge for centuries. Gerald lives on the *Regatta Queen* – an old coastal patrol vessel moored just off the marina. It's a bit of an eyesore, to be honest, and I don't think he's quite what you'd have in mind for lovely young Becca here.'

'I had heard a rumour you'd given him notice to quit his berth,' the Commodore said, turning to Jack.

'We have,' JJ replied on his father's behalf. 'If we can get rid of him, I can get another twenty moorings on that pontoon, and right now we could really do with increasing our capacity.'

'I heard he had some sort of legal right to that mooring,' Judy said.

'Not unless he can find the paperwork to prove it.' JJ almost snapped her head off.

'His vessel's a bloody disgrace,' Pete said, having regained his composure. 'I keep telling you, JJ. Goes against marine safety legislation. We can soon find a legal clause to have it towed away, I'm sure.'

'Jack, you'd know more about Kimble's claim. Is there any truth in it?' Judy persisted.

'Like JJ says, he needs to prove it.' Jack seemed unwilling to be drawn into the discussion. 'Mary's father was not very good at record-keeping.'

'What about your chum van der Plaast?' the Commodore chuckled, turning to JJ.

'What's he got to do with Gerald Kimble?' JJ looked puzzled.

'I hear he's single again. *The Pegasus* is back on the river, so I assume he is, too.'

'I really don't think Becca is Max's type, Commodore,' Natalie giggled.

'I thought Becca and Alex struck up a bit of a rapport when they were in our quiz team,' Chrissie ventured, turning to Craig. 'He's single, isn't he? And probably far more attainable than Max van der Plaast.'

'How old is this Alex?' Pearl demanded.

'Forty-ish, I'd say. He's quiet, intelligent,' Chrissie continued. 'Keeps himself to himself, but he's a polite enough chap, probably just a bit shy. He's renting Stella Markham's houseboat down at Helme.'

'I wish I'd known,' Pearl pouted, 'we could have invited him along tonight, made the numbers up.'

'I really am quite happy as I am,' I insisted, trying to keep my tone light.

'Now listen, Becca,' Pearl smiled, 'the big forty is looming up next year, and I'm just thinking about your body clock. When is the next quiz night, Chrissie?'

I spent the rest of the evening fending off questions about my social life and why I was so sadly lacking in male companions. I conceded I might just possibly be interested in joining Judy for yoga, having turned down every other social activity in the village which involved meeting a man, but Natalie and Rita were both very quick to point out that yoga in the church hall was really just a stretching class for the sixty-plus age group. A real workout was only attainable at the Deane Valley Golf & Country Club. They were both members.

'I'm not particularly keen on gyms,' I confessed. 'Although I do like to exercise.'

'How about rowing?' Jack suggested. 'With the river on your doorstep, it would be silly not to. You can borrow one of our old canoes. Why don't you take Becca down to the boathouse one afternoon and show her where everything is, JJ?'

'I'm busy all week,' JJ replied. 'In any case, I don't have the canoes any more.'

'You don't?' Jack looked puzzled.

'No. We don't use the boathouse, Dad. I did tell you.'

Jack continued to look perplexed, but the conversation rapidly changed direction. Chrissie had a complaint about bin collections – recycling was all well and good, but it should happen on a more regular basis – while the Commodore was keen for a progress report from Pete, who was apparently restoring a vintage vessel. Pete was more than happy to hold the floor, stretching out somewhat uncomfortably in his dark designer jeans as if he was already regretting consuming not just his own dinner but half his wife's as well. He droned on for several minutes about his yacht. I was rapidly losing patience with all of Pearl's carefully selected guests.

'Have you seen what treasures Chapman's currently got in his workshop?' Commodore Stevens asked. 'I was down there last week. The place is an Aladdin's cave of spare parts.'

'Oh, I know,' Pete agreed. 'I have been able to pick up a few bits and bobs from him.'

'I think Pete's converting his boat into a shag pad,' Natalie giggled to Rita. 'It's so hidden away down at Helme Point, goodness knows what he gets up to down there on his days off.'

Judy was very at good engaging Pearl and I whenever she could, as did Craig who, like me, seemed way out of this depth. It was far removed from the dinner party conversations I had enjoyed on a regular basis in London. JJ contributed very little but helped himself to copious amounts of red wine.

Dessert consisted of lemon torte with a raspberry coulis, followed by an overflowing cheeseboard, grapes, and liqueurs, after which Jack finally suggested we retreat to the drawing room for coffee. JJ said he needed to slip outside for a cigarette.

'Fancy joining me, Pearl?' he asked. 'Or are you still pretending to have given up?'

Pearl maintained a dignified silence while Pete sniggered and Judy announced that the church knit-and-natter group were creating a life–sized woolly nativity scene, if anyone wished to contribute an animal or two in time for Christmas.

'A word, JJ,' Jack said. 'My study. Five minutes.'

I instinctively gathered up used plates, wondering what excuse I could use to skip coffee altogether. The strain of the house move, plus remaining impeccably polite amongst such alien company, had left me physically and mentally drained.

I followed Heather back to the kitchen, hoping that if I slipped away now, my absence from the drawing room might not even be noticed.

'Oh, really there's no need,' she insisted. The countertops were overflowing with dirty crockery.

'You'll be up all night clearing this lot up,' I remarked. The dishwasher was whirring away while Nev was up to his elbows in soap-suds at the sink.

Heather almost shooed me out of the kitchen. 'It's our job,' she said. 'I'll be along with the coffee in a tick.'

'Well, at least let me clear some of this stuff for you,' I said, scraping the remains from the plates into the overflowing food waste bin. From the kitchen door I could sprint around to the front of the house and reach the stable block within seconds. I pulled out the wet waste bag and headed out of the back door to the bin store. I doubted anyone would actually miss me, apart from being the butt of the *why-hasn't-Becca-got-a-man* jokes.

As I turned the corner, I smelt the waft of nicotine. Jack had his study at this end of the house, next to his bedroom. Like the drawing room, the study doors opened out onto the garden. The light was on and JJ stood on the threshold of the French windows, cigarette in one hand. I slipped into the shadows against the wall of the house, not wanting to be seen and coerced into re-joining the party.

JJ's voice was slurred; the wine effect. 'I think you're being totally unreasonable,' he said, presumably to Jack in the study. 'You can easily afford to spare a couple of hundred grand. I can pay you back as soon as I can get those extra moorings in place.'

'No, you're the one who's being unreasonable,' Jack retorted from inside. I had to strain my ears to pick out his words. 'If you hadn't insisted on building that ridiculous house and buying yourself a ruddy Aqua Riva, you wouldn't be in this position. I've told you before, the business always comes first. Go and see your mate van der Plaast if you want someone to finance your fancy lifestyle, because I refuse. I'm not bailing you out any more. Do you hear? I'm not lending you another bloody penny. I've got better things to spend my money on now.'

'Like your tart Pearl?'

'I thought we'd already had this out. How dare you speak about Pearl like that.'

'Oh, come on, Dad, be realistic. Why can't you see her for what she is? The woman is a flashy tart. I can't believe you are letting her manipulate you like this. How many other members of her dysfunctional family are going to come crawling out of the woodwork? They're parasites, the whole lot of them. You should call this charade of a wedding off now before it's too late, before she makes you a laughing stock.'

If Jack replied, I didn't catch it. Instead, I heard the opening then slamming of a door. JJ remained in the shadows outside, his body taut. He stubbed out his cigarette on the wall of the house. It was a few seconds before he spoke.

'You think I don't know you're there, don't you, Rebecca?' he called. 'It would all be so much easier if you just left Rivermede now, wouldn't it? Before anyone gets hurt.'

Then, without waiting for an answer, he stepped into the study, drawing the French doors behind him.

Chapter Twelve

Pearl's attempts to launch me into Kerridge society had not been a success. JJ was drunk, his personal insults fuelled by red wine and too many liqueurs. However, there was no disguising his threatening tone. JJ's dislike of my mother stemmed not from a desire to protect his father, but the fact that Jack now had someone else to spend his money on. JJ was used to being the centre of his father's attention.

JJ didn't look like a man who would sit back and hope his problems would disappear of their own accord. I would have to take care, and keep a vigilant watch over Freddy and Pearl. Nick Quinlan's words came back to haunt me. Nick had refused to be drawn when I'd asked, but was JJ already known to the police as a violent man? Was that what Nick's warnings were all about?

As for Pearl's favourite topic of dinner party conversation, I felt mortally wounded. Friends in London knew better than to raise to the bait whenever the subject was mentioned, yet amongst strangers and a totally new gene pool, my mother seemed to think she was justified in promoting my single-status and treating me like a brood mare. Perhaps she and JJ deserved each other.

I'd survived a barrage of Pearl's match-making attempts before. I hadn't spent the last fifteen years since my break-up with Nick living like a nun. Pearl became embarrassingly enthusiastic whenever I so much as mentioned a date, or even dropped a man's name into conversation, so it was much easier to keep quiet. After Nick, I had remained celibate for some time, concentrating on work and developing my mother's brand. Eventually, I'd allowed a few girlfriends to drag me out to a bar or a club, and gradually I had started meeting new people. But I developed an automatic shut-off point. Any relationship that looked as if it might become serious was kept at arm's length, unless of course the man was already unattainable.

My affair with Declan, a married publishing executive from Belfast who flew in and out of London for business on a regular basis, had lasted more than four years. It was a perfect combination of no-strings-attached sex and companionship, conducted well away from Pearl's prying eyes. When Declan mentioned the word divorce, I'd run a mile. I couldn't possibly think about leaving my family, I'd said.

And that, I realised as I retreated to the unfamiliar surroundings of my new home in Rivermede's stable block, was exactly how I had wasted away the last fifteen years of my life. I'd convinced myself that Pearl and Freddy couldn't manage without me, when in fact they were both proving perfectly well that they could.

I was now effectively surplus to requirements. There was absolutely no reason why I couldn't set up my own freelance business in London or look for a full-time job with one of the major publishing houses. Anita was right; I was a good editor and I would find work.

I was at a crossroads, and it wasn't a question of not knowing which was the sensible path to take; the road to London was clearly marked, signposted in big bolder letters. REBECCA GATES GO THIS WAY. I had the perfect opportunity to make a bid for freedom, yet I still found excuses to stay. Could I take the risk that JJ was all bluster? Could I leave my mother and brother at his mercy?

Home truths hit hard. The real problem was that Pearl and Freddy weren't dependent on me; I was dependent on them.

I awoke the following morning filled with new resolve. My life had to change, although I fell at the first hurdle. Despite having my own flat, my own bathroom, and my own kitchen, I had no provisions for Saturday breakfast. I swallowed my pride and wandered back over to the big house.

I followed the wafting aroma of burnt bacon to the kitchen.

Heather was scraping the grill pan at the sink. My cheerful 'good morning' made her jump out of her skin.

'Oh, it's you,' she said, wiping her hands on her apron. She didn't look at all pleased to see me. 'I suppose you want some breakfast, too, do you?'

'Oh, it's fine, I'm happy to get it myself,' I assured her, heading for the fridge. 'I just want some toast and orange juice.'

'No!' She darted across the kitchen, blocking my path. 'Sit down, let me.'

The kitchen table hadn't been wiped from its last occupant which, judging by the amount of crumbs and spillages, I could only assume had been Freddy, unless Nev also ate with the uncontrolled velocity of an eternal teenager.

'Jack and Pearl don't ever breakfast before nine,' Heather said as she gave the surface a ferocious sweep with her cloth. '*And* they always eat in the conservatory or a dining room. I don't like people invading my space.'

I could sympathise with the sentiment. Freddy had been banned on numerous occasions from the kitchen in Battersea. However, I sensed she wasn't just referring to Freddy.

I assured her I fully intended to be self-sufficient. 'Once I've stocked up on supplies,' I promised, 'I'll be out of your hair.'

'Good,' she replied.

She directed me to the local Lidl which had everything I needed. Once I'd bought the basics, I drove on to the nearest M&S, which was only another few minutes along the motorway. I may have overplayed my cooking skills the previous evening; Pearl ate my food because she had little choice, but I wasn't a particularly adventurous cook, sticking to a rotation of easy to prepare old favourites. Now that I didn't have to worry about Pearl's delicate constitution – she was averse to anything too spicy, although I had noticed her consuming Heather's Oriental-themed menu the previous evening with great relish – I could please myself with what I cooked and what I ate.

It was also true that I probably could afford to lose a couple of pounds or two before the wedding. With glamorous competition in the form of Rita and Natalie, I wanted to look my best. I headed for the low-calorie ready meal section and then the fresh soups, perfect for lunches rather than my usual carb-loaded deli sandwich. If I could replicate Heather's wonderful Thai fish soup, all the better. I grabbed the M&S version from the shelf.

With my shopping complete, I headed back to Rivermede, only to discover Pearl sheltering under an umbrella at the top of my steps and knocking furiously on the front door.

'There you are,' she called. 'Where have you been? We're off to Fontwell, to the races. We'll be leaving in ten minutes.'

'Well, have a nice a day then,' I replied, heaving my shopping bags out of the car.

'But you're coming with us,' she insisted. 'It'll be fun. Horse racing. How often do we get the chance to do that?' She noticed my bags. 'What have you been doing?'

'I've been grocery shopping.'

'What do you need to do that for? Heather looks after us.'

'Heather looks after you and Jack,' I pointed out. 'I don't need her looking after me. Besides, I don't think she wants to.'

'She's paid to look after whoever Jack says she has to look after,' Pearl snapped. 'Hurry up and unpack and then you can join us. I'll get Nev to wait.'

'I'm not coming to Fontwell.'

She pouted. 'But I want you to come. It's an outing, a family outing. It'll be fun.'

'No.' I stood firm. The old Becca would have caved in, but the new Becca was stronger. I had to use that fifty metres of gravel which separated our homes wisely. I could live independently yet still keep an eye on my mother and Freddy. It was a frame of mind, not a physical locality. 'You have Jack now, and you and Jack can go and have a lovely day at the races together, and I will stay here finishing my unpacking and then I am going to start work.'

Pearl looked alarmed. 'Work? What work? I told Anita we weren't going to go ahead with the novellas.'

'I know that, but no, Anita hasn't sent me anything. Just

97

because you've quit publishing doesn't mean my work has stopped entirely. There's still your website to maintain, for now at least, and a few fans to placate, but I am also working on a new project.'

'A new project? What new project?'

'Stella Markham's memoirs. You're right, she has got a very interesting story to tell and I'm going to write it for her.'

Pearl's mouth dropped. 'Really? That was just a piece of silly nonsense. Who will want to read that?'

Nev appeared in his chauffeur's suit ready to move the Range Rover out onto the gravel. Pearl watched with a shaking head as I continued to unload my car before retreating to the sanctuary of my new flat.

I'd helped out with the research on a few autobiographies during my early days in the publishing world, before Pearl's career had leapfrogged and become my full-time job. As with all stories, I knew it wasn't so much the content that was important but the way it was told; the magical elements which captured a reader's imagination. Stella's technical accounts of her racing triumph were of little interest to anyone who wasn't an expert sailor, but the human side of her story – the verbal abuse from Owen and the loss of her children – would certainly resonate with a large number of people. But what the story really needed was a happy-ever-after, and so far it was eluding me. An idea had taken shape, but I wasn't quite sure how I was going to pull it off.

By lunchtime, I could feel the beginnings of a headache, so I stopped to heat up the fish soup, hoping it was going to be as delicious as Heather's home-made version. It was. In fact, it was almost identical in taste and in texture. So much so that, despite telling myself it was none of my business if Heather had told a little white lie to Pearl and bought her home-made soup from M&S, or even if Pearl was complicit in the deceit – after all, we had given plenty of dinner parties at Battersea where the food had been provided by caterers – I skipped down to the bin store, brand new rubber gloves in hand, and rummaged through the recycling bin. Alongside four empty cartons of M&S Thai fish soup, I also discovered the cardboard packing for two of Lidl's 'brand new' aromatic roast chickens and an M&S luxury lemon torte.

I wasn't sure what my discoveries proved, apart from exposing Heather as not quite the good cook she, or indeed Pearl, claimed. Heather had made it perfectly clear that she didn't want Freddy or I poking about in her kitchen, but Pearl would be more than happy to keep out of her way. It could well be that Pearl had been just as keen as Heather to impress her prestigious guests, but in Battersea Pearl had never shied away from admitting to using a catering service. I didn't like to think that she had been duped.

The morning's rain ceased to a drizzle. I hoped it was better at Fontwell. Pearl had little time for sport, but coming to Kerridge had opened up a whole new range of interests and hobbies for her. My mother deserved to be happy, and if Pearl was happy, I should be happy, too. There was still the issue of Freddy's impending fatherhood to deal with, but that was really his problem, not mine.

Since my encounter with Nick, I'd spent a great deal of time reflecting on how my relationship with Freddy might appear to others. I'd been as shocked as everyone else when Pearl had announced at the age of 43 that she was pregnant. '*I thought it was the bloody menopause, darling.*' She needed me with her.

While she and Dieter had sojourned in the Hollywood Hills, I'd been sent to a very exclusive boarding school in Switzerland. Non-payment of fees was a heinous crime, and Pearl's termly cheque had bounced spectacularly. I hid my shame well, telling only a few close friends that a family crisis had arisen and I'd been recalled to London.

Pearl was in a complete mess, emotionally and financially, but Freddy gave her the impetus to resurrect her career. She set to fervently penning a series of heart-wrenching historical romances which required intense dedication, peace, and quiet. I loved Freddy. He was an easy, placid baby and I was happy to be left in charge. When Freddy was a year old, I passed my

A levels and was able to take up my place at university, although at Pearl's insistence I remained living at home. I walked Freddy to nursery and later to school; I attended parents' evenings; watched nativity plays. I adopted many of the responsibilities that Pearl should have taken on. It was easy to see how an outsider, someone who didn't know the family circumstances, could possibly have mistaken our relationship.

It was disappointing to realise Nick considered the whole idea that I might have had a child, conceived long before I'd met him, a deal-breaker. Who didn't have 'baggage' these days? What hurt most, though, was knowing that Nick thought I had deliberately deceived him. Did he really believe he was going find Freddy residing in our spare room as soon as we returned from our honeymoon, without any sort of discussion or consultation? I'd loved Nick unconditionally. If he'd fathered a child at eighteen, I wouldn't have walked away. If I'd suspected, I'd have confronted him. I wouldn't have kept my fears to myself and used them as a feeble excuse to sleep with his best friend. What sort of person did that? Nick's suspicions about Freddy's parentage didn't exonerate his guilt in any way; they compounded it.

I sent Freddy a text and suggested that he call in after work and have a meal with me '*to save making any extra work for Heather. Pearl and Jack have gone horse racing. Not sure when they'll be back.*'

He replied he was going for a drink straight from work with some of his new mates from the marina, but promised to be home by eight. I was glad he had already forged friendships but felt even more redundant than ever. Was this how Pearl had felt when I'd refused to accompany her to the races at Fontwell?

Chapter Thirteen

There was little point planning a special meal for Freddy. His idea of eight was more likely to be nine, especially after a few drinks. I checked I had purchased enough ingredients to make a simple pasta dish, and spent the rest of the afternoon on the internet, uncovering all I could about Owen Markham and his Isle of Wight restaurant.

I learned that Owen had recently become a grandfather for the first time. I wondered if Stella knew. There were lots of pictures on his personal and the restaurant's Facebook pages, but the proud granddad omitted to mention baby Ella's parents' names or include them in any photographs. There were numerous Emily Markhams on Facebook, but none appeared to still be located on the Isle of Wight. In any case, Emily could well be married and using another name. As for Tristram Markham, I couldn't find him anywhere online at all.

I didn't hear Jack and Pearl return, but she knocked on the door at seven and invited me over to dine with them. I politely refused. The races had been a disappointment. She looked bedraggled and complained of a chill. At nine, I sent Freddy a text reminding him of his dinner date.

'Sorry. Completely forgot. Left bike at work. Don't suppose you could come and fetch me?'

'Where are you?' I hoped he was at Jolly Jack Tar or The Ship, as both were relatively close.

'Rum Runners in Portdeane.'

Portdeane? Freddy hadn't just gone for a drink straight from work, he'd gone for a swim across the river. How else could he have got there if he'd left his scooter at the marina? I'd had one glass of wine whilst I chopped mushrooms to go with the pasta. I was perfectly capable of driving, but it was seriously tempting to tell Freddy to forget the whole *come-over-for-a-*

chat-and-meal thing and leave him to make his own way back to Kerridge. He was probably already plastered.

I'd only viewed Portdeane from across the river. It had an extensive waterfront of boatsheds, workshops, and offices. It was a busy place compared to Kerridge. Cursing Freddy's thoughtlessness, I headed out to the car. Portdeane wasn't easy to reach by road. The bridge over the River Deane, a mile or so further upstream, had been built during the last century and was currently under repair, and had been for some time, according to Jack. Traffic lights controlled the flow. Portdeane was also in the middle of a house-building boom, resulting in even more traffic controls and numerous mini-roundabouts. It was over half an hour before I pulled up on the quayside

I fought my way through a fug of smokers outside The Rum Runners. Unlike The Ship's regular clientele, the majority of this pub's customers were on the right side of twenty-five. I had to squeeze my way through a noisy throng of youthful bodies to a long table where I spotted Freddy, with his back towards me, his distinctive bleached blond head in very close proximity to another young blonde head.

He sat next to Kimmi, the nubile teenage paddle-boarder we had encountered on the marina. They shared their table with several others, some standing, while a middle-aged shaven-headed man held court. As the pub was so packed, my entrance had been pretty inconspicuous. I tapped Freddy on the shoulder.

'Hey look, Fred,' one of his new mates chuckled as Freddy turned around. 'Your mum's come for you. Is it past your bedtime?'

This seemed pretty rich from a boy who looked barely old enough to drink. I recognised him as one of the lads who worked on the marina.

'She's not my mum,' Freddy drawled, giving me a drunken smile. 'Sorry, Becs, I forgot the time.'

'No worries,' I assured him. 'You ready to go?'

'Yeah, sure.' Freddy drowned the last of his beer.

The shaven man stopped mid-sentence. His voice was heavily accented; mid- European, Dutch or German maybe.

'Are you leaving us, Freddy?'

'Ah yeah, sorry Max,' Freddy apologised. 'Got to go home. My sister's cooking me a meal.'

'Oh, that's a shame.'

'What's a shame?' I asked. 'My cooking, or the fact that you are losing one of your audience?'

He laughed and stood up. He was well over six foot and made an imposing figure. 'I don't think we've had the pleasure.' He held out his hand. 'Max van der Plaast.'

The name rang a bell. This was Kerridge's only eligible bachelor – apart from birdwatcher Alex, who didn't count. Max wasn't bad-looking, in a bulky, muscular sort of way. His eyes were a very clear shade of blue and they assessed me, from top to bottom. A diamond glistened in one ear, while his bare arms were covered with tattoos. His t-shirt and jeans were Armani and Hugo Boss. The watch on his wrist a very large Rolex.

'Becca Gates,' I replied as my fingers crushed under grip. 'I'm Freddy's sister.'

'Ah, so you are also staying with the Robshaws.' Max smiled. He slapped Freddy on the back. 'See you again soon, Freddy, my boy.'

'Cheers, Max,' Freddy replied, 'and thanks for the ride over.'

'Any time.'

'Bye, Kimmi,' Freddy said a little awkwardly to the paddle-boarder, but she had already turned her attention to one of the other youths on the table.

'You should see that guy's boat,' Freddy exclaimed as he flopped into the passenger seat of my car. 'It's like enormous, it's got three bedrooms, proper size you know, flat screen TV, big lounge area, kitchen—'

'So that's how you got across the water, then? I thought you might have swum.'

'No, I mean yeah. We didn't come over on *Pegasus*, we came over on his rib. Max is a mate of JJ's. He was on the marina and he offered to take us out for a spin.'

'Great, glad you enjoyed it. The pasta will be a bit congealed.'

'Oh, I'm sorry. I couldn't really say no, could I? Not when everyone was else was going.'

'Of course not, Fred. I'm glad you've made some new friends. So, who's the girl?'

'What girl?'

'Oh, don't be stupid. The paddle-boarder.'

'Kimmi is Max's daughter. She's staying with him up at his house in Helme. The place is massive, apparently, even bigger than Rivermede. He's got a gym, a games room, private cinema, pool.'

'Have you been there?'

'No, not yet, that's just what the lads say.'

'You need to be careful, Freddy,' I said. I didn't want to sound like I was putting a dampener on his fledgling new friendships, but Freddy had other responsibilities to be thinking of. 'You should be concentrating on your job right now and saving some money. I'm not sure running around after Kimmi is a good thing.'

'I'm not running around after Kimmi,' Freddy replied. 'In any case, it's to my advantage to stay on the right side of Max. The lads say he is often on the lookout for extra crew, and he pays a lot better than JJ, apparently.'

'Crew? You mean on his boat?'

'Yeah, why not?'

'I think you should just stick to working on dry land, Freddy.'

'Oh, it wouldn't be full-time. It's just every now and then. Anyway, you'll be pleased to hear I'm having lessons on the forklift next week. Once I've got my licence, I can start working on the mobile cranes.'

'Cranes?' That was even more alarming than the thought of Freddy setting sail. I wasn't sure Freddy should be left in charge of anything mechanical, not for his own welfare but the safety of others. 'It all sounds highly dangerous.'

He didn't answer. By the time we reached Rivermede, Freddy was asleep.

On Sunday morning, I enjoyed making my own breakfast and then, as watery sunshine broke through the black clouds, I decided to head out for a walk.

I knew from my first brief tour of Rivermede's grounds with Pearl that there was a gate with access to the foreshore. I had a vague idea that if I could walk along the river, in the opposite direction to The Ship of Fools, I would eventually come to the marina and subsequently the marsh at Helme Point, alleviating the need to head up through the centre of the village. I was in my wellington boots, however it soon became quite clear the route was impassable without thigh-high waders.

It was high tide, and a fast-flowing inlet cut through the Rivermede estate. I continued for a little while, hoping that perhaps I would encounter a footbridge or at least a point at which the creek would be crossable. Instead, it carried on into the woodland by JJ's new house. Just as I was about to turn back, I heard a faint swishing on the water, and the sound of oars.

It was Nev, paddling furiously in a canoe, a rhythmic grunt accompanying each stroke, his eyes fixed on the water ahead. JJ may have given up rowing, but it certainly looked as if Nev was on a fitness campaign. I hesitated, wondering if I should call out a greeting. Nev and I were on polite hello and good morning terms, not matey bellows. I didn't want to disturb his concentration, so I shrank back into the trees. For some reason I couldn't quite define, I didn't want an encounter, so instead of continuing on my walk, I turned around and walked back to the house.

Pearl demanded my company for elevenses and we spent a pleasant enough hour discussing wedding bouquets, corsages, and button-holes. I managed to remain remarkably calm throughout. As she had already decided on the designs, it was easier not to express any opinion. I promised to visit the dressmaker in Portdeane by the end of the week for the bridesmaid dress fitting – something I admitted I had been putting off.

'Just ask Vera to make the dress a centimetre smaller in every direction,' Pearl advised. 'That'll give you the incentive to lose that extra weight.'

It was less than six weeks now to the wedding, and the invitations had gone out. There was accommodation to organise for overnight guests and a seating plan. I offered to draw up a spreadsheet, but to my surprise Pearl flipped open her brand-new laptop. She was already on the case.

She seemed disappointed when I mentioned that I would be entertaining Freddy for Sunday dinner and neither of us would be joining her and Jack that evening.

'But Heather does such a lovely roast,' she pouted. 'I've already told her to prepare a meal for four.'

I promised to pop into the kitchen on my way back to the stable block and amend the catering arrangements.

Freddy was late again, this time because JJ, not to be outdone by his friend Max, had apparently been showing off in his Aqua Riva.

'Is that his flashy new car?' I asked, offering Freddy a beer which he took gratefully. He hadn't changed out of his marina uniform – it was still disconcerting to see my brother dressed in another colour other than black, and especially shorts. Freddy hadn't worn shorts since he'd left nursery school.

'*Car*?' This sent Freddy into fits to laughter. 'It's a boat, you dummy. They cost about half a million squid.'

'Oh.' No wonder JJ was in financial difficulties. 'Is it the same sort of thing as Max's van der Plaast's fancy yacht?'

Freddy shook his head and sank onto the sofa. 'No, *Pegasus* is a catamaran. An Aqua Riva is a speedboat. Pearl would love it. It's the sort of thing James Bond would have had back in the sixties, you know when Sean Connery was playing him. Vintage Italian design, handcrafted mahogany with maple inlay deck, leather seating, two 370 hp engines. Apparently, sometimes he lets the lads have a turn at the wheel. I'd love to have a go.'

'Sounds wonderful,' I remarked, having no idea what he was talking about. Freddy seemed to have soaked up nautical terms like a sponge. I asked him whether he knew Nev was a keen canoeist.

He shook his head. 'I've hardly seen Nev since I arrived,' he replied. 'He and Jack always seem to be out, but I suppose if you do like your water sports, this is the place to be.'

'I wanted to see if I could walk to Helme Point along the river this morning, but I couldn't see a way across the creek,' I continued. 'How far up does it go?'

'Just to JJ's boathouse.'

'Is that where he keeps this Aqua River thing?' I asked, wondering if that was why JJ had insisted the boathouse was off-limits. He wouldn't want me anywhere near his fancy speedboat.

'Aqua Riva.' Freddy rolled his eyes in exasperation. 'No, he keeps that in a secure berth at the marina. I'm starving, by the way. When's the food going to be ready? I hope you've prepared something nice. Heather does a lovely Sunday dinner. Last week she made a nut roast just for me, and her potatoes were out of this world.'

It was tempting to tell him Heather's lovely homemade nut roast was more than likely an M&S ready meal and the potatoes were out of this world because they were smeared with delicious goose fat, but I kept quiet. Freddy seemed a little disappointed in the butternut squash risotto I'd lovingly prepared – previously one of his favourites – and after dinner refused to be drawn into any sort of conversation about Ruby, apart from admitting that he had let her know he'd left London. At half nine, he made his excuses and wandered back over to the main house via the kitchen door – hopeful, I suspected, at picking over the remains of the Sunday roast.

Chapter Fourteen

I spent most of Monday working on Stella's memoirs. After lunch, I headed into IKEA in Southampton to buy a few brightly coloured accessories for the tiny kitchen and bathroom.

I didn't return until late afternoon. When I pulled up on the drive, Pearl came flying out of the house as if she had been standing guard.

'Where have you been? I thought you might have forgotten.'

'Forgotten what?' I asked.

'It's Monday, isn't it?' She stabbed me in the chest with an accusing finger. 'Quiz night at the pub. Go and get your thinking cap on. Chrissie and Craig need you. She phoned up earlier to remind you.'

I had my doubts Chrissie had phoned at all; more likely, Pearl had been the one making the call. I knew my mother well. She would be watching out of the window at 6.50pm to ensure I'd left, knocking on my door at 6.55 if she spotted the car still on the drive. Tomorrow morning, she would be bombarding me with questions about my team mate Alex. And if I didn't go, but simply got in the car and spent the evening hiding out in the Rum Runners in Portdeane, which was actually quite tempting, I'd be fending off the same barrage of questions without having anyone to validate my attendance at The Ship of Fools. I didn't doubt she would double-check with Chrissie.

If I went, I could perhaps glean some further knowledge about JJ from Nick. I could also report back that Alex was totally unsuitable marriage material, fabricating a plausible excuse that he was an out-of-work railway engineer (because anyone who worked for Network Rail was the lowest of the low as far as Pearl was concerned) with two former wives and six children. It might just work.

As it was, there was no need for any subterfuge and I felt a strange sense of disappointment to see that Nick wasn't even at the pub. Instead, Chrissie and Craig were joined by the M&Ms – fellow twitchers Mark and Marie – just back from a bird-watching expedition to the South Atlantic and the Antarctic. After brief introductions, Marie spent several minutes expanding on the mating habits of the Adelie Penguin – precocious birds with homosexual tendencies and not beyond a spot of necrophilia, if the fancy took them. At which point, I made a casual attempt to drop Alex's name into conversation. Craig had seen him out on the marsh the previous week, but there was no mention of why he was absent.

'I'm sure Stella said he's got a six-month lease on her boat,' Chrissie consoled. 'I expect he'll be along next week as usual.'

The evening passed pretty dismally. I was able to catch Stella during the break and we made an arrangement to meet up the following week for an update on the book project.

At least I was keeping busy. On Tuesday morning, I received an email from Anita with the good news that she was in negotiations with a major trade union leader who wished to write his autobiography.

'It's going to need an awful lot of editing,' she wrote. 'Are you interested?'

I couldn't think of anything less interesting, but I couldn't afford to turn down work, although it did prompt me to place an ad for my editorial and proofreading services in one of the leading creative writing magazines. It would be good to have choices.

Freddy called into the flat on his way home from work to announce that we'd both been invited to Kimmi's 18th birthday party at the van der Plaast mansion in two weeks' time.

'Max was most insistent you come,' he said. Perhaps eligible spinsters in Kerridge were as rare as the eligible bachelors, although I couldn't imagine a man like Max – I'd Googled him: Dutch; forty-six; divorced, twice; son of the multi-millionaire founder of van der Plaast Marine Engine Services, a major international company with offices in Rotterdam, Marseilles, Stockholm, and Portdeane – would have any trouble attracting female companions.

I had nothing suitable to wear to a house-party hosted by a millionaire, so I spent the rest of the evening looking at cocktail dresses on the internet.

I managed to postpone an inquisition from Pearl until Wednesday morning, when she suggested coffee. She was in a state of great agitation.

'Jack's up to something,' she announced as we sat down in the conservatory. Heather had already set up the ubiquitous tea tray. I wondered if Pearl would ever venture into a kitchen again.

'What do you mean?'

'Oh, I don't know,' Pearl frowned. 'He just seems a bit different here to how he was on holiday.'

'Well, that's understandable,' I assured her. Was Pearl having doubts? It wasn't too late to call off the wedding. We could all return safely to London, Pearl could start writing again…

I quashed such traitorous thoughts. As much as I wanted us all out of harm's way, I didn't want my old co-dependent lifestyle back. And in any case, it was impossible. Beech Mews was sold; I'd handed the keys over to Magda Pepowski myself.

'Why are you worried?' I asked her.

'I'm not worried,' Pearl insisted, 'it's just, well, you know, he's less attentive.'

'There's little else to do on a cruise ship but talk to each other, is there?' I reminded her. 'Here, Jack presumably still has some business interests to keep his eye on.'

'JJ takes care of all that,' Pearl replied.

But not very efficiently, by all accounts. I was quite sure Jack was keeping tabs on JJ. Not that I could confess my eavesdropping to Pearl, but it wouldn't hurt to carry out a little detective work of my own. I did want to hear what was at the route of her concerns.

'Do you think Jack is keeping something from you?' I asked.

Pearl gave a shrug. 'I'm not sure. I suppose you're right, people are always different when they're in their own home. We both have to adjust to living together.'

'He does look after you, doesn't he?' From what I'd seen so far, Jack behaved impeccably towards my mother, but what if that charming veneer was all for show? Was he a different person altogether behind closed doors?

'Yes, of course he does. It's nothing like that all.' Pearl seemed quite indignant.

'Well then, what is it? You had that nice day out at the races, didn't you?'

'It wasn't nice. It was cold and wet, and I hate horses,' Pearl pouted. 'It's just me being silly, Becca. Perhaps I'm missing London. I tell you what, why don't we go into town? Go shopping? I haven't chosen my going away outfit yet.'

'Are you going away?' I asked. In all our conversations about the wedding so far, Pearl had not mentioned a honeymoon.

'We haven't booked anything, but we can't not, can we?' Pearl said, already on her feet. 'Come on, darling, we can go into Winchester and then stop for a spot of lunch or something, what do you say? You haven't told me about the quiz, either. How did you get on? How was Alex?'

'He wasn't there,' I informed her. 'And we lost.'

'Oh, never mind. There's always next week.' She smiled. 'Perhaps we should invite him to the wedding. He can tag along with Chrissie and Craig. Maybe you could have a look for something while we're out, too, for the party.'

'What party?' Had Freddy already told her about Kimmi's birthday? Perhaps Pearl and Jack had been invited, too.

'The evening party,' Pearl said, 'after the wedding, of course.'

Of course. It was all still about her.

'I thought I would just stay in my bridesmaid's dress,' I said.

Pearl shook her head, dismissing my attempt to spoil her fun. 'No, Rebecca, you can't, you really just can't. That won't do at all.'

Despite telling myself that Nick had a perfectly valid reason for avoiding the pub – ie, he didn't want to see me – when I returned from keeping Pearl amused in Winchester, I set off for another walk. This time, I went through the village to the marina and along the marsh path towards to Helme Point.

Over lunch, I had quizzed my mother on what she knew of her new neighbours in an attempt to ascertain if there were any other possible suspects who might appear on a police radar. There were several large detached properties along the river concealed behind security gates, but Pearl had limited knowledge of their occupants. Her weekly activity rota revolved around the same regular companions who frequented the WI, the bridge club, and the choir. She had heard of a wealthy Arab family further up the river, together with a self-made millionaire from the betting industry, and there were rumours of a very dodgy banker. But other than Max van der Plaast, who had a reputation as an international playboy, the residents of Kerridge seemed a fairly unremarkable and law-abiding crowd.

The houseboat was shut up and deserted, although it was evident that Nick was still living on board. Wellington boots guarded the doorway, and a crate of empty beer cans was sitting on deck. I didn't want to analyse why Nick's absence concerned me so much, or why I was so relieved to see that he was still based in Kerridge.

With no sign of Nick, I approached the unimposing workshop on Chapman's Wharf. According to the sign above the door, it was the home of Aidan Chapman, Boat Restorer. The timber shack looked as if it had once been part of a much bigger operation. To one side, a concrete slipway led down to the water. Toxic fumes permeated the air from inside the workshop. A man in his mid-thirties, with an impressive ginger beard and dressed in paint splattered dungarees, was varnishing a wooden hull.

'Are you Aidan?' I asked.

He looked up cautiously. 'I might be. Who are you?'

'My name is Becca. I'm looking for Alex,' I said. 'He rents out *The Solstice*. Do you know if he is about?'

He shook his head. 'I saw him on Saturday. He said he was going to be away for a couple of weeks. When he's back, shall I tell him you were looking for him?'

I shook my head. 'There's no need. Thanks, anyway.'

I was just about to turn away when an old man shuffled into the workshop, blocking my exit.

'You busy, Chapman?' he grunted. 'Bloody decking on the mooring's gone again.'

Aidan put down his paint brush. 'I'll come now, Gerry,' he said. 'Just let me get some tools.'

As it appeared we were all going to be walking back along the same route, we fell into step.

'Bloody Robshaw,' the old man grumbled as we set off. 'He's behind all this.'

'Why do you say that?' Aidan asked.

'It was perfectly all right last night.'

I thought it was safe to assume from the old man's unkempt appearance and belligerent attitude that this was JJ's adversary, Gerald Kimble, Kerridge's least eligible bachelor and owner of the *Regatta Queen*.

'I had heard the marina people wanted the *Regatta Queen* moved on,' I said to Aidan. Sailor Gerry lagged behind. 'Is that what this is all about?'

'Probably. Gerry owns a boat that needs to be scrapped, and the mooring's been falling into disrepair for years,' Aidan explained. 'I believe he and the Robshaws, who own the marina, have a bit of history. Are you a local? I haven't seen you before.'

'I'm just visiting the area,' I replied.

'So, how do you know Alex?' he asked.

I had to be careful. 'We met at the pub quiz at The Ship of Fools. We were more or less forced to be on the same team. I'm staying with relatives.' I thought it wise not to mention which relatives.

113

'Oh, I see. Not my cup of tea that, a pub quiz,' Aidan remarked.

'What's she saying?' the old man shouted. 'Who's she calling a fool?'

'Nobody,' Aidan replied, waiting for him to catch up. 'She was saying she goes to the quiz at the pub, *The Ship of Fools*.'

'I never go to The Ship now,' Gerry said, shaking his head. He had a crown of snowy white hair and grey stubble grew on his scrawny chin. He was a small man, and his heavy overcoat seemed to swamp him. On closer inspection, although I didn't want to get too close because personal hygiene was obviously not top of Gerry's priorities, he probably wasn't as old as I'd first thought; perhaps mid-sixties. 'It's all changed,' he complained. 'Ain't anywhere decent left in the village now.' He gave a nod towards the Jolly Jack Tar on Kerridge Hard, where a boisterous crowd gathered outside. 'That place has gone right downhill.'

I thought I caught sight of the shiny bald head of Max van der Plaast amongst the storm-proof jackets. A couple of people were still wearing buoyancy aids, despite being safely on dry land. Since I'd arrived on the south coast, I'd noticed the sailing fraternity liked to publicise their prestigious status. Yachting was an expensive hobby. If you had it, you flaunted it, seemed an appropriate motto.

As we reached the damaged mooring, Max's distinctive guttural laugh rang out across the quayside. Aidan shared Gerry's disapproving look.

'None of them lot are locals,' the younger man remarked. 'The Heron is about the only decent drinking hole left in the village.'

Gerry shook his head. 'Too far for me to walk,' he grumbled.

'How far is it?' I asked. I hadn't come across another pub on my travels, although I hadn't spent a great deal of time exploring the outer realms of Kerridge.

'It's one of the few pubs in this part of the world that doesn't do food. A real old-fashioned drinkers' pub,' Aidan said. 'It makes a refreshing change.'

'Sounds like something I need to check out,' I said with a smile. 'I'll leave you to your work.'

'You need to get this fixed properly, Gerry,' Aidan said, stepping cautiously onto the rotten wooden decking that was the only means of access to the *Regatta Queen*. 'One morning you could wake up and find yourself adrift.'

'I suspect that's just what the nipper wants,' Gerry replied.

Chapter Fifteen

Although I felt a certain amount of sympathy for Gerry's predicament, the first thing I did when I returned to Rivermede was to freshen up with a shower. I had an evening appointment with the dressmaker in Portdeane.

I had been slightly dubious about the dressmaker's credentials after Pearl had informed me Vera came highly recommended by Rita and Natalie, but my fears were unfounded. Vera, of eastern European extraction and in her mid-thirties, lived on one of Portdeane's many new estates, in a smart terraced townhouse, the top floor of which was dedicated to her design business. Pearl was, quite naturally, keeping her dress top secret although, having spent many hours browsing through bridal magazines, I had a mental picture of the sort of thing she liked.

'Your mother is a woman of impeccable taste,' Vera confirmed. 'She has chosen a very simple, classical design, perfectly suitable for a woman of her age. We will do the same for you. It would be foolish to wear something too youthful.'

Although I disliked the reference to my maturing years, it was a relief to know that Vera and I appeared to be on the same wavelength. Purple would never have been my colour of choice, but she had selected a very pale lilac fabric, which almost verged on grey. The dress would be knee-length and very understated. There was no way Pearl was going to be over-shadowed, which suited me perfectly.

The following morning Pearl waylaid me, as I'd feared she would, for an update on the fitting, before announcing she was off to see 'a man about an owl'.

'An owl?'

'Yes, I saw the ad in the latest edition of Bridal Magazine.'

Nev was already reversing the Range Rover out of the garage and onto the drive. 'It's the latest thing. The owls are trained to deliver the rings. There's a place out in the New Forest that does it. Don't suppose you fancy coming with me?'

'I thought you were preparing for a wedding, not a term at Hogwarts.'

Pearl pouted and continued her path to the car. 'I'm going to meet your Aunt Phoebe for lunch afterwards. She's having a few days in Bournemouth. Call in on Jack later, love, would you? Keep him company. I'll probably be gone for the rest of the day.'

Jack was a grown man, not a child, and unlike Pearl, probably very good at keeping himself amused. However, I'd had too many years of being groomed. After a morning spent answering a few fan queries on Pearl's website – *no, of course Pearl Gates wasn't giving up writing, where an earth had they heard such a silly rumour?* – I wandered across to the house and found Jack in his study. The door wasn't closed. He was engrossed in paperwork; box files and folders were scattered across the desk in front of him, along with pages of yellowing documents.

It was the first time I'd had a proper look in Jack's private domain. Pictures of boats adorned the walls here, just as they did in the hallway. Amongst the artwork, I spotted a couple of technical drawings, presumably mementoes of the Dimmock boatyard.

'Hello, love,' he said, 'just having a bit of a sort through while your mother's out of the way.'

'She thought you might be lonely,' I replied, glad to see that my first instincts had been correct and Jack was more than capable of keeping himself occupied. I wondered if the sudden need to check historical documents had anything to do with Gerry Kimble's claims to his mooring rights, although Jack currently had a map spread out on his desk.

'I'm not lonely,' Jack said with a wink. 'I'm glad of the peace and quiet. You look dressed for an expedition.'

I'd deliberately put on my heavy raincoat and wellington boots as evidence to back up my excuse, if needed, that I was only briefly popping in on my way somewhere more interesting.

'I was planning on taking a walk,' I said. 'You've got some lovely countryside around here, and I've hardly seen anything of it yet.'

'Yes, we're very lucky,' Jack agreed.

'Is that a plan of Kerridge you've got there?' I asked.

'Just the original Rivermede estate,' he replied. 'As you can see, it covered a much larger area back in the 1800s than it does today.'

'So, did your late wife's family own all the land as far as the current marina?' I asked, spotting the creek and, further along, an area clearly marked out for the boatyard.

'Most of it, yes,' Jack smiled. He turned the map towards me so I could get a better look. 'Some pockets have been sold off over the years. I currently rent out a couple of pastures to the north, up here. We originally had some farm cottages, too, but they've gone now.'

'It was a big estate.'

'Too big. Mary's father originally bought it from a wealthy industrialist, but he over-stretched himself. We had to sell off a fair bit of what Mary inherited in order to keep the house. It was her childhood home; we didn't want to let it go.'

Jack rarely mentioned his late wife. A couple of framed photographs had a prominent position on the desk. Presumably this was the one room in the house which hadn't come under Pearl's sweeping new broom. One was a faded colour wedding photograph, a young couple standing outside the parish church in the village. In the other, the same couple posed on the front steps of Rivermede. Jack caught my eye.

'That's me and Mary,' he said, 'back in the day.'

I took a seat opposite him. It seemed as good a time as any to broach a difficult subject. 'Jack, can I talk to you about something personal?'

'Sure, go ahead.'

'I just wondered if Pearl has mentioned anything to you about my father?'

'Ah,' Jack said with a knowing nod.

'You do know he suffered a serious injury and—'

'Shush, Becca, dear.' Jack's smile was calm and reassuring. 'I've got a dodgy hip, that's all it is. I'm not going to end up paralysed or totally dependent on your mother, if that's what you're worried about. I lost my right leg in an accident in the boatyard many years ago. I wore a prosthetic for years, but when my hip started playing up, it made the prosthetic bloody uncomfortable. I gave up wearing it.' He tapped the sides of his wheelchair. 'I can get about much quicker in this.'

'Could they operate on your hip?' I asked. 'It's amazing what can be done these days.'

He gave me a resigned smile, as if he had long accepted his fate. 'There's nothing in the pipeline, my dear.'

I left Jack to continue his sorting. As I was already equipped for a spot of exploration, I decided to head once again for the path that skirted around the Rivermede estate. The tide was much further out than I'd seen before and, as Freddy had predicted, the track and the creek came to a muddy end at a brick boathouse, its doors firmly padlocked. The windows were grubby and above head height; even on tip-toes, I couldn't peep inside.

The only way to continue southwards towards the estuary and the marina was to cross the expanse of mud to a neighbouring field. A series of logs had been laid across the quagmire as stepping stones.

Just as I was about to take my first tentative step across, a dog barked. I turned sharply, only just maintaining my balance and my dignity. Max van der Plaast was approaching through the trees behind me, accompanied by a squat bulldog straining on its lead.

'I wouldn't do that if I were you,' he called. 'The tide's about to turn. You won't get back, unless of course you were planning on walking the long way round.'

I wanted to retort that actually yes, I was, but I could end up looking pretty stupid as I had no idea how to find the long way round. I also wanted to demand what he was doing trespassing on Rivermede property, but my bravado failed. The dog didn't look particularly friendly, although Max was all charming smiles.

'Ah. It is you, Becca, Freddy's sister,' he said. 'I thought I recognised you. I saw you yesterday, too, on the Hard. You should have joined us for a drink. I'd taken some friends over to the Island for the day.'

I had thought I'd made myself invisible as I had sneaked past the Jolly Jack Tar, but obviously not. Unlike me, Max had no trouble peering in through the dirty windows of the boathouse. I saw him sneak a glance. Perhaps he wanted to borrow a canoe. Max looked like he kept fit. Freddy had mentioned he had his own gym.

'Apparently, JJ doesn't keep anything in there,' I said, backtracking my steps to the safety of the grass bank. 'Although I've seen Nev huffing and puffing up the river in a canoe. He looks like he's in training for something.'

Max looked momentarily puzzled then laughed. 'Ah, Neville, yes. No, I have a rowing machine for that.'

'Of course.'

'Still, nothing beats being out on the water. Do you sail?' He had a mischievous glint in his eye.

I shook my head. 'No, not at all.'

'Maybe you are like your brother, a quick learner?' Max suggested. He leaned back against the wall of the boathouse and produced a packet of cigarettes from his pocket. 'Do you smoke?'

I shook my head again. 'No thank you. You've taken Freddy sailing?'

'A couple of times now, although I think it is Kimmi that it is the main attraction, not my yacht.'

Freddy hadn't mentioned he'd been on any sailing trips, but I'd hardly seen him over the last few days. I'd assumed he'd been working long hours. 'Freddy should be concentrating on his job, not girls,' I said.

'They are young, let them have fun,' Max shrugged, as if he didn't care that his seventeen-year-old daughter was luring a twenty-one-year-old father-to-be away from his responsibilities. Europeans were notoriously free and easy with their affections. 'You should let me take you out on *Pegasus* sometime,' Max continued. 'You might enjoy it more than you think.'

'That's very kind of you, but really I'm not a good sailor,' I said. I didn't like the idea of being alone with Max van der Plaast on dry land, let alone at sea.

'Could I tempt you with my jet ski?'

'No, that doesn't appeal either,' I said, forcing myself to smile. 'Sorry.'

'A little English landlubber.' Max seemed amused. 'In that case, I hope Freddy has mentioned the party we are throwing for Kimmi next week? You will come to that, I take it? No water involved, unless you fancy a dip in my pool?'

I was old and wise enough to know that Max wasn't really interested in me. He was simply playing a game. Even if I was charmed by that butch masculinity and seduced by his blatant show of wealth, any dalliance with Max would only end in tragedy. However, men like Max were used to getting their own way and I sensed it would be prudent to remain on his good side – for Freddy's sake, if not my own. I had bought myself a little black dress on my shopping trip with Pearl, not specifically because of Kimmi's party but because a little black dress always came in handy.

'Yes, of course,' I said, as he stepped aside to let me edge past, pulling the dog tightly on its lead. 'I'll see you next weekend. Thank you.'

I carried on for another fifty metres or so before side-stepping into the woods, my natural curiosity taking over common sense. In my green mac, I was well camouflaged. I skirted across JJ's deserted building site and headed back down towards the shore. As I suspected, the doors to the boathouse were open, and the dog stood guard outside. I wondered exactly what in JJ's boathouse required Max's attention. He clearly had his own key. I hurried away before the dog caught a whiff of my scent amongst the lingering continental tobacco fumes.

Chapter Sixteen

A dismal few days followed of appalling weather, squally summer showers which, according to Pearl who was now into all these things, ruined the church fete and Mrs Hathaway's garden party, whoever Mrs Hathaway was.

'Let's just hope it holds off for the yacht club do next Thursday evening,' she said. The yacht club 'do' was a big fundraising event. Fortunately, tickets had sold out long before I arrived in Kerridge and Pearl had been unable to secure any extras. I assured her I was more than happy to stay at home.

Nick was absent from the quiz for the second week in a row, and again I wondered why I felt so disappointed. A horrible longing had crept into my heart, and other places in my body I didn't want to think about it. It was totally ridiculous, knowing how furious our last encounter had left me. Perhaps I should seek out a new man here in Kerridge, but then the ugly head of Max van der Plaast reared into my imagination and I hurriedly dismissed that idea. No relationship ever came without complications.

Fortunately, Marie appeared to have run out of penguin stories. The talk of the day was all about Norah Morland, Mary Robshaw's former nanny and Rivermede's housekeeper-from-hell. Poor Norah had apparently been knocked down that afternoon by the cesspit evacuation lorry as it had rumbled through the village. A handful of Kerridge's more isolated properties were not connected to the main sewage system.

'Goodness me,' Chrissie exclaimed. 'Is the poor woman all right?'

'According to Bill Megson, who was in the graveyard at the time, she was crossing the road at Blind Man's Corner and just walked right out in front of it,' Marie explained. 'The driver was in a right state.'

'And Mrs Morland?' I enquired.

'Dunno, love,' Marie said, shaking her head. 'Sad old dear, she is. Must be in her 90s. Lives all by herself in a bungalow in Clay Kiln Lane. She'll probably enjoy a few nights in hospital.'

We were reliably informed by a member of the team on the next table that Mrs Morland had suffered bruising, but apart from that appeared relatively unscathed. It sounded like she'd had a very lucky escape. Blind Man's Corner was the village's accident blackspot.

'She was putting flowers on Mary Robshaw's grave just beforehand,' another player chipped in. 'You know how dedicated she was to Mary. She was probably still upset, walking off in a world of her own. She's as deaf as post, so she wouldn't have heard the lorry coming. You can never see anything on that bend.'

'You don't need to hear that damn thing coming, you can normally smell it,' Craig remarked.

There was a general consensus that Norah Morland had been devastated by Mary Robshaw's death and had never been quite the same since. I also learned that Mary Robshaw appeared to have been Kerridge's answer to Mother Theresa. There wasn't a voluntary body or local charity she hadn't been associated with. No wonder my mother was so keen to ingratiate herself into village life. Mary Robshaw was going to be a very hard act to follow.

I wondered if Pearl had heard about Norah Morland's accident. She had. The Kerridge grapevine – Judy Stevenson from Honeypot Cottage – had been straight up to Rivermede to tell Jack almost before the ambulance doors were closed.

'We sent a bouquet,' Pearl said, when I broached the subject with her the following morning. 'Jack says we should go and see her when she's home from hospital. She's bound to have heard about the wedding.'

'Perhaps she's expecting an invitation,' I suggested.

'That would hardly be appropriate,' Pearl replied with a

shake of her head. 'And where would we put her on the seating plan?'

The draft seating plan took up the entire conservatory floor. Cardboard cut-out name tags moved from table to table on an hourly basis in a scene that bore more than a passing resemblance to strategic battle-planning in Churchill's war rooms.

'Do we mix and match bride and groom, or keep relatives separate?' Pearl mused, switching Aunt Phoebe next to Anita and then back to Uncle Laurie. Most of Jack's guests appeared to be friends. Apparently, there were very few Robshaw relatives left.

Against my advice – sometimes you just had to make a stand – Pearl went ahead and booked her owls. On Thursday morning, I had my first dress fitting. The wedding was becoming frighteningly real. I combined a second visit to Vera's with a long interview with Stella over lunch in the Sou'wester Café on Portdeane quayside. She'd suggested the change of the scenery. Chloe could manage at The Ship without her, and she'd heard a new café bar had opened up on the waterfront.

'Always good to check out the opposition,' she said.

I doubted the Sou'wester would offer much opposition to The Ship. It was far more café than bar, offering a meagre selection of unappetising sandwiches and burgers. I gave up on the idea of lunch and settled for a coffee. Once Stella had established her business was not under threat, she soon relaxed.

'Did it take a long time to get established after you moved to Kerridge?' I asked.

She shook her head. 'We landed on our feet when we came here. You've no idea what it is like to be ostracised in a community where you'd put your heart and soul into creating a successful business, bringing up your family. I thought people on the island, our neighbours, business associates, were my friends, but I was a social pariah when Owen and I split. Chloe and I had little choice but to leave the island. We knew we wanted to buy a place of our own, and when I saw The

Ship being advertised for sale, I knew it would be perfect. It had always done a bit of food; just pub favourites, really. We came in and tarted the place up a bit, made it look more authentic, gave it a bit of *olde world*e ambiance.'

'And designed a new pub sign?'

Stella laughed. 'Oh, you noticed?'

I smiled. 'It's impossible to miss. Very clever. The locals accepted you and Chloe readily enough?'

'Oh yes. Well, they accepted I was the landlady and my friend,' she made mock speech marks with her hands, 'was the cook. Hasn't always been easy, you know. Prejudice is still rife, even today. Try joining the yacht club. Talk about archaic. It's run by a dinosaur.'

'You mean the Commodore?'

'Yes, Punch Stevenson and his cronies.' Stella nodded. 'Eventually they let us in. I wasn't sure what they were worried about. I made a real effort not to win any of the competitions for the first two years.'

'So, you still sail?'

'Not as much as I'd like to.'

Portdeane's quaint cobbled quayside put Kerridge Hard to shame. After Stella headed home, I spent some time exploring the town's upmarket home décor shops and clothing boutiques, buying a couple of quite striking brightly coloured cotton tops in a moment of sheer frivolity. I was normally a very prudent shopper.

'Eye-catching, aren't they?' the sales assistant remarked, neatly folding my purchases between layers of tissue paper and handing me a sturdy cardboard bag. 'Made by a local designer, Vera van der Plaast.'

I nearly dropped on the spot. 'Vera van der Plaast?' I echoed.

'Have you heard of her?'

'I've heard of Max van der Plaast,' I replied, not wishing to divulge that Vera was currently running up my mother's wedding trousseau. 'Are they related?'

'Vera is his ex,' the shop assistant informed me, 'or at least one of his ex's. The marriage only lasted a couple of years.

She had a lucky escape, by all accounts. You don't want to get on the wrong side of him, that's for sure. Vera still has the scars to prove it.'

I thanked her for my purchases, and the advice, and continued my wander through Portdeane. Away from the waterfront, there was a spacious play park and community hall, together with a modern library. I always felt at home in libraries, and as this particular one was currently hosting the local history exhibition Stella had previously mentioned, I decided to take a look inside.

To my surprise, Judy Stevenson was one of the two volunteers manning the display. It took her a few minutes to recognise me, but when she did, she greeted me effusively.

'Yes, it's Becca, isn't it? Our new neighbour.' She turned to the elderly gent who was her co-host. 'Becca is currently living next door to us in Kerridge,' she said. 'Her mother is going to marry Jack Robshaw.'

'I didn't know Robshaw was getting married again.' The old man looked quite surprised.

'They met on a cruise, isn't that right, Becca?' Judy said. She turned back to her companion. 'It's all happened very quickly.'

'I thought Robshaw was stuck in a wheelchair these days?'

'Oh, he is,' Judy assured him. She gave me a wink. 'But he's still a bit of an old charmer.'

I explained I was interested in learning more about the history of Kerridge and, in particular, Rivermede.

'You're in the right place,' Judy said. 'I'll leave you in Maurice's capable good hands. I've got to dash. Punch and I have to get ready for the fundraiser tonight. Are you coming, Becca?'

I resisted the urge to respond that I was washing my hair. 'I've got some work to catch up on,' I insisted, just in case Judy could put her hands on a spare ticket. 'And a Skype interview with a client, which I can't miss.'

Maurice was quite the raconteur, and provided an entertaining and informative commentary for the visual tour of the River Deane's illustrious past. Smugglers had apparently been the first people to see the benefits of using the river to ply their trade.

'In the lee of the Isle of Wight, the estuary was ideally placed,' Maurice told me. 'The banks were covered in woodland back then; Kerridge was a very secluded spot. The Ship, you know the pub, I take it? That was a notorious smugglers' haunt.'

'Yes. Strange name,' I remarked.

Maurice laughed. 'Back in those days it was just The Ship, but there were many a fool who came unstuck there,' he said. 'You needed to know the tides if you wanted to land your bounty on the old quayside. Get your timings wrong and you'd be stuck on the mudflats. We've a fair share of wrecks in the past and vessels that have been abandoned. High tide, you'd never know they were there, but when the water recedes, you can see the perils of the river.'

After the smugglers had come the boat-builders. As early as 1700, there had been a boatyard on Kerridge Hard, although Rivermede was a much later addition to the landscape. The house had originally been built as the summer home of a wealthy early Victorian industrialist.

'Enrico D'Alba was of Italian extraction, made his money in metals in the East End of London and had Rivermede built as his summer residence,' Maurice told me. 'He liked to sail, and Rivermede had his own landing stage. You can still see the remains at low tide.'

Maurice showed me a picture of Rivermede when it was first built. Victorian ladies in long white frocks took tea on the lawn, while gentlemen in sailing attire strolled along a wooden jetty.

'The D'Alba family sold the property to Ray Dimmock in the 1950s,' Maurice said. 'The first Dimmocks' boatyard was started in the 1920s by Ray's father, Henry, originally renting the land from the D'Albas. He joined forces with another old boat-building family, the Yarrows. Yarrow and Sons were originally based down at Helme, where the Chapman boy has his place now. Have you been down that far?' I nodded.

Maurice pointed to a picture of a flourishing boatyard

which seemed impossible to imagine in the same spot as Aidan Chapman's solitary workshop. 'Yarrows were there long before Henry Dimmock came along,' Maurice explained. 'They were the original Kerridge boatbuilders, but then Henry Dimmock and Joseph Yarrow had a big falling out. It was quite a story, I believe, and something to do with a young lady. But then, they always are, aren't they?' Maurice smiled.

He moved on along the display. 'During the war years, Henry Dimmock built landing craft for the military, and then after the war, when sailing became an affordable, popular pastime, business boomed again. The boatyard patented its own unique yacht designs. You can still see Dimmocks' boats all over the world.'

Besides several pictures of the boatsheds and the workforce, there were also photographs of the annual river regatta, which took place each summer.

Maurice pointed to one particular picture. 'This is Jack Robshaw's first wife,' he said, 'Mary Dimmock, the year she was crowned Regatta Queen.'

These were the days of the non-PC beauty pageant. Mary Dimmock proudly wore her winner's sash over her swimsuit, sitting on the bow of a small sailing dinghy, long shapely legs hanging over the side. There were other pictures of the various regatta queens over the decades – a tradition which appeared to have continued right up until the 1990s.

'Does the sailing regatta still take place?' I asked.

Maurice shook his head. 'It's not the big event it used to be,' he said. 'There are a few races here in Portdeane, but nothing happens up at Kerridge any more. Back in the day, we'd have a starlight parade, all the little dinghies would light up and sail from Dimmocks up to The Ship and back. There would be fireworks, a party on the Hard. I suppose it's all too much to organise now, health and safety and all that.'

'Is this Jack?' I asked, spotting another picture of Mary Dimmock on the arm of a dark-haired young man in a somewhat ill-fitting suit.

Maurice squinted at the picture. 'Oh no, that's Kenny Dimmock, Ray Dimmock's son, Mary's brother.'

'I didn't know Mary had a brother?'

'Oh yes,' Maurice said, moving me along to the next set of pictures. 'See here, Dimmock & Sons in 1970.' The workforce was lined up outside a boatshed. Maurice pointed out Ray Dimmock who stood at one end of the line, while his son Kenny was at the other. 'This is me, here,' Maurice said, a shaky finger picking out a figure in the middle of the back row. 'I was at Dimmocks for thirty years; took on as an apprentice at fourteen and left when Jack Robshaw closed the place down. Lucky for me I got another job with Graystons, here in Portdeane.'

'Is Jack Robshaw in this picture?' I asked, studying the grim faces of the workforce.

'He'll be in there somewhere,' Maurice said. 'Yes, there he is just behind Kenny. He and Kenny were good friends. Jack was never a skilled craftsman like Kenny was, but he had the business skills. That's why Ray Dimmock took him on. You've heard about the accident, I suppose?'

'The accident where Jack lost his leg?' I nodded.

'Jack Robshaw lost his leg and Kenny Dimmock lost his life,' Maurice replied.

'Oh my goodness! I had no idea. How did it happen?'

'There was some fault on the mobile crane,' Maurice said, 'one of the hoists we used to lift the vessels in and out of the water. Boat slipped out of the harness. Kenny and Jack were crushed.' I immediately thought of Freddy. I had every right to be fearful for his safety. Boatyards were dangerous places.

'How long ago was this?' I asked.

Maurice peered at the picture. 'This picture was 1970. The accident would have been only a year or so afterwards. Old man Dimmock was very good at skimping on his maintenance schedules. That crane was always playing up. Had it been anyone else, he could have been in big trouble.'

'What do you mean?'

'Well, if one of the other workers had been crushed, he could have faced charges for criminal negligence. As it was, losing his own son was punishment enough and, of course, Robshaw was well rewarded for his silence, wasn't he? He married the boss's daughter and got the business.'

The history lesson had proved quite illuminating. I had learned some interesting facts about Kerridge's history, and more especially Dimmocks' Boatyard and Jack Robshaw.

Chapter Seventeen

That evening I waved Pearl and Jack off to the yacht club fundraiser, and was just about to crack open a glass of wine and sit down with a microwave meal when a sharp knock on the door of the stable block made me jump.

'Freddy?' I opened the door a crack.

'Hello, Becca, I heard you were looking for me.'

Nick slipped in through the crack before I could stop him. He was wearing an army surplus jacket and a baseball cap, pulled down low over his face.

'Nick, what are you doing here?'

'And what were you doing snooping around my boat?'

'You weren't at the quiz, I was worried.'

'I'm flattered, but I am more than capable of looking after myself.'

'Well, that's a relief.'

His eyes were travelling around the flat. 'This is very nice,' he remarked.

A thought struck me. 'How did you know I was in the stable block?'

'I make it my business to find out things,' he said.

'Have you been spying on me?'

'No more than you've been spying on me.'

'You took a risk coming here,' I said. 'What if Pearl spots you?'

'Pearl is out.' Nick replied. 'As is Jack, JJ, and his trophy wife. They're all at the yacht club playing bingo and eating chicken in a basket. Seriously. And the Muzzlewhites are tucked up in their cottage.'

The conversation had taken a somewhat sinister turn. Nick was behaving very oddly. He really had been spying on us.

'There's Freddy,' I pointed out, although I wasn't entirely sure what Freddy was up to. He could be in his Rivermede quarters wired to his laptop, or he could be down the pub.

'Freddy's at the Rum Runners with Max van der Plaast and his crew,' Nick confirmed. 'You need to warn him off mixing with van der Plaast. That's what I wanted to see you about.'

'You've been spying on Freddy, too?'

'It's for his own good.'

'Is anybody safe in Kerridge?' I tried to keep my tone light-hearted. 'Next you'll be telling me Stella in the pub is really a Russian spy and there's a risk we're all about be poisoned by nerve gas. Who are the Muzzlewhites, by the way?'

'Lurch and his wife, Hev and Nev. Although they could well have adopted new names. It wouldn't surprise me.'

'Oh, come on, Nick.' I loitered by the front door, anxious to keep an escape route clear. Nick was acting totally out of character. This wasn't the practical, level-headed person I used to know at all. What had happened to him? I tried to take stock of the situation. Perhaps I was I the one behaving irrationally. Why did I think I needed an escape route? Nick wouldn't harm me. He might throw the odd insult at me, but this was Nick, the guy who was once my best friend, the man I had been going to marry. A man I didn't know any more, but undeniably, a man to whom I still felt attracted.

Another thought occurred to me. How had Nick made his way into the grounds? Both the main entrance and the river gate were accessed by a key code. And why was he looking like a commando in army surplus? I had too many questions. I felt so confused, wrestling with my jumbled thoughts. In fact, I felt more than confused. I felt faint, lightheaded, black spots danced before my eyes. I took a couple of steps away from the door and reached out for the sofa.

'Becca, are you okay?' Nick's arms were around me in an instant. 'Christ, you look dreadful.' He lowered me onto the cushions. 'Let me get you a glass of water.'

I needed to breathe. That was all. Breathe. Keep a calm head and breathe. Count. Slowly, in, out.

'I want you to leave, Nick,' I said.

'Leave you like this?' He sounded alarmed. 'But you're not well.'

I probably wasn't well because *he* was the Russian agent with nerve gas – not Stella. Realistically, it could just be I hadn't eaten anything all day apart from my diet ration of muesli for breakfast.

He tilted my chin and held a glass of water to my lips. 'There, is that better?'

It was an awful lot better. Perhaps he wasn't trying to kill me. He was being incredibly gentle, and something about those hands on my skin sent tiny, albeit unwelcome, tingles to places they really shouldn't. I wanted him to hold me, hold me tight and never let me go, to make me feel safe and secure, just like the old days…

No I didn't. 'Stop!' I tried to inch away.

'Hey, what are you afraid of? I'm not going to hurt you.' Nick stared at me. 'My God, Becca, you're frightened of me?' He looked shocked and bewildered.

'No, I'm not.' Was I afraid of him, or of my feelings? 'You just don't seem yourself. You're talking nonsense, and why are you spying on us like this?' I wriggled into a seated position, a little further from Nick's clutches. 'I mean, the jacket, the hat, the beard. It's not really you, is it, Nick? And this…' I could think of no other word for it, 'this paranoia, this feeling that everyone out there is out to get us, warning me away from Rivermede, from Max…'

Nick took off his baseball cap and unbuttoned his jacket to reveal a simple Riptide T-shirt. He looked human, normal, far more like the man I remembered. 'I'm on a job, Becca. I'm working, that's all I can tell you. Things happen here that I don't want you or your family mixed up in, okay? I don't think the marina is a safe environment for Freddy to be working in.'

'Oh, I agree,' I said. 'I know about the accident.'

'What accident?'

'The accident at the boatyard, when Kenny Dimmock was killed and Jack lost his leg.'

It was Nick's turn to look completely befuddled. 'What are you talking about?'

'I just found out today. Jack Robshaw inherited the boatyard because he kept quiet about some dodgy machinery. His wife's brother was killed, and—'

'This has got nothing to with dodgy machinery in the boatyard. Anyway, that must have all happened years ago.'

'Yes, it did, but it just goes to show how dangerous these places can be, and proves Jack isn't as squeaky clean as he seems. And then there's this thing with Gerry Kimble not moving his boat. JJ is now threatening him because he wants the extra moorings. Oh, and he also threatened me, us. He doesn't want this wedding to go ahead.'

'Rebecca, you're starting to sound like one of your mother's books. You're talking gibberish.'

'Are you accusing my mother of writing gibberish?'

'No, well, not entirely.' He seemed to have regained a sense of humour. 'Look,' he sighed. 'I can't tell you what I'm doing here because the least you know about it the better, for your own safety. It has nothing to do with dodgy machinery and incidents that happened many years ago, or that old frigate on the marina, although it's interesting to hear JJ needs the extra moorings.'

'He's up to his eyeballs in debt.'

'I can believe that.'

'Oh, and there is something odd about his boathouse.'

'We know about the boathouse.'

'Who's *we*?'

'You know I can't tell you. You need to keep away from the boathouse, Becca.'

'That's just what JJ said. And Max van der Plaast has his own key.'

Now I really had caught Nick's attention. 'How do you know that?'

'Because I saw him.'

'You were at the boathouse with him?'

'No, we met on the path, and afterwards I went back and took another look. He'd let himself in.'

'Becca, you really shouldn't be snooping around Max van der Plaast.'

'No, of course not. Silly me. The only person allowed to do any snooping around here is you. I forgot that.'

Nick sighed. 'How many times do I have to tell you, Becs? I've only got your best interests at heart. I don't understand why you won't believe me.'

'You won't tell me what you're doing here, you won't tell me who you work for, or what's really going on. And you wonder why I don't trust you?'

Nick buttoned up his jacket and returned his cap to his head with a resigned look on his face. 'Stubborn to the last. I don't know what it will take to convince you, Becca, but promise me something at least. Stay away from van der Plaast.'

Without another word, he headed out of the door. I wasn't sure whether I was relieved or disappointed.

I felt decidedly uneasy. There had been a tenderness in Nick's voice, and his touch had awakened feelings I'd thought were dead and buried long ago. Nick's concern for my welfare seemed quite genuine, but this Nick wasn't the same Nick I knew fifteen years ago. We were two very different people.

I still found it hard to believe that a covert police operation, as Nick implied, was underway in Kerridge, centred around Robshaw's marina and Rivermede. On the other hand, it seemed unimaginable that anyone as level-headed and as sensible as Nick would fabricate the story. His behaviour seemed irrational, yet I knew from research I'd conducted for one of Pearl's novels that paranoid schizophrenia came in all sorts of shapes and sizes. People in highly stressful jobs were not infallible, in fact they were very vulnerable to personality disorders. In *Heartbreak in Hawaii* the hero was an eminent but poverty-stricken junior psychiatrist who, while at a conference in Hawaii, met and fell in with the fiancée of another delegate – the director of a failing pharmaceutical conglomerate who needed her money to keep his business afloat. I'd created a diverse selection of patients for Dr Hannover to treat along the way before the ultimate *happy ever after,* including a headmistress and a court judge. Nick was right – my mother could right wonderful gibberish.

I reminded myself how Nick had behaved in the run-up to our wedding. There had been a marked change in his manner, which I had at first put down to nerves before I began to suspect he was seeing Saskia. He'd been on edge, nit-picking, avoiding me, obvious signs now of infidelity, but had his behaviour then been significant of some underlying psychotic condition?

I'd lost my appetite for my low-calorie microwave meal, and instead made a cup of tea and four slices of peanut butter on toast. I sat down with my laptop, determined to undertake some covert research.

Chapter Eighteen

Perhaps I should have Googled Nick earlier. The truth was it had never occurred to me our paths would ever cross. Perhaps I was also afraid of what I might unearth.

I'd first met Nick at university. Pearl insisted she couldn't afford to 'lose me' and the uni I had chosen was within an easy commute of Battersea. Nick was from Yorkshire, exploring London for the first time. His aim had always been to join the police force. We had mutual friends and our paths crossed at various parties, and although there was no denying a mutual attraction, we didn't date. Nick always seemed to have some girl on his arm, and he later told me I always seemed unapproachable and self-contained. In a way, he was right. I had too much going on at home, keeping Pearl on track and helping out with Freddy, to get serious about anyone. I was determined to achieve that degree and I didn't need any additional distractions. When we graduated, he was snapped up by the Met, and we lost touch, despite remaining in the same city.

It was only a year after graduation that I ran into Nick again at a friend's party. For once, he was on his own. Feeling reckless, with that degree certificate firmly tucked under my belt, I made the first approach. On our second date, he confessed he'd just been accepted for a secondment to Yorkshire to be closer to his family – his father had been diagnosed with a terminal illness and his mother was not coping. His younger brother was only eighteen, so somebody had to take control. I totally sympathised; our situations were relatively similar. Of course, he couldn't postpone his move north.

We kept in touch, he came down to London for the occasional weekend, I went up to Yorkshire. Each time I saw him, the spark between us seemed to shine a little brighter, eventually becoming so bright it ignited an intense, passionate flame. I physically ached when we were apart. Within a year, his father was dead, and his mother was coping even less. Nick said he couldn't leave her. I couldn't leave Pearl and Freddy.

Eventually, the police force came to our rescue. The Met refused to extend Nick's secondment. He was rapidly gaining a reputation and they wanted him back in London. His mother, despite her self-proclaimed fragility – I'd met her several times by then and decided there was nothing fragile about her; she could definitely give Pearl a good run for her money – gave in to her ambitions for her eldest boy. Nick came back down south, immediately proposed, and we took a twelve-month lease on a flat.

It was all going so well until Saskia Browning reappeared on the scene.

Saskia was an old friend from my brief stint at the International Academy in Zurich. At eighteen, worldly-wise Saskia was already 5ft 10" tall, golden-bronzed skin, and baby-blonde hair. She was a native Texan and proud of it, with a drawl she refused to extinguish despite the elocution lessons. When I had been recalled by my mother to help with the aftermath of the Dieter situation, I waved a tearful goodbye to Saskia and told her to look me up if she ever came to London – which she did, two months before my wedding.

The school was progressive and forward-thinking, mixed co-ed, and every now and then the inevitable relationship developed between pupils of the opposite sex. Saskia was notorious for breaking sixth formers' hearts, whilst at the time of the whole Dieter debacle I was tentatively seeing a Canadian called Matt Unwin, whose parents, like many others in the school, were working in the Middle East. Years later, Matt, like Saskia, had looked me up on Facebook, and unlike Saskia, I had accepted his friendship request. Matt regularly posted pictures of his family and various vacations. Occasionally, we exchanged reminisces about our time in Zurich. Saskia occasionally commented on his posts.

I'd seen pictures of her kids before, but now, if Nick was to be believed, I had to accept that any resemblance between him and Saskia's eldest was purely coincidental. A quick delve on Facebook soon confirmed that Saskia was married to a hunky brown-eyed Texan called Ralph, and had been for over ten years.

So, Saskia was off the scene, and always had been. I turned my attention back to Nick. Just like Tristram Markham, there was no trace of his existence on Facebook, but in a moment of true inspiration I searched for his younger brother. Jordan Quinlan had been affectionately known as Q, after the James Bond character. He'd been socially awkward, highly intelligent, and a complete computer geek. If anyone would be on social media, Jordan would.

Just as I hoped, Jordan hadn't followed his namesake – or his brother – into the fantasy world of espionage because he had a very prolific online presence. He took regular holidays, and although Nick was never named in any of his brother's pictures, he occasionally popped up.

Some people have all the best jobs, Jordan had Tweeted twelve months ago, alongside a photograph of himself and Nick on a sunny day in Paris. *Off to Amsterdam again for the weekend,* accompanied pictures of canals, windmills, tulip fields. *Guess where we are this weekend? Sweden! Catching up with my big bro in the South of France...*

I wasn't sure what any of the information I had uncovered proved, other than confirming that whatever Nick had been doing for the last fifteen years he had been telling the truth when he had said he hadn't been doing it with Saskia Browning. However, he had spent a considerable amount of time working abroad, which hardly sounded like someone on active police service. So, what was he up to?

I was more than happy to heed his warning about Max van der Plaast, but Freddy had taken a shine to Kimmi. Freddy, as always, needed protecting. I couldn't see the harm, in fact it seemed imperative, that I accompany him to the birthday party. I finished my toast and closed my laptop. Despite my misgivings about Nick, common sense told me it would be wise to remain on my guard.

It was little wonder I slept badly. After a futile morning's work, I headed out for a spot of fresh-air. It was a warm afternoon and Rivermede was bathed in an unnatural aura of calm. Pearl was safely out of the way, rehearsing with the Kerridge Pops Choir, and as the Range Rover was missing, I assumed Nev and Jack were on one of their secret missions. I set off in the vague direction of the rear gardens, which was unchartered territory and lacking the manicured appearance of the lawns at the front of the house.

Despite living in close proximity, I had seen next to nothing of JJ and Rita since I'd moved into the stable block. The rear of the house was their domain and they took little care of its appearance. Rita had an unofficial role on the marina as chief sales adviser, showing potential buyers around high-end yachts and motor cruisers. When she wasn't looking glamorous in the sales room, she was working out at the gym.

I took a track through an overgrown shrubbery and found myself following the line of an old brick wall. I wondered if this was the boundary of the old kitchen garden which Heather and Nev were supposed to be renovating. The wall was a good six-foot high, and the undergrowth so overgrown it was impossible to see how far it extended. Just as I was about to continue through the jungle, I heard voices and footsteps scrunching on the other side. I stopped in my tracks.

'So how much longer do you reckon we're all going to be here for?' Heather hissed in a very thick Midlands accent. 'We didn't mind when it was just the old boy; he was no trouble. Then *she* turns up. Suddenly I've got to pretend I'm a cordon bleu cook while she throws all these fancy dinner parties. Not only that, but she then made Nev decorate an entire flat for the daughter in one weekend, and as for that son of hers, I can't keep up with his appetite. I mean, I know the boy's a harmless idiot, but the girl, well, she's got her wits about her.'

'Don't panic, Heather.' I recognised her companion's voice instantly. 'The boy could be useful, and I can handle the daughter. In fact, I'm looking forward to handling the daughter. Another few weeks and you and Nev can head off to the Costa Del Sol or wherever it is you want to go.'

'Well, it better be soon because Lady Muck's asked me to make the bloody wedding cake and I certainly ain't doing that.'

'What date is the wedding?' Max van der Plaast asked.

'You mean to say you haven't had an invitation?' Heather cackled. 'Gordon Bennet! Somebody's slipped up there. It's supposed to be the 21st June, but I wouldn't worry too much, if JJ gets his way, there won't be a wedding. He seems determined to talk the old man out of it.'

'Oh, I think it's always nice when two people fall in love,' Max van der Plaast replied. 'We all need a little romance in our lives, a little diversion. I'll write it in my diary. Could be a good day. I'd get baking that cake if I were you, Heather.'

I crouched down into the shrubbery. Not that either of them could possibly see me, nor did I think for one minute they would come this way through the undergrowth, but just in case, I didn't want to be discovered. It was no surprise to learn that Heather was not the housekeeping marvel she proclaimed to be, but it now sounded as if she and Nev were involved in something far more sinister. And it involved Max van der Plaast. Nick's paranoia had become infectious.

I wondered how willing Freddy would be to listen to any argument I might put forward for giving Kimmi's party a miss. My brother had been in uncharacteristically high spirits since moving to Rivermede, and without a doubt Kimmi was at the root of it. To my relief, he hadn't as yet commenced his forklift truck training, but he was building up muscles and gaining some colour on his cheeks, although whether that was from his work on the marina or sailing with Max van der Plaast, I wasn't entirely sure.

As I suspected, when I cornered Freddy that evening, my reasoning fell on deaf ears.

'Oh, come on, Becs, what's your problem?' Freddy argued. 'Don't you want to see Max's house? It's massive apparently, way bigger than Rivermede, with all mod-cons. Kimmi says we can use the pool. Why don't you want to come? Got something better to do, like sitting on your own in that flat all evening like *Billy-no-mates*?'

I had visions of the Playboy Mansion. Were guests expected to bring swimming costumes, or was it going to be skinny-dipping all around? If I drove, I would have to stay sober, and therefore any likelihood of being tempted anywhere near the pool, or Max, would be remote.

'Don't be stupid. Nev's going to give us a lift,' Freddy said when I made the suggestion.

'And how are we going to get home?'

'He's going to pick us up. We just call him when we're ready to leave.'

'What if we don't want to leave at the same time?'

'It's only a couple of miles away. You could walk it if you had to. Nev can take you home first and come back later for me.'

'What makes you think I'll want to come home first?'

'Ha-ha.'

I gave in. It was better to be with Freddy than let him loose on his own. As usual, I was letting my imagination run riot. Nick had cast too many doubts into my mind and I needed to look at things logically. Heather and Neville had been employed to look after a single, elderly gentleman, it was no wonder they were disgruntled when the household had increased to four. It could well be I was reading far too much into what I'd overheard in the shrubbery. Perhaps they had a holiday planned in Spain, which was why they were anxious to be away in a few weeks' time. And why wouldn't they be friendly with Max? He was a neighbour.

Pearl could hardly contain her excitement as I prepared to get ready on Saturday evening. There were only so many times I could send her packing from my door. Eventually it was easier to relent and let her sit on the end of the bed.

She couldn't resist the opportunity to advise on my clothes, 'so that's what you bought that dress for…'; my hair, 'up, darling, definitely suits you better up'; and my shoes, 'has to be heels, darling, wedges will never do'.

Freddy's party attire consisted of black drainpipe jeans, Converse, and a badly tie-dyed T-shirt.

Nev was on the drive at the dot of 7.30pm to deliver us to the van der Plaast residence. It was a cloudy evening with a distinctly damp nip in the air and probably not the summer party weather Kimmi had been hoping for. Fairy lights were strung from the trees that lined the van der Plaast's impressively long driveway.

There was no sign of the party girl as we drew up outside the house – vast, modern, and clad in trendy grey clapperboard. A bouncer, baring a startling resemblance to Nev although they didn't acknowledge each other in any way, directed us to the back of the house where the party had spilled out onto the terrace.

The garden was a stark affair compared to Rivermede's lush natural wilderness. Max had opted for the minimalist look, with lots of ornamental stonework, slate, and gravel.

A passing waiter offered Freddy and I a glass of champagne, but Freddy's eyes were already searching the crowd. Kimmi was in the pool room, glass bi-fold doors pulled back onto the terrace.

'You don't have to keep me company,' I told him. 'Go on, run along and play.'

'You sure?' he asked hopefully. 'I expect there's some older people here somewhere that you know. Look, there's Marguerite.'

It was somewhat of a relief to spot a familiar but hardly friendly face. By her side, JJ pretended he couldn't see me. The junior Robshaws stood chatting with Natalie and Pete. There was nothing like a teenage party to make anyone over twenty-one feel very old. If nothing else, we had our age in common. I wandered over. If it wasn't for the fact that Rita was wearing another of her trademark all-in-ones, and JJ looked uncomfortably out of place in a simple grey suit, I might have thought guests had been asked to come in fancy dress. Pete, presumably in an attempt to blend in with the teenagers, was in leather trousers and sported a newly-acquired goatee beard, while Natalie was dressed as a wasp. Not many people could pull off horizontal orange and black stripes.

'We didn't know you knew Max?' Rita greeted me.

'I don't,' I admitted. 'Freddy is friends with his daughter.'

'Have you come along to act as chaperone?' JJ sneered.

'Oh no, I had my own invitation,' I replied.

Right on cue, a muscular tattooed arm draped itself around my shoulders like a predatory python. 'I met Becca on a little walk the other day,' Max said. 'She was down by your boathouse, JJ. I insisted she accompany her brother. Kerridge is hardly party city, is it? It must seem very dull after London.'

'I don't find it dull at all,' I insisted, trying but failing to shrug the arm off.

'What were you doing down by my boathouse?' JJ scowled.

'I was just taking a little walk, exploring.'

Rita fluttered her eyelashes at Max. 'This is a lovely do. You've done Kimmi proud.'

'Thank you, Marguerite, and you look as charming as always. I must go and circulate, I'm afraid. I see more guests arriving. I'll be back for you later, Becca.' He made it sound like a threat rather than a promise. To my relief, he headed off across the terrace.

'Is it true you're writing Stella Markham's memoirs?' Natalie asked. Both she and Rita were in sleeveless outfits; they must have been freezing. I still wore my lightweight beige mac, which completely concealed my very expensive little black dress.

'Stella Markham?' Rita looked puzzled. 'From the pub? What's she ever done?'

'She's only famous because of her husband,' Natalie replied. 'Remember him, Owen Markham, used to have his own TV show years ago.'

'Oh, the cheffy bloke?'

'Yes, that's him. Not been on TV for years now.'

'I've met Owen Markham a couple of times at various sailing events,' Pete said. 'He's a decent chap. Can't you find someone more interesting to write about?'

'Oh, I think Stella is quite an interesting character,' I replied, feeling affronted on her behalf. I should have guessed there might be people in Kerridge who knew Owen Markham

144

personally. Cowes was only a short hop across the Solent, and yacht clubs inevitably shared some kind of affiliation. 'How much of Stella's story are you familiar with?'

Pete gave a shrug. 'Well, not much, obviously, only what one heard at the time. We didn't really want her joining the sailing club, to be honest, when she moved here.'

'Goodness me, what did the poor woman do?' Rita asked with a giggle.

'She's a lesbian,' Natalie enlightened her. 'Obviously that's a severe breach of yacht club rules.'

Pete puffed out his chest as if to make his point. 'She brought the racing world into disrepute.'

I was determined to stick up for Stella. 'Her husband made allegations which were totally unfounded. She broke records when she won the Tri-Island race. I would have thought any sailing club would have welcomed her as a member.'

'Her whole attitude after she won that race stank,' Pete huffed. 'Abandoning her husband and her children like that. We have to uphold moral values, you know.'

'Of course you do, darling,' Natalie murmured, helping herself to another glass of champagne from a passing waiter. JJ looked bored.

I took a deep breath. 'Are you still in contact with Owen Markham?' I asked.

'Our paths have crossed at a couple of sailing events.'

'I don't suppose you know if his children are still on the Isle of Wight? Have you got any idea what they are doing now?'

Pete shook his head. 'I'm not sure about the daughter, but I have a feeling the boy might have gone into the police force.'

Of course, I should have thought of that. If Tristram Markham was in the police force, it might well explain why he was as elusive to uncover online as Nick Quinlan.

I could see Natalie and Rita were anxious to move onto a more exciting topic of conversation. I invented a need for the bathroom and headed off into the house, only to discover JJ following me.

The interior of the house was just as stark as the garden. There was nowhere to hide in the large open plan living space, which was furnished for fashion rather than comfort.

'We need to have a conversation,' JJ said, as I attempted to take refuge behind a large slab of concrete imitating a piece of modern art. It reminded me of one of Freddy's creations.

'Well, that's going to be difficult in here,' I shouted. The monotonous beat of garage music was blaring out from the adjoining pool-room.

'When are you going to put a stop to this fiasco of a wedding?' JJ hissed. 'I suppose you've heard the latest gimmick?'

'I'm not a big fan of the owls,' I admitted, 'but Pearl's already gone ahead and booked them.'

'Owls? I'm not talking about bloody owls. It's this stupid sailing flotilla thing. Anyone would think your mother was the Queen cruising up the Thames. Next she'll demand a forty-gun salute.'

'What do you mean sailing flotilla thing?'

'They hatched it out last night when we were all at the yacht club. Pete was telling her all about the old regattas and how they used to have a torchlight dinghy parade past Rivermede, followed by a firework display. Your mother seemed to think it was a wonderful idea. Pete's organising it for her. She's making my father into a laughing stock.'

For a moment, I almost felt a smidgeon of sympathy for JJ, but it soon passed.

'Sadly, I'm not in charge of my mother,' I informed him. 'If she's set her heart on having a torchlit yacht parade, a torchlit yacht parade she will have.' I gave a hopeless shrug. 'Let them be, JJ. She's happy. Your father is happy. What's so wrong with it?'

'Wrong with it? Everything's wrong with it,' JJ replied, looking more desperate than angry. 'Come on now, how long will it last? If it does go ahead, I'm making damn sure my father signs a prenup. You can tell your mother that from me. If she's after my father's fortune, she's going to be in for a severe shock. She won't get a penny.'

I'd already assured JJ my mother was a wealthy woman in her own right, but it appeared to have fallen on deaf ears. It was on the tip of my tongue to retort that in light of his current overspending, there probably wouldn't be a penny left for anyone to inherit. But before I could respond, Max was bearing down on us.

'Hey, leave the little lady alone,' he said to JJ. 'What are you arguing about now?'

'Her bloody mother,' JJ muttered.

'Ah, the new Mrs Robshaw-to-be,' Max said, placing an arm around each of our shoulders, encompassing us into an awkward group hug. 'I have a wonderful step-mother who keeps my father distracted and off my back. Listen and learn, JJ. Families should make love, not war. Come now, you two should be friends, not enemies, I insist.' Max's licked his lips, as if he was imagining some delicious *ménage à trois*.

Max's gesture of comradeship repulsed JJ as much as it did me, and he eased himself out of the huddle. 'I'm going to get another drink,' he growled.

'Here, let me take your coat now that we're in the warm,' Max said, swivelling around to face me.

Instinctively, I tightened the belt on my mac. 'No, I'm not stopping actually, thank you, Max.'

'You're not? Why not? You are not enjoying my house, my hospitality?' He put on an expression of mock disappointment.

'It's a fantastic house,' I assured him, 'but actually, I'm not in a mood for a party.'

'It's JJ, isn't it? Behaving like a spoilt teenager. He's worse than Kimmi,' Max was already trying to undo the buttons on my coat. 'Come on, relax, more champagne perhaps?'

I slapped his hand away as playfully as I could. 'Sorry, Max, I've got something I need to do.'

'On a Saturday night? What else is there to do in Kerridge but our party?' His laughter was drowned in the music as the door to the pool room swung open and a bikini-clad youngster shimmied towards us, demanding more champagne. With Max's attention diverted, I was able to slither out of his reach.

I thought he might try and stop me, insist I return, but he didn't. In the pool room I spotted Freddy through the narcotic fog, reclining on a deckchair. I decided not to disturb him. He

147

was a big boy and could make his own way home.

I didn't want to call Nev to come and pick me up; Pearl would be agog with curiosity if I arrived home too early. In fact, it would probably be a good idea to stay out for at least another hour. It was an easy walk to Rivermede and, despite the cloudy evening, still light. I decided to call in for a quiet drink at the first pub I came to on my way back through the village.

Chapter Nineteen

The White Heron was located at the junction of the lane that led from van der Plaast's house and the road towards the marsh at Helme Point. It was totally off the beaten track and I couldn't imagine how anyone, other than a local, would ever find it. Even on a Saturday night, its tiny car-park was deserted. There was no fancy beer garden, no board outside tempting customers in with deals of the day or menu of the week. The perfect hideaway.

I pushed open the door. Two men propped up the bar at the far end of the pub; one was reading a paper while the other was studying his phone. Another older couple were playing dominoes. They were the pub's only customers.

Aidan nudged Nick. 'It's your friend again, Alex,' he said. He gave me a shy wave and beckoned me over. Nick looked up and raised his eyebrows questioningly.

'Let me get you a drink,' Aidan said.

I ordered a white wine and pulled up a bar stool.

'What are you doing out this way?' Aidan asked. 'Took my advice, then? Come out for a quiet drink?'

I'd actually done the opposite, which would be quite apparent if I took off my coat. I was far too overdressed for The White Heron. It wasn't just my dress, but my hair, the make-up, everything. Nick took it all in.

'You look, er, nice, Rebecca,' he remarked, slipping his phone back into his pocket.

'Thank you,' I said. I wished I could return the compliment. Nick was looking scruffier than ever and his beard was beginning to compete with Aidan's.

'Were you able to mend Gerry's pontoon?' I asked Aidan.

He nodded. 'Yeah, tried to do a proper job, but if it's

vandalism, not much you can do to stop it.'

'What's all this?' Nick enquired.

'JJ Robshaw's got an awful lot of stock right now and it's not moving,' Aidan explained. 'If he can increase the number of rental berths, it'll boost his income. Moorings are at a premium on this river and Gerry Kimble is taking up a lot of valuable space. He wants the old boy moved on.'

'Can't he just evict him?' Nick asked.

'Gerry says he has a legal right to his mooring.'

'But he doesn't appear to have any paperwork to prove it,' I added. 'Or at least, he hasn't shown anything to JJ yet.'

Aidan looked puzzled. 'So, you do know more about this,' he said. 'How come?'

There was no easy way to break the news. 'I'm staying at Rivermede,' I explained. 'My mother is marrying Jack Robshaw; Pearl Gates is her name. You might have heard of her. Gerald Kimble has been a topic of dinner table conversation.'

'Oh, I see.' Aidan frowned. 'You could have said before.'

I wondered if he meant the first time we'd met, or before he'd bought me a drink. My confession appeared to have killed the conversation. He folded up his newspaper. 'Well, I said I was just popping for a quick half, so best head home,' he grunted. 'You walking back, Alex?'

'No, I'll stay for another drink,' Nick replied.

'You don't have to stay,' I said, when Aidan had gone.

'Seems a bit rude to dash off when you've made such an effort to come out,' Nick remarked. 'I thought Aidan had taken a bit of a shine to you, but obviously now he knows you're about to become part of the Robshaw clan, you've scared him off.'

'If I had my way, I'd have nothing to do with the Robshaws,' I insisted. 'I take it he's not a fan?'

'I don't think many people are,' Nick replied. 'Old hostilities, I think. JJ seems very good at rubbing people up the wrong way. Aidan has a bit of a past, apparently.'

'Really? He's so quiet.'

'It's always the quiet ones you have to watch out for,' Nick said with a wink. 'Anyway, aren't you a bit hot in that coat, Becs?'

'Don't you start.' Reluctantly, I loosened my belt. I was actually stifling in my coat. I saw Nick's admiring glance as I revealed my dress.

'Wow, you really did make an effort. Don't tell me you've just come from van der Plaast's little shindig? I thought that was just for teenagers?'

'God, you really do know everything, don't you?'

'Yes.' Nick smirked. 'Seriously? You were at van der Plaast's? I told you to keep away from him.'

'What I get up to in my own time really is none of your business,' I pointed out.

Nick held up his hands. 'I know. Sorry, I might have overstepped the mark the other day, barging in on you like that. If I behaved erratically, I apologise.'

I acknowledged his apology. 'You were a bit scary,' I admitted.

'Sometimes I find it hard to switch out of work mode and behave like a normal human being.' He smiled. 'So, how was the party? It's not even nine. Why did you leave so early?'

'I wasn't enjoying the company,' I replied. 'For a start, I was old enough to be most of the other guests' mother. And then there's Max. I admit I do find him slightly creepy.'

'God, he didn't do anything to you, did he? I mean, try anything on?'

It was actually quite pleasing to see the look of concern on Nick's face. 'Let's talk about something else,' I suggested. 'Are you able to look something up for me on your police database?'

'What makes you think I have access to the police database?'

'Well, you're something to do with the police still, aren't you? And even if you're not, you must have friends who are still in the force.'

'They're not a public information service.' Nick replied.

'I want to find someone.'

'Oh, we all want to find someone, Rebecca,' Nick's voice

softened. His hazel eyes were watching me intently. It was an old familiar look. I was determined not to fall for it.

'I'm being serious. It's not for me, it's for his mother. There's a chance this guy might be in the police force on the Isle of Wight. I've tried Googling him several times but he doesn't come up. A bit like you, really. Which made me think maybe you're in the same line of work.'

'Have you really been Googling me over the years?' Nick asked.

'No,' I replied honestly. 'I haven't.' His look of disappointment was quite satisfying. 'Have you looked me up? Have you been stalking me, Nick Quinlan?'

His denial came far too quickly. 'No, I haven't. Well, I might have checked once or twice, you know, just to make sure you were okay. And obviously, recently, when I bumped into you here.'

'So, what have you discovered about me on your searches?' I asked, enjoying holding the upper hand once again.

'That you work as Pearl's PA, that you edit books for a living. That you don't appear to have any significant others, and until very recently you and Pearl were still living at number five Beech Mews, Battersea.'

'You make it sound very boring,' I told him.

'Sometimes boring is good,' Nick replied, his face serious again. 'Sometimes boring brings security, and home comforts, stability.'

'Things you've lacked in your line of work?' I asked.

'Yes,' he reflected, 'if I'm honest, things I've lacked, and craved. And missed.'

'Did you miss me?' I asked in a quiet voice.

'Yes,' he said. 'I did.'

We fell into silence. What could I say? I could retort that I'd missed Nick like a hole in the head, but I hadn't. I'd missed him so much I thought I would never recover, that I'd never appreciate sunshine and birdsong ever again, that in the days following our non-wedding I'd wanted to crawl under the duvet and never re-emerge, a chrysalis in a permanent cocoon, locked in stasis.

We were on the verge of bridging a major chasm. Nick's remorse was unmistakeable. The implications of his words, his demeanour, almost wiped out the last fifteen years of pain. We sat there in a state of mutual confusion and contemplation. Where did we go from here?

His phone vibrated. I knew he would check it. He had to. It was his job.

'I'm sorry, Becs,' he sighed, 'I've got to go. Do you want a lift home? You don't look dressed for traipsing through the Kerridge mudflats at this time of night. I've got my car. I knew I might have to dash off.'

'Thanks, yes please.' I gathered up my bag and coat. There was so much I wanted to say, but I needed time to think. It was easier to stick to the present than dwell on the past. 'About that guy I asked you to look up? Would you do it for me? His name's Tristram Markham.'

'Sure. Tristram Markham. I'll see what I can find out'

'Do you want to write it down? So you don't forget?'

'No,' he said, tapping the side of his head. 'It's logged up here. I'll remember it.'

He dropped me off at the gates of Rivermede with a tender peck on the cheek.

'See you around, Becs.'

'Thanks, Nick.'

'It's Alex,' he reminded me.

Chapter Twenty

I spent most of the night restlessly tossing and turning in bed, repeating our conversation in my head. Something definitely shifted between us.

On Sunday morning, I joined Pearl and Jack for coffee in the drawing room. The previous evening, I had promised to give Pearl a full run-down of the party. Jack seemed particularly bubbly, while Pearl couldn't wait to hear the details of Max's mansion. It was no surprise to hear that Freddy had failed to come home.

I was sorry to disappoint her. 'I changed my mind. I didn't stay.'

'What do you mean, you changed your mind and didn't stay? But you were all dressed up to the nines. You didn't come back here until eleven. Where did you get to?'

She had obviously been watching out for me. It seemed keeping secrets – at least, my secrets – was going to be impossible in Kerridge.

'I dropped Freddy off, stayed for half an hour to be polite, and then went to this little pub. I bumped into someone I know so we just stayed chatting.'

'Someone you know?' Pearl was like a hawk, spotting her prey. 'Was it Alex, Alex from the pub quiz?'

'No.' It was so much easier to lie. 'It was someone I met when I went out walking the other day. He was there having a pint and we just got chatting and—'

'*He?*' She swooped in for the kill.

'*He* was there with his girlfriend.'

'Never mind that,' Jack interrupted. 'Let's see what the postman's brought, shall we?'

I'd heard the front doorbell clang but, as was the custom at

Rivermede, with Nev and Heather both on the premises, neither Pearl or Jack had made any attempt to answer it. Jack wheeled himself over to Pearl's side. 'I think we might be in for a little surprise, Pearl darling,' he said.

'A surprise?' Pearl cooed. 'But it's Sunday. There is no post on a Sunday! Oh Jack, I knew you'd been up to something...'

There was a kerfuffle out in the hallway. Nev apparated into the drawing room with his familiar dry cough.

'Sorry to intrude, sir, madam,' he said, 'but there's somebody—'

'Just bring it in,' Jack snapped.

'Uh no, sir, it's not exactly what you were expecting.'

'Oh?' Jack frowned. 'What do you mean?'

'What's going on?' Pearl looked from one of them to the other. 'What were you two expecting?'

'Not this.' Nev's face was inscrutable. 'It's someone asking for your son, madam.'

'Freddy?'

I could make out a waif-like figure loitering behind Nev. She had a rucksack on her back and something strapped to her chest; something that was mewling like a kitten.

The girl looked about fifteen. A horrid realisation dawned. I leapt to my feet. 'Ruby?'

Nev stepped aside to allow Ruby to enter the room. Pearl's face fell. 'What's that?' She pointed to the bundle draped across Ruby's body. 'Is it a puppy? Oh Jack, you did listen when I said I wanted...'

I exchanged glances with Ruby, just to confirm my suspicions. 'A puppy? I don't think so. It's a baby. Freddy's baby.'

'She's called Ivy,' Ruby said with a nod, peeling back some of the swaddling so that we all could glimpse the baby's head.

Now Pearl was on her feet. 'You're saying this is Freddy's baby?'

Ruby nodded. 'Yes. We're at uni together.'

'Come and sit down,' I said, realising somebody had to take charge of the situation. Pearl looked as if she were about to faint, and Jack and Nev were equally as bemused. 'Did you come here on your own or is somebody with you?' I asked, helping to lift the rucksack from her back. She sank down onto the sofa gratefully.

'No. I caught the train to Southampton and then got a taxi.'

'You look exhausted. Would you like tea, coffee?'

'Just water would be fine, thank you.'

Nev was dismissed to fetch water. Pearl sat opposite us in an armchair.

'Freddy is here, isn't he?' Ruby asked. 'I mean, I have come to the right place?'

'Of course you've come to the right place,' I assured her. 'He's just not here, right now.'

I could hardly tell the poor girl that Freddy was probably snoozing off a very large hangover at the home of the local gangster, and for all I knew nuzzling up beside a nubile newly eighteen-year-old.

'How old is Ivy?' I asked, as Ruby revealed more of the baby.

'Just two weeks. Would you like to hold her?'

'Oh, I'd love to.'

I'd always had a thing about babies, more so as I'd got older and the chance of having any of my own grew increasingly remote. Friends knew I was a sucker for babysitting duties, and I was godmother to two children, upon whom I lavished great affection, even though I didn't see them that often. Their mother, Megan, was an old colleague from my early publishing days who had moved with her husband to the US. Maternal feelings were hard to crush.

'So you must be Becca?' Ruby said, placing my niece into my arms. Ivy's face wrinkled, her eyes screwed tight shut. I held her close and stroked her downy head, soaking up the smell of her newness.

'Yes. It's a shame we haven't met before,' I said. 'I take it Freddy does know about Ivy? I mean, he told me you were pregnant, but he hasn't mentioned the birth.'

'I sent him a Snapchat.'

I'd never considered myself old-fashioned, but sending a Snapchat to inform a man he'd just become a father seemed to be taking communication levels to an all-time low. Was this the reason Freddy seemed hell bent on committing hari-kari with Kimmi van der Plaast? Was he upset at being treated so coldly? Did he feel excluded? 'And did he reply?' I asked.

'We're not together any more, so I don't expect anything from him,' Ruby said, without answering my question.

'No, but Freddy has a responsibility,' I pointed out. 'Look, he's come down here and is working seven days a week to provide for you and the baby.' It wasn't strictly true; Freddy seemed to be spending far too much of his time enjoying himself.

'I told him he didn't have to.'

'Perhaps he wanted to?' I suggested.

'I've always brought my boy up to accept his responsibilities,' Pearl interjected. Without leaving her seat, she strained her neck to get a closer look at baby Ivy.

I held her out. 'Want a cuddle?'

'Doesn't look much like Freddy,' Pearl smarted. 'Have you done a paternity test?'

Ruby's shoulders sagged. 'Freddy is definitely Ivy's father.' She lowered her voice to little more than a whisper. 'I haven't slept with anybody else.'

'So, how are you planning to look after Ivy?' I asked, worried by Ruby's seeming immaturity. It seemed incredibly naïve to dismiss Freddy's offer of financial help. 'Are your parents supportive?'

Ruby shrugged. 'My parents are divorced.'

'Well I'm divorced, but that doesn't mean I don't support my son,' Pearl said. 'What sort of excuse is that?' She reached out for Ivy. 'Let me have a look at this grandchild properly, eh? I suppose on closer inspection I can see a bit of Freddy in that nose.' Her face softened. 'What do you think, Jack?'

Before Jack could answer, the doorbell rang again.

'Goodness me, what a morning,' Pearl exclaimed. 'Who's that now?'

'Ah, perhaps this is the post,' Jack said. He wheeled himself across to the doorway to greet Nev, who re-entered the room carrying a large picnic hamper.

'Delivery for you, madam,' he said, holding the hamper out to Pearl.

'Well, I can't take it, can I?' Pearl said. 'I'm holding the baby. Let Becca open it. Who would send us a picnic hamper? Is it an early wedding present?'

'I think you should open it, dear,' Jack said, indicating for me to relieve Pearl of the baby. 'Although I think my gift might have been a little overshadowed.'

I happily removed Ivy from Pearl's arms and sat back down on the sofa next to Ruby. Neville placed the hamper on the floor at Pearl's feet.

'Well?' Jack gave her a nudge. 'Go on.'

Pearl flipped open the lid. There was a little yelp of excitement – from Pearl and from the wriggling white ball of fluff she lifted up onto her lap. 'Oh Jack, you *have* bought me a puppy,' she chuckled. 'So, is this what you and Nev have been plotting? All those secret trips out?'

'Yes.' Jack smiled indulgently. 'You've been on about nothing else since you arrived at Rivermede. Meet Princess Pippadee of Pomerania. They call her Pippa for short.'

'Princess Pippadee.' Pearl picked the puppy up to her face and gave it a kiss. 'Oh my, how thrilling. I've always wanted a puppy.'

I stared at my mother in amazement. Was this really the same woman who had refused to let Freddy and I keep so much as a goldfish? Pets were too much hard work, she always said, although I suppose she now had Heather and Nev to do the pooper-scooping and the wet morning walks, it wasn't such hard work after all.

I handed Ivy back to Ruby. 'I'd best go and fetch Freddy,' I announced. 'I'll be about half an hour. You are planning on staying, I take it?' Ruby seemed to be travelling extremely light for someone with a baby.

She nodded. 'Yes, sure. I want to see Fred.'

Chapter Twenty-One

A world that already seemed surreal became more so with every minute. I headed out to my car in something of a daze, hurriedly texting Freddy to warn him I was coming to pick him up, although not saying why. I stressed the urgency with YOU NEED TO COME HOME NOW.

He didn't reply, but when I arrived at the van der Plaast mansion, the gates were already open and Freddy was loitering on the driveway in front of the house. I leaned across to open the car door.

'What's the rush?' he asked, looking like death warmed up.

'Hop in, you'll see.'

'Max says you should come in for coffee. Why did you leave so early? Max missed you.'

'That I highly doubt,' I replied. 'Just get in the car, Fred.'

Freddy reeked of an unhealthy concoction of stale sweat, alcohol, and marijuana. There was no way he could see Ruby like this. We drove home in silence. I could sense Freddy tensing beside me in the passenger seat. I pulled up outside the stable block and tossed him the keys.

'Go up and have a shower while I fetch some clean clothes from your room.'

'What's going on?'

'Don't argue with me, just do it.'

I slipped into the house through the kitchen door and crept up to Freddy's den on the second floor. His room was the usual mess: clothes, magazines, chargers and leads strewn everywhere; a week's worth of work-wear overflowing from the laundry basket. I rummaged through his drawers until I uncovered clean underwear and a T-shirt. I found a pair of black jeans in the wardrobe – not exactly clean, but certainly less pungent than the ones he had on.

'No time to dry your hair,' I said, glad to see Freddy emerging from the shower in record time. He must have sensed the urgency.

'You are starting to worry me, Becca,' he said, grabbing the clean clothes but regarding my choices somewhat distastefully.

'So you should be worried,' I said trying to contain my anger, which wasn't so much anger as exasperation. Surely Fred could have told me he'd received a message from Ruby about the baby? I'd supported him through all this – didn't he trust me? And then to turn up like this, stinking of sex, drugs, and rock''n'roll, as if he didn't have a care in the world. 'Go on, you're decent now. You've got a visitor in the drawing room.'

'What?' Then he looked really worried. 'Who?'

'Just go, Freddy.'

I'd had enough. There was no right or wrong way of handling his situation. It was unique, but it was *his* situation not mine. Between us, Pearl and I had wrapped Freddy up in cotton wool, protected him, carried him through childhood and into his teens. His faithful back-up team. *Time to grow up Freddy*. He hesitated at the doorway and I could almost see the words on his lips, asking me to go with him into the lion's den. *I'm not your mother*, I wanted to scream. The telepathy worked. He gave me a grimace and hurried down the steps.

Fifteen minutes later, when I hadn't actually moved from the sofa apart from to make myself a cup of tea, Pearl was on the doorstep.

'Can I come in?' she asked, even though she had already opened the door. She clutched Princess Pippadee to her chest.

'How did it go?' I asked.

For once, Pearl appeared to have shown remarkable tact. 'I left them to it.' She said. 'He looked pretty shocked and so awkward when she handed him the baby, as if he didn't know which end was which.'

'I'm sure he'll quickly learn,' I pointed out. 'Would you like tea?'

'Yes please, darling. You make such a better cup than Heather.' Pearl sat down while I got up.

Princess Pippadee was released to explore the flat.

'So, the dog came as a complete surprise, too?' I asked from the kitchenette.

'I told you Jack had been behaving pretty suspiciously, and this is what it was all about,' Pearl said. 'He and Nev had been out looking for the perfect puppy.'

'But you don't even like dogs.' It was on the tip of my tongue to remind her about the whole no-pets-over-my-dead-body arguments Freddy and I had had on numerous occasions in the past.

'How could I not like Pippa?' Pearl cooed like a pigeon, scooping the pooch back up and onto her lap. 'She's adorable.'

'I take it she's fully house-trained, and vaccinated, with a pedigree certificate?'

'Oh yes, came with everything,' Pearl assured me. 'Basket, lead, harness. She's a full Pomeranian. A little dog like this won't be any trouble.'

At least Jack had had the good sense to choose a breed of dog that wouldn't require a great deal of exercise. A short walk down to the river and back would probably be more than enough to tire Princess Pippa, and my mother, out.

By mid-afternoon, some sort of semblance of normality had returned to Rivermede. Heather was informed that there would be another vegetarian for dinner, and Ruby and Ivy were safely installed into Freddy's bedroom. Freddy's empty underwear drawer made the perfect crib.

I was hastily despatched to Portdeane Tesco to buy whatever baby bedding I could, along with a bulk supply of nappies, wipes, and a couple of spare babygros, as Ruby seemed seriously ill-equipped

Trying not to sound like a nosey-parker, I attempted to ascertain what future plans she had in place. Ruby was unforthcoming, either through shyness or because, as I rapidly began to suspect, she had no plans. It transpired, with more prompting from Pearl who was showing remarkable and

161

uncharacteristic restraint, that a housemate had accompanied Ruby to the birth, and less than twenty-four hours later Ruby had been discharged back to her student house. She had little or no baby equipment, preferring to carry Ivy in her sling and sleep with her by her side.

Ruby seemed to think she would manage, although she confessed she and her housemates had had very little sleep over the last two weeks. Ivy was a very grizzly baby. Ruby was determined to breastfeed, despite struggling with seriously cracked nipples. It was not just free and natural, she declared, but also better for the baby.

'Of course it is, dear,' Pearl agreed, 'but is it best for you? You should have seen the state of me after I'd had Becca. My nipples were never the same again. Have you tried putting her on the bottle?'

Ruby had not. I was despatched back to Tesco again, just on closing time, and was able to snatch a tin of newborn formula and a set of bottles from under the security guard's nose.

'It's an emergency,' I pleaded, as he attempted to bar my way. The store manager was more sympathetic as I explained about the arrival of our unexpected guest. She held one checkout open for me and even suggested I might like to purchase a sterilising unit at the same time, which involved more dashing back through the store to the appropriate shelves.

Dinner was a remarkably civilised affair. Ivy and her drawer were carried into the dining room and, with her little tummy full, she slept peacefully as we ate.

'She normally wakes up every twenty minutes or so,' Ruby remarked. 'I've never seen her look so content.'

Pippadee slept equally as peacefully, curled up on a dining chair next to Pearl.

'What advice has your midwife or health visitor given you regarding feeding?' Pearl enquired.

'I've only seen the midwife once since I left hospital.'

Ruby's support network seemed very thin on the ground. By the end of the meal, I could see that Pearl was as concerned as I was about Ruby's situation.

'We have to get her to stay here,' Pearl hissed when Ruby excused herself to visit the bathroom. She turned to Freddy. 'You can't let that poor girl go back to London, to a bedsit. We have more than enough room here for her and the baby.'

'It's up to Rubes, really, isn't it?' was all Freddy had to say.

'Maybe if you asked Ruby if she'd like to stay, it might help,' I suggested, wishing I wasn't sat so far down the table I was out of kicking distance. He still looked as white as a sheet.

'She just wants to get back to her studies as soon as she can. She's heading for a first.'

'How can she go back to her studies when she has Ivy to look after?' Pearl snapped.

'There's a crèche at the uni.'

'But she hasn't even got a pushchair!' Pearl exclaimed, sounding as exasperated as I felt. 'Let's buy the girl a pushchair and a cot; it's the very least we can do. We need to make a list.'

'Her flat's on the third floor. There's no point having a pushchair. She won't get it up the stairs.' Freddy pointed out.

'Even more reason for you to convince her to stay here,' Pearl replied. 'Rebecca, list.'

The list grew over the course of the evening without any contribution from either Ruby or Freddy, who passed on dessert – a wonderful lemon meringue pie, M&S's finest. The new parents retired upstairs as soon as Heather began to clear away.

'I want you to take that girl shopping first thing in the morning,' Pearl told me. 'Whether she wants to or not. I will not have that baby going short.'

I shared Pearl's sentiments, although I pointed out we were in a fortunate position in that we were financially secure and could afford to make the necessary purchases. I reminded her Ruby was a student and obviously in a strained relationship with her parents, who were perhaps not so well-off or able to provide for their grand-daughter. This only fuelled Pearl's determination that Ivy should be spoilt.

By the time I strolled over to the house on Monday

morning, Freddy had already left for work. I'd been hoping to waylay him to ask how things had panned out overnight. I found Ruby in the kitchen, Heather demonstrating how the bottle steriliser worked. Ivy was grizzling hungrily, her tiny fists clenched, her face red.

'Let me take her while you do that,' I suggested to Ruby, who was struggling with hot water and formula milk. The last thing she needed was a wriggling, screaming baby attached to her chest.

Ivy was unswaddled and handed over. I was pleased to see she was in one of the new babygros. When Ruby sat down somewhat dejectedly at the table with the bottle of milk, I offered Ivy back, but instead Ruby handed me the milk. I sat at the kitchen table while the baby guzzled the milk with great gulps. I broke off to wind her.

'She doesn't do that for me,' Ruby complained as Ivy gave a polite burp.

'Freddy was a very windy baby,' I smiled. 'I used to feed him all the time, because Pearl was always working. It brings back all those happy memories.'

'It doesn't make me happy,' Ruby muttered. She rubbed her arm across her chest. 'Look at me. I'm leaking everywhere, so why can't I flippin' feed her? It doesn't make sense.'

'It'll come,' I assured her. 'Just keep trying, take your time. There's no rush, is there?'

'I've been trying for two weeks. I'm knackered, I'm sore, and I look like shit.'

'Then stop beating yourself up about it,' I said. 'Ivy is fine on the bottle. We all want to do the right thing, but if doing the so-called right thing is making you miserable, then you are making Ivy miserable, too. A happy mum makes a happy baby.'

'Yeah, but that stuff costs money,' Ruby said with a nod at the tin of formula sat on the side. 'And all the faff with cleaning the bottles and stuff. Breast is breast. I want to be a good mum.'

'And you will be. You are,' I said. 'But if you are going to put Ivy in the crèche, you'll have to express your milk for the nursery to use. You will still need a steriliser and the bottles, and a breast pump, of course. It'll all add up. Babies are expensive things, that's why you should accept our help. Freddy's help.'

'Maybe I won't send her to nursery until she's on proper food and, you know, normal milk,' Ruby mused.

'That won't be for months yet,' I laughed. Then I stopped laughing. Ruby was staring at me with a puzzled expression on her face. She really didn't have a clue.

'Oh God, I'm useless,' she said, burying her head in her hands. 'Totally useless. I don't know anything. What am I going to do? I'm so bad at this. So unprepared.'

A thought occurred to me. 'Ruby, you have told your parents about Ivy, haven't you?'

She shook her head. 'No. No I haven't. How can I? They didn't know I was pregnant. I hardly ever go home. Like I said, my mum and dad are divorced. My dad ran off with his secretary, and we haven't really kept in touch. Mum works full time. She's got a really good job, she's a solicitor, and she thinks I'm this marvellous straight A student. She's expecting me to come out of uni with a first-class honours degree, not a baby. How can I tell her?'

'Ruby, you have to.'

She shook her head. 'No. I can't.' Tears streaked down her sad little face. 'Freddy was the only person I ever told until I had to go into hospital to give birth, and then like I had to tell my flatmates, but they're sworn to secrecy. I can't tell her, I can't. She'll go mad.'

'Oh Ruby,' I said, drawing her towards me. 'You've been in denial, haven't you? All this time, when you said you didn't want Freddy to be involved and you didn't tell your mum, it's because you've been in denial about being pregnant, just hoping Ivy would go away?'

'Yes.' Ruby nodded between the sobs, her whole body shaking. 'Yes, yes, but now she's here, isn't she? And look, she's good for you, but she hates me. I know she does. She hates me.'

Pearl was right, Ruby couldn't go back to London. She had to stay with us, regardless of her relationship with Freddy. When Pearl emerged for her breakfast at nine, Princess Pippadee tucked under her arm, I asked if we could requisition another of Rivermede's many bedrooms as a separate space for Ruby and Ivy. Pearl instantly agreed.

'It's the only solution,' she said. Ten minutes later, Ruby, Pearl, and I were heading up to the stairs to the first floor.

'Why don't you have the guest room for now?' Pearl suggested, showing Ruby the room I had used when I'd come to stay the first couple of times. 'Becca is going to take you shopping this morning so that you can choose a cot, a pram—' she held up her hand to silence Ruby's protests. 'I know you might not need one in London, but you'll need one here. You'll need a changing table, a baby monitor, a few toys.'

Ruby meekly nodded to everything Pearl said, and even agreed to the suggestion that Ivy should remain at Rivermede with her grandmother while I took her shopping.

She showed little interest in the purchases, happily letting me decide on the design of the cot, the pushchair – the shop assistant recommended one that conveniently converted into a car-seat – and the changing table. Even when it came to selecting additional luxuries like a night-light-cum-mobile, she voiced no preferences.

When Freddy returned from work that evening, he seemed equally subdued and somewhat overwhelmed at the amount of baby paraphernalia that had taken over the house.

'Does it really need all this?' he asked.

'*It* is a she,' I told him, 'and *she* is your daughter. And yes, she does need all this.'

'Even this?' he asked, holding up the entire box set of Beatrix Potter books I had bought on impulse.

'Okay, she probably doesn't need those just yet,' I conceded, 'but she will, one day. One day she'll wake up and demand you read her the story of *Peter Rabbit and the Flopsy Bunnies,* and you'll be very grateful I bought them for her.'

He shook his head. 'You've gone mad. You were always the sensible one, but even *you*'ve gone mad now.' And then, as an afterthought, he added, 'How did it come to this? How did we end up in this mess, Becs?'

'I think it's too late for a lecture on the birds and bees now, Fred,' I replied.

'No, I don't mean that. I mean this, this whole me, you, Rubes, Rivermede mess? What are we doing here? Do you know what I feel like, Becs? I feel like the victim of a shipwreck. I sailed into a storm and now I'm here, stranded on this inhospitable island and I can't see a way off.'

'It's life,' I replied, 'it's what it does to you. You have a plan in your head but then something comes along and screws it all up. God, fate, whatever, but you have to have faith that it turns out all right in the end.'

'You mean we will be rescued?' he asked. 'Is that what happened to you, when you were going to get married and then you didn't, and now look at all you've done for Pearl and her career? That turned out good, didn't it? Is that what you mean?'

It wasn't what I meant at all, but I smiled at Fred and nodded my head. 'Yes, something like that,' I said.

Chapter Twenty-Two

I shared Freddy's despair at the turn of events, and was very impressed by his use of the metaphorical shipwreck. It seemed appropriate given our location, but Rivermede was hardly inhospitable. I craved a sense of equilibrium.

I was struggling to make progress on Stella's autobiography, and I had little enthusiasm to tackle the backlog of emails received in answer to my ads for freelance work. The old adage that everybody had a book in them was not true at all, and although anyone sensible enough to pay for a professional edit was on the right track, you still had to be very tactful. And then there were my feelings for Nick bubbling under the surface. I didn't want to have time to dwell or analyse the effect he was beginning to have on me; the effect he had always had on me.

It was Monday, and quiz night. I hesitated about going. When Nick had dropped me off on Saturday evening, there had been no mention of when we would see each other again, but an awful lot of things had been left unsaid.

Pearl wanted me to spend the evening in the big house. 'We need a buffer. Freddy and Ruby don't seem to be getting on,' she said.

'That's because they've got a lot of adjusting to do,' I pointed out. 'We should give them some space to work things out.'

She didn't look convinced. My love life was no longer top priority.

I decided I had nothing to lose by paying a visit to The Ship. In any case, I didn't want to spend the evening sat alone in the stable block flat.

He was there with the others, a smile on his face as I pulled up a chair. There was no air of tension between us and we kept the conversation banal, which was not that difficult with the M&Ms around. Norah Morland was apparently making a good recovery. Nick had no knowledge of the incident, so the story of her unfortunate encounter with the cess-pit evacuation lorry was relayed for his benefit.

With a full team of six, the Twitchers romped away with the title.

'So, you two obviously know each other from a long time ago,' Marie remarked as the evening came to an end.

'I'm sorry?' I said.

'When we were answering the question about the Maze at Hampton Court, you reminded Alex you'd been there together.'

I hadn't even realised I'd make the mistake. 'Did I? I don't think so. I've been there, that's what I mean, sometimes I say that – we did this, we did that; you know, the royal we.'

'Becca likes to put herself on par with the monarchy,' Nick threw in for good measure. He shot me a warning glance. He obviously hadn't noticed the mistake either.

Marie regarded us suspiciously.

'We're going to have to stop meeting like this,' Nick said, holding me back as the others filed out of the pub. 'Maybe both of us coming here isn't such a good idea. I don't want people asking too many questions about my background.'

'I'm sorry,' I said at once. 'It was just a slip of the tongue. Nobody else noticed.'

'I know, but I don't want either of us being compromised. I'm not keeping my identity secret just for fun, Rebecca.' He had his serious face on again.

'You know I would never compromise you,' I said through a forced smile.

'We're just going to have to tread more carefully,' Nick said, not rising to the bait. 'Perhaps being on the same quiz team is not such a good idea.'

'You want to quit the Twitchers?'

'Not me, you. Last in, first out. Can't you find something else to do on a Monday evening?'

'Why should I be the one to quit? I enjoy the quiz.'

Nick sighed. 'If I quit, Craig and company could become suspicious, start asking awkward questions.'

'Then we will just have to continue as we are, won't we?' I said.

'Becca…'

'Yes, Nick?'

He shook his head. 'Alex. I'm Alex. You see, Becca, it's not going to work, is it?'

'Time is a great healer,' Pearl had told me on the morning of my wedding, when I'd told her I wasn't going to marry Nick because he'd cheated on me with Saskia Browning. 'Everyone gets nervous before a wedding. Goodness me, your father spent all night in the Dog and Duck on the Old Brompton Road. His best man found him slumped in the doorway at seven in the morning where the landlord had thrown him out. Forgive him.'

I'd listened to Pearl's platitudes, inwardly smouldering that she had taken Nick's side when she should have been on mine. What sort of man cheated on his wife-to-be with her bridesmaid? My mother had never liked Saskia Browning, she'd painted her the villain of the piece. She had enticed Nick, connived, schemed, sunk to the lowest depths to get her claws into him because she was jealous of my happiness.

'It's just like *Wedding Veils in the Spring*,' Pearl said.

'It's nothing like *Wedding Veils in the Spring*,' I had retorted. 'This is my life, not one of your trashy novels. Nor do I fancy the vicar.'

In *Wedding Veils in the Spring*, the jilted bride subsequently found solace with the parish priest.

'No, but the point is, dear,' Pearl continued undeterred, 'in *Wedding Veils in the Spring*, it is the bride's younger sister who seduces the groom, jealous of her sister's happiness. And the groom, a very weak young man with an eye for a pretty face, is very easy prey. I agree that there the similarities end.'

Pearl had then resorted to bribes, followed by threats, in order to have her big day. I could not let her down. This wasn't all about me. The months of meticulous planning, the caterers, the band, the disco, the honeymoon...

'When you see him at the altar,' she had finally concluded, 'and you look into the face of the man you love – because I know you do love him, Becca dear – it will all become clear. You will see that ultimately Nick is a good man who loves you and will make you happy. I know he will.'

And so I'd gone along with it. I believed her. I seriously thought when I got to the altar and I looked into Nick's face, I would find regret and repentance. I would find devotion, and all those doubts about his loyalty would be quashed.

I'd had my suspicions about Nick and Saskia for some time. At first, it had just been a mild flirting. Saskia had rented a room not far from our flat. I was glad my best-friend and my fiancé had hit it off. I asked her to be an additional bridesmaid. She was often at our flat, waiting for me when I came in from work. When Nick was on a case, he worked bizarre shift patterns, sometimes sleeping all day and out all night. A couple of times I came in through the front door and found them, heads bent close together, midway through a conversation which stopped abruptly when I entered the room.

Nick denied anything was going on when I interrogated him. I didn't believe him. My self-esteem was at an all-time low. It always was when I was around Saskia. How could he fail to be attracted to that tall, leggy blonde when I was a plain brunette struggling to fit into her size 12 wedding dress? Saskia had perfect teeth, perfect hair, those perfect legs.

I had no hard evidence to back up my suspicions, but the worm grew. A couple of times I caught a waft of Saskia's distinctive perfume *Eau de la Caribe* on Nick's clothes. She used to smother herself in it at school – a distinctive, sickly smell of coconut. Naturally, Nick could never talk to me about what he got up to at work, where he'd been when he'd been on a job all night. In the two-week run-up to the wedding, Saskia stopped coming to the flat. It was guilt. She couldn't look me in the eye. It had happened before with boys at school. This wasn't the sixth form. This was real life and she had got hold of my man.

I threw the accusations at Nick. He denied everything. I wanted to believe him, I tried to keep faith. As tradition dictates, we'd agreed to spend the night before our wedding apart. I returned to Pearl in Battersea, Nick stayed on at the flat. Once I reached Battersea, I remembered I'd left the gifts I'd bought for my bridesmaids in our bedroom, so I popped back to pick them up. He wasn't there. Of course, he could have been having a last-minute drink with friends or entertaining his family who had come down from the north to stay in London. There were all sorts of reasons why he wasn't at the flat, but I could only think of one.

I had walked up the aisle, debating with every step what I would do when I reached the altar, Pearl's words of wisdom re-playing on a loop. I almost did it. I almost went through with it, with Saskia breathing down my neck in her hastily-stitched dress and the smell of her perfume lingering in the air. I would do as my mother said. I would forgive him. When I looked into the face of the man I loved, I would know he loved me and I would forgive him.

'I'm sorry, Becca,' he said. 'I can't do this. I can't go through with the wedding.'

I stared at him, his words slicing through my heart, shattering my dreams into zillions of tiny pieces. He shook his head, pitiful and pathetic.

He was sorry? Indignant rage consumed me. He could humiliate me with my best friend in private, but there was no way I was going to let him humiliate me in front of all these people. This was my day, my wedding, and I was the only one who could call it off. *Yes, he would be sorry*.

I'd squeezed myself into the Jenny Packham wedding dress Pearl had chosen. I'd posed outside the church for the arrival photographs she had demanded. I'd carried the bouquet, handpicked that morning at Columbia Road flower market, and I'd smiled at the guests she had invited. But there the pantomime had to end. My mother's guests could still enjoy the wedding banquet, Pearl could drown her sorrows in the gallons of pink champagne, but there would be no blushing bride sat at the top table.

'You bastard,' I hissed, 'you lying, cheating bastard. All these weeks you've been screwing my best friend, pretending nothing was happening. You're too bloody right this wedding is off. You are the lowest of the low. You're scum, Nick Quinlan, and I'm glad to be rid of you.'

I thrust my bouquet into Saskia's hands with a vehement, '*He's all yours.*'

I had subsequently ignored his phone calls. His letters went unanswered. I'd had fifteen years to get over Nick and move on, but the truth was I hadn't found another man who had come anywhere close to mending my broken heart.

Chapter Twenty-Three

I didn't want to lose Nick again. I didn't want to stay away from the quiz. I wanted to see more of him, not less. I thought we had recaptured something – the old spark, but with a new understanding. It didn't seem fair that I was once again lurching into an intolerable position of not knowing where I stood.

I spent the next couple of days keeping out of everyone's way, ensconced in the stable block. The weather had set in dull and damp again, a fine white mist of drizzle hung over the river. Pearl called in with Pippa, mainly to show off Pippa's new raincoat – she and Pearl had acquired matching tartan waterproofs for their walks around the grounds. Personally, I thought they were both hideous, although I assured Pearl that she and Pippa looked very distinguished. The second time, she called in with Ivy.

'Just giving Ruby a break,' she said, 'the girl looks exhausted. Do you think we should her contact her mother, arrange some sort of meeting?'

The thought had crossed my mind. 'It's tempting,' I agreed, 'but she and Freddy are adults. Maybe just try talking to her again, see if we can convince her to speak to her mum?'

'She doesn't seem to want to talk to me,' Pearl said a little sadly. 'I have tried. Why don't you go over and have a chat with her, Becca? You are so much better at these things than me.'

I was determined not to interfere. 'I honestly think that it's best to just let her and Freddy sort this out,' I said.

Pearl sighed. 'I know you're right. I suppose we shall have to include Ruby in the seating plan for the wedding now. Should she sit with Fred?' She gave Ivy an extra squeeze. 'As for you, little lady, you can be my flower girl. I'll ask Vera if she can run something up. How much will she grow, do you think, in the next couple of weeks?'

I suspected that Ivy would grow a lot, if she continued to guzzle back her milk at the current rate of knots.

'Have you been to see Norah Morland yet?' I asked.

'I think we're going tomorrow,' Pearl replied with a grimace. 'Fancy coming, too, for moral support?'

'I wouldn't mind meeting her actually,' I said. 'Just out of curiosity.'

Pearl settled onto the sofa as if she had no intention of leaving. Any hope of completing a day's work was lost. Princess Pippadee showed her disapproval of being ignored in favour of baby Ivy, by promptly weeing on the floor.

'Oh, naughty girl, Pippadee. Look what you've done to poor Becca's carpet,' Pearl chided.

'You've got to tell her off more firmly than that,' I said, fetching the kitchen roll.

'Heather has bought some marvellous stuff,' Pearl replied. 'It's a magic carpet cleaner and deodoriser. It's very good. Hop over to the house and borrow it.'

'Is Pippa weeing all over the place?' I asked concerned. 'I thought she was supposed to be house-trained.'

'Oh, she is, darling, but we all have little accidents, don't we? Every now and again.'

'Speak for yourself. I certainly don't.' I soaked up the worst of the wee. Pippa started scratching at the door to go out. 'Now what does she want? Don't tell me she's going to do a number two?'

'Quite possibly,' Pearl admitted. 'Can you take her out for a few minutes while I stay here with Ivy?'

The light drizzle had increased to a heavy sheet of rain. Pippa was off down the steps in an instant.

'Go follow her,' Pearl yelled in a panic, 'she's never been outside off the lead. Take my coat.'

'It won't fit me,' I protested.

'Yes, it will,' Pearl replied, thrusting the hideous garment towards me. She was almost in hysterics. 'It's enormous.

175

There's room for two of me.'

'Thanks a bunch, *Mum*,' I retorted, struggling into the coat.

She looked slightly taken aback, then smiled almost shyly before flapping me away. 'Go on, go and rescue Pippa.'

I dashed after Pippa. By the time I reached the flower beds, she was no longer fluffy and white, but bedraggled and muddy. I scooped her under my arm, only to see a figure approaching across the lawn, heading for the house. I recognised the shuffling gait of Gerry Kimble.

'Hello, Mr Kimble,' I shouted, waving to attract his attention. 'What are you doing here?'

He had come from the direction of the riverside gate and I wondered how he had got in. I highly doubted he would have been given access to the code.

'I'm looking for Robshaw,' he grunted. 'Who are you?'

'We met at Chapman's Wharf the other day,' I reminded him. 'My name is Becca.'

'Is he in?' the old man asked.

'Are you looking for Jack senior or his son?'

'Jack senior, of course.'

Jack was usually attacking his crossword puzzle in the drawing room at this time of the morning.

'Follow me,' I said. I could hardly leave Gerry outside in the rain, and in any case, I had to return Pippa to Pearl.

Pearl regarded the puppy and Gerry Kimble with equal distaste. 'You might as well carry Pippa back to the house for me,' she said, refusing to lift the quivering dog out of my arms. 'You're all dirty anyway. Look at the mess you've made of my coat. Take her straight to the kitchen door. Heather can hose her down in the boot room.' Her expression suggested she would like to prescribe the same treatment for Gerry Kimble.

The kitchen door seemed the most appropriate entry point for all of us. Nev was instructed to find Jack while Heather took charge of the puppy. Gerry refused to be relieved of his heavy overcoat.

'I ain't planning on stopping long,' he grunted.

'But you are dripping all over my floor,' Pearl pointed out, refusing to take no for an answer. Beneath his great coat, Gerry wore a knitted jumper and a pair of loose baggy shorts. Pearl raised her eyes to the heavens and said she needed a coffee. I offered to make one for her as Heather was on puppy-cleaning duties. Gerry requested a tea.

When Jack appeared, he suggested Gerry accompany him into the study. I received the impression Gerry might have been a regular visitor.

I made Gerry's tea and a coffee for Jack but hesitated outside the study door. The two men were having a heated argument.

'You won't find it, Kimble, I've looked. Looked and bloody looked. It's not here.'

'She must have kept a copy. She wouldn't have thrown it away.'

'Well, she obviously did.'

'So why don't you stick up for me then? You know darn well that mooring is mine and you know why it was given to me.'

I knocked on the door.

'Come in,' Jack snapped.

The study was in chaos. Gerry was pulling box files off the shelves while Jack watched helplessly from his chair.

'Tea,' I said, smiling brightly.

'You,' Gerry said, slamming a box file onto the pile already on the desk. 'You his secretary or something? You can help us look.'

'I'm not actually Jack's secretary,' I informed him, 'and as I don't know what you are looking for, I couldn't possibly help you.'

'Gerry is looking for the paperwork which he says gives him a lifetime right to his mooring. He insists it is here somewhere, despite me telling him repeatedly that it is not.' Jack's voice was tight, as if he was trying very hard to control his temper.

'Gerry, why don't you just sit down for a minute and have your tea?' I said, attempting to bring some calm to the situation. 'What year did you get given these rights? We need

177

to look at this rationally.'

'I don't think we need to look at this at all,' Jack said.

'Ray Dimmock gave me the rights,' Gerry said, slumping into a chair. 'But Mary made it legal. She got a solicitor to draw up the paperwork.'

'Okay, so what solicitor? I'm sure he'd have kept a copy of the paperwork.' I glanced at Jack. Surely Jack would have looked into this option already?

'Ray Dimmock always used a firm called Kearney and Co in Portdeane,' Jack said, confirming my theory. 'They're not there any more. Haven't been for years. I use Fletchers in Winchester for the business, and they have no records of any document giving Mr Kimble here his divine rights.'

'Mary may have used someone else,' I suggested. 'Can you remember, Gerry?'

The old man shook his head.

'If you wish to help Mr Kimble by contacting every solicitor in the region and asking if they remember drawing up a legal document between him and my wife in the last fifty years or so, you are more than welcome to do so, Rebecca,' Jack said. His face had lost all signs of its usual congeniality. 'Now, I think that has answered our questions for today. Thank you for the refreshments, Rebecca, but our guest is not stopping.'

'Yes, of course, Jack, sorry,' I said, backing out of the room. 'Come on, Gerry, I'll fetch your coat.'

Gerry staggered to his feet. 'I'll tell 'im,' he said, leaning across the desk towards Jack, spittle dribbling down his chin. 'Is that what you want, Robshaw? You turn me off my mooring and I'll tell that boy of yours the truth about his rotten family. Every single little truth.'

'Get out of my house, Kimble,' Jack roared. 'Get out!'

Chapter Twenty-Four

'Goodness me,' Pearl exclaimed, 'what was all that about?'

'I've no idea,' I admitted, easing Gerry into a kitchen chair so that he could finish off his tea. I didn't want to worry Pearl with an account of the scene in the study, and Gerry appeared equally as tight-lipped. Pearl watched him like a hawk while Heather nursed Ivy with a look of distinct disapproval. I could almost hear her complaints about another three mouths to feed – the puppy, the baby, and Ruby, who ate the least of all three.

It was quite clear that Gerald Kimble was convinced that he had a legal right to retain his mooring, and if the evidence couldn't be found, he was prepared to threaten Jack with some sort of exposé. I was intrigued, my natural curiosity aroused. What was Jack covering up? Gerry had called the family 'rotten'. Did this accusation relate to the Dimmocks' boatyard's notorious past, and the accident that had cost Jack his leg and Kenny his life? Was that just one of many incidents caused by Ray Dimmock's disregard for health and safety? Or was it something else entirely? My imagination was running riot. I'd inherited a writer's instinct for chasing a story. Could there be potential material here for some sort of novel? In her former life, Pearl would have been making notes while inspiration struck; instead, she wanted to spend the rest of the day organising a synchronised firework display and torchlight dinghy parade.

As she whisked Pippa off to be blow-dried, I offered to drive Gerry back to the marina. He finished the last dregs of his tea and I handed him his coat. As it was still pouring, I wrapped myself up in Pearl's mac again. There was no point ruining another jacket. Without a word, he obediently followed me out to the garage.

179

There was so much I wanted to ask Gerry, but his demeanour, hunched next to me in the passenger seat, didn't invite conversation. My cheerful opening line, 'You've known the Robshaws a long time I take it, Gerry?' elicited the barest grunt.

After dropping Gerry on Kerridge Hard, I decided to give an afternoon at Rivermede a miss and instead headed for Portdeane Library. If Gerry wasn't going to be forthcoming, it might be worth looking for clues elsewhere. Despite the tartan disguise, Maurice remembered me.

'Back again, young lady?' he said with a smile.

Anyone who referred to me as 'young' was an immediate new friend.

'I can't keep away,' I teased. 'I just wondered if you know Gerald Kimble, who owns *The Regatta Queen* moored up at Kerridge? Did he used to work for Dimmocks, too?'

'Of course I know Gerry,' Maurice said. He drew my attention back to the photograph of the Dimmocks' workforce in early 1970s. 'The Kimbles are an old Kerridge family. That'll be him there, right at the front – probably one of the last apprentices Ray Dimmock took on. He'd have been about eighteen or nineteen when this was taken.'

Gerald Kimble had been a handsome youth. He wore the traditional overalls of the boatyard trainee.

'Do you recall any other serious accidents at the old Dimmock boatyard, besides the one that killed Kenny?' I asked, rather relishing my role of conducting investigative research.

Maurice was very quick to dash my hopes. 'There was nothing else on par with that,' he admitted. 'Of course, there were little things every now and then. A lot of the machinery was very old. Dimmocks was falling way behind with orders, losing customers left right and centre, especially towards the end before Jack Robshaw took over. I know someone who lost a couple of fingers, and another young lad fell off some scaffolding. Broke his back, if I recall.'

'Was there anything that involved Gerald Kimble?' I asked

Maurice shook his head. 'Not that I know of, but it

wouldn't surprise me if something was covered up. As much as I resented Robshaw closing down the construction side of the business, realistically the yard would have needed a major injection of cash to be able to come up to modern-day health and safety standards, let alone allow it to compete competitively. As I said, corners were cut and lads took risks. We all did.'

I could easily envisage the commercial potential in an historic novel based on the workings of a family boatyard, but a catalogue of industrial accidents, which was all I had to go on so far, was hardly likely to catch the paying public's imagination. I was reluctant to let the opportunity for a novel slip out of my grasp before it had even begun to take shape. I needed something more.

'I heard a rumour Gerry has a legal right to retain his mooring on the marina at Kerridge. Do you know anything about that?' I persisted.

'The Kimbles always claimed that mooring was theirs,' Maurice said. 'Gerry's father kept a houseboat there during the war years. We've probably got a picture of it here somewhere. I don't know the whys and wherefores, but as I said they were an old Kerridge family. These things often get passed down father to son without any legal documentation exchanging hands.'

Another dead-end. I tried one more time. 'So, did Gerry lose his job like everyone else when Jack Robshaw took over?' I asked. 'Was there any personal resentment between the two men?'

'Oh no.' Maurice smiled. 'Jack still needed a few lads about the place. The yard continued to undertake repairs and servicing. He kept Kimble on. I think I told you before, there's always a lady involved in these things. Mary had a bit of a soft spot for young Gerry, I believe.'

So, Mary Robshaw held the key to whatever tied Gerry to his mooring. I should have guessed. Mary was known for her charitable works, although a soft spot could mean anything. Was the name of Gerry's boat a coincidence, or a clue?

Maurice had said the Kimbles were an old Kerridge family, so Mary and Gerry would have grown up together. It was hardly likely that a friendship between a lowly apprentice and his employer's daughter would have been encouraged, but it was impossible not to speculate.

Had Mary insisted Jack retain Gerry in the yard and subsequently legalised her father's casual agreement out of loyalty? *Out of love?* Was that the exposé Jack feared?

Maurice directed me to the local history section of the library, and I signed up for a library card and took out a couple of books for research purposes. I felt positively inspired. In fact, I was so busy concentrating on plotting potential scenes for my amazing new novel, my face half hidden under the enormous peaked hood of Pearl's coat, that as I exited the library I walked slap-bang into a man equally as concealed in waterproofs dashing across the car park.

I mumbled an immediate apology and looked up.

'God, Becca,' Nick could hardly contain his laughter. 'What are you wearing?'

'Don't,' I said, peering out at him. 'It's not mine, okay?'

'I should seriously hope not,' he replied.

'What are you doing here?' I asked. 'I thought you rarely left the marshes.'

'I don't.' He fingered his chin. 'I've been to the barbers.'

'That's an improvement,' I said, admiring Nick's newly-trimmed beard.

He grinned. 'What about you?'

'I've just been to the library.'

'Swatting up for the next quiz?'

'I thought you didn't want me to come any more,' I reminded him. Rainwater dripped down onto my nose.

'Well, I suppose you are an asset to the team. I can probably put up with you...' His words were lost as a dark grey van roared into the car park.

There was a huge puddle between us and the row of parked cars. The van could easily have avoided us, but it didn't.

'Flippin' heck, mate!' Nick yelled. We were both drenched, although Nick more so than me because at least Pearl's raincoat was full-length. The van, clearly bearing the logo of *Robshaw Marine Services,* pulled into a distant parking bay.

Nick shook his head in disgust. 'I would ask you if you had time for a coffee,' he said, 'but now I'm so bloody wet and I have to be somewhere in an hour, I need to head back and try to dry off.'

'That's fine,' I assured him. 'Don't worry about it, another time maybe?'

'I'd like that very much, Becs,' Nick said. 'See you at the quiz.'

I watched him head out of the car park and down towards the quayside, before returning to my car. If I wasn't so conspicuous in my very distinctive coat, I would probably have been tempted to follow him – just out of curiosity's sake. I couldn't help but feel the coat had already caused me enough trouble. I couldn't be certain, but the driver of the grey van bore more than a passing resemblance to JJ Robshaw. No doubt he had derived a great deal of pleasure from believing he had just given Pearl a thorough soaking.

I clutched my library books to my sodden chest and returned to my car. Despite the drenching, my waterlogged feet, and the rain drops on my nose, I felt a glowing warmth radiating from my insides.

Chapter Twenty-Five

I didn't want to upset Jack, and subsequently my mother, by opening up a can of worms, so I decided to keep my planned novel project under wraps. The seed had been sown, names, places, dates could all be changed with artistic licence, but common sense told me not to pursue any further real-life investigations. I had the bare bones to work with, my imagination could easily do the rest. Apart from providing the inspiration for an across-the-class-divide love story, which could possibly have no bearing on actual events, the reasoning behind Mary Dimmock's decision to legalise Gerry's claim to his mooring was none of my business. Unless, of course, JJ continued to persecute poor Gerry. In which case, out of human kindness, I would consider it my public duty to get to the bottom of things.

But first, Pearl and I had another public duty – our visit to Norah Morland. Twenty-four hours after his encounter with Gerald Kimble, Jack was still in a bad mood.

'He really didn't want to come,' Pearl whispered in my ear as I joined her on the back seat of the Range Rover.

Clay Kiln Lane was home to Kerridge's meagre stock of social housing – three blocks of semi-detached OAP bungalows located on a steep and pensioner-unfriendly slope. The previous day's wild weather had dispersed and although a stiff breeze left an unseasonal nip in the air, pavements were dry and watery sunshine filtered through the last remaining clouds. Nev had to help wheel Jack's chair to Norah's door, where we were met, to my surprise, by Judy Stevenson.

'I'm Co-ordinator of the Good Neighbours,' she explained.

If my mother had hopes of emulating Mary Robshaw, she'd have to knock Judy off the throne first.

Norah was currently in bed taking a nap and had no idea she had guests.

'We've worked out a rota,' Judy explained, ushering the three of us to Norah's miniscule front room. 'It was the only way the poor dear could come home. I don't suppose we could put you down for a session could we, Pearl?'

Norah's front room was a revelation. There were pictures of Mary Robshaw on every surface, from beaming childhood to blushing bride. It was clear Norah had doted on her young charge, and I could see at once that Pearl was overwhelmed by the presence of her predecessor. No wonder Jack, who presumably already knew the lie of the land, had been so reluctant to come. The last thing he would have wanted was more reminders of Mary's alluring charm after his encounter with Gerry Kimble. My imagination was running away with me again.

'I really don't think I can spare the time,' Pearl said, gazing at the pictures that adorned the walls. 'There's so much to do for the wedding. Some people take years to plan their big day; I've had to do it all in less than three months.'

Judy seemed unimpressed. 'How about you, Becca, could you help out? Just a couple of hours?'

'I don't see why not,' I confessed. 'But she won't know who I am.'

'She doesn't know who any of us are, dear,' Judy replied. 'I wouldn't let that worry you. All you have to do is keep her company. The carers come three times a day. It's just the times in-between we need to look after. Could I put you down for one afternoon next week?'

I could barely contain my enthusiasm. 'Yes, please.'

Pearl looked aghast.

Jack said there was no need to wake Norah, so within ten minutes of wheeling him into the bungalow, we wheeled him out. He remained subdued.

'I need a drink,' he announced as we settled back into the car, 'and a change of scenery. How about we head along the coast to Hooke's Bay? I feel like some fresh sea air.'

'But I've things to sort out back at the house,' Pearl

protested. 'What about Pippa? She'll be wondering where we are. Can't you drop us off at the Rivermede first, Nev?'

'Hookes Bay,' Jack seemed adamant. 'Full speed.'

'Yes, of course, sir,' Nev replied.

We didn't return to Rivermede until half six. We spent the afternoon in a dreary pub watching Jack drown his sorrows. Pearl constantly checked her watch and made no attempt to hide her agitation. It was the first sign of strife I had seen between them. I had tried to keep things pleasant, despising my role as mediator and wishing I was somewhere else entirely. In the end, Pearl and I left Jack to his beer and headed outside, walking along the blustery seafront. Hooke's Bay was a characterless, bleak-looking place, with a scruffy shingle beach.

'They call this the seaside?' Pearl whined. 'Remind me to look at honeymoon destinations when we get home, Becca. Somewhere exotic. I'm tempted to take another cruise.'

'It is a little uninspiring,' I agreed. 'What did you think of Norah Morland's front room? It was like a shrine, wasn't it?'

'Shrine?' Pearl muttered. 'It felt more like a tomb.'

The minute we pulled up on the drive at Rivermede, Pearl instructed me to check up on Ruby and the baby while she rushed to rescue Pippadee, convinced the puppy would be pining from starvation and neglect.

I headed to the guest room and knocked on the door. There was no sound and no reply to my question of, 'Ruby, are you in there?' I didn't want to intrude if Ruby and Ivy were both sleeping. I knew Freddy was home from work because I'd seen his Lambretta parked outside the garage. I trotted up the stairs to the next floor.

I could hear Freddy talking softly in his room.

'Fred, can I come in?'

The room was in its usual state of disarray. Freddy sat on the bed, Ivy balanced awkwardly in the crook of his arm. In his free hand, he held a book – *Peter Rabbit*. His eyes were red.

'Where's Ruby?' I asked, instinctively knowing that something was wrong. Horribly wrong. Freddy had hardly touched Ivy since she'd arrived at Rivermede.

'She's gone,' he said with a sniff. 'She's left us, Becs. What am I going to do? She's gone.'

He nodded to the bedside table. She had left a note.

Dear Freddy, I can't cope with Ivy. I want you and your family to have her, to love and care for her. You can give her all the things that I can't. Ruby.

I stared at Fred, at Ivy, at the note. 'When did she go?' I asked.

'I don't know,' Fred sniffed again, 'sometime this afternoon, I think. I came home from work and Ivy was with Heather in the kitchen. She said a taxi had come earlier, and Ruby had just said she was popping out and could Heather look after her for a bit. The stuff's gone from her room.'

'Have you tried ringing her?'

''Course I have. Her phone's switched off.'

'Oh Fred.' I sat down on the bed next to him. Ivy was asleep, oblivious to the chaos happening all around her, her eyelids fluttering as she dreamt.

'What am I going to do?' he wailed. 'What am I going to do?'

I put my arm around his tense, bony shoulders. He rested his head against my chest, the tears still wet on his cheeks, the lost, lonely little boy he'd always been. There was so much I could have said to Freddy at that moment, but our relationship worked because we functioned at a purely practical level. We didn't reach out emotionally to each other or delve beneath the surface. I was too afraid of the currents.

Given time, he would understand about loyalty, about love, about those irrevocable bonds between parent and child. Instead, I used the words Pearl had said during the trauma preceding Freddy's birth.

'We'll cope,' I promised him. 'We'll look after Ivy. She's part of our family. She's our flesh and blood.'

We used to be three, and now we were four.

It was all change once again at Rivermede. Pearl, as always in times of trouble, pulled on all her powers of resourcefulness and resilience. At her insistence, Freddy phoned around a few college friends until he could find someone who confirmed that Ruby was safely back in her student flat.

'You will need to talk to her,' Pearl told him, 'and she needs to talk to you.'

Pearl was right, but Freddy was adamant he didn't want to put any pressure on Ruby – yet.

'We'll wait until after the wedding,' Pearl conceded, 'but then we'll sort this out properly. Just because she feels like this now, it might not always be the case. We need a solicitor. Ivy needs to be safeguarded.'

It seemed like a plan. Freddy relocated to the sumptuous surroundings of the guest room, and Pearl drew up Ivy's feeding schedule. I promised to sleep over in the house every second night so that Pearl and I could help out with the nocturnal feeds. We all agreed Freddy needed to remain in work.

'If, and when, Social Services come poking their noses into this, as they inevitably will,' Pearl said, showing remarkable good sense, 'you need to prove that you can be a responsible parent.'

During the day, Pearl was happy to take on the main role of Ivy's carer. 'At this age, it's not as if she's in the way, is it?' she said, conveniently forgetting that when Freddy had been that age she'd insisted she couldn't manage without a second, full-time pair of hands.

The weather continued to warm up. The sweet scent of roses and honeysuckle filtered into the stable flat from open doors and windows. Monday came, and quiz night went in a baby blur. The Twitchers would have to manage without me.

'A baby needs fresh air,' Pearl announced on Tuesday morning, strapping Ivy to her chest in her brand-new baby harness. 'Let's take her out for a walk in the grounds.'

'Why don't we take the pram?' I suggested.

Pearl, who had been a modern, progressive mother, was

determined to become a modern, progressive grandmother. 'No, I'll work this thing out if it kills me,' she said, pulling on a strap and nearly ejecting Ivy from her cocoon.

The front lawn was undergoing a make-over in preparation for the imminent nuptials. An area had been cordoned off for the marquee and temporary flooring. We decided to take a walk around the back of the house.

The doors to the study were wide open, a figure bent over the desk.

'Cooee, love, just taking Ivy for a walk,' Pearl called. Her greeting elicited no response. 'Deaf as a post!' she sighed and tried again, striding towards the open doors. 'Jack, love, I'm taking the baby for a walk.'

It wasn't Jack who was in his study, it was JJ. He was sat at Jack's desk looking through the box files.

'What do you think you are doing?' Pearl demanded.

'I could ask you the same question,' JJ replied, hastily closing the nearest box. 'I've far more right to be here than you.'

'Not poking through your father's private papers, you haven't,' Pearl retorted.

'For your information, these papers belonged to my grandfather,' JJ replied. He put the box file back on the shelf. 'There, no damage done, you see.'

'You won't find what you're looking for,' I told him. 'Jack's already looked. And so has Gerald Kimble.'

'You don't know what you are talking about,' JJ sneered. He gave Ivy a disparaging glance. 'I'd heard another member of your family had come crawling out of the woodwork. Is this the little maggot?'

'How dare you refer to my granddaughter as a maggot,' Pearl hissed. 'At least my son can reproduce, which is more than can be said for you. I've heard all about your trips to the fertility clinic.'

I stared at my mother appalled. If JJ and Rita were having fertility problems, this really was not the right time to mention it. JJ's face turned to thunder.

'How dare you,' he snarled. 'If you think for one minute

that this wedding, this fiasco, is going to happen, you've got another think coming. There is no way I am going to let my father marry a poisonous old witch like you. Do you understand? I should have run you over when I had the chance.'

'What do you mean you should have run me over when you had the chance?' Pearl looked appalled.

'It was me,' I explained. 'Last week in the car park at Portdeane. I was wearing your coat.'

'Well, you're just as bad as her,' JJ spat, undeterred. 'You're just a hanger-on. No proper job, no man, and no prospects of either, and that boy, doped up to the eyeballs, lolling around in my boatyard. I can't wait to be shot of the lot of you, and I will, you see. I know people, people who will get rid of people like you, *Mrs Gates*. And that's another thing. I think my father has a right to know what happened to Mr Gates, if he ever existed. Why don't we ever hear about him? What happened to *her* father, or was he another one-night stand?'

My mother puffed up to her full height, just about level with JJ's chest.

'How dare you insult my children,' she said. 'Rebecca is a beautiful, intelligent and talented woman, with a first-class honours degree in Business Studies. She is an excellent PA and a highly respected editor in her own right. As for my son, Freddy, he also has a degree from one of the country's leading academies for the creative arts. As far as I am aware, your only claim to fame is that you once drove a speedboat very fast, and as I've not heard anyone extolling any of your academic achievements, I can only presume that's because you have none.

'And just for your information, your father is fully aware of the circumstances surrounding my first marriage. If you had conducted any research, you would know full well that my husband, Tony Gates, passed away when he was just twenty-seven years old following injuries sustained during a horrific motorbike crash whilst competing in the Isle of Man TT. Subsequently, left on my own with a young child, I managed a successful writing career and have sold millions of books, many of them topping the bestseller lists around the world. Romantic fiction may not be your favourite genre, JJ, but it's very popular amongst the masses. I have made my own fortune and I've managed to keep hold of it, which I think is more than can be said for you.'

JJ placed his hands flat on the desk, leaning forward. 'Did you tell her about the prenup?' he hissed at me.

'Prenup?' Pearl jumped on the word. 'Too right, I'm drawing up a prenup to protect my assets. I don't want you getting a penny of my money. You need to watch your step, young man. Your father is very fond of Freddy and Becca here, very fond. Maybe you need to start showing us a little bit more respect or else I might just drop a few hints into his ear that his hardworking stepchildren might be far more deserving heirs to his empire than a miserable, ungrateful little bastard like you.'

I thought for one moment he was going to strike her, but Pearl swiftly turned away. 'Come, Becca. Let's head for the gardens. There's something very unpleasant in the house right now, and I don't want Baby Ivy anywhere near it.'

There were times when my mother deserved a round of applause. This was the reason why she had made a success of her life, why and how she had pulled herself through the bad times and back into the good. She was industrious, determined, stubborn, and she could give as good as she got. Nobody got the better of Pearl. These were the qualities I admired, and when she exasperated me, irritated me, this was what I had to remember. This was why I loved her.

I struggled to keep up as she stormed off across the back garden towards the shrubbery.

'Goodness me,' she exclaimed when she finally calmed down. She bent and gave Ivy a kiss on the head. 'What a horrid man, Ivy dear, making threats like that. What's this incident in the car park, Becca? You didn't mention anything.'

'That's because it wasn't worth mentioning. He just drove through a big puddle and took great delight in drenching me or you, as I assume he thought I was.'

'Ha, I'm glad it was you not me,' Pearl smiled. 'Well, you know what I mean. You don't think he's serious, though, do you, about *knowing people*? For goodness sake, this is Hampshire, not the East End of London.'

'No,' I assured her, although if Nick was to be believed it was quite possible JJ did have connections with the criminal underworld. But I wasn't going to alarm Pearl by saying so. The car park incident proved JJ had a malicious streak, but I doubted he would really have tried to harm Pearl. 'Are he and Rita seriously having problems trying for a baby?' I asked.

'According to Jack, they are. That's another reason JJ is in a financial mess. You do know he's in a financial mess, don't you?'

I nodded. 'I had heard something.'

'The trouble is, Jack hasn't got the money to bail him out, not any more. He says he's put more than enough into the marina over the years. JJ has managed the whole thing badly, overspent, over-expanded, and of course, he's taken money out of the business for that house, his cars, a speedboat, and now I suppose for IVF.'

Thankfully, Pearl had sought guidance from Roger, our trusted accountant, and the proceeds from the sale of Beech Mews had been deposited into the safest possible investment funds. I was glad she had taken sensible advice, and even gladder she had been able to throw the comment about a prenup back in JJ's face.

We headed on through the shrubbery where the last of the delicate pink rhododendrons' blossoms were falling to the ground on the summer breeze, like confetti.

'Do you know,' Pearl said, blowing a petal from Ivy's head, 'I've never been to this part of the estate before?'

'I think this leads to the old kitchen garden,' I told her, recognising the wall. 'We must be near Heather and Nev's cottage.'

'What do you make of Heather and Nev?' Pearl mused. 'I asked her to make the wedding cake ages ago, but so far I've seen no evidence that she's even started. We've only got a couple of weeks left.'

'Perhaps she wants to keep it a secret from you,' I suggested.

'Perhaps,' Pearl gave a shrug. 'And don't you find Nev a bit creepy?'

'Well yes, I do actually,' I said, 'but I thought you liked them?'

'Oh, I do. I suppose I do, Jack certainly seems very happy with their work.'

'That's not the same as liking them, though, is it?' I pointed out.

We had arrived at a single-storey red brick cottage and the kitchen garden, although there was as much evidence of a flourishing allotment as there was of the wedding cake. It looked as if nothing had been touched in the overgrown beds for years.

'Well, this is a disappointment,' Pearl confessed, looking confused.

'Perhaps the intention was always there, they just never got round to it,' I said, not entirely surprised by the lack of horticultural activity. 'What about the greenhouse? Maybe they've started some plants off in there.'

There were definite signs of life in the greenhouse, and it was a relief to see what looked like a few straggling tomato plants in a grow bag, together with rows of leafy plants in large pots.

I stared at the plants, recognising the foliage with an incredulous sense of dread. No, really? Not here, not at Rivermede in broad daylight, in Jack's greenhouse? It couldn't be. Was this what Nick's surveillance was all about? I gave voice to my fears. 'Mum, I think they're marijuana plants.'

'Oh, don't be silly, even I know that's a tomato.'

'Yes, that's a tomato, but I'm pretty sure this is a cannabis plant.'

Pearl slapped her hand over Ivy's face. 'We can't let her breathe this in,' she hissed. 'We need to get out.'

'It's all right, you can't get high on the plant.'

'Out, Becca, let's get out.'

'No, let me take some pictures.'

'What for? Surely you're not going to put them up on Facebook?'

'Of course not. It's evidence.'

'Oh, we can't involve the police.'

'It's a criminal offence.'

'But what if they're Freddy's?'

'Oh God, I hadn't thought of that.' Freddy had only been at Rivermede for a couple of months, and this whole set-up looked far too established to be his responsibility. I also doubted Fred had the technical knowledge or inclination to cultivate his own cannabis plants, but I couldn't discount the possibility. 'We need to talk to Fred,' I said.

'I'll skin him alive if he's got anything to do with this,' Pearl said, her face grim.

Chapter Twenty-Six

Quite naturally, Freddy denied all knowledge of the set-up in the greenhouse. It was the first time I'd seen him laugh in weeks.

'Naughty Nev,' he chuckled, 'who knew? How's my girl been today?'

We caught him just as he arrived home from work. He didn't exactly greet Ivy with open arms, happy to leave her in mine, but he gave her a tickle, which was a step in the right direction. And I knew that later he would carry out the bedtime routine of bath and bottle, under Pearl's supervision. I realised it was a learning curve, a totally alien learning curve, but Freddy was doing his best.

I left him and Pearl and Ivy to spend their evening together, and retreated to the sanctuary of the flat for a few hours. I would return to the house later for night duty. Within minutes of sitting on the sofa, I nodded off. When I awoke, it was seven and I was starving hungry and my fridge was bare.

I needed food. I didn't want to visit The Ship, in case Stella asked how work was progressing, nor did I want to hop in the car and head to Portdeane Tesco. Instead, I decided to walk to the Jolly Jack Tar, which did a trendy line in gourmet burgers and fish tacos. Being a warm, sunny evening, the Jolly Jack was packed. All the tables were taken with at least a half-hour wait. I added my name to the list for a table for one, then set off along the riverside path towards Chapman's Wharf. The lure was too strong.

I found Nick on his deck. He didn't appear to be doing any surveillance work; instead, he was grilling sausages on a BBQ.

He beckoned me on board. 'How did you know I was cooking?' he asked with an easy laugh. 'Want to join me? I can easily get another couple of sausages out of the fridge.'

'You don't have to,' I said at once. 'I was going to eat at the Jolly Jack Tar.'

'Oh, don't be daft,' he said. 'Now that you're here, you might as well stay. Anyway, I wanted to see you.'

'You did?'

'Yeh, you didn't come quizzing.'

'Were you disappointed?' I asked.

'Extremely,' he replied. 'Even more so Chrissie and Craig. We had a whole round on continental cheeses. It would have been right up your street.'

When he returned with the sausages, and a bottle of wine, I explained about Ruby.

'Sounds like a right mess,' he remarked.

'It is,' I agreed. 'But Ivy is an adorable baby. What else could we do?'

He gave a tense shrug. 'Of course.'

I'd hit his sensitive spot. Family duty. The edge of a tattoo was just visible on Nick's right arm, beneath the short sleeve of his T-shirt. That hadn't been there fifteen years ago. Nor had the muscles or the tan. The outdoor life obviously suited Nick, or perhaps it was the overseas travel. He caught me looking.

'It's a Yorkshire Rose,' he said.

'Very nice,' I replied. 'Is that your only one?'

He pulled his sleeve down as if he was embarrassed. 'Got drunk one night,' he said. 'Have you got any?'

I shook my head. 'No, I've never been that drunk. Freddy's getting quite a collection, though.' I looked around at the scene. 'You're in a lovely spot here,' I remarked.

Across the water, the sun was just beginning to dip into the sky behind Portdeane. Inland, Nick had a view straight across the marsh towards a large grey house, which could just possibly have been the van der Plaast mansion, although Max's New England-style of house wasn't unique in this affluent location. Perhaps it was the millionaire bookmaker's, or the dodgy stockbroker's; any member of Kerridge's criminal fraternity. Even Aidan apparently had a 'past'. Perhaps Nick was observing him.

'I wanted to let you know I found that bloke you asked me to look for,' Nick said, turning the sausages over. 'Tristram Markham.'

'Oh? Thank you.' I had almost forgotten I'd asked. 'Where is he?'

'Still on the Isle of Wight. Parkhurst Prison.'

'He's in prison?' Poor Stella. My one hope of a happy ending – gone.

'He's the Deputy Governor.'

'Ah. That's interesting.'

'Is it?' Nick asked. He came and sat beside me. 'What is he to you?'

I gave him a brief run-down of my attempts to write Stella's story. 'I just thought that maybe if I could get the hold of the children, include their viewpoint, arrange a reunion maybe, it might make the whole thing more appealing.'

'So you want to speak to him?'

'Ideally, yes, but to be honest the book's taking a bit of a back seat right now.'

'Well, you know where he is. If there's anything else I can help you with, just ask.'

'Okay,' I got out my phone and showed him the pictures of the plants in Jack's greenhouse. 'What are these?'

'I think you know what those are, Rebecca.'

'Is that why you're here?' I asked. 'Is that why you're in Kerridge? JJ is farming marijuana. Is that why you've been warning us away from Rivermede?'

Nick's laugh was on par with Freddy's. 'If only,' he said. 'You think I'd be going to all these lengths to hide out here for a couple of pot plants?'

The wine had gone straight to my head. Sitting here on the deck of *The Solstice* was the most relaxed I'd felt in days. I joined him with a seductive giggle. 'Ha-ha, I get it, pot plants. You're so funny, Nick.' I gave him a playful punch in the arm. He didn't look amused. 'Is JJ really the head of a drug cartel?' I asked, warming to my theme and seizing the chance to off-load. 'Goodness knows, he needs money. He could be moving the stuff up and down the river. He's got that flashy speedboat.

He threatened Pearl and I, saying he knew people who could get rid of us. Should we be worried?'

Nick shook his head. 'I doubt JJ would have the guts to put out a contract for your mother's murder, tempting though the idea might be.'

'I'm not sure if that's reassuring or not,' I smiled.

'You know I don't like you being at Rivermede, full stop.'

'So you keep saying.'

I leaned back on the deck, enjoying the warmth of the evening sun and the close proximity of his body. I didn't want to dwell on what Nick was really doing here in Kerridge. He was here, and we were talking, sharing a joke, acting like old friends, casual and without any animosity. That was enough; it was more than enough.

Our arms touched as he stretched out beside me. For a moment, I thought he was going to reach out and kiss me. He turned his face, our eyes met, searching each other for the clues. *Could we, should we…*

A plume of smoke rose from the BBQ. Nick to jumped to his feet. 'Christ, I could have set the whole bloody boat on fire,' he said, flapping the smoke away. 'I hope you like your sausages well done.'

We ate in a comfortable, familiar silence, the silence of people who've known each other for a long time and don't need to make conversation to enjoy each other's company.

'Tell me about Saskia,' I said eventually, when the food was all finished and I'd helped him clear the dirty plates into *The Solstice*'s tidy galley kitchen. The boat's interior was tastefully but sparsely furnished. Nick's laptop and photographic equipment were laid out on a small table, together with a strategically-placed book on coastal birds. 'I was prepared to forgive you, but then you turned around and threw that forgiveness into my face,' I said. 'Why did you do that? Why wait until I was there at the altar?'

'It was Freddy,' he said after a pause. 'I couldn't cope with the idea of Freddy coming to live with us.'

'I don't understand,' I said. 'I don't understand whatever gave you the idea that he would? Do you not think I would

198

have said, I would have told you something as momentous as that?'

'No,' Nick admitted. 'Perhaps now I do, but not then. I was young, stupid, I suppose. I believed her. I had no reason not to believe her.'

'You mean it was Saskia? Saskia told you Freddy was mine?'

Nick nodded. 'Yes. Who else? She said you'd been seeing this boy at school, and then you left without any warning. Then the next minute you were sending her pictures of your baby brother. Why wouldn't I believe her?'

'I left the school because Pearl couldn't pay the fees. You know what kids are like, I was embarrassed. Why didn't you talk to me? If you suspected I was Freddy's mother, why didn't you ask me?'

'I suppose I was scared of the answer.'

'And if he had been mine? Why was that such a big problem?'

'In my job, I could have been sent anywhere, to do anything, you know that. I explained all that when I proposed. I'd got that promotion, I was going to be working on some pretty tough cases.'

'I agree it was hardly the most romantic proposal ever. If I remember rightly, you suggested we should get married so that I didn't miss out on a guaranteed lump sum insurance payout and the full police pension, if anything happened to you on the job.'

'But you still said yes,' Nick reminded me with a smile. 'I was just being practical. I was genuinely worried. What if anything did happen to me? Suddenly it wasn't just you I had responsibility for, it was a six-year-old as well. Or at least, that's what I told myself. I convinced myself, stupidly, that you and Freddy would be better off without me, without the worry and the danger. I didn't want to put you both through it.'

'So, you were being noble?'

'It's what I told myself at the time. On reflection, I was probably being incredibly selfish. The truth is, Becs, I wasn't sure I was ready to take on a child.'

'And naturally, having planted the idea in your head that you shouldn't get married, Saskia was there to pick up the pieces?'

'Yes,' Nick admitted.

Had Saskia really believed Freddie was my child, or had she made up the whole thing to lure Nick away? Saskia had been the one few school friends I'd confided in about my recall to London. I'd confessed to a family emergency, and I could remember forcing her to swear to secrecy, but I certainly hadn't mentioned any pregnancy. I was more worried about the shameful implications of the unpaid school fees amongst my wealthy classmates.

'It seemed as if our life together would just be too complicated,' Nick said. 'I was confused, and Saskia seemed to offer a way out. It was a stupid, cowardly thing to do, and I'm sorry. Truly sorry.'

I believed him. There was something about this new Nick that was very different from the old. He seemed vulnerable, less sure of himself, less invincible.

'I never slept with her,' he said, 'not before the wedding. I never betrayed you, Rebecca.'

I'd been jilted for a bitter misunderstanding. Saskia had broken her promise but exposed the wrong secret.

'We should have talked,' I said.

'Yes,' he agreed. 'Instead, we both went off on a tangent, and now, by some strange, bizarre coincidence, we're here.'

Orange and purple ribbons streaked the sky above Portdeane. Soon it would be dark.

We both spoke at the same time.

'I should be getting back,' I said.

'Stay,' said Nick.

Chapter Twenty-Seven

There was that look on his face again as he searched for the answers he wanted, the answers I wanted to give him. Were we reading the same signals? Were we on the brink of something quite momentous?

The dilemma of wanting something you know you can't have. 'Oh Nick,' I sighed. 'I can't. You know I can't. I have to get back. I'm on night duty, the baby.'

It was the repeating pattern of our relationship. How many times had I said it before on broken dates? I *had to get back.* I had to collect Freddy, from nursery, from school, from a friend's, to babysit while Pearl went on a book promo or a business meeting. The whole reason it hadn't worked out before. Fifteen years later, and the cycle continued.

'Yes, of course. I'll walk you home.' The emotionally charged 'stay' had been replaced with stilted politeness. His whole demeanour had changed.

'Look, it's not that I don't want to stay,' I began, trying to recapture the intimacy of the moment. But it had gone, drifted away on the ebb of the tide.

'Don't make it worse, Becs,' Nick said.

I didn't know what to do. It was the same old story and I was totally torn in two. How could I convey how much I wanted him? Surely I could stay an extra ten, fifteen minutes?

He didn't give me a chance. 'Come on, let's go now,' he said, jumping to his feet, 'before it's too late.'

It was already too late.

A shiny new moon was high in the sky. I was worried about losing my footing on the rough track through the reeds, but Nick led the way, using his torch every now and then to highlight a particularly narrow section of path. We had just skirted around the marina and entered the wooded copse by

Rivermede creek, when Nick came to an abrupt halt, grabbing me and pulling me behind a massive knotted trunk of an oak tree.

'Shush!' he said, clamping his hand over my mouth.

I hadn't heard a thing. I strained my ears, listening. When I'd first arrived at Rivermede, the nocturnal silence had alarmed me. I was used to living in the city, lulled to sleep by the murmur of traffic and late-night revellers. Kerridge had been deathly quiet. Now, I recognised familiar animal noises, a fox, a fluttering bat, a swooping owl, the distant whirr of a ship's engine way out in the Solent, the soft swish of an oar on the water.

A two-man canoe glided along the creek towards the main body of the river. Through the darkness, I could make out the barest details of bulk and size of the rowers. We stayed completely still, Nick's arms tightly around me. He smelt of smoke from the BBQ, of beer, of wine, warm and comforting. The urge to kiss him was unbearable, irresistible. I tried a tentative brushing of his lips and sensed a weakening, but he broke away. I'd lost him.

'Don't, Rebecca,' he hissed.

The canoeists had passed. I willed him to stay close to me, wondering how I could keep his attention. 'Was that Nev?' I asked, as we set off once again through the trees. 'Was he with his double? Van der Plaast has a bodyguard who looks just like him.'

'That's because they're brothers,' Nick replied, keeping his voice low. 'Brian and Neville Muzzlewhite. Brian has worked for van der Plaast for years.'

'The Brothers Grimm,' I remarked.

'They're dangerous guys.'

'So, is Nev working for van der Plaast, too? Is he a mole in the underground workings at Rivermede?'

'Will you stop being so bloody facetious and just take me seriously for once?' Nick came to a halt. 'Max van der Plaast is not a nice man, nor are the Muzzlewhites. They're mixed up in some highly illegal activities. I've tried to warn you, but no, you're Becca-bloody-Gates and you always know best.'

'I'm sorry,' I said, duly chastised. Nick and I had been getting on so well and I'd gone and spoilt it again. 'What is it? Money laundering? Drugs?'

'All I can say is that it's a bit more serious than a couple of marijuana plants,' Nick replied.

'Is JJ involved?' I asked.

'Yes, although I'd say he is complicit, as opposed to proactively involved. I really can't divulge any more information, Becca. Look.' Nick heaved a huge sigh. 'Yes, it's drugs, okay? And something big is about to happen. I can't go into any details, but we've been monitoring this stretch of coastline for some time now. We've got people on the inside of this operation and we know a major shipment is on its way within the next couple of weeks. I am only a very small part of a very large international team, but worst-case scenario, there could be trouble, things could get violent. Do you get the message? The best thing you can do is to get yourself and your family away from Rivermede. At least then, I know you would all be safe.'

'A couple of weeks' time?' I hesitated. 'But Pearl and Jack are getting married in a couple of weeks' time. We can't leave. I know she is planning some sort of honeymoon afterwards, and I suppose I could possibly take Freddy and Ivy away somewhere at the same time, but we can't go before then. There's no way my mother would leave, and I couldn't possibly ask her to postpone her wedding. She's got half of Kerridge coming to this do, plus a flock of doves, a parliament of owls, and don't get me started on the torchlit sailing flotilla and firework display.'

'What?' Nick looked genuinely horrified.

'It's a massive do, Nick. The whole thing is horrendous. She's got an owl delivering the ring; there's going to be an impromptu concert by a cappella choir; there's a jazz band for the evening reception; and now she's organising this sailing flotilla and firework display. There's going to be a whole fleet of boats out on the river come nightfall. She wants to emulate the days of the old regattas.'

'You're joking, right?'

'Sadly not. I'm being totally serious. She's going for the full works.'

'What date is the wedding?' Nick asked.

'Midsummer's night, 21st June. You're invited by the way, for the evening do. Come along any time after seven. It's going to be one big party.'

'Oh God, that's brilliant,' Nick said. 'It's the perfect cover. Are you serious about this sailing flotilla?'

'Unfortunately, yes. I wish I wasn't.'

'It's bloody marvellous.' Nick looked positively animated. 'Who came up with that plan?'

'I've no idea. Nick, what do I do?'

'Nothing.' Nick said. He placed both hands on my arms. 'You can't do anything. You mustn't do anything. It's got to go ahead. This is it.'

'But you've just said we are all in danger. Five minutes ago, you were telling me to get away from Rivermede, now you want me to stay.'

'Rebecca, I'm sorry. I will protect you as much as I can. You know I will. I would protect you and your family with my life, if I had to. You're just going to have to trust me on this.'

Again, that dirty word. *Trust Nick.*

And then, still gripping my arms, he planted a huge kiss on my lips, taking me totally by surprise. 'I love you, Rebecca,' he said. 'I really, really love you. When this is all over, we'll work something out. I promise you.'

Nick couldn't get me back to Rivermede quickly enough. There were no further kisses, just a pledge to stay in touch, leaving me reeling in confusion. What did he mean he loved me? Did he mean he *really loved me*? Or did he mean he loved me because I'd given him a lead in the case he was working on? My head was swimming.

Pearl was pacing the hallway, anxiously waiting for my return. My excuse of slow service at the Jolly Jack Tar didn't fool her one bit.

'You smell like a bonfire,' she remarked.

Baby Ivy wasn't the only one who was restless. I always

slept badly in the uncomfortable single bed in the tiny bedroom Pearl and I used when we were on night duty, one ear alert. I spent most of the night awake, mulling over everything Nick had said.

I couldn't quite believe Pearl could have mixed herself up in such a mess. I'd sensed an air of menace about van der Plaast from the start. It wasn't hard to imagine him as some sort of international criminal. His company had offices across Europe, he had numerous homes, ex-wives, and a fancy yacht. A legitimate business was the perfect cover for his illegal operations, whatever they were. I knew Nev and Heather were not all they seemed. They were all in cahoots. I'd learned from my friend Maurice that the river had always been used for smuggling, and Rivermede was ideally placed not too far from the estuary and with its own creek and private mooring at JJ's boathouse.

Why couldn't Nick give me more clues? '*Something big*' he had intimated, but that could mean anything. *Violence*. By whom? Max? JJ? Were any other of Freddy's marina colleagues aware of what was going on? What if Freddy *was* involved in some, purely innocent capacity? Of all the men Pearl could have met on her cruise, why had she fallen for Jack Robshaw? But of course, if she hadn't, I'd never have run into Nick again. He had stressed the need to do nothing, to carry on as normal. But nothing was normal at Rivermede.

Chapter Twenty-Eight

The next morning, I ascertained from Pearl that Pete from the yacht club was responsible for organising the torchlight flotilla. The local sea scouts were being roped in to help out.

'You mean there will be children, in the dark, on the water?'

'They're not children, they're teenagers – thirteen, fourteen-year-olds,' Pearl assured me. 'Pete's got it all in hand. They're all experienced sailors. It'll be a wonderful spectacle. I can't wait to see your Aunt Phoebe's face.'

I wondered what Aunt Phoebe's face would look like when she realised she was in the middle of a police raid on an international drug smuggling gang? As for Pearl, I didn't even want to think about how she was going to react.

'Why are you looking at me like that?' she snapped. 'I know you don't approve of any of this, but you could at least pretend to be happy for me.'

'Oh Mum,' I gave her tight warm hug. 'I am happy for you. I so want you to enjoy your day.'

A feat which now seemed an impossibility.

I was due to babysit Norah Morland that afternoon. In the morning, I composed a letter to the Deputy Governor of Parkhurst Prison, introducing myself and giving brief details of my book proposal. I gave him my contact details without putting any pressure on him to respond. I decided to send the letter by post, as opposed to email, hoping this would convey my respect for the delicacy of the situation and confidentiality of his position. What I didn't have was a stamp. Neither did Pearl.

'But you always have stamps,' I complained.

She tapped her laptop. 'Who uses stamps these days?' she

replied. 'I used up my last supply on the wedding invitations. Jack might have some.'

Ivy was snoozing in her baby bouncer while Pippadee slept on Pearl's knee. Jack, still more crotchety than usual, was doing his crossword puzzle.

'I might have some in my desk drawer,' he said, without looking up. 'You're more than welcome to have a look.'

I didn't want to snoop, but it was obvious Jack had been sorting through his paperwork again because there were yet more piles of old files on his desk. If a copy of Gerry's legal document had been retained anywhere at Rivermede, surely it would be amongst Mary's personal effects, as opposed to her father's old office papers? I wondered what had happened to Mary's possessions when she died. Were they still in one of the upstairs bedrooms, or boxed-up in an outhouse? Or had everything been thrown away? In which case, there was no hope for Gerry.

I found some loose stamps in the drawer alongside a set of keys. Jack was an organised man. The keys were each attached to clearly-marked plastic fobs – *stable block, JJ's front door, garage, main gate, river gate*, *boathouse. The opportunity was too good to miss. I disengaged the key to the boathouse and slipped it into my pocket.

I wasn't expected at Norah's until two, so there was plenty of time to carry out a recce. After a quick sandwich, I headed straight down to the river, taking a ridiculous amount of time to continually check I wasn't being followed. Although I knew Pearl and Jack were tucked away indoors, I'd no idea what Hev and Nev were up to, and there was always a risk Max van der Plaast could be on the prowl.

Despite skirting through the trees and tiptoeing into the clearing by the boathouse, I needn't have worried. Rivermede's grounds were deserted and there was no whiff of Max's pungent cigarettes in the air. The key fitted the padlock, and I opened one side of the double doors a crack to peer inside. I wasn't sure what I was expecting to see, but it certainly wasn't canoes.

The boats were stacked on racks while lifejackets and oars hung from brackets on the wall. Although six canoes were an awful lot for a man who said he'd given up rowing, I had to assume JJ had lied not because he was hiding a secret stash of contraband, but simply because he was being obnoxious and didn't want me anywhere near his property. As for Nick's advice to stay away, he was probably just being overly cautious, and once again I found myself thrown into doubt about the validity of his warnings.

Perhaps I could take up rowing, after all, although it was far too late now to have any hope of shifting those extra few pounds before the wedding.

I posted my letter to Tristram Markham in the post-box at the top of Clay Kiln Lane. As Judy Stevenson had predicted, Norah Morland, now in her nineties, had no idea who I was but she seemed fairly pleased to see me. She was propped in an armchair in her living room, enjoying an episode of a day-time relocation show on her TV, one arm in a sling and evidence of bruising healing on her face.

I was informed by my departing Good Neighbour counterpart that I would be relieved at four-thirty by the carers, who would come in to give Mrs Morland her tea and then get her ready for bed.

As Mrs Morland was trapped in a world of her own, I decided I could be as bold and as devious as I liked.

'Who is this, Norah?' I asked in a loud voice, pointing to one of the many pictures of Mary Dimmock that adorned the walls. 'She's a pretty girl.'

Norah nodded, her attention immediately diverted from the couple scouring the Somerset countryside for their ideal retirement home. 'That's my Mary,' she smiled.

'Is she your daughter?'

'Oh yes,' Norah nodded. 'That's my Mary.'

'She was married to Jack Robshaw, wasn't she?' I said. 'Were they happy?'

Norah frowned, then with her good arm, struggled to reach for the TV remote on the side table next to her. 'Turn that thing down,' she ordered. 'I can't hear you.'

I switched the sound off completely and added sub-titles before repeating my question. 'She was married to Jack Robshaw, wasn't she? Were they happy?'

Norah scowled at the very mention of Jack's name. 'No,' she said. 'She shouldn't have married him. I told her not to. I said, *Mary, just because your father wants you to marry that man, you don't have to.* Jack Robshaw was a bully, just like Ray, although of course Ray was still grieving. He'd lost Kenny and he blamed himself.'

'Oh yes, the accident in the boatyard. Dreadful. Do you have pictures of Kenny, too?'

'Oh yes,' Norah said. 'He was my little boy.' She raised her good arm again, this time pointing towards the sideboard. 'Take a look in there. I kept all my photo albums.'

It was impossible to know where to start.

'I don't suppose you remember Gerald Kimble, Mrs Morland?' I asked, lifting a stack of albums onto the floor. Norah had collected enough photographs of Kerridge to mount her own local history exhibition.

'Oh yes, he was cheeky little boy,' Norah said with another vague smile. 'Could always make you laugh.'

'He was apprenticed at Dimmocks, wasn't he?' I prompted. 'Back in the day.'

Norah gestured for me to pass her one of the photo albums from the top of the pile. 'That blue one,' she said. 'This is my favourite. Isn't she a proper darling?'

The album was well-thumbed. I pulled up a chair and sat beside Norah as she studied each of the pages.

'She'd have been about sixteen here,' Norah said, 'just left school and working in the offices at the yard. They didn't need a nanny any more, but I stayed on to help around the house.'

'What happened to Ray Dimmock's wife?' I asked.

'She died of TB,' Norah said. 'Mary was no more than five or six and Kenny a few years older. I'd been with the family since Kenny was a baby. Here, see this one, dressed up for the yacht club summer ball, she was.'

'She looks stunning,' I agreed. 'Who's that young man with

her? That's not Kenny, is it?' Neither did it look like Jack Robshaw.

'That's him,' Norah Morland said. 'That's Gerald Kimble. She would have probably married him, if it hadn't been for that accident that took Kenny. If that hadn't happened, there'd have been no need for Jack Robshaw to step in and make himself indispensable.'

Dear Norah. I could have hugged her. After the disappointment of the boathouse, I was so glad my instincts had been proved right. 'So, Mary and Gerry were seeing each other, courting?'

'Oh yes,' Norah said, flicking through some more pages in the photo album. Her eyes had filled with tears. 'She always loved Gerry.'

'And is that why Mary's father gave Gerry Kimble the rights to the mooring?' I asked. 'To make up for Mary marrying Jack Robshaw?'

Norah shook her head. 'Kimbles had always kept on a boat on that mooring,' she said. 'But it was Mary who made it legal, so that he would always be close to his son.'

'His son?' I stared at her. 'Gerry Kimble has a son?'

'Oh yes,' Norah said, swinging the photo album around to show me a picture of Mary Dimmock holding a bouncing baby. 'It was Gerry Kimble's, not Jack's. Mary told me that long ago. Of course, I kept her secret for her. I never told anyone. Jack would have killed her if he knew; her father probably, too. What else could I do? She was my little girl.'

Jack Junior was Gerry Kimble's son. Not only did Norah Morland have several photographs to prove it, and the resemblance between JJ to the young Gerry was unmistakeable, but she also had the deeds Mary had entrusted to her that gave Gerry rights to his mooring for life.

'Mary told me to keep it somewhere safe,' Norah said. 'So, I kept it with the family bible. Nobody's ever asked to see it before.'

I decided, in the light of her revelation, that the family bible was probably the best hiding place for the document to remain.

I took a photograph on my phone.

I suspected Jack knew he was not JJ's father, and I doubted Kimble's threats of an exposé that afternoon in the study were his first. He had been clinging onto his mooring against a tide of opposition for some time, but he'd always have Jack over a barrel. I was convinced if Jack knew the paperwork existed, he would happily share it with JJ, although of course, without explaining the reasoning. The last thing he would want was for JJ to know the truth. But without seeing the evidence, JJ would continue to persecute Gerry.

Norah dozed off when house-buying gravitated into selling antiques, and I spent a relatively pleasant hour immersed in the past. It was only as I came across pictures from Deane River regattas of long ago, including grainy shots of torch lit sailing flotillas, that I was forced to make an unhappy return to the present.

What was I going to do about Pearl's wedding? The satisfaction of being able to prove that Gerald Kimble did have a legal right to remain a thorn in JJ's side was overshadowed by an impending sense of doom. When the two tea-time carers came at four-thirty, I had no desire at all to return to Rivermede.

Chapter Twenty-Nine

I didn't know where I wanted to go when I left Norah Morland's bungalow, although in reality I did. There was only one place I wanted to be and only one person I wanted to be with.

To my immense disappointment, *The Solstice* was deserted. More worryingly, even the wellington boots had gone from outside the door, although there was every possibility that Nick was out somewhere on the marsh, conducting surveillance.

As I walked back through the marina, I saw Freddy sweeping excess hose water into a drainage gulley. The pert figure of Kimmi van der Plaast perched nearby on an empty boat trolley. The rest of the workforce looked as if they had packed away for the day.

'That's good timing,' Fred said, looking up. 'I was just about to call you. I'm going to be late home.'

'But you look like you're finishing up here,' I pointed out.

He reached into his pocket and jangled a keyring at me. 'I've been given the special privilege of parking up *The Caprice* for JJ. He took her out for a spin earlier and couldn't be bothered to put her back into her berth. He was basically showing off to a potential customer, pretending Robshaw Marina provides a valet parking service.'

I wondered if JJ was aware Freddy only had a provisional licence? He shouldn't be left in charge of parking anything, on land or in the water. '*The Caprice*?'

'The *Aqua Riva*,' Freddy said with a grin. 'Come, I'll show you.' I couldn't believe Freddy had been entrusted with JJ's pride and joy. Kimmi followed us down onto one of the pontoons, where the glossy wooden speedboat was moored amongst the gleaming white fibreglass hulls of pristine yachts and motor-cruisers. The boat did indeed look as if it had just motored in from the Riviera with Sophia Loren reclining on its white leather seats. 'Fastest thing on the river, this is,' Freddy said, somewhat proudly.

'It looks very smart,' I admitted. 'Does JJ know what he's doing letting you loose in that?'

''Course he does,' Freddy looked indignant. 'I've only got to move it twenty metres.'

'And when he's done, we're heading over to Portdeane for a drink at the Runners,' Kimmi informed me. 'Isn't that right, Freddy?'

I wondered how much Kimmi knew about the Ivy situation. Kimmi's name had been cropping up a lot less in conversations, but she was obviously still very much on the scene.

'Will your dad be over in Portdeane, Kimmi?' I asked. I didn't want Freddy anywhere near van der Plaast, although it seemed hard to imagine Kimmi herself was involved in any of her father's dubious activities.

'Papa's out of the country for a few days,' she said, pouting provocatively at Freddy. 'I'm all on my own.'

Van der Plaast was away, Nick was away. Coincidence? Unlikely.

'Okay, well don't be too late,' I said to Freddy.

'Sure. I'll be home by eight,' he promised. I was about to say something about that being too late for bath and bed, but Freddy shot me such a pleading look that I didn't. It was impossible to miss Kimmi's gripe as I walked away.

'Why do you let her boss you around so much? She's not your mother, is she?'

I was left with the horrible suspicion that Freddy may not have mentioned Ivy to her at all.

He rolled home at half-eleven. I would leave the admonishment to Pearl. I'd had enough of all of them – of Pearl, of Freddy, although not Ivy; she was the innocent party in all of this. I was fed up of Jack and JJ, Gerry Kimble, van der Plaast and Rivermede, fed up of lies and secrets. I wanted to be gone. I wanted to be the one escaping out of the country for a few days. I longed for a holiday, to sit on a beach and think of nothing, to read a book, to drink cocktails, to swim in the warm sea and not feel like I was drowning under a dead weight of responsibility.

Why did it always come back to me? Why was I the sensible one who had to keep a check on Pearl, to monitor Freddy? Now Nick had added to the burden by dumping this huge responsibility on me to ensure the wedding went ahead without a hitch. Did he not realise the risk he was putting us, me, all under? I now had the additional task of protecting twenty teenagers from Kerridge sea scouts from imminent danger. Why should it all fall on me?

Why on earth was Pearl insisting on this stupid sailing flotilla idea anyway? When had she ever had an affinity to the sea? This had to be Pete's idea. Stupid Pete from the stupid yacht club, and he deserved to be shot, or even worse hung, drawn, and quartered, or strung up from the mizzen mast or some other nautical term, cast overboard with several hundredweight of stones in his pockets.

'Mum, what do you know about Pete?'

'Pete who, dear?'

I was on my way into the house to take charge of Ivy for the day, and Pearl was off for her final dress-fitting. I'd already had mine. Both Vera and I were resigned to the fact that those last few extra pounds were not going to come off.

'Yacht club Pete, the one who suggested you should have this flotilla light show thing for your wedding.'

'What do you mean what do I know about him? He's Natalie's husband.'

'Do they live here in Kerridge?'

'Yes, you know they do. Natalie is best friends with Rita. Why are you asking me all these questions, Becca? What's come over you?' She was waiting for Nev to reverse the Range Rover out of the garage.

'Is it safe, this flotilla thing he's organising for you?'

'Of course it is. Ask Jack. Jack knows him better than me.

Oh, by the way, Jack was asking after Norah. How did you get on yesterday afternoon?'

'Norah's fine,' I snapped, and stormed into the house to interrogate Jack. I'd had enough.

'Pete Wendle? The harbourmaster? What do you want to know about him for?' Jack said, looking up from his crossword. Ivy was in her baby bouncer beside him.

'It's this flotilla thing,' I said. 'Are you sure it's going to be safe?'

Jack laughed. 'Of course it's safe. Pete's got it all under control. He used to organise it back in the day when we had a regatta. You've met him, haven't you? You should go down and see the yacht he's doing up at Helme Point. Wonderful old girl. Of course he knows what he's doing. He's got years of experience.'

'You say he's a harbourmaster? What does that entail?'

'Not much in a little place like this. Just has to keep an eye on things on the water, logs everyone in and out of the estuary, makes sure we all stick to the regulations on the river and obey maritime safety rules. Perfect chap to organise the flotilla.'

My mind should have been put at rest, but of course it wasn't. Why was Pete taking such an interest in my mother's wedding arrangements?

I pulled up a chair. There was no pleasant way of doing this, and I had to offload at least some of my responsibilities before I cracked under the weight.

'Jack, I went to see Norah Morland yesterday.'

'Oh yes, Pearl mentioned it. How was she?' He put his crossword to one side.

'Recovering, slowly.' I took a deep breath. 'The thing is, she told me quite a lot about the history of Rivermede, and about Mary and her brother as they were growing up.'

Jack paused. 'Ah. I see. You do know that Norah is confused a lot of the time, doesn't know what day of the week it is, or what year we're in, or who we are.'

'Yes,' I said. 'I realised that, but it was very interesting, listening to her.'

'I'm sure it was.' Jack's smile was quite forced.

I retrieved my phone and found the relevant picture. 'The thing is, I also found this.'

Jack took my phone for a closer inspection. It took a few moments for the implications of the picture to register. His shoulders sagged a little. 'Ah, I see. I should have guessed. Not that Norah would have told me. There wasn't a great deal of love lost there.'

'She was devoted to Mary,' I pointed out.

Jack nodded. 'Yes, she was. Mary had many qualities. It was very easy to become devoted to her.' His grey eyes looked sad and tired. 'So, what are you intending to do with this, young lady?'

'That's up to you, isn't it?' I said. 'You know Gerry has a right to stay where he is, and JJ needs to stop this campaign to have him moved on. You've always known this paperwork existed, haven't you?'

Jack pushed his crossword to one side and rubbed his temple. 'You're a clever girl, Becca, and I think we understand each other. I don't need to see the original document, it's probably best to keep it where it is, but perhaps you could send me a picture. I'll have to have some evidence to show JJ.'

'Of course,' I said.

Ivy gurgled and wriggled. Her eyes opened and then squeezed shut again. I picked her up and placed her on my shoulder, rubbing her back for comfort.

'She's a dear little thing,' Jack said. 'Babies always bring such joy. It doesn't really matter where they're from, or who they belong to. They just worm their way into your hearts and you love them, whatever.'

His eyes were moist with emotion. I had a feeling he wasn't thinking about Ivy at all.

Chapter Thirty

I paid two more visits to *The Solstice* and there was still no sign of Nick. Freddy stayed out two nights in quick succession with Kimmi van der Plaast. I was at my wits' end. The marquee arrived. The table and chairs were delivered. Vera dropped off the dresses, including a version of mine in miniature for Ivy, together with matching frilly knickers. Where was Ivy in the seating plan? Who was going to be responsible for her throughout the day? Had Pearl given this any thought at all?

'Don't be daft, of course I have,' she bristled. 'Phoebe will look after her.'

Phoebe was unmarried and childless, with even less maternal instinct than Pearl.

An evening escape to the quiz with the Twitchers provided a welcome distraction, although the wedding at Rivermede was the main topic of conversation. Halfway through the evening, Nick walked through the door. My heart gave such a lurch I physically jumped from my seat. I could have cried with relief.

He made a big show of putting his jacket on the back of his chair so that he could bend his head close to mine to speak. 'Are you okay?' he whispered.

'No,' I whispered back. 'I'm going crazy.'

'I have the perfect cure for craziness,' he promised. 'Don't rush off when the quiz ends.'

I had no intention of rushing off anywhere. I really was going crazy. Throughout the evening, our legs touched under the table, he brushed his hand occasionally across mine, innocent physical touches which sent pulses of electricity surging through my body.

We lost the quiz to the close rivals, the Bloodhounds, much

to Chrissie's disgust, but as the regulars began to filter out of the pub, I received lots of good wishes for the happy couple and several shouts of '*see you on Saturday*'. It seemed as if the entire population of the Kerridge really would be at Rivermede on Saturday evening. My mother had made herself very popular, or was the lure of a free party too good for anyone to miss?

'Oh Nick,' I sighed, when we were at last alone in the car park. 'I'm so glad to see you.'

'I never thought I'd hear you say that again,' he smiled, a gorgeous, old familiar Nick smile, despite the beard and untidy hair and the unfamiliar casual clothes. 'What's brought all this on?'

I wanted to say it was the look on his face when he saw me in the pub, when I watched him searching through the crowded bar, seeking me out. *That* was the look my mother had told me I would see on his face at the altar. It was his touch, his tenderness, his everything. It was just being with him and knowing that he wanted to be with me.

'Stress,' I said.

'Don't be stressed,' he said. 'I'm here now.'

It was the most natural thing in the world to fall into an embrace. The tension had been mounting all evening. He held me close, and then he kissed the top of my head, and then I lifted my face to his and our mouths met. I soaked him up, wanting that kiss to last forever, feeling so safe in his arms. Finally, breathlessly, he released me.

'I wish you hadn't headed off so quickly the other evening,' I said. 'I'm going completely mad with worry. I don't think I can do this.'

'You don't have to do anything,' he told me. 'Just carry on as normal. Tell me more about this wedding. What time is the ceremony?'

'Registry office in Southampton at 11am, then lunch in town, some restaurant or other. It's just Jack and Mum, JJ, Rita, me and Freddy, the baby, and my aunt Phoebe and Uncle Laurie.'

'You called her *Mum*. I don't ever recall you calling her

anything but Pearl,' Nick interrupted.

I shook my head. 'It keeps slipping out. She doesn't seem to mind.'

'Really?'

I shook my head. 'I can't really explain it. It's like I didn't used to be able to distinguish between Pearl the writer and Pearl the mother, but now I can. We seem to have grown a lot closer, even though she infuriates me and has done me out of my job, and my home—'

'But brought you here,' Nick pointed out. 'To me.'

'Yes well, she doesn't know that bit yet, does she?' I smiled. 'You're just Alex the Twitcher, the loner from the pub.'

'Yeah well, to be honest I'll be quite glad to see the back of him,' Nick said, fingering his beard. 'So then what, what happens after the ceremony?'

'Rivermede for the vow and ring ceremony at 4pm. Guests have been told to arrive from 3.30 onwards. Then there's the buffet, dancing, and of course, once it gets dark, the boat parade and the fireworks. Can't you at least tell me what to expect?'

'We don't know what to expect,' Nick said. 'We don't even know if it's going to happen, okay? So just try and relax.'

'Help me relax,' I said, seizing hold of him again, 'come to Rivermede with me, Nick, and help me relax.'

'Are you being serious?'

I broke off again. 'I don't know.'

'Listen, Becs, I'm more than happy to come back to Rivermede and have sex with you, in fact there's nothing I'd like more, but...'

'Who said anything about sex? I thought we could do a jigsaw puzzle.'

Nick shook his head, smiling through the darkness. 'Sneaking into Rivermede would be like crossing the lines into enemy territory. It could be fun.'

'It would be fun,' I promised him. 'When we've finished doing jigsaws, we could move on to Jenga.'

'What about this baby?' His voice was serious again, that air of caution. 'Don't you have to look after it?'

219

'It's Pearl's night on, and my night off.' I sneaked my hand under his baggy sweatshirt and onto the bare skin of his torso. I could hear and feel his breath quickening. 'It would just be you and me and the games chest.'

'That's decided then,' he said. He grabbed my hand playfully, entwining our fingers. 'Your car or mine?'

In the end, we took both cars, because neither of us wanted to have to trudge back to The Ship in the small hours or at dawn. Nick left his in the lane outside Honeypot Cottage.

The sense of intrigue was a strong aphrodisiac. I felt reckless, intoxicated, yet I'd only had one glass of wine and a large soda water. I didn't switch on the lights – partly because I didn't want to attract any attention from across the drive, but also because I wanted to create a cloak of mystery. Nick hadn't seen me naked for fifteen years and my body had changed an awful lot in that time. I'd aged and widened, and because I hadn't given any thought to this situation occurring prior to setting out for the quiz, I was wearing very practical underwear. I'd never felt less tempting.

I needn't have worried. We were two people who hadn't had sex for a very long time, and any qualms I'd had about a lengthy sensual seduction were rapidly put aside. Nick threw me onto the bed and we were both scrambling out of our clothes within seconds, barely able to contain our passion. His touch burnt through my skin. My desire was intense, our lovemaking urgent, and over far too quickly.

Afterwards, we lay together, my head resting on his chest, piecing together the fragments of our separate lives over the last fifteen years. Nick, too, carried a little extra weight, although his was muscle as opposed to my blubber, and I felt scar tissue on his thigh that hadn't been there before, perhaps injuries picked up in the line of duty.

Nick confessed he had not had another long-term relationship after our break-up. 'I dedicated myself to my job,' he said. 'It took over my life, to be honest. I've not been without flings, but I never met anyone quite like you, Becca. You were the one, you know that, don't you? The one that got away. The one I let get away.'

I could easily have said the same about him, but I wasn't going to give him the satisfaction. I suspected he knew it anyway. I told him I, too, had thrown myself into my career.

'I concentrated on building Pearl's brand as an author,' I told him. 'It's big business these days. It's not just about the writing.'

'And romance?' Nick asked.

I confessed to my affair with Declan. 'A married man who already had kids and a vasectomy,' I said. 'Every career girl's dream.'

At the mention of the word vasectomy, Nick let out a long drawn-out sigh. We had been spontaneous and very irresponsible.

'I'm just going to pop to the loo,' I said, scrambling out of bed very quickly.

When I switched on the bedside lamp, Nick groaned. 'Do you have to do that?' He tried to hide under the duvet. Too late. I caught sight of the tattoos he had been hoping to conceal in the darkness. A dragon covered the length and width of his back, while a pair of eagle wings stretched across his chest.

'God, you really did get drunk, didn't you?' I remarked, wrapping my kimono around me.

When I returned from the bathroom, we continued to talk, keeping our voices low even though the walls of the stable block were totally soundproof.

Nick confessed it was the tattoos that had been acquired through the line of duty. 'Sometimes you have to do these things to fit in,' he said, while the scar on his leg was the result of a ski-ing accident.

'When did you take up ski-ing?' I asked. Nick and I really did have a lot of catching up to do.

'Only a few years back,' he replied. 'My mother passed away and I didn't have anything to do one Christmas, so I went to Austria. I broke my leg in three places.'

'I'm sorry to hear about your leg, and your mother, of course,' I said. 'How's Jordan?'

'Still cracking the enigma code,' he teased. 'He's fine. He works in the tech industry, as we always knew he would.'

He crept away just before first light, promising to be in touch. We made love again before he left a slower, tender, more careful exploration of each other's bodies and inner desires. We had finally exchanged phone numbers. At least now I could call him, text him, when I needed that reassurance that I could get through the next few days. Somehow, despite the weight on my shoulders, it did feel as if the load had been considerably lightened.

Chapter Thirty-One

Operation Wedding was due to begin in earnest on Thursday. Aunt Phoebe was expected to arrive during the afternoon, along with Uncle Laurie who was travelling down from Suffolk. As principal guests, they had been given accommodation at Rivermede.

On Wednesday, I promised to take charge of Ivy for the day while Pearl over-saw a complete spring clean of the house. Additional help had been hired in the form of Judy Stevenson's Romanian cleaner, who managed to complete tasks at twice the speed of Heather. The wedding cake had miraculously appeared – three layers: one each of sponge, chocolate, and fruit; fashionably coated with butter cream; and adorned with summer sugar flowers. It was highly unlikely Heather had had anything to do with either its baking or its construction, but neither Pearl or I made any comment in front of the housekeeper. The cake was ready, that was all that mattered.

I took Ivy for a walk in her pushchair into Kerridge, and sat on the Hard throwing breadcrumbs to the family of swans which had taken up residence outside the Jolly Jack Tar. The urge to walk along the path to see Nick was almost overwhelming, but we had promised not to see each other again until after Saturday. Nick had things to sort out, people to see, places to go.

Before he left the stable block in the early hours of Monday morning, he had repeated the promise he had made in the woods. 'We'll sort something out, Becs, so that we can be together.'

He owned a flat in north London. It was a heady thought that we could return there together, I could find a permanent job in a publishing house, and we could take up where we left off fifteen years ago. But what would be the aftermath of Saturday? And now there was little Ivy to think about, too. Freddy couldn't cope with her on his own, not if he wanted to hold down a job. And as for Pearl. If anything happened to Jack…

I couldn't think about the future. I just had to get through the weekend.

After we fed the swans, I saw Gerry Kimble shuffling about on the deck of the *Regatta Queen*. One of the lads from the marina was hammering some new boards onto the pontoon, as if it was finally getting the proper repair it deserved. It would appear Gerry and his secrets were safe for now.

There was no sign of Freddy, although later, as I cut back through the village and stopped to take a pause on the bench under one of the huge chestnut trees outside the church, he pulled up on his moped.

'I didn't see you at work,' I remarked.

He tucked his helmet under his arm. 'I got the afternoon off,' he replied. 'Are you heading back to Rivermede?'

It was on the tip of my tongue to demand to know why, if he'd had the afternoon off, he couldn't have looked after Ivy instead of leaving her with me all day. It was pretty obvious where he'd been and who he'd been with, but I couldn't face an argument about Kimmi, not with everything else going on. Reminding him of his parental duties was a more subtle hint, although Freddy wasn't known for picking up on subtlety.

I offered up the pram. 'Why don't you take Ivy for a stroll?' I suggested.

'I'm not taking her down on the marina,' he said at once.

'We've already been down there,' I told him. 'Come on, don't be shy, walk to towards Helme. I'll come with you.' The chance of a glimpse of *The Solstice* was compelling.

'Okay. I s'pose I could.'

'Yes, Freddy,' I insisted, offering up the pram handles. 'You can.'

It was the first time Freddy had taken control of the stroller. I could understand, although not totally sympathize with, his reluctance to be seen pushing his daughter along the waterfront. However, if he was going to make this work with Ivy, he couldn't keep her hidden forever.

As we approached the track to Chapman's Wharf, my pulse quickened. I spotted a familiar figure in a baseball cap, with his jacket collar turned high to hide his face, shoulders hunched, walking purposefully towards a waiting parked car. He kept his head low, deliberately avoiding eye-contact. We passed without a word, although to my surprise Freddy acknowledged Nick with a grunt of 'hello mate'.

'How do you know him?' I asked as we continued onto Chapman's Wharf.

'Seen him around,' Freddy replied. 'Can we go into the workshop? There's a few bits and bobs in there I like the look of.'

'You've been here before?' I asked

Freddy was full of surprises today. 'Yeah, Aidan says I can help myself to anything I want.'

'What do you want with his old junk?' I asked.

'I thought I might be able to make something out of it. You know, art.'

We weren't Aidan's only customers. Eager to sneak a look back into the lane, I left Freddy examining boxes of nautical instruments, while outside, Pete Wendle was picking through the larger bins of spare parts.

'Oh, it's you, Becca,' he said with a smile. 'All set for Saturday?'

'Yes, thank you, Pete,' I replied. 'I hear you're in charge of this flotilla thing. It will be safe, won't it? The scouts will have lifejackets?'

Pete laughed. 'Of course they will, dear. First rule of the water.'

By the time Pete had finished discussing the dynamics of the torchlight parade, Nick and the waiting car had long disappeared.

On our return to Rivermede, I promised to hold onto Ivy for another fifteen minutes while Freddy took a quick shower. I placed Ivy under her baby-gym and opened up my laptop. Anita, who would be staying at a hotel in Portdeane on Friday night in advance of the wedding, had suggested we meet up for a drink. I'd promised to confirm a time.

Amongst some new enquiries for my professional services, I noticed an email in my inbox from somebody called Tilly Markham.

Dear Rebecca, I am replying on behalf of my husband, Tristram, in response to your recent letter. I have been unable to persuade him to contact you, but I feel we cannot let this opportunity slip. Since the birth of our first child, Ella, six months ago, I know Tris has agonised about the rift between him and his own mother. When you have a child, your perceptions change and you begin to see things differently. When I first met Tris ten years ago, Stella's name was not mentioned in the family. It was as if she was dead. Over time I've learned more about her, and, knowing Owen as I do, I share your opinion that maybe it is time for us to heal that rift. I believe our daughter has a right to know her grandmother, and Tris, too, needs to make amends. I don't think Tris would agree to a meeting, at least not yet, but I will be coming over to the mainland next week to catch up with a couple of girlfriends. I was just wondering if there was any chance we could meet up to discuss how to move things forward? He does not know I have written to you, but you can reply to this email in confidence. I look forward to hearing from you, Tilly.

With everything else that had happened over the last week or so, work on Stella's book had taken a distinct backseat. I hastily replied to Tilly that I would love to meet her next week, she just had to name a time and place. It was something positive to cling onto.

Just as I was about to set off to pick up Uncle Laurie from Southampton central station on Thursday afternoon, I received a text from Freddy.

'Going out on Max's boat straight after work. Can you hold onto Ivy a bit longer?'

I furiously typed back that no I could not, and nor could he go out on Max's boat.

'Only going for a couple of hours,' he replied. 'Already at the estuary, can't turn back now.'

The drugs run, if that's what this was all about, was not supposed to happen until Saturday, when the river was full of sea scouts in their dinghies. That's what Nick had said. What if van der Plaast was pre-empting the situation? What if this was it? What if Max was already on his drug run and Freddy was crewing for him? The consequences were too horrendous to contemplate.

I sent Nick a message. 'Van der Plaast is out on his boat with Freddy.'

'Yes, I know,' Nick text back. 'Situation under control.'

That was no help to me and hardly reassuring. Without Nick to hold my hand, calm, sensible Uncle Laurie was the next best thing. Walking with a stick now, he ambled towards me out of the station building and I flew into his arms.

'My dear girl,' he laughed, 'you nearly knocked me flying! Stand back, let me look at you.'

I stood back. He wore a pale linen suit and a Panama hat, and carried the smallest of suitcases. A familiar, trusted figure who represented the security of my childhood. I was so pleased to see him I almost burst into tears on the spot.

'What's this chap like then, this Jack Robshaw?' he asked as he settled into the car. 'Is he a good thing for our Pearl?'

What could I say? 'They seem very happy together,' I confessed. 'But she has given up her career. I never imagined Pearl not wanting to write.'

'She wrote because she had to, because she had to support you and young Fred,' Laurie replied. 'I don't think it brought her that much pleasure in the end. She saw it as a necessity. She's probably ready to retire.'

I'd never thought of it like that. As I drove, I told him about Rivermede, describing the house and the village and how well Pearl had settled in.

'What about you?' he asked. 'Are you happy there?'

'I'm not sure it's where I really want to be,' I admitted. 'But I've got a couple of projects I'm working on right now and I can do it here as well as anywhere.'

'You're writing, too? That's good news.'

Uncle Laurie was pleased to hear Freddy had a proper job, but I realised as I talked that news of Ruby and baby Ivy came as a total shock. Nobody had thought to tell Laurie that Freddy was a father and no longer pursuing a career in art.

'You've all moved on,' he remarked a little sadly. 'Why should you always keep me in the loop? It sounds as if Pearl is finally settled.'

I didn't want to tell him it could all be about to change.

Chapter Thirty-Two

Although Uncle Laurie gave Ivy his nod of approval, Aunt Phoebe was far less complimentary. Over dinner, another aromatic roast chicken, she criticised Pearl for not only allowing such a thing to happen – as if Pearl had any control over Freddy's sexual activities – but then suggested she was aiding and abetting his irresponsibility by allowing Ivy to remain with him at Rivermede.

'What would you have me do?' Pearl asked. 'Give the baby up to the workhouse?'

'You've made it too easy for him,' Phoebe said, 'you both have. Before you know it, he'll be bringing home another one for you to adopt.'

It didn't help that by ten o'clock there was still no sign of Freddy. Phoebe looked smug while I was almost sick with anxiety. I made my excuses and headed out to the stable block. Nick didn't answer my text.

I was on night duty and hardly slept a wink, listening out for Ivy with one ear and Freddy with the other. He rolled in just after midnight.

'Where the hell have you been?' I demanded, bursting into his bedroom the minute I heard his door close.

'Jesus! Don't creep up on me like that,' he replied. 'We went out to sea somewhere, and when we got back to shore Max wanted to hook up with a mate, so we all went down to Helme for a drink.'

'You've been down at Helme drinking? It's midnight, for Christ's sake.'

'It was just a few drinks on this guy's boat. He's one of Max's mates.'

'I don't want you mixing with any of Max van der Plaast's

229

old cronies.'

'God, what is up with you?' Freddy exclaimed. 'Max doesn't have old cronies. We just had a few drinks, that's all. Max's mate is cool. He has a boat on the marsh.'

I stared at Freddy. 'Max has a mate with a boat moored on Helme marsh? What's his name?'

'I don't know his real name,' Freddy said with a shrug, peeling off his trainers. 'I've only been on his boat a couple of times. Max calls him *the Tsar*, but presumably that's just a nickname.'

'*The Tsar*? Is he Russian?'

'No, he's British. Or if he is Russian, he's a got a bloody good English accent. Manchester, I'd say.'

'Manchester? And he has a boat, on the marsh?'

'You're starting to sound like a parrot. Yes. Why are you looking at me like that?'

I refused to think about the implications. Facts first, supposition later. It could be anybody. There was more than one boat moored on the marsh. The estuary was a myriad of creeks and secret hiding places.

'What did he look like?' I demanded.

'God, Becs, what is this? The bloody Spanish Inquisition? I dunno, forty, fiftyish maybe, beard.'

A man with a beard. Fifty? Freddy had never been very good at judging people's ages. Anyone over the age of twenty-five was positively ancient.

'We saw him the other day at Aidan's,' Freddy continued. 'You were with me.'

We'd seen Nick. We'd nearly walked into him and Freddy had said 'hello, mate'. He'd said he'd seen him around. He'd seen him around because Nick was bloody van der Plaast's 'old mate'.

How could I have got this so wrong? Nick wasn't on the side of the law at all. No wonder he acted so out of character. Wasn't *The Tsar* common terminology for police chiefs responsible for special measures? The perfect nickname! I felt physically sick. No wonder Nick had been so reluctant to talk about what he was really up to in Kerridge. He was a fully-fledged, paid-up member of van der Plaast's gang, complete with the tattoos to prove it.

'Hey, are you okay, Becs? You've gone a funny colour.'

I'd been so stupid. I'd allowed him to crawl back into my life. No wonder he'd tried to warn me away from Rivermede when we first met, and then when I'd refused to go, he'd used his charm to seduce me so I'd keep quiet. When I'd spilled the beans about the sailing flotilla, he'd spun me along, feigning surprise. He'd deliberately played with my emotions. Those lies he'd spun about not wanting to take on the responsibility for Freddy, trying to win me over, keep me on his side. I'd always known he'd slept with Saskia. My first instincts had been correct. Why had I ever thought I could trust Nick again when he had already proved himself to be the most untrustworthy, most deceitful person I knew?

I had to pull myself together. 'I'm fine thank you, Freddy,' I said, standing up straight. I was not my mother's daughter for nothing. We'd survived worse.

In the next room, Ivy began her hungry midnight grizzle.

'Look, if you're not well and you want me to do tonight's feed, I can you know,' Fred said.

'Thanks, Fred. You have work tomorrow. I'll be fine.'

A cuddle with innocent and unblemished Ivy was the only shining light on a very dark horizon.

On Friday, the house was a flurry of activity. There was too much going on to stop and think, to dwell, to think of Nick and all the things I wanted do to him next time I saw him. Things which now involved inflicting injury, great pain, and bordered on grievous bodily harm, as opposed to the more pleasant physical activities I had previously envisaged. Of course, it was now highly unlikely I would see Nick again. He would be gone as soon as the weekend was over, off without a goodbye, crawling back under his stone.

Why hadn't I twigged it before? I knew from his brother's Twitter account that Nick had spent a large part of the previous year abroad. The south of France, the Netherlands, Sweden, all those places van der Plaast had his business interests. Nick hadn't been on surveillance, he was van der Plaast's accomplice. No wonder he had uncovered Tristram Markham so quickly – he probably had friends already incarcerated in Parkhurst Prison.

It crossed my mind that I should perhaps now go to the police, but what would I tell them? I had no evidence to back up my theory. I could perhaps shop JJ or Neville for cultivating a handful of cannabis plants, but if the pot plants were linked to the bigger picture, I would be putting us all in danger. More danger.

I had visions of witness protection programmes, of years of hiding, of constantly running and looking over my shoulder. Men like Max van der Plaast would always seek their revenge. No wonder JJ was prepared to take his money to look the other way while van der Plaast's gang used Rivermede creek to transport his illegal cargo. We were all complicit. That's how these people worked.

A whole team of florists and caterers arrived to decorate the marquee, laying tables and arranging party favours. I mooched around in Pearl's shadow as she directed operations. I took Laurie and Phoebe on a tour of the grounds, carefully avoiding the kitchen garden and the greenhouse.

'This all needs a good tidy up,' Phoebe said, stepping through the long grass and gesturing towards the unkempt shrubbery with its overgrown rhododendrons, brambles, and holly bushes.

Ivy came with us, my one source of comfort in the whole sorry mess. After a while, I offered Uncle Laurie the chance to push the pram. Phoebe refused point blank.

'She is your great niece,' I pointed out. Phoebe didn't want to acknowledge any sort of relationship. '*It's bad enough that she kept the boy, let alone give a home to his dubious offspring,*' I heard her hiss to Uncle Laurie at one point.

It was tempting to take Uncle Laurie aside and confide. He was a sensible man, good at dishing out sound advice. He would undoubtedly urge caution, demand hard evidence. I had none, just the horrible knowledge that the guy who had let me down before had done it all over again.

Chapter Thirty-Three

I'd arranged to meet Anita at seven-thirty. Rather than drive myself, I asked Nev to take me and collect me at eleven. He didn't look too thrilled with the arrangement, but was as impeccably polite as always.

'Busy day tomorrow, miss,' he reminded me.

'I am aware of that Neville.' I replied, wondering if he was reluctant to stay out late because he had a final canoe training run through the reed beds.

'You seem a bit on edge,' Anita remarked as I ordered a second glass of wine before she was even a quarter of the way through her first.

'You know me and weddings,' I replied. 'They always make me nervous.'

Anita was pleased to report that the publishing contract had been signed with the infamous trade unionist, and he was now 'all mine'.

'And he can't wait to get the ball rolling,' she told me. 'As a young man, Ian Tate held the country to ransom in the 1980s, and he won't let you forget it. Good luck. He's got two ex-wives and a couple of rather well-known mistresses to pacify, so you'll need all your skills of discretion to keep him on track. I imagine it'll be a bit of a roller-coaster ride.'

'Another one? Just what I need,' I said.

It was actually quite a relief to see Nev waiting outside the hotel at ten forty-five.

Saturday morning dawned sunny and clear. The perfect day for a wedding. My dress hung on the door of my wardrobe, matching shoes lined up on the floor. I peered out of the stable block windows towards the river, where all was quiet and calm. Of course it would be – what was I expecting, a pirate ship and the entire Spanish Armada?

The hair and make-up party had been booked for seven-thirty. The stylist, Charlene, was a close friend of Rita's. Naturally, Pearl and Jack had spent the wedding night 'apart' and Pearl's first floor bedroom was a hive of frenzied activity.

Ivy was fractious, as if she could sense that for once she wasn't the centre of everyone's attention. Phoebe looked on with disapproval while I rocked and jigged her up and down, trying all the usual tricks to calm her.

'Here,' Rita said eventually, holding out her hands. 'You look all over the place this morning, Rebecca. You can ask me, you know. I'd love to have a go.'

Without hair and make-up, I realised Rita was probably a lot older than I'd first thought. Our body clocks were probably ticking away at the same frantic rate of knots. No wonder she was so desperate for a baby. I immediately regretted I hadn't made more attempts to befriend her. We were the same age, living in the same household. I'd had Freddy to lavish those maternal feelings on, she had no-one. Was it so wrong to condemn her and JJ for using whatever means they had to try for a child? If I was in that position, would I have done the same thing?

I felt a few stirrings of guilt that I had only added to their difficulties by supporting Gerald Kimble's claim to his mooring and digging up a past that was long buried. What right did I have to barge in on other people's lives when I knew so little about them?

Within minutes, Rita had lulled Ivy back to sleep.

'You're a natural, Marguerite,' Charlene remarked. 'You must be so excited. I bet the next few months can't go quickly enough for you. It must be amazing, after all those years of trying, to know that you've got your own little one on the way.'

Rita beamed. Instinctively all eyes in the room were on her stomach.

'You mean it's worked?' Pearl was dumbfounded.

'Yes.' Rita looked like a cat with the cream. 'We weren't

going to say anything until after the wedding, because obviously this is your day, not ours, but yes, our last round of IVF worked. Early next year, Ivy will have a little playmate.'

'That's wonderful news, congratulations,' I said, genuinely pleased for her. I would definitely make more effort in future to get to know Rita better. I had been far too judgemental.

'You'll have to make some changes to your lifestyle.' Pearl's lips were pursed. Her thunder had been well and truly stolen and she knew it.

'It looks like JJ's already found a buyer for the Aqua Riva, so when that's sold at least we should be able to get on and get the house finished,' Rita explained. 'JJ's negotiated a good price for her, nearly what he paid. She's not being collected for a couple of weeks, which is just as well as apparently as he's mislaid a set of keys. Personally, I wouldn't be surprised if the one of the lads on the marina hadn't pocketed them and was taking the boat for a midnight spin. Bloody thing has guzzled a whole tank of marine fuel in less than a week. I'll be glad to see the back of it.'

Pearl raised her eyes skywards. 'JJ should be putting his money back into the business, not farting about with that fancy house. Perhaps you ought to remind him about his father's loans, Rita dear, before you go choosing decorations for the nursery.'

'It is a shame JJ didn't think about selling his speedboat earlier,' I said, trying not to think about Freddy and the set of missing keys. Surely he wouldn't be so stupid. 'Then he might not have needed to threaten poor Gerry Kimble to get his hands on those few extra berths.'

'I heard the paperwork had turned up,' Pearl threw in. 'Who found it?'

'Jack, apparently,' Rita said. 'Anyway, that was a business matter. Our private finances are separate. Sailor Gerry will drink himself to death in a few years' time anyway and JJ will get the mooring back.'

'If you're lucky, it could happen sooner than you think,' Charlene added. 'I saw the old boy just the other day, teetering along the Hard, drunk as a skunk. Wouldn't take much, would it, for him to fall in? One push and JJ could have his pontoon back tomorrow.'

'I'll suggest it,' Rita laughed.

All thoughts of potential friendship vanished. Had my meddling actually made Gerry's situation worse? Before I'd poked my nose into things, it had only been his boat that was under threat, now it seemed his life could be in jeopardy. He really would have to watch his step.

'I think Ivy needs to go into her crib,' I said, almost snatching the baby out of Rita's murderous arms.

Rita refused to give up her prize. 'I'll do it,' she insisted.

'Right,' Charlene said, swirling Pearl round so that we could all admire her immaculate make-up. 'Who's next?' She smiled at Phoebe. 'Shall we do the bride's mother?'

'Bride's mother?' Phoebe gasped in horror. 'I'm her sister. Her *younger* sister.'

'Only by eighteen months,' Pearl pointed out. She patted Charlene's arm. 'Don't worry, dear, you're not the first person to make that mistake.'

We were done. Despite my misgivings, I did look good. The bridesmaid dress Vera had designed fitted perfectly and accentuated my curves without making me look dumpy or buxom. Charlene had done wonders with my hair, and my face glowed. If only Nick could see me now...

But he couldn't, and I didn't want him to. I never wanted to see him again. Every hour that passed was an hour closer to the end of the day. Whatever was going to happen in Kerridge would soon be over, and I could begin a new life, yet again.

The doves and the owl were on standby in their cages. The caterers were in full swing, the marquee was a floral fantasy. The vow ceremony was taking place in the open air, under an archway smothered with lavender, love-in-the-mist, and delphinium sprays, to match the wedding bouquets.

Pearl looked magnificent. Vera had created a very simple shift dress in ivory, accessorised with a pure silk lilac pashmina. A fascinator picked up the colours of both. Pearl's trademark honey-coloured hair was softer now, streaked with ash blonde. I was welling up with pride. She looked happy and relaxed, a very different mother from the one I had grown up with, but one I loved just the same.

We posed for photographs on the front steps, and then Freddy took her arm and led her to the waiting car. We had hired a company for the transport as Heather and Nev were needed at Rivermede to ensure everything was ready for when the guests began to arrive.

Freddy looked very grown up. The weeks of working outdoors had filled out his body and tanned his face, so that he'd lost his gaunt, Gothic-ness. His hair was freshly washed and tamed. He looked resplendent in his suit, finally giving in to Pearl's demands and wearing a purple waistcoat to match Jack and JJ. His only rebellion – a loose cravat, not a tie – gave him an attractive, rakish appearance.

The simple civil ceremony took less than fifteen minutes. Pearl had her wish; she was Mrs Jack Robshaw of Rivermede, Kerridge. I prayed to a God I rarely believed in, p*lease, please don't let anything bad happen today.* And then I realised I was really praying to Nick, *just hold off whatever it is you have planned for a few more hours. Please don't spoil my mother's big day. Again.*

Lunch had been booked in a restaurant close to the registry office. I pushed food around my plate while for once Rita ate like a horse. As the waiters offered us champagne, she declined and asked instead for sparkling water, which of course, led to an inquest and the confession of the pregnancy. Jack was overjoyed.

'You've made my day,' he said, much to Pearl's irritation. I saw her give him a dig in the ribs. He dug her back. 'A new generation at Rivermede,' he winked. 'Look how much pleasure Ivy's brought you. They will grow up friends.'

JJ looked appalled at this thought but took the congratulations. I momentarily wondered if the baby would bear any resemblance to its grandfather, Gerald Kimble, and secretly hoped that it would.

Jack proposed a toast, and while we waited for more

champagne to arrive, JJ took me to one side.

'I understand you were the one who found that paperwork,' he said. 'Why couldn't you just leave it alone?'

'Because you were persecuting an innocent old man,' I replied. 'You're a bully. And incidentally, should anything happen to Mr Kimble in the near future, I will make sure the police carry out a full investigation.'

He stared at me quite blankly. 'What's that supposed to mean?'

'It means I know people, too, *Mr Robshaw*,' I replied.

When the meal was over, the moment I was dreading arrived. It was time to return to Rivermede. Was it too much to hope that perhaps we had missed all the action? Perhaps the 'shipment' had arrived early. Perhaps nothing had or was going to happen at all.

Guests lined up on the lawn to greet the wedding party.

'You look stunning,' Anita whispered to me. 'Absolutely beautiful. Are you sure there aren't any eligible men here we can snare for you?'

There were none. Sailor Gerry was definitely off the guest list, and if Max van der Plaast had been issued with an invitation, he had obviously declined because he had his drugs run to organise. And as for Alex the Twitcher, he would hardly turn up now.

Pearl and Jack repeated their vows in front of one hundred and fifty witnesses, and the well-trained owl delivered the rings with precision. The Kerridge Pops Choir rose from the seated crowd flash-mob style. Even I had to admit it was a pretty impressive performance.

I kept a continual lookout over my shoulder. Freddy remarked I was making him nervous.

'What are you so worried about?' he hissed. 'You're not the one making a speech.'

'I'm nervous for you,' I lied.

The sensible, level-headed side of my brain told me I was being ridiculous. The creative, over-imaginative side told me it was perfectly reasonable to expect an entire fleet of gangster speedboats, guns blazing, to roar up the river at any moment.

In the warmth which soon became the heat of the marquee, we ate more food, while the recently released doves re-assembled on the lawn. Pearl and Jack had their first dance. It was a short, awkward waltz to a bad cover of *Thinking Out Loud* by the jazz band Pearl had engaged for the evening's entertainment – an amateur quintet who came on no-one's recommendation but advertised their services in the church magazine. Jack rarely left his wheelchair, and I admired the effort it must have taken to don his uncomfortable prosthetic so that he could partake in the first dance. He and Pearl were good for each other, and I sincerely hoped they would be happy for many years to come.

Chapter Thirty-Four

As dusk fell, I slipped away from the marquee and down to the shore. I'd had champagne with my lunch and one to be polite on arrival, but then joined Rita on the sparkling water for the rest of the evening, conscious that at any moment I might be required to dive into the River Deane to rescue an entire troupe of sea scouts.

All was quiet on the water. The tide was on the rise. Another hour or so and the creek would be fully accessible, the perfect conditions for a landing of contraband. There was no sign of the sea scouts. There was nothing to do but wait. And hope.

I heard footsteps on the gravel.

'Hello, gorgeous.'

I turned at the sound of his voice.

'What the hell are you doing here?'

Nick had his baseball cap low over his head. He wasn't dressed for a wedding. He wore black jeans and a bomber jacket.

'Just hoping for a glimpse of the most beautiful bridesmaid in the world,' he said, sliding his arms around my waist.

'Get off me,' I hissed, edging out of his reach. 'How dare you come here.'

'You invited me, if I remember rightly.'

'You haven't adhered to the dress code,' I pointed out. I couldn't keep the sarcasm from my voice. 'Why aren't you on your stake-out?'

'It could be hours yet,' he said. I took a step back. He looked perplexed. 'What's up, Becs?'

'What's up? What do you mean what's up? I've sussed you out, Nick.'

He stared at me. 'Sussed me out?'

"Freddy went out with Max the other evening. He told me they stopped on the way back for a drink with one of Max's mates, someone Max referred to as The Tsar who has a boat at Helme Point. Do you think I'm stupid? All this time you've been stringing me along, haven't you? Do you know, I seriously thought for one minute a few days ago, that we had something good? That we could be happy together, and yet you've done it again, haven't you? You've lied and cheated.'

Nick shook his head. 'You've got this so wrong, Rebecca. Why would you even think—'

'Oh, stop denying everything,' I hissed. The gate was still ajar. Once on the other side with it firmly shut, he couldn't get to me, he couldn't get into Rivermede. He would be out of my life, excluded like a bad dream. 'Even your name fits, when I think about it, doesn't it? All that old Russian aristocracy, Tsar Nicholas, Tsar Alexander…'

Pearl stood just behind the gate with Pippadee tucked under her arm.

'Rebecca, you left the gate open. Pippa could have got out, she could have been anywhere.'

'Sorry, Mum.'

Nick came to an abrupt halt behind me. Pearl regarded him suspiciously.

'I don't think we've had the pleasure,' she said, holding out her free hand. 'You must be Alex from the quiz.' She stepped to one side, her face impeccably polite. 'Please, come on in and join us for a drink.'

'No, Alex has to be somewhere else right now,' I said. I pushed past her and kicked the gate shut with all the force I could muster in stilettos.

'Goodness me,' Pearl exclaimed. 'What was all that about? Chrissie said he was a bit of an oddball, but there's oddballs and then there's oddballs, Becca. I'd keep well away from that one, if I were you. Do you know who he reminded me of? Nick Quinlan. He looked decidedly shifty, and as for that outfit. What a bizarre choice for a wedding guest. At least, for all his faults, Nick knew how to look good in a suit. And why on earth were you arguing about Russian Tsars?'

241

Why on earth indeed? How could I answer that? 'Quiz question, Mum.'

'Oh, I see. There was Ivan the Terrible remember, he was a Tsar; and Katherine the Great. Peter the Great, too, of course. Talking of which, I hope he's got everything under control at the marina. I've been so looking to the torchlight parade ever since he first mentioned it.'

'Peter the Great?'

'Yes, that's what they call him at the club because he's so good at organising everything. He's just popped out to the get the flotilla started. It should be along in about twenty minutes or so. Won't it be perfect?'

Pete the harbourmaster had a boat moored on the marsh. He also had a beard and was about fifty. Did he have a northern accent? I couldn't recall, but it was quite possible. I tended to switch off whenever he started talking, but we had had that conversation about Tristram Markham… Had I got this all so wrong again? What an idiot I'd been. How could I have doubted Nick?

'Fancy you forgetting Peter the Great,' Pearl chuckled to herself. 'Don't you remember Ivanka the serving girl in *Summer at the Winter Palace*? She could trace her ancestry right back to Peter—'

'Is he from up north?'

'Who, Pete Wendle? Oh yes, you're right, he might be…'

I abandoned her to go in search of Freddy. Why hadn't I thought to interrogate Freddy further about this mysterious Tsar? Why had my mind immediately jumped to Nick and feared the worst? Was it some sort of subconscious revenge for the way he had assumed the worst of me? I didn't know what to do first: run back down to the shore to apologise to Nick, or find Freddy and demand some answers.

My so-called intuition had let me down before. I couldn't risk making another mistake. There was no sign of Freddy in the marquee, although I found Jack anxiously checking his watch.

'Have you seen Nev?' he asked. 'I want him to wheel me down to the front, so I can get a good view of the action on the water later. I don't suppose you could have a quick look for him for me, could you, Becca dear?'

'Yes, of course,' I promised.

It was no great surprise Nev had gone missing. Whatever action was due to take place this evening, I was pretty sure he was going to be in the thick of it.

I wandered into the house, passing Aunt Phoebe pacing in the hallway as Ivy gurgled in her pram.

'Nobody else seems that bothered, but surely she should be put down now?' Phoebe remarked. 'It must be past her bedtime.'

I was glad she had added the second half of the sentence. 'Freddy will do that for you, when I find him,' I promised.

'Oh, Freddy's gone out somewhere,' Phoebe said. 'Took off about half an hour or so ago.'

'What? Did he say where he was going?'

'He was here one minute then he took a call on his phone and went flying off on that scooter thing of his. I don't know why your mother lets him have it. You'd have thought after what happened to your father—'

'Oh Phoebe, do you never give up?' It was all getting too much. 'Why don't you just put Ivy into her cot? She won't bite. I need to go and find Freddy.'

'Really, Rebecca.' Phoebe looked affronted. 'Whatever has got into you?'

I'd only had two drinks; champagne came in very small glasses. I didn't have time to argue. I was already racing out of the door to the stable block. In the flat upstairs, I hastily exchanged my heels for the ballet pumps I had on standby, and then took the steps two at a time to the garage. Freddy's phone went straight to voicemail.

'Fred, if you are there, please pick up. It's urgent. Please call me.'

I could only think of one reason why Freddy would head off at the drop of a hat. Kimmi van der Plaast. My stupid, stupid brother. Didn't he realise that now he had Ivy, he only had room for one girl in his life?

Freddy couldn't afford to get mixed up in any of van der

243

Plaast's illegal activities, not tonight. Whatever happened later, he mustn't get caught. I headed straight through the village to the van der Plaast mansion. The gates were firmly shut and, although it was impossible to see the house from the road, every combination of buttons I pressed on the keypad failed to gain a response.

I returned to my car, slammed it into reverse, put my foot on the accelerator, and headed with a growing sense of dread to the marina.

Chapter Thirty-Five

My throat was dry, my heart was racing. There was a police roadblock at the top of the lane that led down to the Hard. I wound down my window.

'Sorry, miss, we can't let you through.'

'But I need to get to the marina.'

'The marina is closed. I suggest you head on home.'

I shoved the car into reverse. It was some consolation to know that if I couldn't get through, Freddy couldn't get through. On the other hand, it definitely indicated the police were expecting something to happen tonight. How could I have been so stupid as to doubt Nick? Back in the village, I took the rutted track that led to Chapman's Wharf. If I couldn't get to the marina one way, I would try another.

I parked my car outside Aidan's workshop. It was all very quiet, and very dark. There was no sign of life on *The Solstice*, but then I already knew Nick was prepared for a night of nocturnal activities.

I used my phone to light my way along the gravel path. Up ahead, the rusty bulk of the *Regatta Queen* partially blocked my view. I could hear voices on the water. I recognised Pete's bellow. He was issuing instructions from one of the pontoons. The sea scouts had formed an unruly circle, struggling to keep their torches alight as sails flapped in the gentle breeze. Pete wasn't happy.

'Get a bloody move on,' he shouted. 'George, you lead. This is shambolic. I thought I'd trained you better than this.'

I definitely caught traces of a northern accent – Liverpool perhaps, as opposed to Manchester, but it was there and it was enough. The marina itself looked deserted, but if Pete was The Tsar then Nick and his men would be hiding out here somewhere. Perhaps they were already dealing with van der Plaast and Neville at another point along the river? Meanwhile, Pete was just twenty, thirty metres away, balancing precariously on the edge of a mooring, and he'd been swigging champagne all afternoon.

It would only take one push. I thanked Charlene the beautician for putting the idea into my head. Pete was smug and bumptious and, Tsar or not, he was the man who had sold my mother this stupid idea of having a sailing flotilla, regardless of his motive. That was all the excuse I needed.

Pete looked puzzled as I approached. 'Becca, what are you doing here? The lads are just about to set off now. I've just phoned Natalie and told her to let everyone know…'

I gave him a shove, he opened his mouth to say something, I shoved again, he wobbled, 'what the hell…' and then toppled straight into the water.

'Man overboard!' one of the sea scouts cried, unable to contain his glee. The others joined in with various cat-calls. 'Mr Wendle's in the water.' 'Somebody save him!' 'No, leave the old sod to drown…'

Pete splashed and spluttered, reaching out fruitlessly as his sea-scouts sailed away from him as instructed, forming a perfectly co-ordinated straight line. Gerald Kimble, aroused by the commotion, appeared on his deck.

'What's going on?' he called. 'Is someone in the water?'

'Don't help him, Gerry,' I yelled, running towards the *Regatta Queen*. Pete swam frantically towards the old frigate. 'That man is a dangerous criminal and the police will be here any minute now to arrest him.'

Just as I reached the start of Gerry's pontoon, I was grabbed from behind. I struggled, dug my elbows into the chest of my attacker, and kicked his shins.

'Becs, it's only me,' Freddy hissed, spinning me round. 'What the hell are you doing here?'

'Looking for you,' I hissed back. 'Where's Kimmi? Have you seen Max?'

He shook his head. 'Kimmi wanted me to launch the Aqua Riva and meet Max down at the estuary. But I couldn't get to the mooring. The woods around the creek and lane are heaving with police.'

'Have you taken the Aqua Riva before?' I demanded.

'We might have taken it for a spin or two.'

It was probably the least of my worries. 'Where is Kimmi now?' I demanded.

'I don't know. She ran off. She must be trying to get to the estuary on foot. Why the hell did you push Pete Wendle into water?'

'Because he's the Tsar, isn't he?'

Freddy shook his head, 'No, he's the harbourmaster.'

'What?' Before I could even begin to contemplate the implications of being wrong again, a shower of golden stars lit up the sky in an ear-splitting explosion. The fireworks had started early at Rivermede.

Another second explosion closely followed, throwing a burst of colourful confetti into the night air. As the sky illuminated, I saw the canoe swiftly and stealthily following in the wake of the line of little boats, and all hell broke loose on the marina.

Bodies appeared from everywhere, from within the dry stacks, from behind the boatsheds.

We both realised at the same time what was happening.

'Jesus, run!' Freddy shouted. 'He said this might happen. We've got to head for Chapman's Wharf. We can hide out on *The Solstice*. He said to go there if anything went wrong.'

'Who said? Who told you that?' I gasped, already knowing the answer but not wanting to face the horrible truth. At least he had offered Freddy an escape route. He wasn't all bad. A crook with a heart. My heart, shattering into zillions of tiny shards all over again.

I stumbled over the uneven stones, losing my footing in the ruts of the track. A screeching flare zoomed into the sky. Within an instant, searchlights appeared on the river, their beams picking out the line of the dinghies, picking out Pete thrashing in the water. And then as they swung in the opposite direction, they picked out a figure, the familiar bulk of Max van der Plaast, lurching towards us along the shore, followed by a chasing pack.

Freddy pushed me off the path and into the squelchy mud of the reed bed with an urgent, 'Hide.'

There was nowhere to hide. It was impossible to run through a reed bed, and *The Solstice* was still a couple of hundred of metres away. I squelched through no more than ten, fifteen metres, before my progress was halted by the thickening mud. I looked over my shoulder to see Max van der Plaast grabbing Freddy by the tails of his morning suit.

'Nice outfit, boy,' he grunted, 'but it's about to get ruined.'

Max had a gun, and he pointed it at Freddy's head.

This wasn't happening. This was a dream, a nightmare, one of those awful realistic nightmares where you feel genuine fear and can't run because your legs are made of lead, or trapped in mud, as mine were. I couldn't make a sound, I daren't move. I was frozen with fear in a slowly sinking hiding place, watching a scene from the worst kind of TV show being played out in front of me, all to the accompaniment of a pyrotechnic multi-coloured light show, willing myself to wake up safe in my bed in the stable block, or even better back in Battersea. The Kerridge nightmare over.

The chasing pack had stopped twenty metres of so away from where Max stood with Freddy. I crouched low, clasping hold of handfuls of the reeds to haul myself free.

'I want a boat,' van der Plaast shouted. He was out of breath, panting hard. Another ear-splitting shower of fireworks lit up the sky, making a spectacular mockery of his threat so that he had to start all over again. 'I want a boat. You get me a boat and I let the boy go.'

'There's nowhere to go,' one of the pack retaliated. 'We've got the estuary covered and upstream is surrounded. There's no escape, van der Plaast. We've already got your haul. You are completely cornered. Give yourself up and we can talk.'

Van der Plaast laughed. 'You want this boy's blood on your hands?'

A figure stepped forward. He was dressed differently to the other officers in their black uniforms. A figure in a bomber jacket with a baseball cap on his head. 'Give yourself up, Max.

Let the boy go.'

Van der Plaast's grip on Freddy tightened. 'You. I should have guessed. Maybe I'll save my bullets for a traitor, not a stupid boy.'

There was a rustling further along the track, accompanied by a sob. 'Papa, please.' Kimmi scrambled up onto the path. She must have been hiding out somewhere in the reeds like me. 'Papa, please let Freddy go.'

Van der Plaast said something in Dutch to his daughter. The tearful girl shook her head and made to move towards him, but one of the police officers lunged for her. Van der Plaast twisted Freddy to his knees, and then Nick darted forward. I covered my face with my hands, squeezed my eyes tight shut, and then heard the shots.

For a split second, everything went quiet and then Kimmi screamed. I heard a scuffle, scrunches on the gravel, grunts, shouts, and thuds. I opened my eyes. Two men were down and surrounded on the shore by half a dozen officers. Kimmi was being restrained, while Freddy remained on the path, curled in the foetal position, hands over his head, dazed but safe.

I clambered out of my hiding place, sacrificing my ballet pumps to the mud.

'Freddy!' I cried.

'Oh Becs,' he stuttered, tears streaming down his cheeks as he unfurled himself. 'I thought I was a gonner.'

'I thought you were, too,' I wailed with relief, clinging to him.

The shoreline was in chaos. There were paramedics, officers in riot gear everywhere. Kimmi continued to cry, breaking her sobs every now and then to swear in Dutch.

My eyes searched the throng for Nick. It took seconds to register that he was the second man down.

'I have to go and see Nick,' I gasped to Freddy.

'Who?'

'The police officer in the baseball cap. The guy who saved you. Was he your Tsar?'

The guy who had been playing a double bluff, undercover, risking his life to fight crime. *My hero*. Every single emotion

249

escalated into one. Love, compassion, grief, gratitude, relief. Nick had saved Freddy's life.

Freddy nodded. 'You're saying he's police?'

I nodded. 'Yes, Freddy. It's Nick, my Nick.'

'Your Nick?' Freddy looked even more dazed and confused than ever.

The jagged pebbles stabbed my bare feet as I approached the huddle on the strip of shingle. A paramedic was already administering a drip. An ambulance crew was rushing towards us along the gravel track.

I could see and smell blood.

'Take all civilians out of the way,' a gruff voice commanded from the huddle.

'I need to know if he's going to be okay?' I cried, as an officer reached out to restrain me.

'Is that you, Rebecca?'

'Yes, it's me, Nick. It's me.' The huddle momentarily gave way to allow me to crouch down beside him. I could see he was in agony; his face was deathly white. Blood was pouring from a wound in his leg, his bad leg, the leg that already bore the scars of his ski-ing accident.

'Get the bloody stretcher here quick,' the paramedic yelled.

'I'm sorry about your dress,' Nick rasped, 'you looked so lovely earlier on…'

'It's only a dress,' I replied, tears rolling down my cheek. 'I can always have another one.'

'A white one next time, eh?' he croaked, and then one of Nick's fellow officers hauled me out of the away.

Chapter Thirty-Six

'Stop screaming, Becs,' Freddy said, holding me close. 'You can't do anything, you have to let them go.'

Was I the one who was howling, making that awful animal noise? I thought it was Kimmi having hysterics, but Kimmi was quiet now, already being led to a waiting police car.

A physical pain tore through my entire body. The sense of helplessness was crushing. There was absolutely nothing I could do. *Please, please, please let Nick be okay.*

The ambulance sped away from the quayside, sirens blaring, lights flashing.

'What hospital will they take him to?' I screeched to the nearest officer. 'You have to tell me.'

But he didn't. He didn't have to tell me anything. 'It's classified information,' he replied. 'You two need to come with us. We'll need statements.'

'I just want to go home,' Freddy said, his teeth chattering. He was still in shock. We were both in shock.

We were given blankets and then bundled into a car. At Portdeane police station, I confessed I knew Nick from long ago, hoping for some sort of sympathetic ear, but the interviewing officers remained tight-lipped. They wanted facts, not romantic speculation. The operation to apprehend Max van der Plaast was part of a much bigger, international enterprise. Nick was just one of many officers involved, and Freddy and I, we were mere minions, bystanders who had unwittingly got in the way. I couldn't believe I had been so stupid as to doubt Nick. He had warned me right from the start that Rivermede wasn't safe. As the evening wore on, it dawned on me we were all very lucky to have escaped relatively unscathed.

While I waited for Freddy to finish being questioned, I saw

a bedraggled, wet Pete Wendle staggering into the police station supported by two officers. He swore at me through the glass partition. He's going to file charges, I thought, here goes. I am going to be charged with attempted murder, but there was no re-call to an interview room. Presumably the police had more pressing matters.

At three o'clock in the morning, Freddy emerged, and we were told we could go. We caught a taxi back to Rivermede. News of the arrests on the marina had filtered through to the newlyweds, and Pearl was waiting for us in the drawing room, beside herself with worry, all thoughts of a wedding night in the luxurious surroundings of a nearby country house hotel abandoned.

'Oh my goodness, what has happened to you two?' she cried. She was wrapped in her old familiar padded dressing gown, although her face was still fully-made up. 'Freddy, look at the state of your suit, and Rebecca, where are your shoes?'

She swamped us with affection, hugs, tears, offers of tea, coffee, brandy. But for once Heather was not on hand, and I ended up making my own cup of tea while Pearl sat at the kitchen table, her arms draped around Freddy, running her fingers through his hair and repeating a relieved, 'my dear, dear, boy,' over and over again.

Freddy wanted to see Ivy.

'But she's asleep,' Phoebe protested when she was awoken from her bed in the night-duty room.

'I don't care,' Freddy said, grabbing his daughter from her cot and clutching her to his chest. 'I just want to hold her.'

I knew the feeling. I was too tired to explain everything to Pearl, too exhausted to face further questioning. The stable block flat had never seemed so welcoming, and yet so surreal. I slipped off my ruined bridesmaid dress, left it on the floor, and fell into bed.

The police arrived at Rivermede at first light with search warrants. They didn't disturb me in the flat, and I sensed little would be gained from rushing to enquire for news of Nick. Instead, I watched from the window as JJ was led away and bundled into a car. Later, when the coast seemed clear, I ventured over to the house.

Pearl, Jack, Freddy, and Rita congregated in the drawing room, together with Uncle Laurie and Aunt Phoebe.

'Ah, there you are, Becs,' Phoebe said, as soon as I arrived in the room. 'I've a train to catch at 3 pm. I trust you can run me to the station.'

My car was still at Chapman's Wharf. How ironic that when I actually wanted Nev to apparate into view, he was nowhere to be found.

'I'll call you a taxi,' Jack said, pre-empting the necessity for making excuses. 'I think Becca needs to stay here with Pearl and Fred.'

I agreed. Freddy still looked shell-shocked, Ivy was harnessed to his chest.

Rita attempted to find excuses for JJ's involvement in van der Plaast's schemes.

'I warned JJ not to trust him,' she said. 'We were perfectly content until he turned up in Kerridge. JJ was happy with his lifestyle. I never wanted the new house, the speedboat. That was all to keep up with Max. Max encouraged him to overspend, to get into debt. I should have listened to Vera, she tried to tell us what he was really like.'

'JJ has always been very headstrong and impetuous,' Jack tried to console her. 'He was a bit like his mother in that respect.'

'Why can't he have been more like you?' Rita whined. 'You will get him a good lawyer, won't you, Jack? Someone who can vouch for the family? Perhaps we can claim JJ was led astray.'

'I suspect it's going to be a lot more serious than that,' Uncle Laurie told her.

'So do I,' Jack confirmed. 'Sadly, I don't think stupidity counts as an adequate defence.'

'That's a shame,' I said, looking at Freddy. Max had been very good at masquerading behind his veneer of respectability, but it didn't exonerate JJ's or Freddy's involvement in any way. They had both, however unwittingly, become involved with an evil man whose criminal activities ruined the lives of

253

thousands of people.

Freddy admitted he'd been naive, swearing to me in the taxi back from Portdeane police station that he'd had no idea exactly what Max had been mixed up in. Kimmi had caught his eye and his common sense had vanished in the wake of her paddleboard.

'What did you really think he was doing on all those sailing trips?' I asked.

Freddy shrugged. 'Sailing. We just sailed,' he said. 'I never saw any drugs from start to finish, Becs. I promise you.'

I desperately wanted to believe him. I just hoped a jury, if it came to that, would believe him, too. I couldn't allow myself to think that far ahead.

Nick had been in the perfectly positioned stake-out, the ideal spot to watch everything arriving in and out of the river, maintaining his contact with Max. The fact that I had doubted him – twice – made everything so much harder to bear. Even the consolation of hearing that Pete Wendle had been arrested did little to absolve my guilt.

Rita took a phone call from Natalie. Pete had been on van der Plaast's payroll after all. A harbourmaster who was prepared to look the other way was the perfect ally for an international drugs smuggler – although Natalie remained insistent that Pete's idea of the sailing flotilla had nothing to do with the Max's plot. Pete was being altruistic.

'He wanted to give Jack and Pearl a memorable send-off,' Rita relayed.

'Well, he certainly did that,' Pearl grunted.

An officer called to the house to inform us the boathouse had been cordoned off and was out of bounds. The canoes had been taken away as evidence.

'It's where they hid it,' Freddy said, when we were alone again. 'It must be. That's what they were doing, Becs. Going down the river on the canoes and hauling the stuff back from a drop-off point.'

Jack discussed the situation with Laurie. As always, Laurie's presence was calm and reassuring, a steady rock in a time of turbulent waves.

'I suspect both your son and young Freddy here will need good solicitors,' Laurie told Jack. 'I know a few people in London, but obviously if you have somebody in mind here...'

'My solicitor does little more than fend off breach of contract enquiries when an engine breaks down or a mast collapses,' Jack grunted. 'He knows nothing about criminal law.'

'Call London,' Pearl insisted, her face filled with fear. 'I want the best for Freddy. As for JJ, that's Jack's shout.'

Jack gave a resigned sigh. 'We'll lose Rivermede over this,' he said. 'I'm not a bottomless pot of money. But thank you, Laurie. JJ should have the best representation there is.'

The caterers had boxed up the remains of the wedding banquet and the left-overs sat in the fridge. Nobody was particularly hungry, but we sat in the dining room, as was the Rivermede custom, and picked at the buffet.

Like a rat leaving a sinking ship, Rita made arrangements to spend a few weeks with her parents in the Channel Islands.

I remained in a state of flux. Police officers returned to interview Freddy. I surreptitiously accosted every officer who came to the house, not wanting to alert Pearl or Freddy to my concern for Nick. As predicted, I received no answers to my questions. They were not 'at liberty' to divulge any information. I retrieved my car from a deserted Chapman's Wharf, together with my phone. I called Nick's number, but it was no longer recognised. My mood fluctuated from frantic panic to stoic calm. Nick was strong. It would take more than a bullet to put him out of action. So, why wouldn't anyone tell me what was going on?

I returned to the police station at Portdeane.

'But you must know what happened to this guy, he was one of your officers,' I insisted.

'It's nothing to do with us, love,' the desk sergeant said. 'It's all being handled by the bigwigs in the organised crime squad up in London.'

'Can you give me a contact number?'

'Google it,' they replied.

I scoured the press for news, but surprisingly little was reported. The local south coast evening paper told of several arrests following a major '*drugs haul retrieved during an undercover operation*', but it made no mention of a shoot-out or named anyone involved.

Judy Stevenson called in to offer commiserations to Pearl and Jack. I made a tray of tea and Pearl suggested we retire to the conservatory. Outside on the lawn, the contractors were dismantling the marquee. Pippadee stood on her hind legs, scratching at the window pane, watching the action. Judy reported that a previously unknown mother had swept in from the Netherlands to whisk Kimmi van der Plaast off to an island in the Dutch Caribbean. Freddy didn't seem too upset by the news.

'Ivy and I don't need people like Kimmi in our lives,' he said.

Judy seemed to know far more about what had happened on the marina than we did. Apparently, Gerald Kimble was a local hero. Firstly, because he had rescued a drowning man from the water on Saturday evening. And secondly, now that it was common knowledge that the drowning man was part of a major international drugs ring, Gerry was commended for holding him captive on the *Regatta Queen* until the police arrived.

'How he knew, I've no idea,' Judy continued, lowering her voice. 'But apparently, he said he saw the ghost of Mary Robshaw running along the quayside, shouting instructions at him, poor old soul. Anyway,' the voice raised again, 'to think all this was happening under our noses. I had no idea Kerridge was such a hotbed of criminal activity. That so-called writer who was renting Stella Markham's houseboat, was involved, too. Did you know him? Alex somebody, I think. Chrissie and Craig Sutherland were quite friendly with him.'

'Alex from the pub?' Pearl exclaimed, retrieving an over-excited Pippadee from the windowsill and placing her protectively on her lap. 'I knew he wasn't a writer as soon as I saw him.'

'He and van der Plaast were as thick as thieves,' Judy

continued. 'Isn't it awful to think we welcomed these people into our community? Apparently, he was the mastermind behind the whole thing.'

'No, he wasn't,' I butted in, unable to stop myself. Somebody had to stand up for Nick. I could let the ghost of Mary Robshaw take the credit for passing on top-secret intelligence to Gerald Kimble, but I was not going to have the Kerridge rumour mill insinuate that Alex from the pub had played any part in van der Plaast's scheme. He had to be recognised for the hero he was, undercover or not.

Freddy rolled his eyes. 'I thought I told you all this, *Mum*. He was the guy who got shot. He was just pretending to be a writer. He was part of the drugs squad, working undercover. He'd been staking out the estuary and following van der Plaast for months.'

Judy's mouth dropped, although she didn't look quite as shocked as Pearl. My mother had gone white, although that could have been because Freddy had referred to her as 'Mum' for the first time since he'd been about five. Despite the recent traumas, or perhaps because of them, our family dynamic had well and truly changed.

'Anyway,' Freddy added for good measure, giving Ivy's discarded pacifier a quick lick before popping it back into her waiting mouth. 'He was the one who saved me, and he isn't called Alex at all. His real name is Nick, he's Becca's Nick.'

'Becca's Nick?' Pearl's look of horror turned into one of triumph. '*That Nick?* I knew it. I told you, Becca, didn't I? I told you he reminded me of Nick Quinlan. Oh my goodness. Nick saved Freddy?'

'Yes,' I said, wiping a tear from my eye. I sniffed. I'd been holding everything together for far too long. What harm was there in telling the truth now? Freddy had just blown Alex's cover to the Kerridge gossip queen. '*And* he got shot, and they won't tell me where he is, or how he is doing.' I crumpled, finally giving into the trauma of the last few days.

'Oh, Becca darling, why didn't you say?' Pearl immediately placed Pippa on the floor and gathered me into her arms. 'No wonder you are pining away.'

Judy was agog. 'So, you knew this man, Alex? You knew he was a police officer all along?'

'I just need to know he's safe,' I blubbed, never having felt so wretched or helpless in my entire life. This was worse than the non-wedding day by far. 'Or even alive, the police just won't talk to me—'

'Fred, go and fetch your Uncle Laurie,' Pearl ordered. 'He's with Jack in the study. He'll know what to do, or who we have to contact to find out.'

Freddy trotted off like an obedient puppy, while Pippa, the disobedient puppy, scratched at my legs in an attempt to return to her rightful place on Pearl's knee. Pearl shooed the dog away and held me tight.

Chapter Thirty-Seven

I was very grateful for Pearl's support in ascertaining news of Nick. However, sensible Uncle Laurie was very quick to quash any hopes we could actually discover anything new.

'I don't want to put a dampener on things,' he said, immediately doing just that, 'but I suspect any undercover officer engaged in an operation like this will need to remain incognito while the investigation is still ongoing.'

I didn't like to point out that as Judy Stevenson was now fully aware of Nick's identity, any hope of him remaining incognito was already dashed.

'If he's injured,' Laurie continued, not just dampening my spirits but completely drowning them, 'he will need time to recuperate. Worst case scenario, he could be very seriously ill, or even... on life support.' Another word hovered on his lips, but he stopped himself just in time. 'Apart from anything else, an officer involved in this sort of level of investigation will need a thorough debriefing. It is highly unlikely he will be allowed to communicate with any witnesses or anyone currently under suspicion.'

'I'm not under suspicion,' I pointed out.

'No, but Freddy is obviously implicated,' Laurie replied.

Pearl gave me a sympathetic smile. 'There must be something we can do, Laurie?'

'There's no harm trying to make some enquiries through official sources,' Laurie agreed. 'I suggest your first port of call should be the police station at Portdeane.'

'I've already tried them,' I told him. 'They won't tell me anything.'

'It's such a shame we don't have any inside contacts,' Pearl remarked. 'Someone who could make discreet enquiries on our behalf. Who do we know in the local police force, Judy? Is

259

there anyone at the yacht club who might know someone high up in the county constabulary?'

Judy was already gathering up her bags to leave, as if she couldn't wait to head off to spread the news. 'I really don't think it would be appropriate to impose on anyone's goodwill,' she said. 'And even if there was, there's all sorts of confidentiality issues involved.'

Confidentiality never seemed to have bothered Judy before. However, Laurie agreed she was right.

'What about the family, Becca?' he asked. 'I don't suppose you still have contact with any of them?'

I shook my head. 'Both Nick's parents are dead.' I thought of Jordan's prolific tweeting and grabbed my phone. He hadn't posted anything for at least a week. Should I message him? I was prepared to try anything, although my fingers trembled so much that a message which should have taken thirty seconds to compose, ending up taking about fifteen minutes. I didn't want to disclose too much information. I simply announced who I was – *Nick's old friend Becca.* I explained I'd bumped into Nick recently but hadn't heard from him for a while. *Could you just let me know if he is OK?*

Naturally, I expected an immediate reply. Naturally, I heard nothing.

Freddy said he needed to return to work. Uncle Laurie had been in touch with his favourite firm of solicitors, and appointments had been arranged. JJ was released on bail and skulked in his apartment, having been warned to keep clear of the marina. Even his offer to co-operate fully with the police didn't put him back in his father's good books. He admitted he'd allowed Max van der Plaast to use the boathouse as a holding point. Consignments of drugs had been smuggled up the river, as Freddy had predicted, via Neville and his brother, Brian. The drugs remained hidden in the hulls of the canoes in the boathouse until it was safe to move smaller batches on.

Neville had denied everything, although Heather had owned up to cultivating the cannabis house in the greenhouse, '*for medicinal purposes*'.

The sales office on the marina remained closed while Jack ordered a full audit of the entire operation, although work in the yard had to continue. There was plenty for Freddy to do.

The following day, I dropped Laurie off at the station for his journey back to Suffolk. On my return to Kerridge, I plucked up courage and knocked on the door of JJ's apartment. In all the weeks I'd been at Rivermede, it was the first time I'd paid a visit.

He was unkempt and unshaven. The resemblance to Gerry Kimble was uncanny.

'What do you want?' he grunted, barely opening the door more than a crack.

'I'm trying to find out what happened to the undercover officer who was shot the night Max van der Plaast was arrested,' I began.

JJ looked totally bewildered. 'How the hell should I know?' he asked.

'I just thought you might have heard something during your interviews with the police.'

'What? Like they'd give me an update? I didn't even know somebody had been shot.'

'Yes, it happened on the beach.'

'Well, at least they can't pin that one on me,' JJ said. 'There's 150 witnesses who can confirm I was here at Rivermede all evening, attending some bloody farce of a wedding. You lot must be well pleased with yourselves.'

'*You lot*? What's that supposed to mean?'

'You, your mother, your brother. This is just the excuse the old man needed, isn't it, to disinherit me?'

'Is that all you really care about?' I asked.

'I've worked my guts out to keep that bloody marina afloat these last twenty years,' JJ snarled. 'He had offers, you know, to sell out. He had good offers, people wanted to buy shares which would have provided some sort of investment. But no, he wanted to cling onto it all, retain the family business. Some bloody family we've turned out to be. He's not even my real father. Did you know that? My mother told me that years ago. They were always arguing. He might tell you differently, but their marriage was a sham.'

Now it was my turn to be confused. 'You mean you know Jack's not your father?' No wonder JJ had vented his anger on my mother that afternoon in the study. JJ really was fearful of losing his inheritance.

'Yes, that's what I just said, isn't it?' JJ frowned. 'Do you mean you know it, too? How can you know? He would never have admitted it.'

I decided it would be prudent to say nothing more. 'Okay, so you don't know what happened to the policeman. That's fine, I'll try somewhere else.' I turned to leave. 'Thanks, JJ.'

His hand was on my shoulder. 'Not so quickly. How do you know Jack Robshaw isn't my father? Who told you?'

'I just guessed,' I lied. 'I mean, there's a lot of animosity between the two of you, and you don't look anything like him for a start.'

'Well, you don't look much like your mother,' he pointed out.

'Oh, JJ,' I said, wondering how I could prepare him for the worst. His strained relationship with Jack didn't excuse his behaviour, but it might account for his self-destructive lifestyle. 'I'm sorry all this is happening to you right now. I'm sorry you're in this shit with van der Plaast; I'm sorry Rita's left you; I'm sorry Jack's not your father.' I took a deep breath. 'Norah Morland told me.'

'Norah Morland? Norah told you? Did she tell you who my real father was?' I could have been mistaken, but there was a sense of optimism in JJ's voice as if although he knew Jack wasn't his father, he didn't know the whole truth. Was he hoping for some sort of sensational reveal? If so, I'd just dug myself into a very big hole.

To my utmost relief, JJ's phone rang. 'Don't go anywhere,' he ordered, turning away from the door to answer it. 'Hi Reets, look I can't talk now, okay, yes I'll sort it. I'll look at flights…'

I took the opportunity to make my escape, and fled.

Freddy came home from his first day back at work in a

positively cheerful mood, swooping Ivy into his arms from where she had been laying contently on the conservatory floor beneath her baby gym, guarded by Pippadee.

'I'm not going to face any charges,' he announced. 'The police phoned today.'

'Oh, that's such a relief,' Pearl cried.

'Who did you speak to?' I demanded.

'I dunno, I didn't get the guy's name, he just said I wasn't going to be charged with anything, although I might be called to give evidence if it goes to court.'

'But won't that be dangerous?' I demanded, 'Testifying against an international drug smuggling gang?'

'Would you rather I was charged with aiding and abetting them?' Freddy retorted. 'How would that look when I apply for full custody of Ivy?'

It seemed as if the tables had been turned. He was now being the sensible one and I was acting totally irrationally.

'Oh, and he also said you're not to worry.' He added it almost as an afterthought.

'Who said I wasn't to worry?'

'The guy on the phone,' Freddy replied.

I stared at him. 'What?'

'He said, tell your sister not to worry. Although I didn't think you were going to be charged with attempting to drown Pete Wendle, not now he's come out as part of Max's little gang.'

Nick. At last a glimmer of hope. It had to be Nick. Not to worry was pretty ambiguous. More clues would have been helpful. 'Did you recognise his voice?'

'Oh, I know what you're thinking,' Freddy said, 'but it wasn't your Nick. He was Northern, wasn't he? This guy definitely didn't have an accent. In fact, he sounded quite posh.'

'Nick can sound posh when he wants to,' I argued. 'Give me your phone. I want to check the number.'

'The number was withheld,' Freddy said, shaking his head. He tossed the phone towards me. 'Sorry, Becs, but you're more than welcome to check, if you don't believe me.'

I didn't want to believe him. Nick knew where I was. He knew how to contact me, so why hadn't he? Didn't he realise how much I cared? Didn't he understand how much his silence hurt? One cryptic clue that he was still alive – if that was it – in nearly a week wasn't enough.

'You know what you should do,' Pearl said, patting my arm in solidarity. 'Work, sweetheart. It was my cure-all. Immerse yourself in your job. Concentrate on finishing Stella's memoirs and starting that biography Anita's passed on. Start at eight in the morning and work 'til eight at night. It got me through my dark days. It might do the same for you.'

I didn't want to admit Pearl might be right, but two days later the pain of 'losing' Nick had been temporarily lessened by a burst of enthusiasm for completing Stella's story. I was actually itching to get started on my fictitious family boat-building saga, but I couldn't justify beginning that until I cracked on with my paid work.

I kept my appointment with Tilly Markham, a slim petite woman in her mid-thirties. We met on neutral ground at a coffee bar in Southampton. Tilly explained that Tristram and his sister had been told by their father that Stella had wanted nothing to do with them. He had fed the children lies, cut Stella out of their lives, and ensured they believed she had chosen Chloe over them.

With everything else around me falling apart, it didn't occur to me not to try and reunite Stella's family.

'From what I understand, it wasn't like that at all,' I told Tilly. 'Stella desperately wanted to keep in touch, but Owen wouldn't let her. He made a big thing out of his cheating accusation, which was nothing but a technical complaint by another team. And then, when he'd failed to discredit her for that, he used her relationship with Chloe to turn everyone against her. Friends, relatives. They all took his side.'

'I had no idea,' Tilly said. She had brought along her daughter Ella – a few months older than Ivy, and equally as placid and adorable. I had to stem the tide of broodiness; over the years I'd told myself I didn't want children. I was self-sufficient, self-contained, I'd had Freddy to lavish with affection, I had my godchildren, but Ivy's close proximity, coupled with Rita's pregnancy, had awoken those dormant maternal feelings. My embittered hormones had become rampant.

'Do you think Tristram would be prepared to meet Stella?' I asked, watching enviously as Tilly bounced Ella on her knee. 'And what about Emily? Are you in contact with her, too?'

'Oh yes, she's a nurse in Portsmouth. Neither Tris nor Em have much to do with their father, to be honest. We see him at family occasions, birthdays, Christmas, but he's not the easiest man to get on with. I don't think Emily would take a great deal of persuasion to come round, to agree to meet her mother. I can't believe we left things as they were, we should have been more pro-active. The trouble is, the longer you leave a wound to fester, the worse it gets.'

'I can relate to that,' I said.

'I think Tristram should see Stella first, before we involve Emily,' Tilly suggested. 'Boys do tend to be more forgiving, don't they?'

'Do they?' I had no idea. I offered to have a chat with Tristram to prepare the ground. 'Do you think we can arrange to meet up again in a couple of weeks?'

'Good idea,' Tilly said. 'I'll have to check my shift pattern. Tris and I are juggling jobs and childcare. We never seem to have the same days off, but I'll give you a call when I get home and I've studied the diaries.'

'You work in the prison service, too?' I asked.

Tilly laughed. 'No,' she said, 'I'm in the police. I'm a family liaison officer on the island. I work with victims, people caught up in crimes, those left bereaved. Believe it or not, holding families together in times of strife is supposed to be my specialty.'

'Oh, I believe it,' I said, because I believed in karma, in good things happening to good people, and I had been good. I had been patient and industrious, and I'd concentrated on my job. But there was only so much weight one pair of shoulders could bear, and I couldn't let the opportunity slip through my hands. 'Before you rush off,' I said, 'I know it's a bit of a long shot, but I don't suppose I could ask you a favour?'

Chapter Thirty-Eight

Six Weeks Later

Wednesday lunchtimes were always quiet in The Ship of Fools. I sat outside on the terrace overlooking the river, soaking up the late summer sunshine.

'You want another one?' Stella asked, picking up my empty glass and tipping out a drunken wasp.

I glanced at my watch. 'Maybe just a small one,' I said.

It was only my second visit to the pub since Pearl's wedding, and Stella was very keen to retain my custom.

'Have it on the house,' she said. 'It's good to have you back in circulation.'

It felt good to be back, too. I'd hardly left Rivermede in the last few weeks, apart from taking the occasional walk along the river with Ivy, or to stock up on groceries. Judy's Romanian cleaner remained on permanent loan, but the house was proving far too big for Pearl to manage on her own and I was already resenting the crown of head chef. With JJ's legal bill likely to run into thousands, Jack had resigned himself to selling the marina. I didn't see why Rivermede couldn't go under the auctioneer's hammer, too. Freddy was hurriedly taking driving lessons, but for now JJ was acting chauffeur.

Our doorstep conversation regarding his paternity issues remained unresolved. Fortunately for me, but sadly for her, Norah Morland had taken to her bed the day after JJ and I had had our confrontation. Norah had never fully recovered from the trauma of her collision with the cesspit evacuation lorry, and she had subsequently passed peacefully away in her sleep. By the time JJ returned from a futile trip to Jersey to save his marriage, Norah's bungalow had been cleared by the council and all evidence of JJ's relationship to Gerry Kimble destroyed.

'Have Pearl and Jack started the honeymoon yet?' Stella asked.

'Yes. I finally managed to convince her it was safe for her to go,' I smiled. 'They're cruising around the Far East as we speak.' I glanced at my watch again.

'You're looking anxious, Becca,' Stella said, 'are you sure everything is all right?'

'You know me,' I smiled. 'I can always find something to worry about.'

'Well, at least you're putting weight back on,' Stella remarked. 'When we first saw you a few weeks back, you looked positively peaky.'

'Don't tell Pearl,' I laughed. 'She'll have me back on the pre-wedding diet. Maybe I shouldn't have that second drink after all.'

'Go on with you, it's only a soda water,' Stella grinned. 'I'm bringing it right out,'

She disappeared back into the pub. Out on the river, a lone canoeist was heading upstream, paddling against the outgoing tide. Freddy had talked about buying a kayak, something he and Ivy could do together when she got older. He seemed quite settled now in Kerridge, bearing little resemblance to the feckless young man who had arrived from London just months before. He'd requisitioned some space in Aidan Chapman's workshop, disappearing for hours with Ivy in tow. Apparently, he'd already sold two pieces of 'nautical art'. He'd even asked Stella about renting *The Solstice*. 'We can't stay at Rivermede forever,' he said. 'We need a place of our own.'

Pearl had looked dismayed when he'd mentioned the idea of moving out. 'But who is going to look after Ivy for you, when you're at work?' she demanded.

'She can go to nursery. There's one in the village,' Freddy said. 'Or I'll pay a childminder.'

'Ivy should be with family,' Pearl was adamant. 'Becca, don't you agree? Family is always best.'

I conceded my mother had a point. 'If you want to be more independent, you could always move into the stable block,' I suggested.

'How would that help?' Fred asked. 'You've only got one bedroom.'

'Maybe I could move out to *The Solstice* instead.'

The perfect writer's retreat. The idea took hold and refused to go away, sustaining me during long lonely days. In between my furtive scribblings about scandalous south coast river folk, I made a start on transcribing Skype interviews with Ian Tate, who revelled in recounting anecdotes from his trade union glory days, naming and shaming politicians still alive and those long-dead, careers he had ruined and wives he had seduced.

The tide was high, and the River Deane looked its best as it curved through the countryside, the lost reminders of its past, just like its more recent illegal activities, well hidden beneath its still waters. It was almost impossible to imagine this serene stretch of coastline had paid host to Max van der Plaast's illicit business dealings and the horrific events of his capture.

'Here you go,' Stella said, placing the glass of soda water on the table. 'The last of the big drinkers. Are you going to start quizzing again soon? The Twitchers need you. It gets boring when the Bloodhounds win every week.'

'I might,' I said. 'I could do with some light relief.'

'My book getting you down?' Stella looked put out.

'No, you're nearly finished,' I assured her. 'I've a couple of other things on the go right now, but the one I should be concentrating on, the one I'm getting paid for, is proving to be not nearly so enjoyable.'

A car pulled into the pub's empty car park.

'More customers,' Stella said. 'A bit late in the day, but I best get back to the bar.'

'No, Stella, wait here,' I said. I recognised the couple getting out of the car, even if Stella didn't. Tilly carried Ella on her hip while Tristram looked up and caught my eye. I beckoned him over.

'Friends of yours?' Stella raised her eyebrows.

'We've only become acquainted quite recently,' I said. 'But I believe you might have met before.'

269

As the apprehensive trio made their way onto the terrace, realisation dawned. Stella reached out and clutched hold of the table. I stood up and took hold of her arm for support.

Tilly spoke first. Tristram seemed equally as lost for words as his mother. 'Hello Stella,' she said. 'My name is Tilly, and this is your granddaughter, Ella.'

'My granddaughter?' Stella turned to me, her face a mixture of perplexed, befuddled joy. 'I'm a grandmother?' She edged around the table.

She didn't need my support any longer. 'Oh my goodness, my dear boy, how you've grown.' She stumbled forwards while Tristram stooped to take her in his arms.

'Hi Mum,' his voice broke. Stella laughed, and then she cried, and then she laughed again. She looked to each of us in turn, incredulous, delighted, overcome. 'Oh my, I'm a grandma,' she repeated again.

Tristram placed his daughter in Stella's arms.

'Oh Becca, you did this? You did this for me?' Stella couldn't control her emotions, her voice quivered, her eyes filled with tears. 'You found them? Where's Chloe, can you go and fetch Chloe?' She shook her head, wiped away the tears, sniffed. 'No, not Chloe. You won't want to meet Chloe, will you? Not the right thing to do, must do the right thing.'

'No, Mum, it's fine,' Tristram said. 'We'd love to meet Chloe, wouldn't we, Tilly? But first, I think what we'd all like now is a drink.'

'Silly me,' Stella said, balancing Ella on one hip and wiping her face with her apron. 'Of course we must have a drink. At least you're in the right place for that. Come inside. Oh my goodness, Becca. How did you keep a secret like that?'

'I'm very good at keeping secrets,' I smiled.

She continued to hold Ella while Tristram followed her into the pub. Tilly hesitated.

'Are you coming in with us?' she asked.

I shook my head. 'I think it's a private moment,' I replied. 'I'm going to slip away, but we'll be in touch, yes?'

Tilly nodded. 'Did you get any messages?'

'Oh yes,' I said, 'thank you.'

'Good luck,' she said, and gave me a hug before following her family into the pub.

I'd orchestrated one happy ending. Now it was time to write my own. Two weeks after I'd first mentioned my predicament to Tilly Markham, she'd sent me an email. *I've found your man. I've been assured that he is alive and kicking and is currently recuperating at a rehab centre in the north of England.*

Tilly had told me not to raise my hopes. She confirmed Uncle Laurie's supposition that Nick couldn't afford to jeopardise an ongoing investigation by communicating with potential witnesses. The whole case against the drug smuggling cartel could collapse. Nor could he afford to risk his own personal safety. A man like van der Plaast had far-reaching tentacles into the criminal underworld. Nick's identity had to be protected.

She had been sympathetic and realistic, promising to pull strings to find out what she could, but nothing more. As a parting shot, she added that if our relationship was as strong as I believed, a man like Nick, used to covert operations, would find some way of contacting me.

Be patient, she urged, *these things take time*.

I checked my phone daily, hourly, every fifteen minutes, waiting, hoping, daring myself not to look. I interrogated Freddy when he came home from work to ascertain if he'd received any more messages. I reminded myself each morning of the sensitivity of the situation, of Nick's injuries, of the whole hundred and one reasons why I hadn't heard from him, and then I received a new follower on Twitter - ATwitcher. At last the lines of communication were open.

As snippets of information began to filter through, I felt guilty that I'd thought of my own predicament as opposed to Nick's. His injuries had been life-threatening. He'd lost a great deal of blood. It was little wonder I hadn't heard from him.

He wasn't physically able to leave hospital to come and see me, but as soon as he could, he would, he promised. He could only text during Q's visits, borrowing his brother's phone. His direct messages made me smile; he sent emojis and Snapchat photos which made me feel lightheaded, like a teenager in the first throes of love. During one of Q's visits, he was able to make an excuse to visit the bathroom, and we were able to talk at last. The very sound of his voice, so solid and reassuring, sent waves of relief crashing through my body. My knees nearly buckled beneath me. We were going to be okay.

'How long before I can see you, Nick?' I asked.

'I don't know.' Nick was honest enough not to make promises he couldn't keep. 'There's all sorts of issues involved here, Becs. Police procedures.'

'Can't I come and visit you?'

'I'd love you to,' he said, 'but they wouldn't let you in.'

'Can't you sneak out and see me?'

'I'm at the other end of the country.'

'Can't you fabricate an excuse? Some sort of family emergency?'

'They know I don't have any other family.'

'But you do. You have me. You have *us*.'

'What's that supposed to mean? Are Freddy and Pearl desperate to see me, too?'

'Freddy and Pearl would love to see you, Nick, but that's not what I mean. Something's come up. Things have changed.'

The situation had changed. I was changing, rapidly. I was putting on weight and I was barely eating a thing. I couldn't remember the date of my last period, although I'd never been particularly vigilant at keeping a check on these things. Nick and I had had unprotected sex. I was no better than Freddy.

Just before I'd set out for The Ship of Fools to reunite Stella with her son, I received the message I'd been waiting for.

'Saturday at six. *The Solstice*. Q is springing me out of jail. I've got a twenty-four-hour pass.'

Chapter Thirty-Nine

I spent most of Saturday trawling through the first draft of Ian Tate's manuscript, determined to keep my mind occupied. I took Pippadee for a long walk, far longer than she was used to – so far, in fact, that I ended up carrying her home. Ivy accompanied Freddy to Chapman's Wharf. Rivermede was eerily empty and quiet.

At five forty-five I set off in the car. I passed Freddy by the church, wheeling Ivy home in her pushchair. I pulled over and wound down the window.

'Will you be home for dinner?' Freddy asked. With Pearl away, we had adopted the habit of eating together in the kitchen.

'I don't know,' I replied.

'Okay. I'll see if JJ wants to share a take-away.'

Freddy and JJ had formed an unlikely allegiance. JJ was also working seven days a week. He was back on the marina, selling off as much stock as possible. He seemed suitably humbled, a different man. Perhaps he had come to his own conclusions about Gerald Kimble.

'Maybe you could try cooking something?' I suggested before driving on.

The car park outside Aidan's workshop was occupied by a large white Audi. The driver had his head bent over a book. The passenger seat was empty.

Nick sat on one of his old deckchairs waiting for me, a pale-faced, clean-shaven Nick, with short, neat hair, speckled with grey. He struggled to stand up when he saw me approach. I broke into a run, nearly knocking him over as I flew into his arms.

'Careful,' he half-laughed, half-winced. 'I'm not quite as strong as I used to be, Becs.'

'Does it still hurt?' I asked, momentarily drawing back and glancing down at his leg. I noticed the stick propped by the side of his seat.

'Not now you're here,' he smiled. He buried his face in my hair, brushed his mouth across my lips. 'This feels so good,' he said. We held each other as tight as we dared.

'I was so worried about you,' I said, the emotional impact of the last couple of months finally finding its release in a flood of tears.

He kissed them away. 'I'm so sorry. It's a hazard of the job, I suppose, getting shot.'

'I've bought wine,' I told him, finally breaking away to retrieve the bottle I'd stolen from Jack's secret supply in the boot room fridge.

He shook his head with a look of regret. 'I can't drink. I'm on too many pain-killers.'

'I can't drink either,' I said, putting the bottle of wine down on the deck.

'Oh? That's not like you, Becca, what's up?'

I took a deep breath. 'Sit down, Nick.' There was no easy way to say what I was going to say, and I needed to say it before I chickened out. He stumbled back into his canvas chair while I took the one opposite. I leaned across and took hold of his hand.

'You're not going to believe this, Nick, but I'm pregnant.'

His mouth dropped. 'Becca, that's not funny. You're joking, right?'

I shook my head. 'No. A night of unprotected spontaneous sex has its consequences. It was totally irresponsible of us, both of us. And Freddy will have a field day when he gets to hear about this, considering the lecture I gave him when he told me about Ruby.'

'Yeah, but they're a couple of teenagers. They're allowed to be irresponsible.'

'Freddy is not a teenager.'

'Yes, but at your age, we knew the chances were slim.'

'What? You think all women of thirty-nine are over the hill and can't get pregnant?'

'It was what I was banking on,' Nick replied, his face inscrutable. 'Are you sure?'

'Oh yes. I've done a test. In fact, I've done several tests.'

His eyes travelled down my body to my stomach. 'God, I wasn't expecting this,' he said.

'Well, neither was I, frankly. But I am expecting Nick. *We* are expecting.'

He broke into a smile. 'Oh, wow. Well, that's amazing. That's fantastic.'

'Is it?'

'Yes! Of course it is.' He let out a long breath. 'I never thought I'd have a family. I'd given up thinking about it, to be honest. That's just wonderful news. This is the best family emergency ever.' He leaned back in his chair, his face a picture of astonished bliss.

'You're pleased?' I said hesitantly, trying to suppress a goofy grin but failing miserably.

'I'm over the moon,' he replied. 'Oh Becs. Right,' he leaned forward again and squeezed my knee, 'I was going to save this for another day, but I might as well say it now anyway. Let's go for a walk.'

I helped him up.

'The thing is,' he began, as we walked slowly along the path away from the wharf towards the marsh. 'I'm retiring. This case was always going to be my last. I can't carry on working now anyway. My wound turned septic and there were all sorts of complications. It'll take ages to get my fitness back and, if I'm honest, I'm just sick of the whole business. I've had enough. I'll receive a full pension with all the benefits. I'll get a lump sum, plus additional payments for being injured in the line of duty.'

'Goodness me, I thought for one minute you were going to say something romantic,' I teased. 'This is starting to sound like another proposal.'

'That's because it is,' he said. 'It is another proposal.' He came to an abrupt halt. 'I want to finish what we started fifteen years ago.'

Now I was the one faced with the totally unexpected. My

stomach flipped over in excitement. I'd hoped for a pledge of support, but I hadn't anticipated a total commitment. 'Are you serious?'

'Totally,' he nodded. 'Obviously, your news has expedited the situation, and although I'd love to marry you tomorrow, I can't. We can't, not until this case has come to court. I'll warn you now, it could be months, but as soon as the court case is over, and I'm out of the force and living a quiet life well away from Rivermede, then we can get married.'

'Away from Rivermede?'

'Yeah, I was thinking I might buy my own boat. I thought about taking some sailing lessons and seeing a bit of the world. Kerridge has whetted my appetite. What do you think?'

'Um, I'm not much of a sailor really, Nick, and it wouldn't really be very practical with a baby, would it?'

'Oh yes, the baby. Of course, when I came up with that idea, I didn't know about him, or her,' he added quickly. 'I suppose travelling around the world isn't an option any more. And I suppose you'd probably prefer to stay here, too, close to Pearl and Freddy, especially now that he has his own baby?'

'Oh, it's not that. Mum has Jack now and Freddy is all grown up. He can manage Ivy. They don't need me.' I was free, and the idea of Nick and I being together at last, was making me reckless. I'd spent too many years not daring to dive beneath the surface, but now I was braver and ready to take the plunge. 'Nick, about Freddy...'

He put his finger to my lips to stop me. 'Shush. I love you, Rebecca. You, the whole package. Freddy, Pearl, they're your family. They're part of you and they make you who you are. They make you complete. You wouldn't be the woman I love without them.'

'But you saved his life, Nick. Words can't express my gratitude.'

'I don't need your words,' he said. 'I know what Freddy means to you and, believe or not, he means an awful lot to me, too, Becca.'

And then, on the path in the middle of the marsh, amongst the reed beds and the dirty brown rivulets of the estuary, he lowered himself painfully down onto one knee. 'Let's do this properly,' he said. 'I love you. I love you with all my heart, and I'll always love you. I want you to be my wife, regardless of your madcap family and this crazy place we find ourselves in. I want to have you, to have and to hold from this day forward, for better, for worse, for richer, for poorer, in sickness and in health, to love and to cherish. Will you marry me?'

I didn't hesitate to answer. 'Yes,' I said. 'Yes, oh yes please, please let's get married, but can we do it very quietly? Just me, you, and a couple of witnesses?'

Nick laughed as I helped him to his feet. 'You mean you don't want a marquee on the lawn, a choir, doves, and an entire sailing fleet?'

I shook my head as he took me in his arms again. 'No, Nick,' I said, immersing myself in the warmth of his body pressing hard against mine. 'I only want you, although I might want the fireworks afterwards.'

'It will be my pleasure,' Nick said, 'to provide the fireworks.'

We stood wrapped in each other for some time. Eventually, Nick broke away. 'Seriously, Becs, I need to be honest with you. We have to keep this quiet, okay?' He placed his hand on my stomach. 'We might not even be able to get married until after this little one comes along.'

'That's fine. We do single parenting quite well in our family,' I assured him.

'Yes,' he smiled. 'You do. You do it very well, and I know I'm leaving this little one in very safe hands, but you won't be a single parent. We're doing this together and it will work out. I will keep my promise to you.'

'It's fine, Nick,' I assured him. 'I can wait.' And I would wait, for as long as it took, because I trusted him. Implicitly.

We turned back towards *The Solstice*. 'Will you have time to come back to the stable block tonight with me, to practise the fireworks?' I asked.

'I was worried you might say that,' he replied. 'I'd love to, but I'm not totally convinced I'm up to it, and what do we do with Q?'

'Give him the key to the boat?' I suggested.

Nick shook his head. 'The police cleaned it out. There's nothing on it. Stella can re-let it, or maybe I'll ask her if she wants to sell it to us? I liked hanging out here, pretending to be a writer. In fact, I reckon I've got a few stories to tell. I've spent the last twenty years fighting international crime all over the world, although I'd probably need to engage some sort of professional to polish my books off for me.'

'I quite fancied hanging out on *The Solstice,* too,' I told him. 'Are you only marrying me to save paying my ghost-writing fees?'

'No, I'm marrying you because I love you, Becs,' he said, squeezing my hand.

'Perhaps we could smuggle Q into Rivermede?' I suggested.

'It wouldn't be the first time smugglers have used Rivermede,' Nick agreed.

'Are you serious, about this book writing thing?' I asked.

'Why not? Would you help me?'

'I'd love to,' I laughed. '*My Husband, The Ace Detective.* Pearl will be so pleased.'

Epilogue

Pearl

'Goodness me,' Pearl said, rolling over and reaching for her mobile phone. 'Who on earth is calling at this hour? Don't they know what time it is?'

Beside her, Jack grunted. *The Majestic Oceans* had just docked in Singapore. Tomorrow, they would begin their long journey back to Rivermede, and Pearl was actually wondering, with all the fuss that had gone over the last few weeks, if she could possibly broach the subject of buying a little place in London. By the time she'd put aside a lump sum each for Becca and Freddy, she still had money in the bank from the sale of Beech Mews; more than enough for a bijou *pied-a-terre*. The marina was already under offer, and JJ's half-finished house had to be sold anyway. She and Jack didn't need to stay at Rivermede any more. Perhaps Jack could sell off the entire estate, apart from the stable block. Then they could have their main house in London and a holiday home on the river.

As much as she had enjoyed her coastal sojourn, Pearl was missing the city. The constant smell of rank mud, the wafting aroma of dried seaweed, it wasn't to everyone's taste. Plus, Sunday morning lie-ins disturbed by the clanking of rigging and the whine of a jet ski. Battersea had been an oasis of calm and civility in comparison; sitting in the village square with croissants and coffee...

In London, surely they would be able to find a surgeon prepared to do something with Jack's dodgy hip? Jack may have resigned himself to never dancing the tango again, but Pearl hadn't. She knew Jack well enough by now. He suffered

279

his crumbling joint like a penance; he'd forced Mary into a loveless marriage, and this was the cross he had to bear. Ridiculous. Nobody was forced to marry anyone in the 1970s; it was a time of freedom and liberation, and it appeared Mary Dimmock had been very liberal indeed. She'd married Jack because she knew he'd provide her with a home and be a good father to the child she already carried. Who wouldn't choose Jack over Gerald Kimble?

Jack was drowning in a quagmire of self-pity and regret. Pearl needed to get him away from Rivermede and all its memories. She'd heard of women like Mary before. Charity didn't begin at home, it began in everyone else's; a kind heart and an insatiable sexual appetite. Goodwill wasn't the only thing Mary had spread around Kerridge, if Dolly Hathaway at the gardening club was to be believed. Dolly used to volunteer at the county hospital, when such a thing existed, and had fond memories of her time on service at the STD clinic. Mary Robshaw had been a regular visitor.

Now what would I call that book? Pearl thought. She felt invigorated. Time away on the cruise had given her a whole bevy of new ideas. She'd missed this, the tossing and turning at night, planning scenes, creating conversations. Her characters kept her awake, reciting their lines. She'd already began to jot down some notes on her iPad. Becca would be proud of her. Pearl hadn't thought she'd actually miss writing, but she did, and the social scene that came with it. As much as she'd enjoyed participating in village life, she didn't feel totally accepted by the hierarchy of the WI, and she'd never got the hang of bridge. Becca would enjoy being back in the thick of things, too. There would be so much more to do in the city.

Of course, there was Freddy and the dilemma of what to do about him and Ivy, bless her little heart, but Freddy had grown up a lot in the last few weeks. Amazingly, his marine artwork had taken off; it was even possible he could actually make a bit of a name for himself. For the first time in the entire twenty-one years since his birth, Pearl felt proud of her son. It had taken a long time to get there. She loved Freddy with all her heart, but he had repelled every maternal move she had ever made. It was almost as if he knew.

In the beginning, Freddy had seemed like her salvation, a beacon of hope at a time of bitter despair. She had conceived by careless accident, her relationship with Dieter already approaching its inevitable end. And then, just as she was beginning to accept the idea of the child growing within her, the results of her final tests and scans had come through. The doctors announced that Dieter's poor little baby, if it even survived to full-term, would have no quality of life. The decision was hers and only hers to take, but she had listened to the medical advice and made the agonising choice to have a late termination.

And then, as she lay empty and wan in her hospital bed, she'd had to listen while Becca, already recalled from Zurich, made her tearful confession. Becca might just have missed a period, or two, or possibly three, but in fact probably about six – she'd never been very good at keeping account of these things. A boy in the sixth form – and no, she had told no-one. No-one at all. Beneath the layers of baggy jumpers, the firm hard mound in Becca's stomach was already visible. While she had sobbed apologies and garbled nonsense about giving her baby up, Pearl knew there was only one thing to do.

They had made a pact, mother and daughter.

'He's our flesh and blood,' Pearl said. 'Neither of us can do this on our own, but together we can make it work.'

And they had, for all those years, sharing Freddy's care and ensuring Pearl's career blossomed. They had functioned like a well-oiled machine until Freddy had left home at eighteen, the age when in the natural pattern of evolution, fledglings flew the nest. There had been only one moment in between when Pearl thought Becca might possibly waiver, when she had been about to get married and set up home on her own. But Becca had assured her then she would never dream of taking Freddy from Pearl.

'You legally adopted him,' she said. 'I couldn't take him, even if I wanted to. And I don't. He's yours. He's my brother, not my son.'

281

Pearl would have to ensure Ivy was tied to Freddy with the same watertight bonds, in case Ruby ever came back into their lives. She knew how these things worked. You had to make sure everything was legal.

The phone wasn't going to stop ringing. She braced herself. She could only imagine it had all gone pear-shaped again. She'd tried to warn Becca against it. Who'd have thought all these years later Nick Quinlan would come back into their lives? Pearl knew trouble when she saw it. Just as well she and Jack would be back in the UK in a few days' time, providing shoulders to cry on. She only hoped Becca wouldn't fall into quite so many pieces this time round.

The only good she could see coming out of the whole shambolic mess was another idea for a new book. *My Undercover Lover*, the tale of a charming but manipulative police detective who seduces an old flame in order to help him crack a case. She'd pitch the idea to Anita as soon as she got home. She was itching to get started.

'Becca darling, have you any idea what the time it is? I thought we had this rule about not calling after ten?'

There was a pause on the line. Becca sounded unnaturally cheerful for someone who had just been jilted by the same man for the second time.

'Sorry, Mum, but you'll never guess what…'

THE END

By the same author:

The Theatre of Dreams

Fantastic Books
Great Authors

CROOKED
CAT

Meet our authors and discover
our exciting range:

- Gripping Thrillers
- Cosy Mysteries
- Romantic Chick-Lit
- Fascinating Historicals
- Exciting Fantasy
- Young Adult and Children's
  Adventures
- Non-Fiction

Printed in Poland
by Amazon Fulfillment
Poland Sp. z o.o., Wrocław